DEGREES

HS Chandler

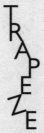

First published in Great Britain in 2019 by Trapeze Books,
an imprint of The Orion Publishing Group Ltd
Carmelite House, 50 Victoria Embankment,
London EC4Y 0DZ

An Hachette UK company

1 3 5 7 9 10 8 6 4 2

A CIP catalogue record for this book is
available from the British Library.

ISBN (Paperback) 9781 4091 7821 7

Typeset by Born Group

Printed and bound in Great Britain by Clays Ltd, Elcograf S.p.A.

www.orionbooks.co.uk

For Evangeline

You always have a choice
You always have a voice
Never settle for less than you know you're worth
And know you're worth the world to me

I love you, little Squishy McBoo

I

Edward Bloxham lay face down in a pool of blood and sunshine on the stone-tiled kitchen floor. He hadn't moved or made a sound for several minutes. Maria stared at his body as she folded the newspaper that had been left on the kitchen table, and deposited it in the recycling bin. Slowly wiping a tea towel around the inside of a mug, she wondered how she was going to get the stains out of the pale grouting. Leaving a second mug in the sink, she picked up the chair leg from where it had been resting on Edward's head, and poked her forefinger into the tangle of human tissue caught around the protruding metal bolt. The sturdy wood had proved a remarkable makeshift weapon. Even in the absence of medical training, there was no mistaking the greyish-tan mess of brain displaced from inside her husband's skull. The vertical crack in the back of his head was four inches long, a bubbling stream down his neck. It was time to call the authorities, but her garden looked so idyllic through the kitchen window in the mid-afternoon light that it was hard to motivate herself. She performed a rough mental calculation. The number of gardening months per annum – eight in a good-weather year – twenty days of gardening per month, four hours per day. Multiply that by the fifteen years since she'd stopped working, and Maria had clocked up some ten thousand hours bending the earth to her will, producing the only colour and beauty in her life. Now it would go to ruin. Perhaps that was the most appropriate ending, anyway. Husband deceased. Plants dead. The predictable seasons of her life disappearing.

Maria ran her hands, one after the other, up and down the chair leg, drinking in the sensation of Edward's life-giving cells ebbing between her fingers. For nearly two decades he had been the dominant force in her life. Now, just one week before her fortieth birthday, she had caused his death, soon to be celebrating that milestone as a single person. Behind bars, most likely, but single.

There really was an awful mess on the floor. After pressing a tea towel into the wound, she stepped over his body, gently knocking the pantry door shut with her elbow as she walked into the hallway where Edward's jacket hung from the hat stand. Sliding a sticky hand into his inner pocket, Maria withdrew his mobile, marvelling at how sleek it was compared to the cheap plastic block she had hidden away. There was no need to bypass any of his personal security settings. Edward had never needed any. Maria was the only person in the house with him, and at work it was just his secretary. Simple and routine. That was the world he liked. The world he had liked, she corrected herself, as she dialled 999.

'Which service do you require?'

Odd to think of what was about to descend as a service. The word suggested help or usefulness. It was too late for that.

'I've killed my husband,' Maria replied. 'So whatever you think is best, really.'

The woman on the end of the line didn't miss a beat. Credit to her. She took Maria's name and address, then launched into a series of questions about Edward's current physical state.

'He's lying on the floor completely still,' Maria said. 'I haven't moved him since. He's face down.'

'Is he breathing?' the operator asked.

'I split his head open,' Maria replied. 'So no.'

2

'The police and ambulance are on their way. I need you to ensure that the doors are unlocked. Do you have any dogs at the property?'

Maria sighed. No, no dogs. Nothing that might require any of her love or time. Nothing that might have loved her back.

'Just me,' she said, walking to the front door and opening it wide. Birdsong and the smell of freshly mown grass distracted her. She watched gulls swooping through the sky towards the Somerset coast, smiling at the knowledge that her husband would never again complain about them damaging the paint-work on his Volvo. In the distance, sirens sang their two-tone song as the police navigated the lanes to the house. Maria wondered where she ought to be. It seemed wrong to be standing over her husband's body as they arrived. The sitting room seemed too distant; how callous to be found lounging in an armchair amidst so much drama. The driveway seemed more logical. She stepped through the front door, untroubled by the neighbours. Leylandii hedges had long since ensured privacy from both sides, and the generosity of the plot their picture-perfect, five bedroomed house occupied meant they never heard or saw the people living either side.

The gates. She hadn't considered them. Walking back into the hallway, Maria pressed the button. Edward had another gate controller on his key set, but that would be in his trouser pocket and she wasn't prepared to start rummaging there. Returning to the driveway, she watched the last of the gates' progress. They stood fully open, impressive wrought ironwork forming swirling scrolls that Edward had been so proud of. Maria remembered the day they'd been installed. The man who fitted them had handed her the electronic key fob delightedly, offering her the chance to be the first to close them. They had swished together over the gravel driveway in perfect synchronisation.

'There, that'll keep you good and safe,' the man had said.

Just like that, her cage had closed. She could see out, of course. The road beyond still meandered into the distance. The neighbours' houses still sat in the centre of their well-tended lawns. Birds still flew overhead, nesting where they chose. Nothing had changed, except that her world had shrunk imperceptibly more, and she hated her life to an even greater degree.

A police car swerved onto the driveway as another drew up outside the gate, followed by an ambulance. Maria watched as a policewoman exited the nearest vehicle and began walking cautiously towards her.

'Are you Mrs Bloxham?' she called.

'Yes, hello,' Maria said.

'Ma'am, I need you to put down the item you're holding,' the policewoman instructed, keeping her distance.

Maria raised her hand. The chair leg rose before her face as if magically attached to the end of her arm. A few strands of Edward's hair fluttered in the breeze.

'Sorry,' she said. 'I didn't realise I was still holding it.' She placed it gently at her feet on the gravel. 'Edward's in the kitchen.'

Another police officer appeared at the policewoman's side and they walked towards her together, then two paramedics climbed out of the ambulance.

'I'm PC Mull,' she said. 'We need to get inside to your husband, Mrs Bloxham. Can you confirm if anyone else is in the property?'

'I'm all alone,' Maria said.

'And are there any other weapons we should know about?' PC Mull asked.

Maria cocked her head. The officer meant the chair leg, of course. It hadn't occurred to her that it was a weapon. A while ago it was just a broken piece of furniture awaiting repair. Now it had assumed a new purpose. What a dramatic change, she thought. Rather like her. From housewife to murderess – that's what the papers would call her when they got hold of it – in one swift move. Then there would be Edward's obituary. Prominent ecologist, an expert on climate change, champion of British wildlife and seabirds – the credits rolled on and on – author, broadcaster, local hero. They would report that he'd been bludgeoned to death in his own home. Bludgeoned. Such an onomatopoeic word. She'd never considered it before hearing the sound of wood upon skull today.

'Mrs Bloxham?' the police officer prompted, taking a step forward.

'Absolutely, no,' Maria said. 'No other weapons.'

'Good. I'm going to ask you to raise your hands now, ma'am, and please don't move as I approach,' PC Mull said. The words weren't spoken unkindly but they were an order. Maria knew one when she heard it. Raising her hands slowly, she caught sight of her crimson palms and realised she looked frightful. PC Mull stepped close and patted her down. Satisfied there was nothing concealed beneath her clothes, the policewoman nodded at the paramedics who swiftly entered the house accompanied by a further officer from the car that had parked beyond the gates. 'Thank you. Now I'd like you to bring your hands together behind your back. I'm going to handcuff you. The cuffs will feel tight but you should tell me if they cause you any pain.'

They were all being terribly polite, Maria thought, given what she had confessed to. A man lay dead on her kitchen floor and here she was being respectfully referred to as 'Mrs Bloxham'. That wouldn't last long. Not when they saw his body.

'I'm going to ask you to remain here while I go inside. My colleague, PC McTavish, will hold you. I have to instruct you not to move, or attempt to move. Do you understand?' PC Mull asked.

'I do,' Maria replied.

Another car pulled up, this one unmarked, as PC McTavish took hold of Maria's cuffed wrists. A man climbed out, his clothing as anonymous as the vehicle he'd arrived in. He pulled on gloves, looking left and right as if he was sniffing the air, Maria thought. Catching the scent of blood. He opened the back door of his vehicle and took a bag from the seat, walking directly towards Maria without making eye contact. Bending to the ground, he inspected the chair leg.

'Photograph it,' he called back to a woman who had alighted the vehicle after him. She plodded heavily up the driveway, camera banging her chest from a strap around her neck, and did as she'd been told. Ten or more snaps later, the man giving commands picked up the chair leg and placed it inside the bag. 'Label it and start an evidence log,' he said, handing it to the photographer who began walking back to the car. The policeman in charge took his time acknowledging Maria, checking his watch first and greeting the police officer who was restraining her.

'Sir,' PC McTavish said deferentially.

'McTavish,' the senior officer nodded. 'Has she resisted at all?'

'No trouble as yet, sir,' PC McTavish confirmed.

Maria kept her face as straight as she could. The concept that she could be regarded as any sort of threat in resistance terms was both laughable and oddly pleasing.

'My name is Detective Inspector Anton. Was it you who called the incident in?' he asked.

'Yes,' Maria said. 'What will happen next?'

'We'll be assessing the scene,' Anton replied.

'Where will I be taken?'

Anton stared at her. She lowered her eyes to meet his. He was five feet five inches tall, she decided, wondering if his below average height for a man had hampered his progress in the police force. He was looking at her strangely. Maria glanced away.

'Mrs Bloxham, you told the emergency operator that you'd killed your husband, is that right?' he asked.

'It is,' Maria said.

DI Anton paused. 'You seem very calm.'

'Do I?' Maria asked, meeting his eyes again.

'Would you turn around for me, please?' Anton asked.

PC McTavish released her so that Maria could comply. She did so, noting that the roses along the driveway border needed pruning. She wouldn't get the chance now. No one would care for them like she had. If they weren't cut back hard enough, the blooms would be depleted next spring. She felt the weight of regret setting in and tears formed unexpectedly in her eyes.

'Bag her hands, PC Cooksley,' Anton instructed the photographer as she reappeared. Cooksley pulled bags from her pocket and slipped one over each of Maria's hands, fastening the tops with tape. 'We're preserving the evidence, Mrs Bloxham, in the event that you have any defensive wounds or debris under your fingernails. Do you believe you have any injuries the paramedics should attend to?'

DI Anton was fishing. There was no concern in his voice.

'No,' Maria replied. 'I'm unhurt.'

PC Mull appeared from the front door, calling DI Anton over. The pair disappeared into the house. Maria didn't care what the police did inside. It was bricks and mortar, just a conveniently arranged shelter from the elements, devoid of sentimental value. She could happily walk away from it and never set foot inside again. It didn't matter how beautiful the architecture was, or how many bedrooms there were. Deep pile carpets and triple glazed windows didn't make a home. The generous square footage had only ever provided additional space for her to clean and extra walls to stare at.

A bead of perspiration left a glistening trail from the corner of her left eyebrow down her cheek. Maria waited until it descended to her jaw then raised a shoulder to wipe it away. DI Anton would enjoy seeing her sweat. It would tick all those stereotypical criminal behaviour boxes – guilt, fear of discovery, the subconscious desire to confess her wrongdoings. Maria would save them the drama. She had no intention of saying anything other than that she had killed Edward. Deliberately, too.

DI Anton reappeared and strode across to stand directly in front of her. 'Mrs Bloxham, I am placing you under arrest. You will be transported to a police station where you will be given an opportunity to consult with a lawyer and later questioned regarding the attack on your husband.'

'I already told the lady on the phone what I did,' Maria said. 'I don't think I'm going to need a lawyer.'

'I'm cautioning you, and it's important that you listen.' DI Anton raised his voice a notch. Apparently he didn't like being interrupted. 'The paramedics will be exiting your house in a few minutes and we need to remove you from the vicinity before that happens. Do you have any medication that you need us to collect from the house? I can't guarantee when you will be able to re-enter.'

'No,' Maria said. 'I don't need anything from inside. I'm finished with that place.'

'What about your husband? Any pre-existing medical conditions we should know about?'

'He was perfectly healthy until today. I'm sure his GP can confirm that,' Maria said.

'Sir,' an officer called from the doorway to the house, 'the helicopter's three minutes off. They're just establishing a clear landing area.'

'Right, we need to move you now, Mrs Bloxham. If you could start walking towards the police car just outside the gates,' Anton said.

'Is the coroner coming by helicopter?' Maria asked. 'I was wondering when they would arrive.'

'The coroner?' Anton frowned. 'The helicopter is an air ambulance, Mrs Bloxham.'

'That seems like a waste of time in the circumstances.'

'Presumably you'd prefer we didn't bother,' DI Anton commented, checking his watch again. 'We have to go. You are under arrest for attempted murder and I'm taking you into custody immediately.'

'What?' Maria asked.

'Mrs Bloxham, I'm going to have to insist that you move towards the police car right now,' Anton said.

'You said attempted murder,' Maria replied. Beneath her feet, every shard of gravel made its presence felt through her slippers. The day was suddenly sweltering.

DI Anton raised his eyebrows. 'Sorry, I obviously wasn't clear enough. Your husband's still alive, Mrs Bloxham, although having seen the injury I can understand why you assumed otherwise. A surgical team is waiting to operate immediately.'

She shook her head, tried to reach out for something to steady her, succeeding only in tightening the handcuffs around her wrists. 'No,' Maria whispered as her knees forgot how to keep her upright. DI Anton ordered the other policeman to help him catch her, and she felt them take the weight of her body before she hit the ground.

'Please be too late,' Maria murmured, as darkness took her.

2

Day One in Court

'My first love. My darling.' That was what Isambard Kingdom Brunel had called the Clifton Suspension Bridge. Lottie's recollections from school history lessons were patchy, but that snippet had lodged in her brain, returning unbidden whenever she drove into Bristol. She'd lost count of the number of times she'd used the gravity-defying structure to cross the Avon river, and her stomach still complained if she dared look the 250 feet down into the valley. Putting her foot on the accelerator, conscious that she couldn't be late, the continuing butterflies she felt had nothing to do with vertigo and everything to do with being thrown into a new situation. No one she knew had ever done jury service. She'd read the letter a dozen times before it had sunk in. Trying to second-guess the rush hour traffic, Lottie took the road that skirted the river, focusing on the grand Victorian warehouses that lined the water as she entered the city, with their ornate arches and perfect geometry. The surrounding glass and steel office buildings framed the historic buildings more than detracting from their beauty. She rounded College Green where the vast arc of Bristol's City Hall made a triangle with the Cathedral and the road that swept down to Harbourside. Lottie wanted to lie on the grass, wander through the shops and treat herself to lunch at one of Bristol's multitude of tea rooms.

Instead she headed north and hoped there would be a space left in one of the central car parks. Her day was destined to be spent inside, away from the blue skies and burning sunshine, separated from all the city had to offer, and she couldn't have been any more nervous if it had been her on trial.

An hour later, Lottie found herself staring around the courtroom, feeling underdressed in her short-sleeved white shirt and navy trousers, and wishing she'd tied up her long hair. The jury service letter hadn't specified anything more formal, but many of her fellow jurors were in smart work suits and ties, or formal blouses and skirts, in spite of the August heatwave. And if the surroundings weren't daunting enough, the judge and barristers looked entirely alien in their voluminous black gowns and stiff grey wigs. Her husband, Zain, had been right. Lottie was out of her depth. The only comfort was that the man beside her looked just as uncomfortable, checking his watch every few minutes. Twelve of them had been selected from the jury pool by number, like some ridiculous game of human bingo. Her Honour Judge Downey – a sweet-looking but sharp-eyed woman – had told them to sit down until all the seats were filled. The attention was intimidating.

The man in the seat next to Lottie's raised his hand, causing a sudden shift in attention towards him. He was one of the few jurors close to Lottie's age, and physically striking enough to turn heads anywhere. His body language – leaning back in the seat, legs spread wide – said he knew it, too.

'Yes,' Her Honour Judge Downey said. 'Do you have a question, Mr . . .?'

'Cameron Ellis. I don't have the time to be here. I'm self-employed, got a carpentry business. I did phone the court last week and explain,' the man said.

Lottie was amazed at his boldness, complaining in front of a room full of lawyers and police. He was maybe a couple of years older than her, but at twenty-six the thought of standing out in front of a crowd still made her stomach shrivel.

'I appreciate your situation,' the judge replied, 'but I'm afraid there are a good many self-employed people in the Bristol area. We cannot excuse all of them from jury duty. You will receive a daily financial allowance to assist. Before you are all officially sworn in, does anyone else have a question?'

Lottie took a deep breath, wishing she didn't have to speak up, but knowing her husband would be furious if she failed to get herself released as he'd instructed. His job was all targets, deadlines and bonuses, which as far as Lottie could make out simply meant endless stress and an expectation that his home-life would operate like a well-oiled machine. Additions like jury duty didn't fit into that picture anywhere. She raised her hand. The judge nodded at her encouragingly.

'I'm Charlotte Hiraj. I've, um, got a three-year-old to look after so, you know, I should probably not be here and I'm not sure I'm the right person for this anyway,' Lottie mumbled.

'Childcare expenses are paid for the hours you're in court, so you won't be out of pocket. Jury service can seem ominous but it doesn't require any special knowledge on your part,' the judge replied.

Lottie shrunk down in her seat. Next to her, Cameron Ellis was still tutting. Jury service it was for them both, then. Two weeks of stunning weather would be wasted in dark rooms with people she didn't know, listening to words she wouldn't understand. Zain was going to be unimpressed by her absence whether or not he had to foot the childcare bill himself.

A woman in the row in front of Lottie was asked to stand, then handed a bible and a card. One by one they took the oath until it was Lottie's turn. She chose to affirm rather than swear on a holy text. A childhood spent drifting between foster homes had knocked any possible faith out of her. Heat rose in her cheeks as her name was called and she was instructed to read the words on the card.

'I do solemnly, sincerely and truly declare and affirm that I will faithfully try the defendant and give a true verdict according to the evidence,' Lottie said. The words seemed absurdly antiquated, yet they resonated with the gravity of the task. The idea of judging another person felt unpleasant. Lottie had made enough mistakes in her own life to be uncomfortable passing judgment on anyone else, yet the long-absent buzz of adrenalin through her veins was electrifying. The opportunity to legitimately sift through another person's dirty washing, to watch them answer questions and figure out who was lying and who was telling the truth, was captivating. It occurred to her that being on a jury might be like watching the most compulsive daytime TV ever, just with less audience heckling.

She pushed the card back towards the usher and retook her seat as the eyes that had been watching her shifted mercifully to the man on her right. Directly across the courtroom from the jury benches were rows of seats filled with curious onlookers. Some were clearly press, their identification lanyards hanging like medals around their necks, as they recorded whatever sliver of misery was to be played out in the courtroom. Behind the press seats was an odd collection of humanity. Two elderly people whispered together behind their hands. A row of four older teenagers who might have been students, practised looks of boredom. A middle-aged woman mopped her face with a handkerchief, clearly not built for the heat the summer had brought. Still wearing his sunglasses, one man was furiously sketching. A few seats down, police officers sat with their arms folded, waiting for the real action to begin.

The woman in the dock was asked to stand, and the court clerk sitting below and in front of the judge read out the charge. There was a moment of silence before the full weight of the case became clear.

Attempted murder.

The silence was stifling. Lottie was amazed at how quickly her sunny Monday morning had darkened. Edward Bloxham was the victim's name. She recognised it at once. The national news had covered the story extensively, a wife accused of trying to kill her husband. TV reporters had stood outside the scene of the crime clutching microphones and speculating on events, against a background of police officers coming and going. The local papers had been even more full of it, with fewer equally salacious stories to fill their columns. Lottie had read a sample of the victim's writing in the *Bristol Post* – something about seagull nesting habits on the south coast. She'd turned the page at that point. Harsh, perhaps, but there were some things she just couldn't get excited about. Now she was to hear every detail of the man's life and near death.

'To the charge of attempted murder, do you plead guilty or not guilty?' the court clerk asked.

'Not guilty,' the defendant replied, eyes cast downwards. No fuss.

'Just goes to show you never can tell,' an older female juror muttered.

Lottie allowed herself a glance at the defendant's glass box, situated in the rear of the courtroom, where the woman who was about to face trial sat listless, shoulders hunched. She looked not dissimilar to the lady who ran the bakery section of Lottie's local supermarket. A background person, Lottie thought, briefly ashamed at how quickly she'd formed an opinion, but there it was. In a line-up of likely suspects, the female in the dock would surely be the last chosen. Perhaps that was the brilliance of her criminality, her air of dull, mid-life irrelevance.

The prosecuting barrister got to her feet. She was tall and incredibly thin, with stick-like legs and a suit so well tailored to her flat body that she looked like a posh ironing board. Her brown hair was tied up beneath her wig, and she wore square-sided black glasses that screamed control freak to Lottie.

'Miss Pascal,' the judge said. 'Is the prosecution ready to proceed with the trial?'

'I gather from my learned friend defending, Mr Newell, that there is some legal argument before the case can be opened to the jury,' Miss Pascal replied, sounding both terse and bored. The defence barrister – Newell – was sitting closer to the jury, writing notes and keeping his expression carefully neutral.

'Is that correct, Mr Newell?' the judge asked.

Newell got to his feet slowly and smiled at the judge. 'It is, Your Honour, although I'm afraid I can't say quite how long it will take. I suspect the jury will not be required until after lunch.'

He was in his fifties, Lottie guessed, with smile lines creasing out from the corners of his eyes, and fingertips stained blue with ink that might never be entirely erased. He reminded her of Mr Willoughby, a favourite teacher who had made the most disruptive elements in her class believe that physics really could be interesting. He'd never needed to raise his voice to make a point or quieten his students. Being respected was a side effect of being liked, Lottie decided, as Mr Newell pulled up his gown, which had been making a slow escape down his shoulders.

'Very well,' Judge Downey replied. She turned to face the jury. 'Ladies and gentlemen, in your room you will have access to the necessities to make your waiting time bearable, but you cannot leave the court building while the trial is in session. There will be times when I have to ask you to leave the courtroom. Sometimes we must undertake work without you present. Much of it is administrative and I'm sure you'd all rather be drinking coffee and reading newspapers while it takes place.' There was a ripple of laughter as the judge paused. 'This case will attract media attention.' Lottie redirected her gaze to the members of the press, pens poised. 'You must disregard anything you hear save for the evidence presented in court,' the judge continued. 'Do not discuss the case outside the jury room when all twelve of you are gathered together. You must also not use social media to comment on the trial or you may find yourselves in contempt of court which can result in imprisonment.'

'Might as well just lock us all up right now,' Cameron muttered.

The judge turned over a sheet of paper and continued. 'Should you be approached regarding this case, whether by a witness, a member of the press or anyone else, decline to speak with them and report it to a member of court staff. Please now retire to your jury room. This would be a good opportunity to elect one of you as foreperson, to speak for you in the courtroom. You will be informed as soon as the case is ready to restart.'

A male juror in a pin-striped business suit, who had been attached to his laptop and mobile from the second they'd arrived that morning, raised his hand. He didn't bother to introduce himself.

'How long's the trial likely to take? I have to schedule meetings later this month,' he explained.

Miss Pascal the prosecutor stood up. 'Your Honour, the current time estimate is two weeks.'

The judge put the lid on her pen, a gesture that clearly indicated she was ready to do something else. 'The jury should make no plans for the next fortnight, and it would be wise to ensure there is nothing in anyone's diary for a week after that which cannot be cancelled if necessary. That will be all for now.'

The court usher motioned for them to follow her. The defence barrister, James Newell, sent a half smile back towards Maria Bloxham who met it with a blank gaze. Lottie tried to imagine being in her shoes, trusting her fate to twelve strangers. Everything about the courtroom was unnerving. There was nowhere to hide. It was designed like an inward-looking box. The jury seats lined a wall directly opposite the press and public seating. The dock where the defendant sat was at the back and to the right of the jury's line of vision. At the front of the court was the judge's desk, elevated several feet higher than anyone else. In the centre were the lawyers' benches, with the defence seated closest to the jury and the prosecution on the far side. Everyone could see everyone. Even with the high ceiling and grand scale of the room, it felt claustrophobic. The furnishings were modern enough, but there was no mistaking the sense that crime and punishment was an age-old business that hadn't really changed in centuries. It was like theatre in the round, with the outcome dependent on who gave the most compelling performance.

Lottie wondered what would happen if she called in sick the next day. The judge would surely just replace her. Her normal home routine would continue unbroken. Shopping, cleaning, cooking, childcare. Without her at home during the day, it would all just pile up to be rushed in the evenings. With Zain already so pressured, feigning illness was looking like the best solution for an easy life. The problem was that no one had told them what to do if they were ill. Presumably the absence of a clearly set out procedure implied that such a situation was supposed never to arise. Worse than that, she'd already asked to be released from jury duty, so an unforeseen sickness was bound to be viewed with scepticism. It suddenly seemed probable that a police officer would end up knocking her door and escorting her back to court whether she liked it or not. It was no good. She was stuck with it. Zain would just have to understand. Now that the decision had been made for her, Lottie found herself more excited by the prospect than she'd anticipated. A younger her would have loved it, she thought. Perhaps it was a chance to find that girl again.

3

They were shown to their jury room and told to settle in. In the centre was a long wooden table around which twelve chairs were positioned. Having ascertained lunch preferences, the court usher left them to their own devices. Lottie made herself a cup of tea and went to sit at the far end of the table next to one of the other younger jurors. His head was already in a book, and she left him reading quietly as she used her mobile to avoid the awkwardness of sitting silently. There were no messages. She hoped that meant her son Daniyal had settled okay at the childminder's. Lottie glanced up briefly. Everyone else seemed perfectly at ease, a group of five already putting the world to rights across the table as if they'd known each other for years. Wandering over to sit with them would mean they'd expect her to join in, which seemed pointless given that she had nothing to contribute. She stayed where she was and flicked through the photos of Daniyal in her phone gallery instead. The man who had sat beside her in court – Cameron Ellis – threw himself into a chair opposite and began making a phone call.

'Excuse me everyone, my name is Tabitha Lock,' an older woman bedecked with perm and pearls said. 'Can I suggest we all put away our mobile devices and get on with business as the judge directed.' Her request was met with silence. 'I would like to offer myself as jury foreperson. I've chaired a number of committees in my time and I'm very good at assimilating information and organising people. I must say, I think the case is going to be fascinating.' Lottie figured Tabitha was in her mid sixties and unused to hearing the word no.

'Perhaps we should introduce ourselves,' the suited businessman who had asked the judge for the trial time estimate replied. He adjusted his watch as he spoke. 'So we have some idea who we all are, and who we want to represent us.'

'Well, if you really think that's necessary. Perhaps anyone else interested in the post could indicate as much during their introduction,' Tabitha sniffed.

There was a muttering across the table from Lottie that escaped the jurors at the far end, but it was a clear 'For fuck's sake' from Cameron. Lottie concentrated on stirring her tea.

The businessman took the reins. 'My name is Panagiotis Carras. My friends call me Pan. I'm a fine art auctioneer, and I have no desire to be jury foreman but I think it's a job that'll require someone taking the middle ground. I've got a lot of work to do when we're not in court, so forgive me if I don't socialise.' He looked at the next person around the table.

'Gregory Smythe, retired civil servant,' a well-spoken older gentleman said. Lottie thought she spotted some food dripped down his tie. Probably single, she thought. If he'd had a wife at home, she'd never have let him go out like that. 'If Mrs Lock would like to be foreperson, that's fine with me.'

'It's Miss Lock,' Tabitha interjected, 'but thank you.'

'Jennifer Curry,' a quiet voice continued. 'Or Jen. I'm just a housewife. I don't think I should be foreperson, so probably Tabitha, Miss Lock, is okay for me if no one else wants to do it. The judge talked about lots of rules. I'm not sure I caught them all. Can we go through those, too?'

Lottie sat up straighter in her seat. Just a housewife? How depressing to hear it said like that. Jennifer Curry looked to be in her early fifties, perhaps her late forties if she wasn't taking good care of herself. Lottie hated the thought of getting to the point where she referred to herself as 'just' an anything. She stared down at her own hands, that for the last three years had done little except change nappies and prepare food, recalling the girl she had been, full of ambition. At school, at several schools in fact, she'd been the prettiest there. Popularity had made her bold. When everyone wanted to sit next to you, the world felt like a wonderful place. Teenage life was scored in terms of numbers of friends and the extent of their admiration. Where other girls were getting better grades, she was confident that her looks and personality would bring her the things she wanted in life – some sort of unquantified success involving money, travel and glamour.

She'd moved schools too often to make long-term friends, but during each brief episode she'd been sought-after in the pecking order of good-looking boys. Shifting between carers and homes had meant that little else was achieved during her education. Lottie left school with few qualifications but happy in the knowledge that her cheeky grin and self-assurance would win the day. It had taken no more than a year for reality to dull her smile. Good looks got her positions in retail and hospitality, but not much else. She found a job, and got bored. Went to parties and got drunk. When that got tired, she went to other parties where the doors were locked early and not opened again until dawn, and illegal highs came as a side order with your drink. She'd avoided a variety of addictions only because of the toll they would have taken on her looks, and from the need to pay her rent. By the time she understood that the rails were necessary to progress steadily in life, she was already off them – until Zain came along. Now she was married to a pharmaceutical company area manager, but without much else to say for herself. She, too, was nothing more than a housewife.

For a second Lottie contemplated suggesting herself as foreperson. Five years ago she wouldn't have given it a second thought. The sharp-edged cockiness of her early twenties that had allowed her to heckle, joke and lead had drooped, then dissolved. Baby-brain had softened her wits, that's what her husband Zain occasionally teased. Lottie told herself to forget putting her name forward. No one was going to be interested in anything she had to say.

'Agnes Huang,' the woman next to Lottie said. 'Can you believe it's an attempted murder trial? I thought we might end up doing something boring like, I don't know, car theft. This is much better.'

'I'm not sure "much better" is how I'd phrase it,' Gregory commented. 'Tragic, perhaps.'

'I could be foreperson. It sounds fun,' Agnes ignored Gregory and continued. The Chinese woman folded her arms and directed a challenging stare towards Tabitha. Lottie compared the two. Perhaps the women were a match for one another, but judging by the looks on Gregory and Jennifer's faces, they would be happier with a known quantity in charge, and that known quantity came with a middle England accent.

'I suggest a vote at the end, when everybody's said their bit,' Tabitha answered. 'How about you, dear. It's Charlotte, isn't it?' She smiled like an officious grandmother and motioned for Lottie to speak up.

Caught between wanting to tell Tabitha that nobody had put her in charge yet, and shrinking under the table to avoid making a fool of herself, Lottie opted – as she always seemed to these days – to comply. 'Call me Lottie,' she said spontaneously. It was the name she always used in her own head, a throwback to a time when her life still seemed full of possibilities. Here, with these strangers, she could be anyone she wanted to be, again. 'I've got a three-year-old son, so I'm not working at the moment,' she said. 'I'm planning to, though, soon. I'm not going to be a housewife forever.' She blushed, wishing she'd phrased it better, hoping Jennifer Curry hadn't been too insulted. All she'd been trying to say was that she still had dreams. One of them was to see a bit more of the world. She'd been on one long-distance trip, even if the circumstances had been unexpected. Her husband had organised a visit his family just before their son was due. It had turned into a longer stay than she'd thought, and Lottie had ended up giving birth in Pakistan. Her husband's parents had been delighted to see their grandson the day he was born, even if Lottie had missed the support of her own midwife. It had been worth it at the time to have made Zain so proud. They hadn't returned to England until Daniyal was a month old.

'And do you have any thoughts about who should be foreperson, Lottie?' Tabitha asked, bringing Lottie's attention back to the matter at hand.

'Not really,' Lottie replied, sitting upright and pretending she hadn't just been daydreaming. 'I think Pan's right, though, it should be someone, you know, open minded.' She looked to the tall, skinny male seated at the end of the table next to her, the one who'd been absorbed in his book, diverting any further attention from herself. He was the only person younger than her, no more than twenty-one Lottie estimated, and had opted for the compromise of wearing jeans but ironing them, smartening up his look by adding a striped shirt.

'Okay, my name's Jack Pilkington,' he muttered.

'Sorry, can't hear a word,' Gregory said. 'Speak up.'

'Pilkington, Jack,' he repeated. 'I'm a student at Bristol Uni. Latin and Arabic.' He was so softly spoken that everyone around the table was leaning forward. Lottie could hear him swallowing, as if punctuating his sentences with his throat. His shyness was painful for Lottie to watch, her own confidence having seeped into supermarket trollies and baskets of washing over the last few years. No one even looked at her any more. Passers-by didn't notice you when you were pushing a pram. It didn't matter what she wore, how she did her hair, or how long she spent doing her make-up. The pram was like an invisibility cloak. Motherhood had stolen her identity.

'Latin's not a lot of use these days, is it?' a tattooed man from the other side of the table asked. 'Guess it's all right for you posh lot to waste three years of your life though. What exactly qualifies you to be in here? Shouldn't let students do jury service, if you ask me.'

Jack stared at him, then picked up his coffee and took a sip. Cameron stepped in, managing to sound both half asleep and irritated at once.

'No one did ask you, so it's my turn.' The tattooed guy gritted his teeth at the dismissal. Cameron smiled in reply and slowly poured a few extra drops of milk into his coffee mug. 'I'm Cam Ellis. Self-employed carpenter in case any of you need any jobs done. I'd rather be working, or on the beach, or anywhere but here. I don't want to be foreperson. The daily allowance for jury duty isn't enough to bother with that, especially with how bad the coffee is. Does that cover it?'

Jack looked gratefully across at him, the attention firmly removed from his university degree subject. Cameron was tall with the sort of build and skin tone that could only belong to a man who either spent all his time at the gym and abusing tanning machines, or who did a hard physical job and spent much of his time outdoors. His denim shirt had seen better days, but it flattered his broad frame and set off his blue eyes, and he moved with an assurance that was unmistakably alpha male. Agnes Huang was staring at him openly, and even Jennifer Curry seemed to have perked up as he spoke. He was the type of man who attracted attention without making

23

any effort at all. Lottie had been too nervous to notice much about him in the courtroom, but it was hard now not to see the effect he was having on all the women under sixty in the room. Lottie included.

Legs wide apart and outstretched, he let one arm hang to the side of his chair as he held his coffee mug with disregard for its handle. Everything about him was casual and taut at the same time. The cords in his neck tensed as he swallowed, and the flex of his jaw gave Lottie a tiny buzz low in her stomach. He slid his eyes sideways, meeting Lottie's boldly before flicking his eyes up and down her body. She looked away, aware that she had been caught staring, shifting her focus to the next person around the table.

Samuel Lowry was an insurance clerk from Burnham-on-Sea. 'I'm fifty-nine,' he said. 'I live with my sister and our three dogs. It was four, only Potts passed away last year . . .'

'Garth Finuchin,' the tattooed man interrupted. His bulk suggested more muscle than was really there, and he held his arms away from his sides to enhance the impression of strength. 'I may not have a degree in some fancy waste of time, but I reckon I've got more life experience than anyone else in this room. Makes sense for me to be foreman. More of a bloke thing anyway as it's a murder.'

'Attempted murder,' Tabitha added, 'and I don't see that gender plays any part in it.'

'Witnessed much violence at the WI, have you?' Finuchin asked, rewarding himself with a bark of laughter.

'I'd have thought it was more important to elect someone who might communicate well with Her Honour,' Tabitha continued.

'Absolutely,' Gregory nodded. 'Not that I'm prejudging.'

'Well, of course you two are going to stick together,' Finuchin smirked.

'Could we please just get on with it?' Cameron asked, sighing loudly. 'At this rate, the accused will have served a couple of years before we've chosen a foreperson.'

'The lawyers call her the defendant, not the accused,' Tabitha said. 'We should try to get to grips with the proper vocabulary.'

The final two jurors – Andy Leith and Bill Caldwell – both declined the opportunity to be elected as foreperson. Lottie didn't blame them. Joining the contest between Tabitha, Agnes and Garth felt more like inviting a vote for least disliked rather than a show of confidence.

'Shall I preside?' Gregory asked, smiling around the table. 'Let's each have a scrap of paper and write the name of our choice for foreperson.' There was no dissent as he ripped up a sheet of paper and passed the sections around.

'What if we don't want to vote for any of them?' Cameron asked. 'Not that I'm saying it applies to me, just so we know what to do.'

'Ruin your paper,' Pan said. 'Write a cross or something. Let's get on, though. Some of us have work to do.'

Lottie allowed herself a half-smile across the table at Cameron who raised an eyebrow in reply. He was trouble, Lottie thought, writing a cross on her own piece of paper and folding it tight. They all handed their scraps to Gregory who opened them into a pile then set them out one by one in a line on the table.

'One vote for Garth Finuchin,' Gregory said

'Fucking typical,' Finuchin muttered.

'Two votes for Agnes Huang.' Gregory frowned but continued slightly louder. 'Five votes for Tabitha Lock and four ruined papers. Miss Lock it is then. Congratulations.'

Tabitha bowed her head as if touched and humbled. 'Thank you so much,' she said. 'I won't let you down. Now, I think the first thing I should do is remind us all of our duties.'

'Clean underwear every morning?' Cameron muttered. Jack let out a yelp of laughter and Lottie masked a snigger with a pretend yawn, which she realised immediately might have come across as even ruder than Cameron's joke.

'We were just in court together, so I think we're all up to speed with that,' Pan said. 'I've got emails to attend to so if there's nothing new, I'll need some space until the judge calls us back in.'

Lottie longed for a large glass of wine in spite of the two hundred or so calories it would cost her. Some days you just had to give in to your cravings. Jury politics were much more complex than she'd imagined. It was intimidating, yet she found herself intrigued by the lawyers and judge. She was terrified of humiliating herself with ignorance but there was no denying the importance of the job the jury had been given to do. She sighed. There would be no alcohol to sooth her nerves until she got home. Until then the best she could do was make herself a cup of tea. She walked across to the kettle. Jack, the student, followed.

'Take no notice of Mr Finuchin,' Lottie told him quietly as they poured insufficiently hot water onto tea bags. 'I'm not sure he really gets the point of further education.'

'He's probably right,' Jack muttered, shaking his head at the floor and reddening. 'My mother thought I should study the classics but I wanted modern languages. It was a compromise.'

'Oh,' Lottie replied, trying to inject some reassurance into her voice. 'Well, the Arabic will be useful, I bet. Interesting to put on your CV when you're job hunting.'

Jack stirred his tea without answering. 'Do you think she did it? The defendant, I mean,' he whispered. 'Only she looked so, I don't know, pathetic.'

'Those are the types you have to watch,' Cameron said over Jack's shoulder as he grabbed a biscuit from a paper plate. 'It's always the quiet ones who turn out to be psychos and maniacs. This whole thing's a true crime TV drama waiting to be made.'

Lottie watched him devour shortbread and lick his lips, keen to respond with something insightful and interesting, or no one would want to get to know her. It wasn't that difficult, she told herself. She chatted to people all the time at toddler group, and never felt out of her depth. Everyone on the jury was in the same boat, landed with strangers in the middle of the summer when they'd all rather be elsewhere. She just had to relax and stop being so insecure. In the middle of drawing breath to tell Cameron he shouldn't judge the defendant by her looks, the door to the corridor opened and the usher beamed at them. 'Ladies and gentlemen, Her Honour Judge Downey has requested your presence back in court.'

Cameron and Jack made for the doorway as Lottie quickly tidied the abandoned cups, telling herself it was ridiculous to be worried about the mess when no one else seemed to care. Some habits were hard to break. Lottie wondered how she could possibly be expected to decide something as critical as whether or not the defendant was guilty, and which mistake was worse – setting a guilty person free, or wrongly condemning an innocent one to prison?

4

Maria Bloxham surveyed the courtroom through the smudges on the inside of the glass dock. She liked them. They told a story of a cleaner who was either too distracted or uncaring to be fastidious. No one should obsess about cleaning. She'd wasted so many years worrying about every mark on the carpets and straightening the towels. It had all been for nothing.

James Newell, her barrister, walked into the dock and took a seat next to her as the public gallery began to fill.

'So the jury will come back in shortly. After that the prosecution will open their case, which means Miss Pascal will summarise the evidence against you. She'll only give her version of the facts and will probably make you out to be extremely manipulative. Don't expect anything she says to be either fair or balanced,' he warned.

'You'll respond though?' Maria asked. 'We should have a chance to put our side, too.'

Newell shook his head. 'That's not how it works at this stage, I'm afraid, but I will be able to give a speech at the very end of the trial which is much more valuable. It'll be one of the last things the jury hears before considering their verdict.'

'But they'll be thinking the worst of me from the outset,' Maria said. The tension she had tried so hard to banish began flooding back in.

'The system is set up so that the prosecution puts its case first as the burden is on them to prove their case. After that, we can call our own witnesses and you can tell your story. It'll take a while and you should be ready for delays. Court cases rarely run smoothly.'

'So are they allowed to say whatever they like about me?' Maria asked.

'If they break any rules, I'll object. Otherwise it's up to the prosecution to run their case as they see fit. Try to focus on something else during the speech. Miss Pascal is likely to disregard any mention of your defence. Any last minute questions?'

'No, I'm fine,' Maria said. 'Although it's a bit hot in here.'

'You should feel it with this wig on,' he smiled. 'Listen, it's not too late,' Newell said, suddenly serious again. 'We could still run a psychiatric defence. It's much more usual in cases like this. The judge would criticise us for lateness, but I'm sure I could make her understand . . .'

'You want to tell the jury I was suffering from an abnormal mental state. It would mean endless hours with psychiatrists, and that would be intolerable for me. I appreciate you're trying to give me the best possible chance, but I won't pretend I didn't understand what I was doing.'

Newell nodded, acknowledging defeat gracefully. 'All right then. I'm hoping the judge will keep the court days short. It'll be unbearable in here by the afternoon.' He motioned for the prison guards to take their place next to Maria, then went back to the lawyers' benches. Most of what Maria could see was a wall of backs. It hardly seemed fair. Surely, she thought, she should be able to look at the faces of the people who were talking about her.

Only when everyone else had gathered did the jury enter. They must hate her, Maria thought. All they'd have heard so far were press reports from when she was first arrested. Headlines had ranged from the creative 'The Would-Be Widow' to the plodding 'Suburban Violence Rages in Bristol.' Her age had been given as anything between thirty and fifty. Various witness testimonies had apparently been uncovered, detailing a history of shouted arguments and vehicles screeching late at night from their address. Maria had been sympathetic to an extent. The press had to make something up. The truth of her life was far too dull for the public to bother buying it.

She sighed. It didn't matter what anyone thought. The only real crime was that Edward hadn't had the good grace to simply die. Ed, she reprimanded herself. She could call him Ed now. He could never complain about the abbreviation again. He'd once had a secretary who'd called him Ed three times in a row. Her employment had been terminated the next day. Since then, every other secretary had been firmly instructed to only ever address him as Mr Bloxham.

Her Honour Judge Downey cleared her throat, finished writing a note, and looked up at the prosecutor. Imogen Pascal – that was what Maria's barrister had called her – was a tough one. Maria recognised the same ambition that had previously shone in her husband's eyes. The drive to be the best, craving recognition. The nasty creep of failure just over your shoulder if you ever paused for breath. In contrast, all Maria had done for at least a decade was to stop and smell the roses in her garden. She wanted to tell Imogen Pascal that mediocrity wasn't so bad. Excelling only meant there was a greater distance to fall.

Miss Pascal stood up, flawless in a grey woollen suit beneath her gown.

'Members of the jury,' Imogen Pascal began, 'this case, whilst serious, is factually quite simple. The defendant,' she turned flamboyantly with a wave of her arm to the dock in which Maria sat, 'made a serious, forceful and deliberate attempt to end her husband's life. That much, I can tell you now, is not in dispute.'

Heads turned. However much Maria willed herself not to move, it was inevitable that she should meet the jurors' eyes. They looked bewildered. How could Maria not be disputing that she had tried to kill her husband? That was what they wanted to know. Miss Pascal's description of pure brutality was not what they were expecting. Presumably they thought Maria would claim it had all been some dreadful mistake, that she'd believed her husband to be a burglar. Or perhaps that she had been swotting a fly with the chair leg and aimed badly. Maria frowned to deaden the grin that was threatening to spread her mouth wide. No. No excuses. Maria had wanted her husband dead. The truth was that she had prayed for it, fantasised about it. Seeing him bleed on the kitchen floor was all her Christmases come at once.

Imogen Pascal, having wrung every drop of melodrama from her pause, tapped a pen on her notepad twice, drawing all eyes back to her before continuing the prosecution's opening speech.

'Allow me to set the scene. The defendant and Dr Edward Bloxham had been married for eighteen years. Edward Bloxham is a man of impeccable character. He works – I should say worked . . . the injuries he received at the defendant's hand were so severe that he will never recover – as a consultant ecologist. He advised both governments and industry on the ecological impact of manufacturing. In his free time, he presented a video blog on the effects of global warming on British wildlife with more than half a million subscribers. Dr Bloxham had written books, and appeared on both the radio and television. He was the champion, if you like, of the grasshopper, the robin and the field mouse. He did his best to prevent harm from coming to those small creatures, until he himself was struck down in a calculated act of violence.'

In spite of the high-sided glass of the dock and the wall behind her, Maria could almost hear the jury foreperson as she mouthed a single word, 'Shame'. Just like that, they had convicted her. It hadn't required the chair leg, the brain damage or the blood on Maria's hands. Just the field mouse. Imogen Pascal was clever. Maria had never had cause to think about it before, but criminal barristers weren't really employed for their legal skills. They were psychologists. They slid their hands into your chest to pull your heartstrings, creating moral outrage from the least obvious misdemeanours. She wondered how her own barrister, James Newell, would respond. He had none of Imogen Pascal's cutting edge. Quite the opposite.

A man in the press seats was sketching her again, the constant scribble of his pencil irritating the people around him. Maria could see their foreheads crinkling into frowns. What would the picture show? She wouldn't buy the newspaper to see, although she was free to do so. The judge had allowed her to live in the community awaiting trial, provided she resided at a bail hostel. One room with a hard bed and a broken chest of drawers, next to a shared bathroom and opposite a kitchen barely fit for the purpose. Maria had been put on a curfew, allowed out only between the hours of 8 a.m. and 6 p.m. Her lawyers had impressed upon her that she shouldn't break the rules under any circumstances. Most importantly, she was under no circumstances to attempt to contact Edward Bloxham. That one was beyond irony.

The press artist's sketch would not be kind. Maria knew every line on her face, every sag of skin. At forty she looked fifty. Her long hair was tied in a plait and wound into a bun at the back of her head, brown shot through with dried-up grey. Moisturisers and hair dyes were a waste of money, her husband had said, and given that she wasn't earning any, how could Maria have expected Edward to have spent his cash on such vanities? Likewise appointments at the hairdresser. Foolish, conceited women, sitting for hours staring in mirrors as their hair was imbued with false colour and they were flattered by people who only wanted their money, he said. True beauty was a wonder of nature. It couldn't be bought in a salon. There was no point Maria going, he'd made that crystal clear. You couldn't make a silk purse from a sow's ear. Over the years that had become one of Ed's favourite phrases.

'You will see,' Imogen Pascal persisted, 'the weapon with which the near-fatal blow was dealt, and hear about the tremendous force that was employed. The prosecution will prove that the devastating attack on Mr Bloxham was not dealt in self-defence, as Mrs Bloxham will claim, but in fact while her unsuspecting husband had his back turned to her. She chose to strike when he could not possibly have fought back, then she calmly telephoned the police and waited on the driveway for them to arrive. The only emotion she showed was when she found out that her husband was still clinging to life, at which point, ladies and gentlemen, the defendant fainted. Dr Bloxham did survive, but just barely. His blood is on the defendant's hands, and no amount of the excuses you'll hear in this courtroom can wash them clean.'

Miss Pascal sat down. Maria was tempted to applaud. The prosecutor deserved it. Her performance had been spectacular. In his absence, Edward had taken on a saintly air that made even Maria feel rather sorry for him. The attack sounded as if it had been planned over a period of weeks or months, as if Maria had lain in wait until he'd finally turned his back on her. The blow to his head seemed so brilliantly aimed and delivered that she might have practised with a baseball bat and dummy to perfect it. She liked the idea of that.

The jurors were pale faced and uncomfortable. At least two had been wringing their hands in distress. Others had closed their eyes at the height of the prosecutor's speech. Some of the men had looked Maria square in the face, trying to get the measure of her. Perhaps they were wondering if their own wives were waiting at home harbouring the same bloodthirsty desires. The shock, at least in part, was that a female could do such a dreadful thing, Maria thought. Had the defendant been a man accused of beating his wife to within inches of her life it would have been just another incident of domestic abuse gone too far. There would be neither shock nor incomprehension. But a woman consciously and purposefully attacking a man was an unacceptable perversion of day-to-day violence. It was intolerable.

The jury left. Bail was extended until the following day. Maria's barrister, James Newell, motioned for the prison guards to release her from the dock. Suddenly she could breath again.

'Are you all right?' Newell asked, pulling his wig from his head and running a hand through his hair. 'That was a bit rough.'

'I'm sure Miss Pascal was just doing her job,' Maria said. 'Tomorrow's another day.'

He pulled her aside into a quiet corner, setting his pink-ribboned brief down on the floor and shoving his hands into trouser pockets. 'You know, Ms Bloxham, you don't have to be so stoic. It's all right to be scared, these proceedings are overwhelming at the best of times and frankly . . .' he broke off, searching for the right words.

'It's going to be difficult, isn't it, claiming self-defence in these circumstances?' Maria asked.

'Difficult, but not impossible. It'll largely fall to you to convince the jury that you needed to strike your husband in the manner you did,' Newell said.

'I understand,' she replied. 'I'm just not sure how to explain what my life was like. I don't think they'll believe me. Sometimes I can't believe it myself.'

'One day at a time,' her barrister said. 'Let's worry about that when we've got through the prosecution case. You're not on your own here. Let me walk you out.' He held the heavy courtroom door open for her.

Maria paused at the top of staircase. 'Is it hard for you, defending people accused of crimes like these?'

James Newell sighed. 'Sometimes it makes me rather sad,' he said. 'Like everyone, I have moments when I'd prefer to be by a pool reading a good book. But the truth is that everyone deserves a fair trial and a proper defence. If you're asking me about your case specifically, you should know I consider myself a reasonable judge of character.' He gave a modest smile. 'We're going to fight this as hard as we possibly can. Not just because it's my job, but because I want to see justice done.'

'I wasn't asking your opinion of me,' she rushed to reassure him. 'I didn't mean to put you in a difficult position.'

'That's all right, Ms Bloxham. If I were in your shoes, I'd want to know that the person representing me believed me too.' He motioned towards the exit and Maria continued down the stairs.

'Thank you,' she said, before heading towards the sunshine, wishing she'd never started the conversation. As reassuring as it was to know he was on her side, it made her feel so much worse about lying to him.

Maria made her way down Small Street and into the pedestrian walkway Exchange Avenue, avoiding the late afternoon café users and tourists buying cheap trinkets they didn't need and would never look at again. Her new, lightweight mobile buzzed in her pocket. She still wasn't used to the vibrate function. It seemed excessive when a ringtone did the job perfectly well. The solicitors' firm had insisted that she buy a phone to facilitate communication before the trial, but calls were few and far between. A man bumped into her as she pressed the button to take the call. Maria recognised him as the person who'd been sketching her in court. He glanced back over his shoulder, smirking as he sauntered away. Maria stepped into the shaded mouth of an alleyway and answered her phone.

'Maria, how are you holding up?' a soft voice asked at the end of the line.

'Ruth, I saw you in court. It would be better if you'd stay away. Knowing you're watching makes it harder, not easier,' Maria said, poking her head out of the alleyway to check the man had gone.

'You need a friend to get you through this. No one's tough enough to cope on their own,' Ruth replied.

'I made a decision,' Maria said. 'I want to be able to look myself in the mirror and know I finally stood up to him. I'm going to stand in that courtroom and tell the world I wish I had killed him.'

'You can't put it like that,' her friend said gently. 'The jury won't like it.'

'I have lawyers to advise me what I should and shouldn't say, and I've had enough of living a lie. I'm glad Ed's never going to walk or talk again. I'd have preferred him to have died, but the state he's in is the next best thing. I won't apologise for it and I won't dress it up. If he had a grave, I'd be dancing on it.'

'Maria, don't talk like that, you'll end up convicting yourself,' her friend said.

The man who'd bumped her wandered back past the end of the alleyway, peering into the shops opposite.

'Damn,' Maria muttered, shrinking against the wall.

'Maria, are you okay?'

'Listen, I need you to stay away tomorrow,' Maria insisted.

'But I can support you. I still think I could help.'

'This is my life and it's my decision. I want to do it alone. This *should* be hard, showing some backbone after years of weakness. It's my way of gathering up the shreds of my self-respect and weaving something usable out of it,' Maria said. 'You of all people should understand that. Let me stand on my own two feet. If I can't even do that, I might just as well plead guilty.'

5

Zain was late home. Normally Lottie would have been irritated, but today it gave her additional time to make sure dinner was ready, then get Daniyal bathed and in pyjamas ready for a cuddle and a book when his daddy walked in.

Lottie had compromised on half a glass of red wine which allowed for a guilt-free serving spoon of pasta. She hadn't stopped since leaving the court. Shopping, picking Daniyal up, cleaning, cooking. The house was looking nice though, which should make it easier to break the news to her husband that she was going to be on jury duty for the next fortnight.

Topping up her wine glass with an extra splash as she flicked through a recipe book, she looked for meals that could go in the slow cooker before she left each morning.

Daniyal's scream hit her at the same time his head butted into her stomach.

'Mummy, mummy, help, help . . .'

She lurched forward, one arm around her son, just managing to stay on her feet, as the wine bottle sploshed liquid over her chest and hand. Losing her grip on it, she covered Daniyal's face before it could hit him too. The bottle tumbled down her blue shirt, soaking the white bra beneath, leaving her eyes stinging and her face dripping. It was half empty by the time it hit floor and smashed, leaving her standing in a crimson puddle.

'Daniyal, what happened sweetheart?' she asked, as she lifted him clear of the mess and reached for the kitchen roll.

'There was a spider at the bottom of the stairs. I had to jump over it to get through the hall. Shall we try and catch it, Mummy?' he suggested, wide-eyed.

'What a mess! Is that wine all over him?' Zain asked from the kitchen doorway. 'Don't let him get any of that in his mouth.' He strode through, avoiding the glass, grabbing a tea towel and wiping Daniyal's damp hair. 'I think it might be more sensible if you didn't drink until after he's gone to bed.'

Lottie turned to the sink, running water into her hands and rinsing the wine off her face.

'It was an accident,' she murmured. 'I'll give him another bath.'

'No, I'll do it. You need a shower yourself. I didn't say it wasn't an accident. It's just that some accidents are avoidable. Come on Danny.'

'There was a spider, Daddy,' Daniyal reported, his face beaming as his father finished rubbing his hair.

'Really?' Zain asked, picking the boy up and carrying him out of the kitchen.

'Yes, it was huge. I was really brave and I jumped over it . . .'

The two of them disappeared up the stairs as Lottie began unbuttoning her shirt.

'My day was fine,' she told thin air. 'Quite interesting, actually, thanks for asking. And yes, this shirt is ruined. Never mind. Doesn't matter. Yours are all clean and hanging in your wardrobe.'

She tossed the shirt into the sink and ran the cold tap over it. The mark had turned an ugly shade of purple with a brown rim. Lottie considered trying white wine or salt to get the mark out, before picking up the dripping wet cotton and thrusting it into the bin. On a different day she might have wasted hours of her time soaking and treating the stain.

Not today, though. Tiredness had taken over. Zain could get his own dinner out of the oven. She wasn't hungry anyway. Shutting her eyes as she spent a few minutes dabbing her bra with a cloth, she wished the day was already over and that she could just go to bed. There was still a tricky conversation to be had with Zain, and she hadn't quite figured out the right words yet. The oven beeped. She turned it off while taking cutlery from a drawer and setting the table. Lottie looked longingly at what remained of her wine. She was entitled to finish it. It was ridiculous to throw it down the sink, whatever Zain's views were. Whirling round to pick up her glass from the counter, she stubbed her bare toe on the edge of a drawer she'd failed to shut properly.

'Oh fuck,' she hissed, reaching for her throbbing foot.

'Charlotte, mind your language!' Zain tutted. She looked up to where he stood in the doorway with Daniyal in his arms.

'I'm sorry, I just stubbed my toe. It's been one thing after another and I . . .'

'He wants you to put him to bed.' He lifted Daniyal towards her. 'He never settles down for me.'

'He's not rational when he's tired,' Lottie said quietly as she took him. 'It's not personal. Danny's just around me more than he is you. There's a plate in the oven. Use the gloves. It'll be really hot by now.'

'Why aren't you eating?' Zain asked, shrugging off his suit jacket.

'Not hungry,' she said. 'Leave everything on the table. I'll come back down and clear up after my shower.'

Taking the stairs slowly, avoiding knocking the injured toe, she sang a nursery rhyme to Daniyal. He stroked her hair, laying his head on her shoulder and humming along with her. Tucking him into bed, she kissed his cheek and smiled down at him.

'Were you okay without mummy today?' Lottie asked softly.

'Yes, but the carrots in my snack were a bit squishy so I hid them under a cushion,' he replied, rolling over to grab his favourite toy from the stack of furry animals next to his pillow.

Lottie laughed and pulled the duvet up over his shoulders. 'So do you think you'll be all right going there for the next couple of weeks while I'm busy?'

'Sure,' he said, 'they let me jump around much more than you. I jumped from the third step today and no one told me I'd hurt myself.'

'Good for you.' Lottie did her best not to frown as she responded. 'Sleep now, little man. Got to be up early again tomorrow morning.' Closing his door save for an inch in case he called out in his sleep, she imagined the scenario from his perspective. The childminder's was more fun because there was no mother constantly fussing over him. Did she really tell him he might get hurt every time he jumped off some steps? Perhaps she did. Maybe Daniyal was ready for a break from her just as much as she needed some time out from her routine.

Sliding a hand into the shower to get the water running, she shed the rest of her clothes and stared at her naked body in the full-length mirror on her wardrobe. With a hand still sticky from the fermented grape juice, she felt the tautness of her neck, slim and smooth. Her shoulders were tanned with the thinnest of strap marks after a month of wearing summer tops. Gently she ran her hand over the flesh of one breast, still pert even after breast feeding. Her stomach was in good shape. The stretch marks were fading, and an iron will to resist sugar had left it just about flat. Then there were her legs, her pride and joy, long with defined muscles, always immaculately hairless. At nineteen her legs could turn almost any man's head, whether she was wearing jeans or a mini-skirt. She wondered how so much could have changed. They were the same legs.

She was the same person. Now those legs were just limbs that walked her from one place to another.

'Stupid girl,' she told herself in the mirror. 'Zain's right. What the hell's wrong with me?'

Lottie pulled her hand from her body abruptly enough to scratch the surface of her skin, closing her eyes at the image of the frowning woman in the mirror. The shower would bring her back to her senses. Anticipating the heat and relief, she stepped in, tipping her head back to greet the warm water, already reaching for the shower gel.

The freezing spray hit her chest first, leaving her gasping. She screeched, reaching out to turn it off, succeeding only in knocking the shower head down to the floor from where it began spurting upwards, soaking her in an icy stream. Two baths and there was no hot water left for her. Turning towards the door she realised she still reeked of wine. There was no choice but to endure the chill. Gritting her teeth, she grabbed the shower head and forced herself to accept the cold water pummelling her skin. Half a minute later, she was climbing back out and clutching a towel, grateful to the extraordinary heat of the summer for rendering the upper floor of the house overly warm in the evenings. Now she had to go back downstairs and clean up from dinner, and the floor needed mopping as well or the whole kitchen would stink in the morning.

Zain was sitting at the table, his empty plate pushed away to make space for the newspaper.

'You all right?' he asked without looking up.

'Sure,' she said. 'You want anything else?'

'Coffee would be good,' he replied, turning a page.

Lottie watched him from the corners of her eyes as she put the kettle on and loaded his plate into the dishwasher. With premature flashes of grey at his temples, Zain looked older than his late thirties but he carried it well. He was lithe, the golf course keeping him in shape, and he moved with a confidence Lottie had once felt she matched. Now it was a characteristic she envied. Filling his mug with boiling water, she stirred in milk and half a teaspoon of sugar, the way he liked it, putting the cup down in front of him.

'I decided to do jury service,' she said, grabbing a cup to make herself a green tea.

She heard him flick the paper shut and push it across the table before picking up his mug.

'But we discussed it,' he said. 'I thought we agreed that the best thing for Daniyal was for you to get yourself excused. I've got back-to-back meetings for the next couple of weeks. What happens if he suddenly gets ill and can't go to the childminder?'

'It's only two weeks. There's no reason to think he'll get ill in that time,' Lottie said.

'Charlotte, you promised you'd get yourself released. I even offered to write a letter for you to explain the circumstances.'

Lottie bristled. She didn't need her husband writing a letter to make excuses for her. At some point, not only had she lost confidence in herself, apparently her husband had lost confidence in her as well.

'I thought being on the jury would be interesting,' she said. 'So I didn't ask to be released. This is important. It's a citizen's duty.' Lottie concentrated on the hot water she was pouring to cover the lie. It was ridiculous to have created an untruth from something that might have saved a row, but she was damned if she would give him the satisfaction of knowing she'd done what she'd been told.

'I think the phrase is civic duty. And in case you've forgotten, the reason I go to work and you stay home is because of our commitment to our child and this house,' Zain replied. 'We also decided to try for another baby. Daniyal's the right age to deal with a sibling now and my career's going well, but you're still drinking and now there's this jury thing . . .'

'You decided it would be a good time for another baby, Zain. I didn't agree anything, and even if I had, half a glass of wine and two weeks jury duty is hardly going to make a difference,' Lottie said, ripping off a piece of kitchen roll to clean the water mark her mug had left. 'I want to be more than someone who just looks after a family.'

'This argument again?' he sighed. 'Our lives work because we agreed on different roles. Couldn't you just make it easy for me? I have enough conflict in the office all day. I don't need to come home to it as well.'

'There's no conflict,' Lottie said. 'I'll do everything I usually do. Daniyal will be fine at the childminder for a fortnight. If anything happens, I'll take responsibility for making alternative arrangements.'

'I don't want alternative arrangements, I want the normal ones. Do you have any idea how much pressure I'm under at work? I'm trying to make up for several other offices that are underperforming whilst training new staff members. The least you could do is make sure everything here runs smoothly.'

'It does run smoothly. I got called for jury duty, Zain. You're reacting as if I booked myself onto a two week cruise. You can't just tell them you're not going to do it. And for the record, I don't feel ready to have another baby yet. I'm just getting my life back so you're going to need to have a rethink . . .'

'Getting your life back? What exactly is so terrible about raising our child? Listen to yourself. We had the chance to move to Pakistan and live with my family. You'd have had help from my mother with Danny, I had a great job offer there, and you said no. So don't moan about your life. I work every hour I can to support this family. If we don't have another child now, then when?'

'I'm not giving you a time estimate. This is about my body!'

'I think I'm entitled to a say, don't you?'

'Actually no, I don't. You said you were okay with the decision not to move to Pakistan, so don't throw that in my face now.'

'We're going to have to talk about this another time. I'm not prepared to argue with you tonight. I've got several reports to read before a meeting tomorrow, so work's not over for me yet. Enjoy the rest of your wine. The floor needs . . .'

'I know,' she said. 'I'll run the mop over it now. You go and get your work done.'

He picked up his bag from the hallway and retreated into the lounge, slamming the door behind him. Lottie took the mop from the utility room. Jury service would be good for her, she decided, as she squirted detergent into a bucket and filled it with warm water. Anything but more housework was as good as a holiday. She wouldn't let Daniyal down. Being a mother was the most important job in the world, but she mattered, too. Feeling alive again mattered. If Zain was too wrapped up in his own work to see what she needed, she would make some changes on her own terms, whether he approved of them or not.

6

Day Two in Court

Baking in the heat of the jury room, Lottie pulled her chair into a corner and flicked through a magazine that had been abandoned in a pile on the floor. The date on the cover was December two years earlier. She imagined all the bored fingers that had turned the pages, then closed her eyes before getting sucked into endless housekeeping articles. She'd had enough of domesticity, and it wasn't even ten in the morning.

Lottie had made sure her daily tasks were completed, knowing it would be easier to go to court if there were no compromises at home. She'd checked that Zain had a shirt ironed for the next morning before searching her own wardrobe for an appropriate outfit, settling on a long green skirt and white shirt. Keeping her make-up as natural as possible, she determined to fit in with the group, sure they wouldn't approve of either short skirts or too much eyeliner. After that, she went through her diary and emailed cancellations to all the toddler groups she'd planned to attend over the next two weeks. The break would do her good. There were only so many renditions of 'The Wheels on the Bus' that one person could stand without suffering long-term psychological damage.

Now she was stuck in a stifling room with eleven strangers and not looking forward to what the day might bring. Actually, ten strangers. Someone was late. Lucky for them, the day was starting with yet another delay.

'Anything good in there?' Jen asked brightly.

Lottie held out the magazine half-heartedly. 'Not much, but help yourself. I've finished with it.'

'So where do you live then? We're in Redcliffe, near Temple Meads train station. It's a bit busy but an easy walk from the city centre.'

'Abbots Leigh,' Lottie replied, glancing around to see who else she could talk to. Jen seemed nice, but she didn't want to get stuck in dull conversations about her family. That was exactly what she wanted to get away from.

'Lovely village, very quaint, lucky you. I suppose you come over the Clifton Bridge in the mornings then. Nothing like that view, is there? Costs a fortune to keep it in good repair, of course.'

'I'm sure,' Lottie murmured. 'Time for a cup of coffee, I think. Enjoy the magazine.'

'Hold on,' Jen said. 'Let's exchange numbers. It might be helpful, I thought, in case either of us was ever late for court, or if you fancied going out some time?'

'Oh yeah, sure,' Lottie mumbled, as Jen pushed her mobile forward and waited to get Lottie's in return. She punched her number into Jen's contact list with a sinking stomach. This was what she was. A housewife, destined to be friends with other housewives. All of them dull together. 'Thanks. I'm going to go and get coffee now.'

She stood up abruptly, and joined Jack – the Latin and Arabic student she had felt so sorry for yesterday – at the coffee table. His clothes were already limp with sweat, his hair sticking to his forehead. Lottie sympathised. Her skirt was clammy against her legs, and she wished she'd brought her antiperspirant stick in her handbag to freshen up at lunchtime. Daily news bulletins

47

were announcing deaths from over-heating, and comparing the south of England with various desert regions across the world.

'Word of warning,' Lottie said. 'Don't eat the biscuits. They're the ones from yesterday.'

'I'm a student. Even soft biscuits are a luxury I can't normally afford,' Jack smiled.

The door opened and Cameron walked in. He was wearing the same shirt as the day before, and his eyes were bloodshot. It was either partying or trouble, and he was sufficiently attractive that any number of women would be willing to keep him up all night. Lottie recognised the signs. She'd been an expert on clubbing and arriving home after sunrise before meeting Zain. He'd rescued her from a steep downward slope and given her a new life, something of a Cinderella story. It wasn't that she wanted to sink back into her former partying days – she had motherhood to thank for that change – more that the memories represented an irrecoverable time. She would never again be so carefree. The real issue was that her life now was so staid and predictable in comparison. She struggled to find things to look forward to.

The recently elected Tabitha addressed Cameron from the head of the table where she sat surrounded by willing cronies, Gregory, Agnes and Samuel. 'Mr Ellis, I'm afraid you're rather tardy. We were supposed to arrive no later than 10 a.m. I'm not sure the judge would appreciate one of our number keeping the court waiting on the second day.'

'So you've already been into court, but were sent back out to wait for me, is that right?' Cameron asked, filling a mug with coffee and slopping it everywhere, evidently not the least bit concerned about cleaning up after himself.

'No, as a matter of fact, but that's besides the point. This is a very serious case and as foreperson I should remind you of your . . .'

'Remind me all you like, lady, but you're not my mother. If the judge has something to say to me, I'm sure she'll say it. Don't make the mistake of telling me off again.' He took his phone out of his pocket and stalked away to the far end of the table, throwing himself into a chair and directing his attention towards his mobile. There was a ripple of shocked murmuring around Tabitha, with the foreperson reassuring her admirers that she was quite all right.

'Sorry, I'm on a business call, would you mind being a bit quieter?' Pan Carras asked, putting one hand over the end of his mobile.

'Or you could go somewhere else,' Cameron replied without looking up.

'Maybe you should go somewhere else,' Agnes Huang snapped.

'Do you want me to tell you where you can go?' Cameron smirked.

'Really,' Gregory Smythe blustered, getting to his feet. 'An apology is required.'

'Stay out of it, granddad,' Cameron said. 'While we're not in court I can say what I like to who I like.'

Gregory took a step forward to respond as Tabitha put a calming hand on his forearm. 'Perhaps this is best left,' she whispered to him. He looked thunderous but retook his seat. The Tabitha support act reformed quietly at the end of the table, exchanging dark glances.

Lottie watched Cameron texting furiously. Something was wrong. He was hammering the touchscreen of his phone, jaw clenched tight. He was frustrated. The easier way for her to deal with it would be to focus on what she was reading and mind her own business, but she wasn't interested in easy any more. Easy had made her sluggish and pathetic. She wanted to make friends, and that meant reaching out. Everyone had bad days. Setting down the magazine, she approached him, determined to repair the damage to the atmosphere for all their sakes.

'Hey, there are a few biscuits left. Can I grab you some?' she asked quietly. 'The sugar might make you feel better. Always works for me.'

'It's Lottie, right?' Cameron replied.

'Yes,' she responded, pleased he'd remembered her name.

'Okay Lottie, I've got legs to walk across the room and hands to take whatever I want. Just because you've finally escaped from your little two-up-two-down doesn't mean you have to find some replacement for your kid to fuss over,' he said. 'What I really want is to be left alone.'

The rest of the room stared on in stunned silence.

'Just trying to help,' Lottie muttered, her cheeks blazing. Jack averted his gaze. Cameron Ellis might be good looking but he was rude and aggressive. Whatever mood he was in didn't excuse him speaking to her like that. He wouldn't get another chance. He might be the person closest to her age on the jury, but he could look elsewhere for conversation from now on. If there hadn't been other people in the room, she'd have told him exactly what she thought of him.

Lottie knew what her husband would say, hating that he was right. She was out of her depth. She'd imagined lengthy conversations, trying to get to the heart of the truth in the trial, finding others equally interested in seizing an opportunity to make a difference, but on her wavelength. It was obviously not to be. The older jurors had already banded together. Jack, the student, was sweet but looked even more lost than her. Better to wait for jury service to be over and stick with the young mums' brigade at toddler group, accepting her limits. Better still to just keep quiet.

7

Maria took the stairs up from the Crown Court reception area, avoiding the solicitors hurrying to meet clients and catching snippets of the barristers' conversations as they swished past. She studied the emotions on the faces of life's other losers. Victims there to give evidence, defendants waiting to be sentenced, everyone hoping their particular judge had woken up in a good mood. It was fascinating, encompassing all the stresses and strains Edward claimed to have protected her from. She'd missed out on so much. Friends had been left unmet and unmade. Mistakes equally, from which she might have learned. And she – foolish, ridiculous, duped she – had done nothing about it until far too late. Better late than never, though. If revenge was a dish best served cold, hers had been on ice for a decade.

As if catching glimpses on a speeding train, she walked past the conference rooms that were dotted around various floors, in which today's line-up was alternately crying, shouting or huddling in conversation. The building was incredibly busy, with multiple sentencings that day. As a result, most of the rooms were full. Maria's barrister, James Newell, had found them a tiny space that had presumably been a broom cupboard in a former life, and they squeezed into it.

'Sorry about the delay. The prosecution is struggling to find a date when their psychiatrist can be here. How are you feeling today?' Newell asked.

'Very well, thank you,' Maria replied.

A knock at the door interrupted them, and Imogen Pascal poked her head in, with DI Anton standing close behind her.

'James, a word please,' she said. Maria's barrister excused himself and went outside, leaving the door ajar. Maria watched their exchange through the crack. It sounded polite enough, but the body language was tense. James Newell's arms were folded. Miss Pascal handed him documents which he skimmed as she spoke. He shook his head at her. Imogen Pascal's hands went to her hips. Maria leaned forward in her seat to see more of their exchange, bringing DI Anton into view. He was standing a metre behind the prosecutor, right hand in his trouser pockets as he wiped his left on his hip. He was perspiring badly, darkening patches already spreading beyond his armpits. He wasn't watching the exchange, though. His eyes were aimed downwards. Maria moved across the room to get a better view. From side on she could see much more clearly. DI Anton couldn't take his eyes off Imogen Pascal's buttocks. Maria doubted he even realised he was staring quite so openly. She stepped closer to the door, intrigued. No doubt he'd been on endless police courses designed to stop that sort of behaviour which just showed how little human demeanour was truly controllable. It had been half a lifetime since Maria had stared at anyone's buttocks. She wondered what the attraction really was, having spent a considerable amount of time avoiding looking at Edward when he was naked. That was mainly sagging white skin and spongy flesh. To be fair to DI Anton, Miss Pascal was rather more shapely. The police officer turned his head and caught Maria staring. She raised her eyebrows at him. He frowned and glared at her, making a show of coughing to cover his scarlet face, then moved to join the conversation between Pascal and Newell, turning his back to Maria. She sat back down, grinning.

James Newell reappeared a few minutes later clutching sheets of A4 paper and a bundle of photographs.

'What was that about?' Maria asked.

'A new statement,' Newell said, putting a bundle of paper-work on the table between them and rubbing his forehead. 'The police made a further search of your home. I suspect they were looking for anything that might counter your defence and the extent to which we say your husband controlled your life. They found this.' He held up a photograph of a mobile phone. Square, basic, and obviously cheap, without the frills of a camera or advanced functions, it had served Maria well enough over the years. 'You'll be asked about it if you give evidence. Think carefully before you answer. It's a pre-paid phone, no contract, and the police have been unable to produce any call records for it. We call them burners. As they can't be traced, they're commonly used by drug dealers. Now it might be that it's not yours, but they have also given us a statement stating that your fingerprints and no one else's were lifted from it. Do you recognise it?'

Maria took the photo from him, running her fingertips over the mobile in the picture. That silly piece of plastic had been the greatest risk she'd taken in the last half decade. She nodded.

'Yes,' she said. 'It's mine. It was tucked into an old pair of gardening shoes in my bedroom. They must have searched hard to find it.'

Newell ran his eyes down the police statement, speed-reading. 'They claim it was in your wardrobe,' he said. 'Any reason why you'd hidden it there?'

'The police will suggest I put it there so they couldn't find it, won't they?' Maria asked.

James Newell nodded. 'Quite possibly.'

Maria sighed. 'It was the one place Edward never ventured. By the time he'd got rid of all my clothes he didn't like and replaced them with his own choices, he didn't need to go into my wardrobe any more. Or so he thought.'

'Can you tell me where you got it?' Newell asked.

Maria stared at the photo. The mobile brought back so many memories. The idea had come as she'd been cleaning the lounge one day. She'd dismissed it as ridiculous at first. Just another pipe dream in a world where she had nothing of her own. Pulling the cushions out from the couch she'd found a treasure trove of coins. Thirty-eight pence in all. It had been so long since she'd held cash in her hand that she'd spent some minutes just turning them over, studying their faces. Slightly sticky, they nonetheless shone of freedom.

Hard for anyone else to imagine, she thought, as she smiled at James Newell in his bespoke suit and cufflinks. Hard to comprehend in this century, that a situation could have arisen whereby an adult female had no contact whatsoever with money. It hadn't always been that way. When Edward had first proposed to her, she'd owned a car. An exhausted run-around on its last legs, but it got her from A to B, usually. After they'd married it had failed its MOT and Ed had insisted she get rid of it until he found her something safer. In the meantime, the bus system around Bristol was good and it would save them money to be running only one vehicle. Maria had been impressed by his common sense, and by how much he'd cared for her safety. Then the months had slipped by. It was hard for her to do a week's shop using the buses. Thoughtful as ever, Edward had signed them up for internet grocery deliveries. It was perfect. Maria did the weekly meal plan and gave Edward a list of the ingredients she needed. He completed the order and paid on his credit card. Her every stress and strain was taken care of. She had no conscious memory of when the scales had tipped. By the time the landline in the house had been unplugged she had known there was a problem, but there was no sudden awakening. She had practiced wilful blindness for a while. Maria despised herself for it. That destructive human tendency to close one's eyes and believe that somehow, miraculously, everything would turn out all right, had rendered her useless and indecisive.

By the time she needed – not just wanted, but really needed – access to a phone, it was beyond her capability to get one. Until the pennies. Discarded, forgotten, fallen into a different realm, those coins had become her obsession. She checked the couch every morning as soon as the driveway gates had closed behind her husband's car. Two pence here. A celebrated ten pence there. Occasionally coins turned up in the rim of the washing machine. Once, only once mind, she had taken a pound coin from Edward's trouser pocket as she'd hung them up for him at bedtime. She hadn't slept that night, lying sweating in a pool of guilt. Coppers and small coins were one thing. Anything larger than a twenty pence, he'd miss.

Seven months, one week and two days later she had amassed the grand sum of twenty pounds. The woman who looked at her in the mirror that morning had glowed victorious. Her trip to the local newsagent was less exhilarating. Maria had attempted to disguise herself, looking ridiculous as she'd left the house in a winter coat during the summer, headscarf and all. She'd returned to the bedroom and stripped it all off when she realised that no one in Stoke Bishop had the slightest idea who she was anyway. Twice she'd set off but returned home, convinced her husband had some sixth sense and would know what she was up to. Finally, as she was changing her clothes for the last time, she'd caught sight of the criss-cross scarring on her thighs. That was what did it. Off she'd gone to the shop, pennies in a paper bag, to buy a line of communication with the world.

The photograph of the mobile phone sat on her lap, fraying at the edges already where she had gripped it too hard with wet palms.

'You're sure they can't tell if I used it, or how often, or who I called?' Maria asked her barrister.

James Newell sat quietly, studying her. 'They can't prove anything,' he eventually confirmed. 'No doubt they've tried. It was a good choice of phone if you wanted secrecy.'

Maria looked up at him. James Newell might be quieter and less showy than Imogen Pascal, but he was equally astute. His blue eyes and soft voice hid steel beneath sensitivity.

'Then it is mine, but I never had the nerve to use it,' she lied.

'All right,' Newell said. 'But Maria, at the moment we're struggling to find anything that backs your version of events. The jury only has you to rely on, so if there's anyone at all you confided in about what was happening in your life, or who might have witnessed anything, now would be the time to tell me.'

'It's just me, I'm afraid,' Maria lied. 'The way it always has been.'

Newell folded his arms, staring at the photograph of the mobile phone. 'You're sure there's nothing else? What you've described experiencing during your marriage was appalling. No one would blame you if you'd reached out for help. When people are pushed to their limits they make bad choices. If there's anything you're not telling me because you're worried how it'll look, you'd be better off discussing it. Some corroboration of your version of events, even if not every aspect of it is ideal, is better than none at all.'

Maria smiled sweetly at him. James Newell was mild mannered and kind, but he was nobody's fool. He knew she hadn't told him everything. 'We'll just have to make the best case we can with what we've got,' she told him.

He sighed deeply, picked up the new statements from the desk and slid them into a folder. 'I don't want you to suffer more than you already have. A prison sentence would be . . .'

'I don't want to talk about it,' she said quickly. 'One day at a time. That's how I endured my marriage. That's how I'll get through this trial.'

He nodded. 'Very well. I'm going to ask the judge to adjourn today to give me the chance to read this new material carefully and decide if we need to do any further work before proceeding. The jury will be sent home for the afternoon. We'll start again in the morning. Do me a favour, would you? Have another think about what we've discussed. If there's anyone, anyone at all, who might be able to tell the court what your husband was really like, we need to call them as a witness.'

'Thank you, Mr Newell,' Maria said. 'I'll consider that.'

She wouldn't. She was quite clear about that. The jury was going to be presented with a version of events on her terms, and her terms alone. Her not guilty plea required some additions and a few omissions. Getting other people involved was only going to decrease her chances of acquittal. Maria didn't need a law degree to have reached that conclusion.

8

Day Three in Court

Bristol was heaving with commuters rushing from overcrowded multi-storey car parks to offices. The intense sun had scattered overheated cars along the curb-side, smoke billowing from beneath their bonnets, exacerbating rush-hour chaos. Pedestrians clutched bottles of water as they walked, fanning themselves with newspapers. Lottie was tense from the heat before she even arrived, but at least she was there early, thanks to her childminder's strict parental drop-off-and-don't-linger rule. Yesterday had been completely wasted. Lottie had wanted to hear from witnesses and explore the issues in the case. More importantly, she'd wanted to go home with a sense of purpose but all she'd felt at the end of the day was bored and alone.

A crowd of banner-wielding protestors was gathered a few metres from the court, and several police officers were keeping them restricted to a single area. Edward Bloxham's face appeared on their boards, with declarations of grief over the man who had been such a leader of the green community. Lottie did her best not to read and be swayed by them, but she couldn't avoid hearing the chants of 'Justice Now!'. Seeing Cameron Ellis leaning against the wall outside the Crown Court doors didn't improve her mood. She put her head down and sped up to go past him.

'Lottie,' he called as she headed for the door. 'Hey Lottie, wait up.'

She gave in, aware that pretending not to have heard him was ridiculous given that Cameron had jogged to within a metre of her.

Gritting her teeth, she turned to face him. 'What?'

'Listen, I know you don't want to talk to me. I was well out of line yesterday. You were being nice and I behaved like an idiot. I got here early to say I'm sorry, before they stick us back in our sheep pen,' he said. 'Let me make it up to you?'

'No need,' Lottie replied. 'You've apologised. We can leave it there.' She moved closer to the doors, doing her best not to make eye contact with him, the embarrassment of his previous nastiness still raw. A ten second apology didn't make up for humiliating her in front of the other jurors. As far as she was concerned, Cameron Ellis could stay out of her way for the duration.

He managed to step ahead, hands in the air in a gesture of surrender. 'A thousand apologies wouldn't make what I did any better, but that's not how I am normally. Please, let me buy you a decent coffee to start the day. If nothing else I can save you from another cup of the dishwater they're serving, okay?' Against her better judgment, Lottie sighed and paused. 'Great,' Cameron said, 'I know a fantastic place just around the corner. Follow me.'

'I didn't say yes,' Lottie said, glancing at her watch.

'You didn't say no,' he grinned. 'And yes, we do have time. Take the free coffee and run if that's how you feel. Just give me another chance. I was having a really bad morning, and I didn't sleep all night worrying about it. You can spend the next half hour finding as many swear words as you can to yell at me if you like.'

Lottie smiled in spite of the irritation she still felt. Cameron Ellis could be as charming as he was horrible, but Lottie knew how a bad day felt. She'd been having a lot of them lately.

'Now I really am taking that smile as a yes. Come on, if we don't get moving you'll change your mind again,' he said, as he held out a hand out to let her walk past him.

'You're going to have to work a lot harder for me to actually forgive you,' Lottie said as they began to walk together. 'And I don't need half an hour to think up the swear words. I had them all in my head yesterday. Some of us are just better at minding our mouths than others.'

'Fair comment,' he grinned. 'I guess I owe you more than just a coffee.'

'Coffee's a start,' she said, softening. 'As long as it's followed by a lot more grovelling.'

They went to Corky's Café and chose an outside table to watch the slow progress of the traffic. A trickle of sweat ran down Lottie's back and she wished she'd worn a darker top. By the end of the day the cotton would be see-through if the temperature kept up.

Lottie turned her attention to Cameron who was ordering their coffee. She shouldn't have given in that quickly, not after he'd been so unpleasant, but he seemed genuinely sorry. The truth was that the jury room, as cramped and fascinating as it was, was a lonely place. Making a friend, even one with a snappy temper, was better than having no one to talk to at all, and she wasn't tempted by the thought of joining Tabitha's fan club. The others all seemed so dull. Jennifer was nice but uninspiring. Agnes Huang was odd. Cameron, if nothing else, seemed more alive than all the others.

He sat down and pushed a full cup towards her, offering sugar as an afterthought. 'What do you make of it so far?' he asked.

'Being on the jury?' she clarified. He nodded as he drank. 'I don't really know what I expected in the first place. It's like being removed from reality. You're there to sit quietly, watch and judge someone else. I'm not sure how comfortable I am with that.'

'Me too. It's interesting, but what if we get it wrong?'

'I guess that's what the judge is there for, to make sure we've got all the information we need. But there's a lot they seem not to be telling us, and all the rules! We shouldn't even be talking about it. I feel like I'm fourteen again and my best friend just told me who she fancies. How do you not go and tell someone else?' Lottie asked, ripping open a packet of sugar and emptying the granules around the edge of her saucer.

'I'm not sure I want you on the jury if I'm ever accused of anything, if you think this is on the same level as fancying someone,' Cameron laughed. 'Are you going to actually eat any of that sugar, or . . .'

'Old habit,' Lottie smiled, feeling self-conscious and pushing the saucer to one side. 'I used to take sugar, now I just like playing with it. Therapeutic or something I suppose.'

They sipped in silence.

'So is your little boy missing you?' Cameron asked. 'This must be tough on him if he's used to being with his mum every day.'

'He's doing okay,' Lottie said, wishing they could just talk about the trial. She'd been enjoying being something other than a mother for a few minutes. Good of Cameron to take an interest, though. He'd obviously listened when she'd introduced herself, which was more than most people did when she talked these days. 'He likes his childminder. She looks after other boys his age, so I suppose it feels like a club.'

'What about you? When you're not being insulted by morons like me, how are you finding the juror experience?'

'Well, the moron pretty much ruined my day yesterday,' Lottie raised her eyebrows at him.

Cameron winced. 'Okay, I deserved that.'

'Other than that, it's somewhere between awful and fascinating. A bit like being unable to look away from a car crash.'

Cameron laughed. 'It's weird, right? I've never done anything like this before. And this case! I can't get my head around why the defendant would have tried to kill her husband. Surely if you're that fed up with your partner, you just pack your bags and leave.'

'It's not always that easy,' Lottie said. 'All relationships are different.'

'You can't tell me you're not married to someone rich and successful,' Cameron grinned.

'What makes you think that?'

'Really?' he asked. 'You're playing me.'

'I have no idea what you're talking about,' Lottie said.

'You're beautiful,' Cameron replied. 'You must have had your pick of men.'

'You're going to swing from yesterday's insults to that level of flattery without even flinching? Wow, you're something else,' Lottie said, tipping her head to one side and staring open-mouthed at him, sure he was making fun of her. Then again, it wasn't altogether unpleasant being complimented by a good-looking man, even if she hadn't forgiven him for his previous outburst.

'Just making an observation. Too much?' he grinned.

'And then some,' Lottie answered, wiping her forehead with a serviette, the coffee a mistake in the heat, she realised.

'So what's the story?' Cameron asked. 'You're bright and funny, so you seem kind of young to be married with a child. Was it true love?'

'My husband's just a normal guy, and thanks but you're overdoing it. My life consists of looking after my three-year-old and housework. Most of my socialising is done at a toddler group,' she replied, wondering why Cameron had asked if it was true love in the past tense. Had she given the impression of not being happily married? She was sure she hadn't admitted anything so personal. She did still love Zain. They were happy most of the time. Content. Only that wasn't quite accurate. Zain was content, and she didn't have any specific reason not to feel satisfied, except she wished her husband would lay off the pressure to have another baby. That was the last thing she wanted right now.

'So is parenting enough for you? I'm not insulting you again,' he looked serious for the first time that morning, 'but you're confident – you spoke up in court on the first day when most people would have been too intimidated to try – and you're outgoing, even if I did screw up your attempt to be friendly yesterday.'

Lottie stirred the remnants of her coffee unnecessarily to avoid having to meet Cameron's gaze. The woman he'd just described was the opposite of how she felt. What he had done, though, was put into words exactly who she wanted to be again. She felt a warmth inside that had nothing to do with the sun's harsh burn on her skin. It had been too long since anyone had looked at her and seen a person with attributes other than femininity.

'Morning,' a man called out as he marched past, saving her from responding. 'It's getting quite late, by the way.' Lottie looked up to see Gregory tapping his watch at them. She checked the time on her mobile.

'The Sergeant-Major's on our case. He's right about the time. We should get moving,' she said, picking up her bag.

'Let's finish our coffee first. If he's the Sergeant-Major, Tabitha has to be royalty,' he grinned.

'Queen Tabitha,' Lottie laughed. 'We really shouldn't start giving them nicknames. It's hard enough to take most of them seriously already. Come on, drink up, I really don't want to be late.'

'Do we have to go? I can't stand the thought of being locked up all day when it's this sunny out here,' Cameron replied.

'I know what you mean,' Lottie said, draining her cup and standing up. 'I could have taken my son to the park for a picnic. How about you? No one to tempt you away from work on a day like this?'

'Long story but the answer's no,' Cameron said. 'I didn't get as lucky as your husband.'

'Don't start again. There's an overkill point at which I simply won't believe a word you say.' Lottie shook her head and pointed at her watch. 'How come you're so much perkier than yesterday?' she asked as he finally got to his feet.

Lottie jumped as Cameron grabbed her wrist and pulled her towards him. A cyclist raced past her, scraping her back painfully with his handle bar, but Cameron had rescued her from the worst of it. Stepping away, she distanced herself from Cameron's chest, hoping she didn't look too much like a blushing schoolgirl, and trying to ignore how solid Cameron's torso was.

'Thank you.' She rubbed her back.

'That's all right. Bloody idiot trying to beat the traffic by using the pavement. Are you hurt? Do you want me to take a look?'

'No,' she said, 'I'm fine, really.' She began to walk back towards Small Street, doing her best to appear more composed than she felt. 'You were about to say . . .' she prompted.

'Right, yesterday. The whole jury service thing threw me. It's tough being self-employed. I'm losing work because of this case but I realised last night there's nothing I can do, so I might as well make the best of it. Got to treat it like an enforced holiday.'

Side by side, they left Quay Street and turned towards the Crown Court.

'Does it bother you, everything we're going to be shown and told? What are we supposed to do if there are words we don't understand or it doesn't make sense?' Lottie murmured, taking her bag off her shoulder and preparing to hand it to the security guard for checking.

'Are you kidding?' Cameron grinned.

'Don't laugh at me. It's fine for you. You obviously don't get nervous about anything,' she frowned.

'I wasn't laughing at you,' he said quietly as they left security behind and made their way towards the jury rooms. 'But you're being ridiculous. You think anyone in that jury room is smarter than you? They're not. You've seen through all of them already. We're here to judge the defendant as ordinary members of the public, and while I don't think you're ordinary at all, just what part of that are you not qualified for?'

'Thank you,' she muttered softly as they plunged into the semi darkness of the jury corridor. Those few words of support were all she'd needed. Such a shame her husband hadn't been able to say them, and how kind of Cameron Ellis, in spite of his obvious faults.

He opened the jury room door and stepped back to let her enter first. The chatter faded into silence. Lottie steeled herself against appearing either guilty or embarrassed. She should be able to go for coffee with a member of the opposite sex without anyone reading more into it. Surely.

Tabitha had a larger crowd around her today. Her usual crew of Gregory, Agnes and Samuel had been swelled with the addition of Andy Leith and Bill Caldwell.

'Good morning,' Tabitha said. 'Thank you for getting here on time, Mr Ellis.' Cameron managed to smile and not bite back, for which Lottie was grateful. 'However, we are concerned about jurors meeting outside of this room. It might give the wrong impression. You know we're forbidden to discuss the case unless directed to when we're all together.'

Lottie looked at Gregory who had the decency to appear embarrassed about having tattled.

'It was just coffee,' Cameron said. 'I was rude to Lottie yesterday and making up for it this morning.'

'I see,' Tabitha said. 'I think we can accept that. In future, though, perhaps we should all agree not to meet privately. The temptation to pass the odd comment about the case would be too strong for most of us.'

Cameron winked at Lottie as he passed her to put his newspaper down. Lottie caught Just-Jennifer staring openly at Cameron's backside as he sat. Perhaps all that boring housework had left her Jennifer, like Lottie herself, yearning for distractions. Easy to understand why she was captivated. Cameron was wearing sufficiently tight jeans that little was left to the imagination. Flashing him a brief smile in response to the wink, Lottie focused her attention to her mobile.

'Morning,' Jack the student said, joining them at the coffee table. 'You two caused quite the stir. Lucky for you Tabitha hadn't called the jury police in yet.'

Her Honour Judge Downey settled the courtroom into silence and asked the prosecution to begin presenting their evidence. Imogen Pascal got to her feet. Her face, Lottie noted, was make-up-free today. It made her look stark. No frills.

'Your Honour, the prosecution calls its first witness. Dr Edward Bloxham.'

James Newel, the defence barrister, got to his feet immediately. 'Your Honour, the description of Dr Bloxham's injuries can be read to the jury. There's no need for him to be brought into the courtroom.'

'Dr Bloxham is being brought in whilst the medical evidence relating to his injuries is read out, to assist the jury who will be able to see the extent of his injury for themselves,' Imogen Pascal responded.

Newell flexed his jaw. 'There are photographs of the injuries. This is an emotive and dramatic overstepping, and frankly a rather cheap move,' he said to the judge.

Imogen Pascal got to her feet. 'My learned friend, Mr Newell, needs to watch his language. This is neither cheap nor any sort of move. I won't be spoken to like that.'

'Could you please both remember where you are? I appreciate that we're all hot and uncomfortable, but normal courtroom courtesy still applies. Mr Newell, the physical trauma Dr Bloxham suffered is a key factor in this case.' The judge dabbed her forehead delicately with a handkerchief. 'I cannot direct the prosecution how to present their case. Dr Bloxham may be brought in, Miss Pascal, but only while you are presenting the evidence that relates to his altered physical condition.'

'I'm obliged, Your Honour.' Imogen Pascal inclined her head.

The courtroom door opened. There was a pause before a wheelchair arrived, pushed by a uniformed nurse. Lottie couldn't help but stare, much as she wanted to look away. She felt a shameful wave of nausea, wishing her reaction wasn't so unkind. No human being should ever feel that others couldn't tolerate the sight of them. The chair was pushed to a halt below the witness box where the jury could see Edward Bloxham clearly. There were audible intakes of breath from around her. Lottie pushed her nails into her palms to keep from making such a noise herself.

It was a wonder that Edward Bloxham had survived the attack. One side of his head was caved in. You could fit half an orange into the dip in his skull. Below the area where the blow had been struck, his eye had dropped and his mouth was turned down. Slumped over in his chair, there was no hiding the fact that he was drooling and that his hands were shaking uncontrollably on his lap. Eventually Lottie looked away, finding that many of the heads in the jury row below her had turned their attention to the back of the room. Maria Bloxham wasn't looking at her husband. Instead, she was staring towards the courtroom egress. Perhaps, Lottie thought, the defendant recognised that the egress to the outside world might soon be closed to her forever. Whatever she was thinking, Mrs Bloxham was good at hiding it, or perhaps she naturally had a cold personality. Had that made it easier when she'd tried to kill him, Lottie wondered, looking back at Edward Bloxham.

Miss Pascal picked up a sheet of paper from her file and began to read.

'Ladies and gentlemen of the jury, I'm going to read you a statement. The defence does not dispute the facts contained in it. It is from a consultant neurologist, Dr Manse, from the Bristol Brain Centre at Southmead Hospital. It states as follows: Edward Bloxham suffered a blow to the head causing severe haemorrhaging and loss of tissue to the parietal lobe. This is the area of the brain at the rear of the skull and processes sensory information, as well as interpreting visual information and performing language and mathematical functions. These functions are now severely impaired. In addition, his vision has been substantially reduced and he has been rendered incapable of speech. Other vital organ functions have not been affected, although there has been reduced response to brain stimuli testing. He will not recover to any greater extent than he already has.'

Lottie looked back at Edward Bloxham. She would sooner have died than be left in such a state. Anyone would.

Miss Pascal continued. 'The damage from bleeding within the brain has left Dr Bloxham unable to walk or control his arms. He will require twenty-four hour nursing care. His muscles will gradually atrophy until he is bedridden. As a result of Dr Bloxham's inability to communicate since the injury, it is not possible to form a concrete view as to his level of consciousness.

He may be in pain and aware of his injuries, without the ability to express that distress or discomfort.'

Imogen Pascal put down the statement she had finished reading. 'The usher is handing out a bundle of photographs which you may refer to when considering the evidence in this case.' Along the row of jurors came the blue bundles. Lottie took hers and put it straight down on the desk unopened. 'They do not, I'm afraid, quite do justice to the extent of the injuries. Bearing that in mind, Your Honour,' she directed to the judge, 'I would like the jury to come into the main area of the courtroom to inspect Dr Bloxham's injuries themselves.'

'Oh my God,' Jack the student muttered. 'Please say they're not serious.'

Lottie felt the same. It was one thing looking from a distance and hearing the statement read out. It was another thing entirely, inspecting the damage up close and personal.

'It's an unusual request, Miss Pascal,' the judge said.

'The photos don't show the full 360 degree effect of the injury,' Miss Pascal responded. 'This is the only way for the jury to get the whole picture, and it speaks for itself in terms of the force and direction of the blow.'

The judge nodded and a court usher motioned for the jurors to circle around Edward Bloxham. Tabitha went first, moving slowly across the courtroom, all eyes on her. Credit to her, Lottie thought, for keeping such a neutral face as everyone waited for her to react. Only when she neared Dr Bloxham did she crack, her mouth a little 'o' of shock as she inspected the damage. Gregory followed, head bent, clutching a handkerchief. The heat wasn't making the morning easier for any of them. Next up was Jen, biting her bottom lip and looking shaky. After that went Pan, head up, direct, then the line moved fluidly. Only Garth Finuchin, the tough man bedecked with tattoos, spent what seemed like an indecent amount of time staring at the injuries, circling the wheelchair clockwise then anticlockwise, leaning over to get every perspective. Lottie felt nauseous at the poor man being displayed as if it were some Victorian sideshow. A whole section of his skull was caved in. His hair had begun to regrow in tufts, and one ear stuck out at a bizarre angle from below the missing bone and flesh. Tabitha was clutching her chest as she retook her seat, and Jennifer was openly crying. Garth was staring with open hatred at Maria Bloxham. Lottie caught Jack wiping his face with his sleeve and wondered if he was perspiring or crying. Her own hands were shaking as she retook her seat.

As the nurse wheeled Edward Bloxham out of the courtroom, Lottie stared at the floor where his chair had been. There was a patch of saliva where he'd sat as they had paraded around him. How terrible, Lottie thought, to be left in such an inhuman state. She'd wanted to try to the case fairly, to hear all the evidence before deciding it, but there were some things that defied explanation. Whatever Maria Bloxham had to say for herself, it would be a poor excuse for leaving another human to rot away in such a living hell. Hard to imagine that a decent person was capable of such evil. Reserving judgment was all well and good, but she couldn't deny her feelings. What Dr Bloxham had been subjected to was savage. Despicable. It was all but impossible to imagine what he could possibly have done to justify such an assault.

Lottie glanced back at the defendant. She caught the tiny smile before Mrs Bloxham could cover it. It could have been a grimace, Lottie knew that was what many people would have seen, but to her it had looked like satisfaction. As the expression had flashed across the defendant's face, her shoulders had dropped and her chin had lifted fractionally. It was more than just pleasure. Something closer to triumph. She hadn't just disabled Dr Bloxham. His wife had condemned him to a lifetime trapped inside a body filled with pain, humiliation and misery. All that without reducing the number of years he might live. It spoke of either an uncontrollable hatred, or plain evil.

9

Ruth Adcock had kept notes of every call she'd ever taken in her capacity as a counsellor. They were a point of reference for future contacts. It also provided a good sounding board for assessing the advice given. Occasionally things went wrong and callers took a more dramatic and permanent way out, appearing in news reports or obituaries with the label 'deceased'. Those were the records Ruth spent the most time re-reading, wondering if there was more she could have said or done, if different words could have prevented the tragedy. The truth was that many suicides were not preventable. It didn't make the reading of her call logs any easier, though. Then there were some calls she remembered second by second, word by word, for no identifiable reason. They just stuck. That was exactly how it had been the first time Maria called. She replayed the exchange in her mind, as she had a thousand times before.

The phone rang. Ruth noted the time and date of the call in her records before answering. 12.15 p.m., 4 August 2013.

'My name is Ruth,' she said into the electronic void. 'I'm here for you. Take your time. This is a safe space. You don't have to give your name, or any details at all.' She paused, leaving the caller to find whatever words they could. Eventually, hearing nothing, Ruth began to speak again. 'This is hard, I know. Reaching out feels like climbing a mountain. We just need to make contact. One noise, something so I know you're still there. It doesn't matter what it is.'

The sound came hard and fast. The caller was retching, the phone clattering as it dropped from their fingers. Ruth waited patiently. Minutes later the phone was retrieved and a croaky voice sounded a million miles away.

'Hello,' the voice whispered.

'It's all right,' Ruth replied. 'I'm still here. I'll be here whenever you need me.'

That's when the sobbing began, wringing the oxygen from the air. For all her training, Ruth struggled with others' pain, with treating rather than consuming it. Counsellors should empathise rather than sympathise, that was the rule. Good luck with that, she'd always thought privately.

As the sobs faded into hitched breaths, Ruth spoke again. 'Why don't you tell me your name?' she'd asked. 'Not a surname, keep your details secure. Just a first name, or any name you want me to call you. I'll be able to remember you, and I'll think about you. I promise.'

'Maria,' she said. 'I have to go now.'

'Just one more minute,' Ruth said. 'You don't even have to talk. Go if you're in immediate danger of course, but otherwise let me tell you a bit more about the phone line. It's confidential and aimed at victims of abuse, but we talk to anyone who needs us. When you phone you'll either speak with me, Gemma or Ellen.' She paused. A muffled sniffle came from the other end of the line. 'You can just call us and talk, or we can recommend other places where you can get help in person. There are doctors who will see you without asking your name if you need that, or shelters if you have to get away from a situation urgently.'

'Can't,' Maria said. The sobbing had stopped. What was left was a voice completely detached from emotion. Privately, Ruth thought she preferred the sobbing.

'Do you have children?' Ruth asked. She wanted to keep the woman on the line. If she couldn't find some means of connecting, Maria might never phone back. And she needed to, Ruth thought. Some people's silence screamed of loneliness. 'I don't, but I've always wanted them.' There was no reply, but Maria hadn't hung up. That was good. 'I'm not married, though. Everyone assumes you are, or thinks you should be, when you have children, especially at my age. Are you married, Maria?' A noise came from the other end of the line that sounded confirmatory. Ruth noted that there was probably a husband involved. 'I've never been very good at relationships myself, but I think it's better to be alone than in a bad relationship. I really believe that. Does that make sense to you?'

'I have to hang up,' Maria said. Ruth knew she was losing her.

'All right. Just one last thing. We don't have enough resources to cover the lines at night, but there's someone here seven days a week, from 9 a.m. until 9 p.m. Please phone back. I'd like to think that we can help you, Maria,' Ruth said.

'I left it too late,' Maria muttered. The phone line beeped in place of a goodbye.

Ruth sipped a cup of jasmine tea as she made her notes of the call, staring as she often did at the photograph of her older sister when a new caller made contact. Gail had been twenty-six when she'd begun a relationship with Rory, a teacher, who was two years her senior. Eighteen months later, desperately in love, she'd married him. Ruth was in the final year of her post-graduate degree when the news came that Gail was in hospital. There had been a fall, a head injury, her mother wasn't clear on the details.

The hospital visit was tense, Rory being less than welcoming, as machines had blipped the seconds away and helped Gail to breathe. It was a junior doctor who'd taken their parents aside and asked if they were aware of other recent fractures not explained in Gail's medical notes. Ruth recalled her parents' bewilderment, absolutely genuine. They had no idea how Gail could have suffered a broken wrist, cracked ribs, three fractured toes, and never have mentioned the injuries. Ruth knew. She knew the second she burst into Gail's room and asked Rory about the injuries. He'd looked away before answering, gruff with her, dismissive. Her parents hadn't believed it when Ruth shared her theory. Gail loved her husband. He was a teacher, of all things. Why would he have hurt their daughter? None of it made sense. All of it too awful to contemplate. Ruth waited patiently for her sister to recover consciousness so she could explain the injuries herself. She never did. Rory disappeared under a cloud of suspicion but nothing could be proved. And Ruth's life had changed forever. Not because of Gail's death specifically, not even because her sister had found herself in a violent relationship. But because she'd never told them. Not her mother, or father, or sister. She hadn't come to them for help when she'd need it most. Gail had never told a single soul.

It took a decade before Ruth felt adequately qualified and equipped to open the helpline. Now she couldn't imagine doing anything else, not just because of her dedication to the task, but because of the number of people out there who needed help. More than she'd ever imagined when she'd started out. And every time the phone rang, for a fleeting moment, she heard her sister's voice at the end of the line, making the call she'd never made, getting the help she'd never asked for. The phone line was Gail's legacy.

10

Day Four in Court

By ten thirty the next morning, the jurors were gathered and ready to get started when the usher stuck her head around the door.

'Brief delay, I'm afraid. The judge is hearing an urgent bail application on another case. Shouldn't be too long.' She disappeared before anyone could ask for clarification of the exact time estimate. It had become clear that time had a different meaning inside the court building, and the phrase 'not too long' could mean anything from ten minutes to several hours. Waiting was the normal order of the day, with little to do except watch the clock and wonder what was happening elsewhere.

'Morning, Lottie,' Jen said. 'Did you come over the bridge this morning? I heard on the radio there was a terrible traffic jam. I'm guessing you missed it as you're on time.'

'I got the bus actually. My car's in for its MOT today, but the traffic was fine, thanks,' Lottie murmured, side-stepping away with her mug of coffee. She didn't want to make small talk. Her commute had been spent counting down the minutes until she could get back into the jury room to talk about what they'd seen the day before. Taking a seat between Cameron and Jack, she wondered how to broach the subject with them.

'Do you suppose she's on bail . . . the defendant?' Sergeant-Major Gregory asked no one in particular.

'I hope not. Bristol's not safe with a woman like that on the loose,' Agnes Huang responded bluntly.

It was an opportunity to get involved in the discussion. Lottie steeled herself for criticism and took the leap. 'But we haven't heard from the defendant, yet,' she said, wondering why she was taking the side of someone who had inflicted such stomach-churning injuries. She'd lost half a night's sleep wondering how a woman who appeared so mild could suddenly turn feral. Lottie was both horrified and intrigued. The only conclusion she'd reached was that there had to be an explanation for Maria Bloxham's behaviour, unless she had simply lost her mind, and that wasn't Lottie's impression having studied her in court yesterday. 'I just don't think we should assume what type of woman she is yet,' she added, her voice trailing off into an almost inaudible mumble.

'I certainly wouldn't want her living next door to me and my sister,' Samuel Lowry chipped in.

'I'm sure your dogs would protect you,' Cameron muttered into his newspaper, just loud enough for Lottie and Jack at either side of him, to hear. Lottie responded by nudging his foot with hers.

'You never know what people are capable of,' Garth Finuchin said, flexing his tattoos, too many of which were on show courtesy of a sleeveless T-shirt. Lottie was glad she wasn't going to be sitting next to him in court all day. The best anti-perspirant in the world was no match for the temperatures that week.

'What we're all capable of,' Jack said. Lottie smiled at him. He was in classic student-wear, complete with ripped jeans and a top proclaiming some political slogan that Lottie vaguely recognised but couldn't place. His delivery had been soft and well-intentioned, but the effect it had on the room was certainly not.

'I'm sorry, it might just be my more mature years, but I am certainly not capable of that sort of violence. I also believe we should expect better of our fellow human beings than that which we witnessed yesterday,' Tabitha said.

'You don't think that pushed to your limits, you might be capable of more than just jam-making and crochet?' Cameron asked her, keeping his voice light, without lowering his newspaper an inch.

'That was rude,' Gregory bristled on Tabitha's behalf. 'You're suggesting Tabitha is no more than some clichéd version of a pensioner. I didn't see you volunteering to be jury foreperson.'

'And you lot are assuming the defendant's some 1970s BBC drama version of a criminal, because you've seen the injuries and her husband has the word doctor in front of his name. I think we should all just keep our thoughts to ourselves at this stage.' No one spoke for a good twenty seconds, then the silence was papered over with the lifting of mugs, and fingers tapping on mobile phone screens.

Cameron lifted his newspaper a little higher in front of his face and went back to reading what Lottie figured were the sports pages. She caught herself. That was another assumption. The world seemed to be full of them. Cameron Ellis, however, was refusing to be drawn into everyone else's outrage. He was happy to have an opinion that didn't match the group's, and had no problem expressing it. Lottie wished she could be more like him. Perhaps if she could talk to him about yesterday, it would help her put the injuries into perspective. She longed to ask if he was really so open-minded about the case, or if he was just playing devil's advocate to the Tabithas.

Lottie herself felt torn. She'd been desperate to talk about the case the previous evening, but had felt the weight of the judge's warning too heavily to break the rules. When Zain asked her about the charges, she'd explained the restrictions

78

on discussing matters at home. He'd responded by telling her she was taking it all far too seriously.

'Fine. It involves an assault,' she'd said, as she emptied an assortment of stones and twigs from Daniyal's coat pockets.

'I don't see why you have to be secretive about that. Sounds like a normal Friday night in Bristol to me. Drink and drugs involved?' Zain had asked.

Lottie paused. 'I can't say any more,' she'd replied, wishing she could tell him that she'd felt sick to her stomach when Edward Bloxham had come into the court. Wishing she could explain that she'd hated herself for thinking exactly the same as Queen Tabitha, Just-Jennifer and Agnes Huang. How could a woman do such a thing? A woman. Pour me another glass of stereotype and make it a double, she'd thought. What difference did it make that a woman had committed such an offence? But it did change things, in a million minuscule, ridiculous, outdated ways. Zain wouldn't be able to understand. How could she expect him to, when Lottie was at a complete loss herself?

Finally they were called into court for the trial to start again. An eerie hush remained in the courtroom, as if Edward Bloxham hadn't left. Lottie checked up and down the two rows of her colleagues. Not one of them was looking towards Maria Bloxham. It would have been easier, Lottie thought, if the defendant hadn't been there at all. Her presence felt malevolent given the evidence they had already seen. Imogen Pascal, today bedecked in pale grey with dark pinstripes, had forsaken her stern glasses in favour of contact lenses. It was a softer image, one that made her more likeable.

'Your Honour,' Miss Pascal began, 'we will begin today playing a video blog, popularly known as a vlog for the internet savvy among us.'

She motioned pressing a button at the usher who was operating a laptop linked to a large screen at the front of the court. James Newell got to his feet before the film could start to play.

'Actually, Your Honour, the defence is not satisfied as to the relevance of this evidence. It has no bearing on the facts of the case.' He sat down.

'Miss Pascal,' the judge said, pushing her glasses down her nose and peering over them. 'Could you summarise what we are about to see, and explain the relevance to the charge of attempted murder.'

'Absolutely,' Pascal said. 'The contents of the blog are of no direct factual significance, which is why we will show only a brief clip. The relevance is for the jury to witness the man Dr Bloxham was prior to his injury, to compare with the man they saw yesterday. It is also pertinent in balancing whatever picture the defence later paints of Dr Bloxham. In that regard, if the defence can confirm they will not seek to sully the victim's character in any way, then we can agree not to show the video.' She paused and raised her eyebrows in James Newell's direction.

James Newell didn't bother to answer the question. 'Is the prosecution really claiming it's impossible for a man who likes wildlife to be cruel and abusive to his wife? This tactic really is laughable,' he said.

'What's laughable is running a defence with no corroborative evidence,' Imogen Pascal countered.

'May I remind you both that the jury is in court listening to this exchange. Keep your comments to yourselves. As far as the video goes, keep it brief, Miss Pascal. Make your point and move on,' the judge ordered.

Imogen Pascal nodded once more at the usher who pressed play. There was a flash of pixelation across the screen, then a man's face appeared, close up and beaming.

'And today, at my favourite time of the year, I have a rare treat for you,' Dr Edward Bloxham told them through a digital time-warp. He leaned down to the floor and rummaged, lifting a piece of cloth up first, then bringing a tiny squirming creature into view. It lifted its nose to sniff Bloxham's hands then tipped its head to one side.

A gush of air crossed the courtroom as the viewers cooed over the baby hedgehog he displayed. Edward Bloxham held a morsel to its mouth and let it nibble. 'The loss of woodland and meadow to building projects in England is having a dramatic effect on this creature's habitat. We are seeing fewer babies born, and more adult hedgehogs are dying leaving orphaned young. The next generation will be lucky to come across one of these beautiful, shy animals. It is vital that we conserve areas for them to mate and thrive.' He put the snuffling baby back in its box and sat up to continue addressing his audience, at which point the screen turned blank.

Imogen Pascal continued. 'That video blog was recorded and put online by Dr Bloxham five days before his death. Now the prosecution calls Dr Gibbs, forensic investigator, to give evidence.'

The usher disappeared outside to summon the witness.

Lottie let out a long breath. Dr Bloxham's injuries were so life-changing that the video might as well have been sent from beyond the grave. He was never going to hold another hedgehog, nor speak so passionately into a camera to send his thoughts out into the world. He would probably never even understand the outcome of the trial at which he was the undoubted centrepiece. Lives were shattered so quickly. She wondered what Mrs Bloxham's intentions had been as the blow was struck. Was it fear, anger or a more complex emotion that had made her raise the chair leg? Jealousy, frustration or greed? Lottie felt melancholy. If she had been shocked at the injuries yesterday, today she felt the toll of the loss. Seeing Edward Bloxham talking and smiling was so much worse than just perceiving him as a victim and a patient. The idea that such an engaging and passionate man could be left halfway between life and death was heart-breaking. The weight of the jury's task suddenly felt enormous. They weren't just reaching a verdict. They were to pick through the dirt of the Bloxham's marriage, sorting the bones from the treasure.

'Clever,' Cameron Ellis muttered from beside her. Lottie turned to look at him, unsure if he was talking about Dr Bloxham himself or the vlog. The court door opened and a woman walked in, taking her place in the witness box before Lottie could clarify Cameron's meaning.

Dr Gibbs swore the oath then gave her professional credentials, explaining that she had examined both Dr Bloxham's injury and the scene of the crime. It had been her remit to oversee all the forensics in the case, from DNA to blood spatters. Lottie didn't envy the woman her job.

In Dr Gibbs' hands was a long plastic bag. She placed it on the witness stand in front of her as Imogen Pascal began asking questions. 'What did the injury tell you about the attack, Dr Gibbs?'

'The most notable feature of the injury was that the skull itself was not merely fractured, but that the metal fixture normally securing the chair leg to the seat had permeated the skull and entered the cranial cavity, forcing out a section of tissue. That level of force is almost invariably lethal. It is only because the injury was to an area of the brain which allows the vital organs to continue functioning that Dr Bloxham is still alive.'

'What about the angle of the injury? Did you infer anything from that?' Miss Pascal asked.

'It's high up on the skull. Given that Dr Bloxham is approximately the same height as the defendant, she must have raised the chair leg very high into the air, substantially above her own head, enabling her to increase the force of the blow. Bringing it down onto the top of his skull with so much force not only damaged the skull, but also caused his facial features on one side to slip as a result of skin slackening, nerve and muscle damage.'

Lottie felt sick.

'Is there any evidence that the defendant intended a lesser injury, for example, to temporarily incapacitate Dr Bloxham while she fled the house?' Imogen Pascal asked.

'I don't believe so,' Dr Gibbs replied. 'This was a very substantial blow. The angle of the strike at the rear of the skull is relevant. If you look at photograph number 3 . . .' Dr Gibbs opened the bundle of photos on the desk in front of her. Lottie leaned forward and opened the booklet, her stomach lurching as the injury appeared supersized and in glorious technicolour. It was all she could do not to immediately close the pages again. 'Here you see the injury from behind. It is slightly to the left of the centre of the skull, with a triangular shaped indent. The positioning means that Dr Bloxham would not have been aware of the chair leg being raised because the weapon would not have been noticeable at either side of his peripheral vision. He was attacked squarely from behind and could not have defended himself. The injury also indicates that there was no sound prior to the attack. Had there been, the victim would have been in the process of turning his head as the blow was struck, and the injury pattern would not have run straight down the back of the skull.'

'Do you have the weapon with you?' Miss Pascal asked.

'I do,' Dr Gibbs said. 'The defendant's fingerprints and DNA were found both in the blood at the end and along the lower shaft, confirming that she had held it with both hands. There were other fingerprints on the article also, none at the bloodied end though, but one expects that with furniture which has been used over a number of years, and this piece was approximately thirty years old.'

The chair leg was given an exhibit number and handed to the defence to inspect before being passed to the jury. Tabitha took it first, taking her time examining it, removing her glasses and writing notes on her pad as she turned it around. By the time it reached Lottie, the plastic bag was slick from sweaty palms. She handled it with her fingertips, holding her breath. The blood was still visible on the end, although it had long since blackened and dried, leaving a powdery residue in the bag. What made her skin crawl was the hair clumped and matted around the metal edge. The end of it was sharp. You'd be hard pressed not to foresee just how much damage it would do, whether the exact angle of the blow was deliberate or accidental. As she passed it down to Agnes Huang, Lottie watched her wrap both hands firmly around the base of the leg and draw her arms back, as if ready to take a swing. From behind, Lottie could see Agnes's muscles flexing with the weight of it. The chair leg was old and dense, nothing flat-packed or light-weight about it. Swing that and you were making a choice, she thought. Swing that, and you really meant it.

Imogen Pascal sat down and James Newell got to his feet.

'Dr Gibbs, the amount of force used might indicate a number of different motivational factors, none of which you can assess, isn't that right?' he asked.

'I'm not sure exactly what you mean,' Dr Gibbs replied.

'I mean the amount of force used might have been affected by anger, or equally from fear, or a number of other emotions,' Newell said.

'I don't think I've indicated any one specific emotion,' Dr Gibbs countered.

'No, but you stated that the blow was delivered while Dr Bloxham's back was turned, implying that it was an unprovoked attack. My point is that your view is rather simplistic. It assumes that a fight is a stand-alone event, and that a person only defends themselves in the midst of action,' Newell said.

'Yes, that's how I see it,' Dr Gibbs said.

'Which ignores the possibility that the blow might have been landed to prevent a later event, or the prospect of future harm,' Newell said.

'My learned friend is asking this witness to speculate,' Imogen Pascal interjected.

'I'm exploring an alternative scenario,' Newell responded. 'But I'll move on. Dr Gibbs, can we agree that the metal on the chair leg was what caused the bulk of the damage to the skull?' he asked.

'It certainly caused the skull to split fully rather than just fracturing but remaining closed,' Dr Gibbs said.

'Using such force, it would have been almost impossible for Mrs Bloxham to have ensured that one specific part of the leg came into contact with the skull. The chair leg might easily have turned as she raised it or swung it,' Newell said.

'I suppose so,' Dr Gibbs said.

At the back of the courtroom, Maria Bloxham shifted in her seat, giving a tiny shake of her head and frowning. Lottie wondered if she was recalling the precise moment she brought the weapon down on her husband, the reality of what she had done sinking in.

'And thus, it might be the case that Maria Bloxham had not intended such a dramatic injury as in fact resulted,' James Newell finished.

'That's a possibility but I can't speak as to what was in the defendant's mind. My evidence is purely scientific,' Dr Gibbs finished.

'Quite so, thank you,' Newell said, sitting down.

Dr Gibbs was allowed to leave.

'As it is now half past twelve, we will adjourn for lunch,' the judge said.

'He didn't like hedgehogs,' a voice came from the rear of the court.

Her Honour Judge Downey frowned. There was a mass turning of heads. 'I'm sorry, did someone say something?' the judge asked.

'He said they were flea-ridden vermin,' Maria Bloxham went on, louder this time. Lottie watched as the defendant got shakily to her feet and put one hand against the glass.

'Mrs Bloxham, you will have an opportunity to present your case later on. For now, I must ask you to sit down,' the judge said.

'But it's a lie,' Maria replied, her voice rising in pitch. Lottie was surprised by how insistent she had suddenly become, having shown so little interest until then.

'Mr Newell,' the judge said. 'Please caution your client that she should sit down and remain quiet. I do not want to have her forcibly taken to the cells.'

Newell turned around and motioned at Maria to sit down.

'I once brought an injured hedgehog indoors and he . . .' Maria said.

'That's enough, Mrs Bloxham,' the judge raised her voice. 'Sit down at once or I'll have you removed.'

The dock officers stood up and took the defendant by the arms, guiding her back to her seat. James Newell intervened.

'Your Honour, if the jury could retire, I'll have a word with my client,' he said.

'I think you'd better, Mr Newell. I don't want any repeat of that sort of disruptive behaviour in my courtroom,' the judge snapped, standing up and leaving through the door behind her.

They returned to the jury room thoughtful and quiet. Gregory, Tabitha, Samuel and Agnes were in a huddle by the time Lottie entered. They had even foregone their usual rush for tea and coffee. She took her mobile from her handbag and headed for the toilets, staring in the mirror as she waited for her phone to spring into life. Running a fingertip lightly up the vertical line between her eyebrows, it was hard not to wonder about the frown on Maria Bloxham's face as she'd made her case about her husband and the hedgehogs. She had been adamant. Absolutely perplexed, Lottie thought, that no one was listening to her. When the prison guard had pulled her hand from the glass, a perfect sweaty handprint had been left. Yes, the courtroom was sweltering, and yes, the heat must have been exacerbated inside the glass box where she'd been sitting. Still, Lottie couldn't help but wonder if the sweat wasn't more than that. Lottie pressed her own hand against the mirror, waiting long enough that its outline was easily visible as she pulled away. The ends of her own fingers had made the smallest and lightest of marks. Not so with Maria Bloxham's. Her fingertips had shone white through the pane, widely spread, perspiring to the very tips, pressing them with so much force and intensity. She had been furious, Lottie realised. Her outburst had been inevitable. Like the sweat on her palms, there was no physical means of holding it inside. Was that anger an indication of an unstoppable temper, or was it the frustration of seeing her husband fool everyone inside that courtroom?

I must not judge, Lottie told herself. Not so soon. Not any aspect of it. Whatever the cause, Maria Bloxham's reaction in that moment – her frown, her insistence, the sweat on her palms – had been real, not acted.

Her phone buzzed, and her heart sank. She'd been in court for hours, and missed messages from Zain when they had an important evening ahead of them. No doubt her husband was frantic waiting for her to acknowledge them.

'Coming home to prep for tonight. Is dinner jacket back from dry cleaners? My mother emailed about birthday present

87

for Daniyal. Send suggestions for her to order online. I need dentist app't. Can you make for me? Thks.'

Of course her husband's dinner jacket was back from the dry cleaners, Lottie thought. Not that he'd been to collect it. That was one of her jobs. And why should Zain have to make his own dental appointment? Easier to get her to do it. Daniyal's birthday was still two months away, but her mother-in-law would expect a response today. It was less hassle to comply. Just a few more items on her to-do list. A week earlier she might not have noticed, she thought, as she ran her fingers through her hair, lifting the heavy strands to get some cool air through, so why was it bothering her so much now? Perhaps because she was part of something bigger, for once. Maybe because she realised she had something to offer beyond the walls of her home. Or that she had been able to cope with the boredom of her life until she'd walked into this bizarre, intimidating building and remembered what it was not to be bored? It felt as if she was waking up from a fairy-tale length sleep.

Running her hands under the cold tap, she dried them on a paper towel and returned to the jury room in search of a drink and a distraction. She was overthinking things.

'It's absolutely ghoulish,' Gregory blurted as she walked in. 'To think that such a nice man could be so badly treated.'

'And in his own kitchen. Makes you feel as if you're not safe anywhere,' Tabitha added.

'If my husband did that to me, I'd want the death penalty,' Agnes Huang added.

'You know, we really should wait and hear both sides,' Jack said quietly, opening a battered copy of Thomas Hardy's *Far from the Madding Crowd* and settling in his chair.

'Oh, get real,' Garth-the-tattoo replied. 'Bloody namby-pamby students. What the hell do you know about anything?

You've gone from a comfy home with mummy, to a school for big kids where you sit around all day discussing theories. This is real world stuff, mate.'

'Mr Finuchin,' Tabitha said, 'There's no need to get personal, although I'm inclined to agree that Jack's view of this may not be as adult as ours. It's a life experience perspective. I think we're entitled to be drawing some conclusions from what we've seen this morning.'

'I just meant that it's all been one sided so far,' Jack said. 'I thought we were supposed to wait until the end before leaning one way or the other.'

'No one's taking sides, young man,' Gregory said. 'But we all saw that weapon. There's no doubt in my mind as to what that woman intended.'

'You can't convict her like that,' Jack said.

'For God's sake, I bet the boy's a bloody vegan,' Garth muttered.

'He's not a boy, he's an adult and we're all equals in this room,' Cameron interrupted. 'So lay off. The instructions were clear. We judge at the end. You're entitled to your opinions, but keep a lid on for now.'

'Tabitha is foreperson,' Gregory bristled. 'If she's comfortable with us talking about this . . .'

'Then I'm sure when I explain that to the judge, Tabitha will face no criticism at all,' Cameron said.

Tabitha coughed. 'Perhaps we should all take a breather,' she said. 'Apparently, the most innocent of conversations can be misinterpreted. We were simply running over the evidence in preparation for reviewing it at the end of the trial. Thank you for your input, Mr Ellis.'

'Happy to help,' Cameron said, slipping into the chair next to Jack's and winking at him. Jack smiled back and Lottie grinned behind her mobile.

'Very heroic,' she whispered to Cameron once conversation had struck up again.

'Bunch of judgmental bastards,' he replied.

'I didn't mean to start anything,' Jack said.

'You were right to tell them,' Cameron said, laying a friendly hand on Jack's shoulder. 'Someone's got to play fair.'

The usher appeared and relayed the news that they were free to go home for the weekend. Lottie packed her bag and got ready to leave. Cameron picked up the magazine she'd left on the floor that morning and held it out to her.

'You okay?' he asked as the others left.

'Sure, it was just incredibly sad watching the video,' she said. 'And then actually holding the weapon . . . that made me a bit queasy.'

'I know, but there's another side to this thing. There must be, or I guess Mrs Bloxham would have pleaded guilty by now. Listen, I heard you tell Jennifer you came on the bus. Why don't you let me drive you home? It's been a tough day.'

Lottie took a moment considering it, but shook her head.

'I'll be fine,' she said. 'I don't want to put you out.'

'It's no bother. We've finished early. I've got nothing else to do,' Cameron said.

Lottie rearranged her bag on her shoulder. 'Actually, my husband wouldn't like it – me being dropped home by a man. He's a bit sensitive about things like that.'

'You mean jealous?' Cameron laughed. 'It's not as if you're doing anything wrong. Surely you should be free to get a lift instead of public transport?'

'It's not that big a deal, just not worth having to explain who you are. My husband's protective over me and we have the sort of neighbours who like to curtain twitch,' she replied.

'Okay, but you should probably dump that magazine in a bin before you get home. I wrote my mobile number on the cover, in case your bus breaks ever breaks down and you need rescuing. Secretly, of course,' he added quietly.

Lottie's stomach dropped an inch and she felt a rush of adrenalin that ran straight up her spine, leaving her light-headed.

'Idiot.' She laughed it off, wondering what to do with the magazine. It seemed like an overreaction to take it out of her bag then and there. She could leave it on the bus, she decided. There was no harm in her having Cameron's number, anyway. Just in case she ever needed it.

'Come on, the least I can do is walk you to your bus stop,' he said.

He walked ahead of Lottie though the door as she stared at his outline. A head taller than her, with the sort of body that would turn heads in any bar, she wondered what his story was. It was hard to believe Cameron didn't have someone at home waiting for him. The summer sun was bringing out highlights in his brown hair, and he suited jeans and white T-shirts in a way that screamed American carbonated drinks adverts. Lottie was willing to bet that there wasn't an inch of spare flesh on him. Plenty of muscle, but no fat. Nothing soft. He reminded of her of an animal that way. Not that she'd been thinking about his body, she told herself, as she tried to banish the image from her mind. Just as well he wasn't dropping her home. Her husband really wouldn't appreciate her spending time with a man like Cameron Ellis. Not that the subject was going to come up. What her husband didn't know, couldn't hurt him.

II

Zain Hiraj held out his sleeve for Lottie to fasten his cufflink. 'Could you do these for me?'

'Sure,' Lottie said, putting her own bracelet aside to help. She knew Zain didn't really need her to do it for him, but he liked it when she did. He'd insisted on changing all his shirts from button sleeve to cuffs when he'd made area manager for the pharmaceutical firm. At least since then it had been easier to buy him birthday presents. She made sure each cufflink was turned to the same angle, and that the cuffs themselves were sharply folded. Zain liked to look sharp. He was a good-looking man, with perfect skin, high cheekbones and toothpaste advert teeth. As a husband and father he had a traditional outlook, but Lottie had known that when she'd married him. He had a passion for ticking boxes. Nice house – check. Pretty wife – Lottie stared at herself in the mirror. Yes, she was pretty, no denying it, even if these days it seemed to mean less and less. Check. Child (a son, for extra points) – check. Then there was the non-stop professional ladder Zain was climbing.

Tonight was the annual sales dinner. Zain's team was nominated for an award, which might mean a luxury golfing weekend for him and his sales executives. More importantly, it was a chance for Zain to make a good impression on the bosses, some of whom were flying in from the United States especially.

Lottie ran straighteners through her long hair. Zain had asked her to wear the floor-length emerald green dress that made her stomach look washboard flat and accentuated her bust. It was showy but he'd always admired her in it, and it was his night. Personally, she'd have preferred a hot bath and an early bed. Lottie had sneaked a large glass of wine before Zain got home, taking another cheat night from the diet, hoping the alcohol would make her evening marginally more tolerable. Conversation at company events was always stilted and she usually ended up nodding politely for several hours until she could remind Zain that they really had to get home to Daniyal.

The babysitter arrived and Lottie spent a few minutes giving instructions in case of an emergency, before going to kiss Daniyal goodnight. He was fussy and whining, not his usual self at all. Lottie laid down next to him and stroked his face. He wrapped his arms tightly around her neck, messing up her hair and smudging her make-up. Lottie didn't care. She had missed him while she'd been at court. It was a good feeling to get home each day, desperate to hold him in her arms. She hadn't realised how much she'd needed some distance, to feel that love for her son afresh.

Zain poked his head around the bedroom door. 'Lottie, the taxi will be here any minute.' Daniyal picked his head up from the pillow, waking again and struggling to get out of bed.

'I have to get him to sleep,' Lottie said. 'He'll get upset if the babysitter tries to do it.'

'You should have done that before starting to get ready. Now your hair needs doing again.'

Lottie smoothed it with her hands. 'Just ask the driver to wait a few minutes. I can get Daniyal to sleep, I promise. My hair will brush out.'

'We can't be late,' Zain reminded her, as if she could have forgotten.

'We won't be,' she replied softly.

Zain closed the door. Lottie tickled her boy gently under the chin and kissed him on the nose. 'Right, now, mini-monster. Song or story?' she asked.

'Song,' Daniyal decided.

'Okay. Close your eyes, though. Deal?'

'Deal,' he said. 'But more kisses.'

'I think I can do that,' Lottie said, cuddling up to him, kissing his cheeks and forehead as he curled up. She murmured a gentle song while he fell asleep in her arms, cursing as the taxi beeped its horn from the road. Creeping out of his bedroom, she held her breath but he didn't wake again. A quick dash of extra lipstick and running a brush through her hair, she hoped Zain would forgive her for looking less than perfect.

'So you remember who's on our table?' Zain asked, brushing non-existent specks off his trousers.

'Yes, I do. It'll be fine. I've done this before,' Lottie said quietly, staring out of the window, enjoying the fact that the cloudless night had left the stars visible. It had been too long since she'd bothered to look up at them.

'And what we discussed about the golf?' He checked his watch for the fifth time since they'd climbed into taxi.

'Hmm?' Lottie murmured, changing position to get a better view of a man and woman who seemed to be arguing at the roadside. The world was suddenly filled with new possibilities. The most stable relationship was a powder keg ready to blow. Except hers. Zain was a steadying influence. Set in his ways, even though he had yet to reach middle age, he knew what he wanted and where he was going. These days he also decided who Lottie should be and how her life should pan out. It wasn't his fault. Lottie had to take responsibility for letting him make decisions for her.

'Charlotte?' he said, barely hiding his irritation. He was allowed to be stressed, she told herself. It was a big night in the pharmaceutical sales calendar.

She stifled a yawn. 'Yes, I've got it. When you're away from the table, let slip that you won the golf club tournament. You don't want to be seen showing off but it's the sort of thing they like.'

'You don't have to sound so weary,' he whispered, throwing a quick glance in the driver's direction.

She considered telling him he was being childish. He shouldn't have to impress the bunch of bores who made up middle management. Certainly she shouldn't have to play along with it. It was pathetic really. She settled for shrugging and staring out of the window once more, wondering where Maria Bloxham was spending her Friday evening, and if she was struggling with her conscience or lying awake terrified at the prospect of a prison sentence.

'I know you don't enjoy these dinners. Just try to keep smiling. The impression we make is important. It's a chance to stand out in the crowd . . .'

Lottie let her mind drift as Zain continued explaining the significance of the forthcoming hours. She didn't need the lecture. Company events were intimidating enough, not because of Zain's bosses who, by and large, were pleasant and not at all interested in Lottie. She very much doubted they could tell one employee's partner from another after a few drinks. What bothered her was how tense Zain got about all the things she was supposed to do, or not do. Sticking to safe topics of conversation was a specific rule. Things she really knew about to avoid silly gaffs. Lottie wasn't sure Zain's bosses wanted to hear about her expertise in changing nappies on the go, but that was the only specialisation she had these days.

'Are you ready?' Zain asked as the hotel lights appeared in the distance.

'Yes, absolutely, got it. Mr Mason's wife just left him so don't ask after her, and Mrs Johnson's rash is to be ignored at all costs,' Lottie said.

'You look great, by the way. Why don't you go to the ladies' when we arrive to touch up your mascara, then you'll be perfect?' Zain said.

'Thanks,' Lottie murmured, knowing she'd forgotten to put mascara in her purse. She'd pretend to go and do it anyway, for Zain's sake. He worked hard all year. The least she could do was play along. In the toilets, she managed to borrow some mascara from another woman and went to join Zain at their table.

'That's better,' he said, as she sat down. 'Jeff, Alex, this is my wife Charlotte.'

She shook hands and introduced herself to the men and their wives. Zain was pleased with himself, his voice louder than normal and his laugh more jolly. It was a positive sign that her husband had been moved up onto a senior management table. Another year like the last, Zain had told her, and he was in line for promotion. Tonight was meant to seal it.

The first course passed without Lottie saying a word. She'd got smiling through boredom down to an art.

'I absolutely love your eyebrows,' one of the wives said during a lull in conversation. 'Where do you get them threaded?'

'Actually, I do them myself,' Lottie said, taking a long sip of wine. 'I find it easier.'

'The things women talk about,' either Jeff or Alex said with a side-wink at Zain. 'I wish my day could be spent worrying about eyebrows, not that the mortgage would get paid!' He won himself a round of laughter for that, the women joining in at their own expense. Lottie felt as if she'd been slapped. She was so much more than a female who could only talk about beauty treatments. The fact that she was spending time raising a child didn't give anyone the right to speak down to her.

'In fact,' Lottie said, addressing the women at the table, 'I haven't had time to worry about my eyebrows recently. I'm doing jury service at Bristol Crown Court at the moment.'

'Jury service!' the other wife had said. 'Aren't you finding that rather challenging?'

'Not challenging, but there's a lot involved. The trial might go on for some time,' Lottie said, draining her glass. 'We've only heard the forensic evidence so far.'

'The case is nothing serious though, presumably,' one of the Jeff/Alex duo said. Lottie decided she no longer cared which one was which. 'Bit of shoplifting? My wife's an expert on retail. She'd be perfect for that jury.'

Lottie was pleased to see that even the other wives couldn't produce a convincing laugh at that.

'It's an attempted murder, quite high profile, actually. There's been a lot of media coverage about it. Beats having a boring office job, any day.' She smiled and picked up a wine bottle, refilling her glass.

'I'm surprised they don't vet people for jury duty,' Jeff/Alex sneered. 'It's always seemed odd to me that any Tom, Dick or Harry can be allowed to decide such complex matters. Some minimum level of education or work experience should be required.' He leered at Lottie. She willed herself not to take the bait.

'Oh, I'm sure they explain everything in very simple language,' one of the wives said. 'Isn't that right, dear?'

Lottie gulped her wine, unsure which was more offensive. Being called simple or referred to as 'dear'.

'Charlotte was telling me there are plenty of impressive people on the jury. There's a fine art auctioneer, apparently. I'm guessing with a good mixture of intellects it balances out,' Zain said before she could respond. She knew he hadn't meant to be quite so insulting, but it was a shame he couldn't just have trusted her to stick up for herself without pandering to his bosses.

'The complexity of the case is what I'm enjoying. The sense that I'm a part of a bigger process. It's okay being at home while Daniyal's young and still needs me, but I can't think of anything worse than spending the next thirty years of my life simply looking after a house and a husband.' Lottie said.

She was gratified that her comment finally shut them all up. The wives were suddenly deeply engaged in fiddling with their food, while Jeff and Alex were stony faced, glaring at Zain. Taking a deep breath, she tried to find the right words to soften her outburst. Even she wasn't sure quite where it had come from. It was almost certain that the Jeff/Alex wives didn't work for a living. She'd meant to shut them up, not to cause quite such shocking offence, and she hadn't even meant it. Lottie saw the merit in providing a stable home and family environment, and in supporting the people you loved. It was just as valuable a contribution to society as any other job, more so in lots of ways. Raising a happy child, working your fingers to the bone with washing, cleaning and household administration was sure as hell no easy option. The truth was not that being an at-home parent was a lessening of stature, only that she had been unable to find the value of herself within the role. Lottie was opening her mouth to apologise when Zain interjected.

'I'm afraid you might be overthinking the importance of jury duty, sweetheart,' her husband said, a warning hand on her knee signalling the end of the conversation. 'And you're maybe a bit stressed out with it all.'

She glared at him. Overthinking her importance? Why? Because she was, in fact, worth so little? Zain was right about one thing. She was stressed out. Not because of the rigours of jury duty, though. She was stressed out by how insignificant she'd become. How had she been reduced to the status of a misbehaving, troublesome hanger-on? The old Zain would never have spoken to her like that. He used to like her spark. She could make him laugh. He'd admired her. The balance had shifted. As he had done better in life, the seesaw of their relationship had tipped to leave him in the air and her in the mud. Her husband couldn't even see it.

'If you say so,' Lottie replied, emptying her glass and reaching for bottle to refill it again. Zain smoothly removed the bottle from her hand and put it back on the table. 'I need to check my lipstick. Excuse me.' She stood up and made her way out to the toilets, ignoring the fact that she felt rather wobbly, and fixing a smile on her face until she was safely locked into a cubicle. Their rudeness, their patronisation, was insufferable. Even worse, the women seemed to be encouraging it. Her husband – whether or not he was just sucking up to his bosses – had no right to belittle her. She took a few deep breaths to steady a vague sense of spinning. Dinner had been stodgy so she'd pushed it around on her plate until it looked as if she'd eaten some of it. Thank God at least the wine had been half-decent, but it was going to take several more glasses to drown her anger.

Lottie pulled her mobile from her bag, going to her contacts file where she had stored Cameron's number under the word 'Carpenter'. Zain wasn't given to checking her mobile, but there was no point asking for trouble. She typed in a few words, then deleted them.

Cameron would be out, and he wouldn't want a text from her moaning about some stupid dinner anyway. She contemplated phoning one of her other friends, mentally crossing out names in her head. What was she supposed to say? That going to a black tie dinner and drinking wine while a jazz band played in the corner was terrible? Right now everyone she knew would be watching television, washing up or tidying away stray toys. At least Cameron seemed to understand her. Ridiculous, really.

He was little better than a stranger, except that after just a few days he felt like more. She began texting again, determined to simply take the risk and reach out to him. After all, he'd left her his number. He wouldn't have done that if he hadn't wanted her to use it.

'Bloody awful evening,' she texted. 'Surrounded by morons who think all I am is a face with no brain. Can't wait to get back to court on Monday.'

She pressed send, then pulled a mirror from her bag and touched up her eye make-up. Cameron would be busy, she told herself. His phone was probably switched off or out of battery. Or he was in a bar and wouldn't hear it.

When hers buzzed with a reply, her pulse went up a notch. She opened the text.

'I'm guessing people underestimate you all the time. Their loss. Smile sweetly knowing they're the idiots. Let's have breakfast Monday. 9.15 a.m. at the Knife & Fork, Cabot Circus. I'm buying.'

She read it three times before responding.

'Okay. But I want a full English.' Shutting her phone off she flinched, imagining her husband's reaction if he knew what she was doing. Cameron was right, though. It was Zain's loss, and it had been too long since she had been made to feel interesting. Not that Zain didn't appreciate her. He did, in his own limited way, even if he'd been a jerk over dinner. Squashing a rising sense of guilt, Lottie switched her mobile on once more and deleted the text messages. Better not to leave them there and open to misinterpretation. Smoothing her hair, she prepared to return to the table, hoping that the music was now loud enough to make talking unnecessary. It didn't have to be a ruined evening. There was plenty of wine and dancing still to come. Whatever anyone else thought of her, she was entitled to live her life while she was still young enough to enjoy it.

12

The Cabot Centre was the quietest Lottie had ever known it, but then she'd never had a breakfast date there before. Not a date, she corrected herself. A meeting. With a friend. A colleague, almost. She wandered past the chain stores, cash machines and rows of plastic seating offering shoppers a place to put their feet up before continuing their commercial pilgrimage. It was the same as any other large shopping centre, she supposed, although she didn't get out of Bristol very often to see other cities. In fact, she couldn't now recall the last time she'd been anywhere. There was a trip to Cardiff to visit a few of Zain's distant relatives but that was what . . . eighteen months, two years ago? Zain travelled regularly with work, so the last thing he wanted to do at weekends was get back on the road. She might feel the same if she were constantly disappearing off to London, Manchester or Edinburgh. Her husband complained about it, but never passed the travel on to more junior members of his team. Pausing outside a travel agency, she stared at the pictures in the window. Safaris, gothic European cities, expanses of white sand, and here she was in the Cabot Centre, feeling as if she was doing something exotic. How utterly pathetic of her.

Turning away from the window, she looked upwards instead, through the high glass ceiling to the clear blue sky above. There was a cinema here that she never went to. Zain preferred to download films at home. There were restaurants she'd never visited. In fairness, most of them served burgers and listed twice-fried chips as a speciality, but even so, they ate out very rarely these days. Easier to stay at home with a young child. There was a whole life she wasn't living.

'Zain's a good man,' she said aloud, realising she was seeking to persuade herself rather than to compliment him. They'd met at a corporate event when she'd been handing out goodie bags with the usual useless, branded debris inside. It was her fifth week working with the promotions firm and she was fed up already, wondering why she'd taken a job that involved so many hours of standing around in stilettos, largely ignored by the crowds. Then a man had walked past and slapped her scantily skirted bottom. Another man had stepped in, berating the offender, demanding an apology on Lottie's behalf. It had taken her breath away, the sense of being protected, viewed as more than just an accessible body.

Zain had made sure she was all right, offered to get her coffee, and waited for her to finish her shift before taking her for a meal. Lottie remembered being impressed by his well-cut suit and manicured nails. He was older than her by more than a decade, but suddenly that seemed reassuring rather than awkward. Zain paid the bill, walked her to his car, and held the door open for her. No man had done that before. It was a habit her husband had maintained until they'd been married a few months, but then, like so many pre-marital benefits, it had drifted from always to occasionally to never. Likewise with his cooking dinner for her, or bringing home flowers for no reason. Or saying thank you. Familiarity might not always breed contempt, but it was a sure-fire path to laziness.

Lottie began walking again, fiddling with her wedding ring, the heat so intrusive she was even sweating beneath the thin band of gold on her finger.

Zain had found her, rescued her from pointless, back-breaking jobs, interrupted her cycle of self-destruction, and given her everything she thought she'd wanted. Then slowly he'd begun taking her for granted. There was no malice, no nastiness. The problem was that there seemed to be no emotion in it at all. No wonder he wanted to travel, even if all that awaited him at the end of each journey was yet more sales meetings. However dull, if the alternative was talking to Lottie about her day, who in their right mind would choose the latter?

'You look a million miles away,' Cameron said. She jumped, putting one hand on her chest, laughing at her own reaction. 'Sorry. I really did startle you. Next time I'll shout from a safe distance. Give you time to prepare.'

'I think I'm a bit tired,' she lied. 'I don't know what I was thinking.'

'Well, I hope you were thinking about either waffles or pancakes, because I need all the sugar I can get if today's going to be anything like Friday.' They walked to the door of the Knife & Fork. Cameron held it open and stepped aside for her to enter first. Smiling her thanks, she headed for a table near the back of the restaurant and sat down.

'You regretting getting called for jury service already?' she asked, wishing Cameron hadn't worn such a tight T-shirt, or at least that she could stop staring at the shapes his muscles made beneath the thin fabric. She hated it when men ogled her, now she was doing exactly the same.

'Not regretting, exactly,' he said, picking up two menus and handing one to Lottie before reading his own, 'but it's hard to watch so much misery without ending up miserable yourself.'

A waitress scuffed her trainers along the tiled floor, yawning as she greeted them. 'Decided yet?' she asked.

'Latte and scrambled eggs on sourdough,' Lottie said, liking how the word sourdough sounded, feeling more cosmopolitan than she had in an age.

'Black coffee and the pancake stack with bacon and maple sauce,' Cameron said, handing the menu back to the waitress. 'Do you want to talk about the dinner or shall we just drown our sorrows in caffeine?'

Lottie shook her head, playing with her serviette, trying to think of something entertaining to say. The silence was too reminiscent of the taxi journey home with Zain. They'd barely spoken all weekend.

'That good, was it? Let me guess. Lots of suits worn by men who should have gone a jacket size up a decade ago. Food less than hot by the time it was mass-delivered to your table. Wine that hadn't been left to breathe long enough, and music better suited to a nursing home.'

Lottie surprised herself by laughing out loud, stifling the sudden noise with her hand and snorting instead.

'That was pretty close, except the wine wasn't bad. Were you hiding behind the curtains or something?' she asked.

'No, but every corporate dinner is the same. I had a job with an insurance firm straight out of college. The struggle was not to get pissed and embarrass yourself. No wonder I became a carpenter. I still have nightmares about desk jobs.'

Lottie grinned, tried to hold it, but a grimace took over. She crumpled as tears filled her eyes.

'God, I'm sorry. What a total fool I am,' she said, dabbing at her eyes.

'Don't do that with me,' Cameron said. 'Save the bravery bullshit for people who can't be bothered to really listen.' He offered his own napkin as a backup.

'Please don't be nice to me. I'll only cry more,' she turned her head to the wall as the waitress returned balancing mugs and plates, glad of the chance to pull herself together as cutlery and sugar was also plonked on the table. When she looked back, Cameron was waving a forkful of pancake dripping with syrup in her direction.

'Eat it,' he demanded. 'Doctor's orders, or some such crap.'

Lottie smiled, taking the fork and enjoying the sweetness of the batter while she figured out what to say. She swallowed, taking a deep breath and preparing to speak.

'No,' Cameron said, raising a hand and shaking his head. 'You're going to eat everything on your plate and drink the coffee. No explanation necessary. Forget it until your stomach's full. Agreed?'

'Agreed,' she said, her shoulders relaxing as she gave up the effort to find the right words.

They ate in silence, until Cameron began talking about his favourite pancake toppings. Lottie smiled politely until she wasn't being polite any more and had genuinely forgotten the humiliation of her tears.

She finished first, having let Cameron do most of the talking. As he tucked into the final mouthful on his plate, she wiped her lips and folded her serviette onto her plate. 'I feel like I have no value,' she said. 'I felt it when I first started jury duty, then again at that bloody dinner Friday night. I lashed out at someone who patronised me, so now Zain's pissed off. I know I'm being ridiculous and that I'm really lucky, but I can't help it. I don't want to be this person who just looks after other people, while everyone else has all the adventures. Some days it's as if I'm physically shrinking.'

Cameron squeezed her fingers, then pulled his hand away, sitting back in his chair and folding his hands behind his head. Lottie watched him watching her, and waited for him to say something.

'I don't believe people make themselves feel small,' he said quietly, rocking slightly on the rear chair-legs. 'Human beings aren't programmed to do that. So I guess the question is – who's making you feel that way?'

Lottie looked away from him, reaching for the salt shaker and tipping a small pile of granules onto her hand, sifting through them with a perfectly painted fingernail.

'You don't have to answer that,' Cameron continued, setting his chair to rest and leaning across the table, taking hold of both her hands and leaving the salt in a trail across the wood.

Spilled salt, spilled sorrow, Lottie thought vaguely. Should have thrown it over my left shoulder. Some superstitions never left you. She wondered how Cameron's hands could be so warm but not the least bit sticky. Hers, she was sure, were damp with sweat, not that he seemed bothered.

'At the risk of sounding like a complete tosser, you're more than just a wife and mother. You and Jack, as far as I can make out, are the only two people on that jury who haven't been suckered into convicting that woman based on a bloody hedgehog. It takes a lot of guts to go against the crowd, but you're doing it. And you stood up to me when I was an idiot. To be honest with you, I was almost too intimidated to try apologising. I'm glad you forgave me.'

'I didn't stand up to you,' Lottie replied quietly, wondering when Cameron would release her hands, realising she was hoping he wouldn't any time soon.

'Yes, you did. You weren't stroppy about it either, and the next day you tackled me head on about it, with real self-respect. So think about it. Who in your life is making you feel less than you are?'

The shop doorbell – a sweet old-fashioned touch – jingled. Lottie pulled her hands back instinctively, looking up at the newcomer, doing a double-take.

'We should go,' she said quietly, bending down to pick up her bag from the floor.

'Hey, sorry, if I was out of line tell me. I just don't like seeing you upset. You deserve more than you're getting from life at the moment,' Cameron said.

'No, no, you were being lovely,' she rushed. 'It's the woman who just came in. I'm sure I saw her in the court before. I'm worried she might be a journalist.'

Cameron took a quick look. 'She doesn't look like a journalist,' he smiled. 'I don't recognise her, but we should get going anyway. Mustn't get told off for being late again. Maybe we should stagger our arrivals so no one figures out we've been on a breakfast date.'

That word again. Lottie avoided his eyes, waving at the waitress for the bill.

'Give me a moment, I've only got my credit card. I didn't have time to stop at the cashpoint this morning,' Cameron said, reaching into his pocket for his wallet.

'It's okay, I've got cash,' Lottie said. 'We really ought to get out of here. I'm certain I recognise her. Of all the cafés in the city, she had to walk in here,' she murmured, flicking her eyes over the bill as it arrived and leaving a twenty on the table. 'Come on.' She hustled out with Cameron behind her, striding past the shops towards the nearest exit. 'Don't you think that's weird, her choosing the same place as us to eat this morning?' she asked over her shoulder to Cameron. 'Who comes to the Cabot Centre this early on a week day?'

'Hey, Lottie stop.' He put a gentle hand on her shoulder until she came to a halt. 'Who knows, maybe she did wander into the courtroom at some point, but I didn't see her. Everyone looks the same to me wearing sunglasses. I certainly don't think she was spying on us,' he smiled.

'How can you be sure?' Lottie asked.

'Because we weren't doing anything. What's to see? Two people who are on a jury together getting an early morning coffee on their way to court. We didn't talk about the case, so we've done nothing wrong. What is it you're really worried about?'

Lottie blushed, no hiding it. She felt as if they were doing something wrong because she'd lied to her husband about her reason for heading into the city early, having made the arrangements from Zain's work celebration, of all places. Cameron hadn't done anything wrong, but she had definitely crossed a line.

'I think I just have hangover hypersensitivity. It always takes me two or three days to recover properly,' she said, shaking her head.

'I probably didn't help, holding your hands in public. I didn't even think about it. Sorry. You're married and that was too much. I won't do it again.'

'I wasn't complaining. For the record, I really appreciated what you were saying,' she said. 'We should get to court now.' She began walking again, this time at a more measured pace than before.

'Really? So I can hold your hand again sometime?' he laughed.

'Now you really are being inappropriate,' she said. 'Don't push your luck.' She laughed back, wishing the thought of him touching her weren't quite so thrilling. Wishing she didn't want him to quite as badly as she did.

'You'll be missing out if you say no,' he grinned. 'I'm something of an expert with my hands.'

'Not one more word,' Lottie said, trying to keep a straight face.

'It's worth being in trouble with you just to see you laugh,' he said. 'But fine, I'll stop. For now.'

They crossed the road together at a jog, with Lottie grateful for the distraction of the traffic, pushing her guilt aside. It felt good to be laughing again. It felt great, in fact, for the first time in ages, just to be alive.

13

Day Five in Court

Maria Bloxham's face in the court toilets' mirror was white with a hint of avocado. She had once painted her own downstairs toilet walls exactly that shade. Her skin colour was understandable. Regular meals were a thing of the past. The legal proceedings acted as a natural appetite suppressant. None of it was conducive to looking or feeling healthy. The press were starting to take more of an interest in the case with every passing day, and they had taken to gathering at the court doors to snap photos of her walking in each morning. It made her feel naked. Not just naked, if she was brutally honest. It made her feel violated. They yelled questions at her, knowing she couldn't and wouldn't answer. Now the protestors were also a regular event at the court doors morning and afternoon, baying for blood. She'd taken away their precious wildlife crusader. He would never write another magazine article about green energy, or have his photo taken as he posed thigh deep in a river, checking fish stocks. There would be no more fan mail for her to answer on his behalf, no more fêtes for him to open, no more guest lectures at universities. Her husband had earned an absolute fortune and never given a single penny of it to the charities he spoke so highly of. It was all sitting in some savings account somewhere – half hers, her lawyers had told her – just as long as she wasn't found guilty.

Think about the money, she told herself. Think about a future. She splashed cold water over her face. Today the prosecution's psychiatrist was due to give evidence. In his appointment with her, he had spent his time issuing false reassurances, befriending then prying, making soft accusations with false smiles. Maria had closed off from every insipid attempt at cajoling a confession from her. The results had not been good. She took a deep breath and prepared to spend another day watching her future unfold as she perspired in her glass box.

Professor Jasper Worth was still smiling when he took the oath and regaled the court with his qualifications and experience. He was a global expert in criminal psychiatry, apparently, who had been involved in some of Europe's most well-known and bloody cases. Imogen Pascal was almost curtsying by the time he'd finished.

'Is it right that you met with the defendant to assess her mental state, Professor Worth?' Miss Pascal asked.

'I did. That meeting took place some weeks after she was arrested,' Worth replied. He swiped his forehead with the back of his hand, the heat in the room assuming almost tangible weight. 'I had been given access to the case papers including the forensic evidence, and also to Maria Bloxham's medical records,' the professor said. 'Mrs Bloxham came to our suite of offices. It is designed to be a comfortable space where patients can feel relaxed and at ease. Given how little Mrs Bloxham disclosed during our conversation, I would say that our approach did not work.'

'Could you take us through the detail of your consultation with her please, Professor,' Miss Pascal said. Her voice was sugary sweet. Maria hated it.

'Indeed. I began by explaining my role, then I asked Mrs Bloxham to give me her version of events of the day when the police were called to her property. She was unwilling to share this,' he said.

'Did Mrs Bloxham provide you with any information at all about how she came to leave her husband so badly injured?' Miss Pascal asked.

'I asked questions designed to engage her in a discussion, using non-threatening subjects such as her family and childhood. She was monosyllabic answering those, so I moved on to general life-preference questions to start a more natural conversation.'

'Life-preference questions?' Pascal asked. In fact, the prosecutor understood the psychiatrist quite clearly, Maria thought. This was a rehearsed script. Perhaps not every question and every answer, but they knew exactly what they were going to cover during his evidence and what information he was going to convey to the court. James Newell had warned her that the morning might seem nothing short of theatrical. It was exactly that. Professor Worth was a different man to the person she had encountered during their 'session' as he'd called it. Maria had had little choice as to whether or not she went. It wouldn't look good if she refused, her lawyers had warned. It was imperative that the jury sympathise with her. And yet as soon as Maria had settled into the comfortable, over-sized chair in Professor Worth's office, as soon as he had opened his well-educated but condescending mouth, the only face she had been able to see was Edward's. She had felt like a child once more, like a silly infant whose opinions were obviously pointless and inevitably wrong, only this time she had seen red during the questioning. For almost the first time, she had given her anger words.

It was bad timing, she accepted that. Perhaps Professor Worth hadn't deserved it, although she couldn't silence the internal voice telling her that actually he might be the sort of man that needed answering back occasionally. But all in all, it was an inopportune moment for her to have chosen to refuse to be downtrodden any longer.

'Conversation starters,' Professor Worth explained in the jury's direction, 'relatively inconsequential questions, about the weather, favourite foods, reading preferences, travel experiences. The subjects that allow most adults to sustain a dialogue that is soothing and where there can be no perception of a right or wrong answer.'

'What did you establish from the defendant in response to those questions?' Miss Pascal asked.

'When I asked her what hobbies she enjoyed, she replied gardening. When I asked what books she liked, she did not respond. Likewise when I asked her favourite season, and so on. I did however observe that she was becoming increasingly stressed during the process of being asked those questions. Her hands were closing around the arms of the chair, her knuckles whitening. She was exerting substantial force.'

'How did you deal with that, Professor?' Miss Pascal crooned.

'I asked if she would like me to undertake some relaxation therapy with her and I also checked whether or not she was suffering from any form of pre-menstrual tension or post-menstrual stress,' he replied. 'That may sound very personal, but with female subjects it is only fair to establish that they do not have temporary chemical or biological factors which might affect them on that particular day, and which I should take into account when formulating my report on their mental state for the court.'

'May I ask if the defendant responded to that question?' Miss Pascal asked.

'She did respond, in fact. Mrs Bloxham looked me directly in the eyes for the first time during our session together, and told me – I quote – to go fuck myself.'

The shock displayed on several of the jurors' faces was rather comical, Maria thought. How many times had each one of them heard that phrase before? How many times had they used it, or at the very least thought it? They could read it, hear it on the television, see it graffitied on walls. Yet here they were, confounded by a forty-year-old woman using it against a professional, whilst sitting in a leather chair, in a slick office? Surely the sky was about to fall in.

One of the jurors, a young woman, notable for her looks, turned around in her seat, gazing in Maria's direction. They locked eyes. Maria knew she should look away – her barrister wouldn't appreciate her being so bold – but what she saw on the woman's face was genuine appraisal. Not judgment or disgust, more puzzlement and interest. Maria wanted to smile but kept her face blank and neutral. There was a chasm between them that couldn't be overcome with normal social gestures. The woman, and the eleven seated with her, would decide her fate.

Letting her eyes sink slowly towards the floor, Maria returned her attention to the man in the witness box, hoping he would be finished soon, as weary of him now as the first time she'd met him.

She raised her eyebrows and allowed herself a brief shake of her head at the ridiculousness of it all, her nose letting loose a drip of blood, the heat trapped within the dock too much for her body to handle. The prison guards at her sides had already stripped off their jackets and removed their ties, sweat stains marking their armpits. Maria put one hand to her face, dragging the back of her wrist along her upper lip and staring at the bright streak as she pulled it away.

Her blood. Edward had hated it. At first he'd refused to acknowledge or speak about it. Then as the months of their marriage had banded together to become years, he had insisted on regimented diarisation so he could anticipate when she would be menstruating. One rainy February morning, she had walked into their bedroom to find him clearing the en suite cupboard of tampons.

'Edward, what's happening?'

'I've chosen a more appropriate method of sanitary protection for you,' he'd said.

'That's ridiculous,' Maria had protested. 'I've always used those. It's what I'm happy with.'

'I've done some research,' he'd said, stripping off the plastic gloves with which he'd been handling the items. 'With internal vaginal products there's a risk of toxic shock syndrome. It can be life-threatening. You probably haven't heard of it.'

'I have, actually,' Maria said softly, 'but it's very rare and there are clear symptoms. I think I'd know if there was a problem.'

'Napkins are cheaper, too,' Edward continued, as if she hadn't uttered a word.

'But you're wasting money by throwing away what I've already bought,' Maria said, her voice firmer, sharper.

'Is that an excuse?' Edward asked. 'It sounds like an excuse for wanting to insert those nasty capsules into yourself each month. Do you like the way they feel inside you? Is that why you're arguing with me?'

Maria had blushed with painful ferocity.

'Of course not, why would you think that? It's just easier. I know it might seem strange for you, as a man. I can see how it might be an odd concept,' she had murmured, trying to soothe him.

'No, no,' Edward had said. 'It's not hard for me to imagine. My intellect allows me to perform that very easy task. In fact, it's all too easy to conjure in my imagination. Five days each month where you stuff those awful things up inside you . . .'

'Edward please stop, you're being vile,' she'd said.

'I'm vile?' He'd paused, laughed, stepped into her face, '*I'm* the vile one? It's a simple request, Maria. After all, I'm the one who pays for all this. I buy it, have it delivered to the door so you don't have to bother to so much as get to the shops. Let's be rational about it, shall we? There are new products in your cupboard. You will get used to them in time, and you'll have the added benefit of knowing I find them tolerable. I have no desire to argue with you. It's not like you to be so difficult. Presumably that revolting time of the month is upon us again.'

Maria had bitten her tongue. Edward wasn't going to back down. Continuing to argue was, she knew, the least sensible option.

'All right,' she'd said.

He had merely picked up his bin bag containing her tampons and walked out into the bedroom.

'Oh, and it might be best during your monthly for you to sleep in the spare room. That concession on my part is for your comfort. I recognise that your temperature goes up at that time, and I think it best if you have your own space. You sweat and leave the sheets sticky.' He had left.

Maria had waited until she heard Edward was downstairs then checked what he had left her. It occurred to her, for the first time, that whenever he bought her anything, he left it on the very bottom shelf of her cabinet shoved to the back. Maria didn't know why it had taken her so long to figure out why. Perhaps in haste, she'd assumed previously. Perhaps because he didn't know how she liked to organise her things. But Edward never did anything carelessly. When he bought something for her – deodorant, toothpaste, soap – she had to kneel down to reach it. Through that simple action she was made humble, grateful, had actively to acknowledge his generosity on her knees.

There they were, the packages so large it was impossible to miss them. The sort of sanitary napkins she remembered from her school days, when girls taken unawares had to go to the sick bay and ask the nurse for assistance. About an inch thick and approaching half a foot long, she knew they were not only the cheapest product he could have found, they were also the most obvious. Any hope of wearing trousers with them was laughable. Not that she went out anywhere anyway, but those things were the final nail in the coffin. They would bang against her legs as she walked, she'd thought. And wasn't that what he wanted? For her to be aware every second of her period that she was outcast, that she was disgusting to him.

Maria went to close the vanity cupboard door, noticing the tiny cardboard pack balanced on top of the sanitary napkins. She reached a hand in slowly and drew the packet out. Razor blades. Five of them, kept safe in a small plastic case. Maria fought the urge to open them and run her finger tip along to test their sharpness and feel the sting of the cold steel. Was he taunting her, or rewarding her for good behaviour, she had wondered, walking back into their bedroom and staring at their one framed wedding photo that sat on Edward's bedside table. Hard to believe she had ever been so hopeful, or so naive. Maria had balanced the razor blades on her lap as she'd sat on the bed contemplating spending the remainder of her years living with a man who dictated what sanitary protection she could wear.

'Go fuck yourself,' she'd thought, staring at her husband in the photograph. She remembered glancing at the doorway to the hall, suddenly convinced she would find Edward standing there, somehow able to hear what she had said in her mind.

It had become her silent mantra. When she awoke and saw that photograph first thing in the morning. When he'd asked her to leave their bed so that he didn't have to sleep next to a menstruating woman. When he'd refreshed her supplies of sanitary towels, each time shoving them to the bottom to get her – and keep her – on her knees. Go fuck yourself, she'd thought, every single time. But she hadn't left him. She had nowhere to go and no means to support herself. Then there were the marks on her legs. Edward would declare her to be at serious risk from self-harming. If she dared to leave, he had promised her institutionalisation. Maria had been left in no doubt that he meant it.

Imogen Pascal waited for the jury to recover from the shock of hearing what the defendant had said to the psychiatrist. 'What happened after that?' she asked Professor Worth.

'I asked her why she was so angry,' he said.

'What was her reply?' the prosecutor continued, teasing the story out.

'She kicked away the coffee table in front of her – just a few inches but it was a deliberate action, picked up her handbag, and stormed out,' Professor Worth said, raising his nose a couple of inches on his final words, signalling the dramatic end to his story.

'So presumably you were unable to reach any conclusions as to Mrs Bloxham's mental state,' Imogen Pascal said.

You bitch, Maria thought. You know he has. You've read his report, multiple times. The jury, though, has to have its pound of flesh delivered on a legal silver platter. Timing really was everything.

'Not so, in fact,' Professor Worth replied. 'A trained professional can read a remarkable amount in a short period of time with a patient. My assessment of the defendant is as follows.'

There was a fractional movement, a transition, as every single body in the courtroom – save only for James Newell and Maria – leaned forward in their seat. What was the secret of her madness? They were all desperate to know.

'There is no evidence of a psychiatric illness. Mrs Bloxham was in control of herself at the time of the offence, as she was in my office until she lost her temper. At the point when she became furious with me, she was actually baring her teeth.

There is no history of mental illness in her medical notes. Some teenage self-harm, but no report of that continuing after the age of eighteen. It's a phase many young people go through. It can be a cry for attention and is rarely serious. Often when the teenager goes to university, gets their first job or a steady partner, the self-harm stops immediately.'

'So that self-harm from nearly twenty years ago has no relevance now, that's your assessment?' Miss Pascal reiterated.

'None at all. In fact, Mrs Bloxham has not had cause to attend her doctor for several years. She is physically healthy, of a good weight, and I observed the muscle tone of her arms and lower legs to be good, which is consistent with what she told me about enjoying gardening. She is competent, and her intellect is within normal parameters,' Professor Worth said.

'So as far as you were able to observe, did the defendant display any symptoms of a mental illness that might mean she was not responsible for her actions when she attempted to kill her husband?' Miss Pascal asked.

'Other than a woman who can turn from reasonable and self-possessed one moment, to flying off the handle the next. A woman who, I believe, does not like being questioned, perhaps especially by a man. No defensive wounds were reported to the police, and when she was given a chance to explain her version of events, she chose to remain silent. The police interview is blank,' the professor said.

'Blank?' Imogen Pascal asked, the tiniest fragment of carefully choreographed faux shock in her voice.

'Blank on her part. She was questioned but offered no explanation, no answers, no expression of remorse. Also, perhaps more telling, no tears, no questions, no fear. A long, self-controlled blank. It is my opinion that Maria Bloxham is not mentally ill. She is, I believe, responsible for the injury to her husband, in both legal and moral terms.'

Imogen Pascal nodded reverently at the professor, swept her gown to one side, and sat down. James Newell stood up, his eyes focused on his notebook.

'Moral terms, Professor?' he asked, so quietly that even the judge had to lean in to catch his words.

'I meant only that . . .' Professor Worth blustered.

'How many years have you been a qualified psychiatrist?' Newell asked him.

'Twenty-two,' Worth bristled in reply.

'How many court appearances in your professional capacity in that time?' Newell continued.

'Too numerous to count. Certainly hundreds,' Worth said.

'And at what stage did this courtroom convict people on the basis of your moral judgment?' Newell asked. His voice was raised. Maria looked up. She had spent several hours with James Newell, not only at the court but in conference in his legal chambers. He'd never raised his voice before.

'I wasn't implying that this was a forum for morally based decision making. Only that Maria Bloxham was able to tell right from wrong at the time of the offence,' Professor Worth said. He had taken a half-step back in the jury box, and was fiddling with the notes on the desk in front of him. Imogen Pascal's cooing and coddling suddenly seemed an age ago.

'You believe she was able to tell right from wrong at the time of the alleged offence? But you weren't there, Dr Worth. Your interview with Maria Bloxham ended before she recounted those events to you, so unless you have some sort of psychic ability we don't know about, I'm not sure how you've reached that conclusion.'

'That's ridiculous,' Worth muttered, glancing to the judge.

'As is diagnosing someone's mental state from a single interview after reading a few statements,' Newell responded. 'Do you believe it's possible for a person to be under so much stress that they effectively break, driven to using extreme violence, even when they're not suffering a specific psychiatric illness?'

'Yes,' Worth said, 'but I'd expect some evidence of that.'

'And because Maria Bloxham lived in a nice house and never troubled her doctor, you've decided that cannot be the case?' Newell asked.

'I made my decision based on the problem she has controlling her anger, as I witnessed first hand,' Worth said.

'Have you considered that what you see as a non-threatening environment might not be perceived the same way by the people you examine?'

'These are procedures developed from years of professional work, and I don't appreciate having my standards questioned . . .'

'Spare us the righteous indignation, doctor, there's too much at stake for that,' Newell said, hands on his hips, his gown spreading out behind him like voluminous black wings. To Maria's delight, it looked as if he might suddenly fly away.

'I object to the tone my learned friend is taking with this witness, Your Honour,' Imogen Pascal interjected.

'Your witness can look after himself,' James Newell replied.

'I think that's enough for one day,' the judge said, setting her glasses on the desk. 'Apparently the heat is getting to us all. Perhaps tomorrow we will return with cooler heads and more civil tongues. I'm adjourning until 10.30 a.m.'

The tea and coffee in the jury room remained untouched. The Tabitha gang – seven of them now – were whispering in one corner. Cameron was leaning to mutter into Jack's ear. Pan was on his laptop already, as if the trial was merely a minor distraction in his busy working day. Lottie's head was full. She was too hot. Her feet were swelling in her sandals.

'I thought that professor man was quite clever, didn't you?' Jennifer asked as Lottie poured herself a glass of tepid water. 'He seemed to be pretty clear on the defendant's personality.'

'I'm not sure,' Lottie replied blandly, avoiding another confrontation. The truth was that she hadn't particularly liked the psychiatrist. He'd reminded her of that generation of GPs she used to see as a young child. White, middle-aged, supercilious males, ever so slightly sneering.

'Are you all right? You look a bit off colour. Probably the heat. I keep meaning to ask if we can have a couple of fans in here to keep the air moving around,' Jen said, looking around the room as if the fans were magically going to appear.

'Good idea,' Lottie said. 'Actually, I think I do need to sit down. Excuse me.' She slipped away, finding her bag and fanning herself with a deserted newspaper, hoping Jennifer wouldn't follow her. She knew she wasn't being kind – Jen was making an effort – but Lottie wanted to make conversation with someone whose life was entirely different to her own.

Taking out her phone, she considered who to text first – Zain to say she would be on her way home soon, which might do something to repair the bad atmosphere between them, or the childminder to see if she could pick Daniyal up in time for a trip to the park before tea.

'Sick of me yet or are you free for the afternoon, given they've let us have an early day?' Cameron asked quietly.

'We had breakfast together three hours ago,' Lottie said, slipping the mobile back into her pocket. 'I'm not sure we've got much left to talk about.'

'No talking then,' he said. 'How about a drink somewhere? I know a great pub on the coast. Breeze in your hair, sun in your face. No more talking about blood and death.'

She checked her watch to buy thinking time. An afternoon in a pub garden, or extra time at home doing what she usually did? The decision wasn't as hard as it should have been. Over the course of the morning, the answer to the question Cameron had posed in the café had repeated through her head. Who was responsible for making her feel small? *Zain.* Not deliberately or consciously, but there it was. She had a right to be happy and appreciated, and she wasn't going to pass up any opportunity she had to feel those things again.

'I'll have to get home at normal time,' Lottie replied.

'Suits me. I'm catching up with Jack for a drink tonight. Meet me in the multi-storey car park, second floor, row A,' he said.

Lottie grinned as he walked out. Cameron made her feel better about herself. He never talked down to her, and he was easy company. Why shouldn't she go for a drink with him? As long as they didn't talk about the case, they were doing nothing wrong. It wasn't as if she was going to let things go any further than simple friendship. She knew where to draw the line.

14

They drove west towards Portishead, then south down the coast, the sun enticing hoards of visitors to the sand. Ice-cream vans, bucket-and-spade vendors and unofficial cafés littered the entrances to the car parks, colouring the landscape in every shade of plastic imaginable.

'I love Kilkenny Bay,' Cameron said, lowering his window and allowing his right elbow to hang out, catching the breeze. That's why it was more tanned than his left arm, Lottie realised, wondering when she had first noticed the difference. 'I used to come out here all the time when I was a teenager. We'd wait until the tourists had given up for the day, bring some beers, light a fire on the beach.'

'Sounds idyllic. Where are we going?' Lottie asked, pulling her hair back from her face as the incoming breeze whipped it back and forth.

'Right here,' Cameron said, pulling off the road into a car park and pointing up to an old windmill. 'It's been converted into a pub. Follow me.' They walked round to the back of the building where it overlooked the sea. Part of the structure had been modernised with a curved glass façade. 'You get us a table on the decking and I'll get the drinks.'

Lottie watched him go, enjoying the way his T-shirt stretched across the top of his shoulders, trying not to let her gaze meander down the length of his body, and failing. Once he'd disappeared inside, she found a table and stared out across the waves. It felt good to be outside without worrying about watching a roving toddler. She could listen to the waves instead of responding to constant demands. Tipping her head back and closing her eyes, she let the sun bake her skin.

'You belong in the sunshine,' Cameron said quietly, brushing a strand of hair from across her cheek as he sat down. He poured tonic into gin and ice and handed it to her. 'This okay?'

'You're a bad influence. I can't remember the last time I drank in the middle of the day. If I start giggling, you'll have to throw some cold water over me,' she smiled.

'That would be my absolute pleasure,' he grinned, raising his glass to hers. 'Cheers. Here's to meeting you. How can I regret being called for jury service now?'

'You mean it's not enough that you're serving the community, sacrificing your time for the greater good?' She tilted her head, knowing the sunlight was catching her face and showing off her smooth, newly browned skin.

'That too, of course, but it might not have been quite the same if I'd ended up sitting next to Tabitha,' he said, stretching his arms above his head, tautening the muscles in his upper arms and chest.

'You mean you're not tempted by the thought of whispering the sorts of comments into Tabitha's ear you do into mine?' Lottie caught a drip of water from the outside of her glass and licked it from the end of her finger. A little light-hearted flirting was okay, she told herself. Nothing serious. No one was going to get hurt by a bit of banter.

'I'm not sure Tabitha smells quite as good as you, but I'm willing to give it a go if you think it'd loosen her up a bit,' he replied.

'Please, stop!' Lottie said. 'There are some things I don't want in my imagination.'

'Come on, it's a great idea. Or would you be jealous?'

'Maybe I'd be relieved,' she raised her eyebrows, turning her wedding band slowly on her finger and rubbing at a smudge on the gold. 'No more tutting and sighing without you next to me. I might actually be able to concentrate for a few minutes at a time.'

'You know what you do with your hands is a huge giveaway about what's on your mind,' Cameron said, nodding towards her fingers.

Lottie stopped fiddling and looked up at him. 'How so?'

'Give me your right hand,' he said, holding out his left, palm upwards on the table.

'Is this some sort of trick?'

'No, I work with my hands all day. I understand how important touch is. Come on, a little trust.' He pushed his hand an inch further towards hers.

'Fine,' Lottie said, placing hers palm up on top of Cameron's.

'Our hands are one of the most demonstrative parts of our body. They're a defence mechanism, our first point of contact and the things we use to incite a sexual reaction either in ourselves or in other people,' he said quietly.

'I'm not sure where this is going,' Lottie said. 'Is there a punch line?'

'No, no, this is real.' He turned her hand on its side and reached out his own to shake hers. 'We have all sorts of rules about touching each other with our hands that completely change the meaning of what we're doing, and yet it's still the same five fingers in play. You meet a stranger, or your boss, the first thing you do is reach out a hand to shake. You don't think about it. It's not personal, in fact if you don't shake hands you might be considered rude.'

'Go on,' Lottie said, picking up her glass with her free hand and taking a sip of gin.

'We can hold a friend's hand without it meaning anything, because we regulate the pressure of our fingertips.' He wrapped his fingers around hers to make the point. 'But if we use our fingers differently, hold hands in a different way, the meaning and the sensation becomes something else. Intimate, intense.' He turned her hand so that his palm was flat against the back of her hand and slowly eased his fingertips between each of her fingers, pushing all the way through until he could close his fist around hers. Lottie's stomach registered the shift in tension, forcing her to take a sudden breath in. 'It's to do with the act of opening up a part of someone else's body, forcing a sort of submission.' She knew he could see the effect he had on her. Flexing her fingers she tried to release her hand, but he kept hold, turning her hand palm up again in his own. 'We use our fingertips to give pleasure. A single touch can affect our whole body.' He ran his nails in a circle around her palm, issuing a shock of sensation up her arm and down through her core, then he trailed his fingers up the soft inner flesh of her arm to her elbow. Lottie put down her glass, laying her free hand over his to stop the caress.

'I get it,' she said, extracting her hand and wrapping it around her glass to cool it down. 'I still don't see what the relevance is to me.'

'Our hands are show our mood. We bite our nails when we're nervous, tap our fingers when we're impatient, and fiddle with things when we're stressed. Like your wedding ring.'

'Maybe the band's just too tight in this heat,' Lottie challenged him.

He didn't take the bait. 'Do you know you frown whenever you touch it?' he asked, his voice little more than a whisper.

'You're overthinking it,' Lottie replied, wondering if he was right, wanting to touch the ring immediately but too self-conscious to do so. The idea that she was so transparent was embarrassing, and she really should have argued with him, but that was just going to invite further scrutiny of her marriage. She opted for diffusion instead. 'It was a good excuse to hold my hand, though, right? How long had you been planning that?'

He laughed, all smiles, the seriousness gone, letting the moment drift away on the light wind blowing off the sea. 'You got me,' he said. 'I'll have to try something more subtle next time. I hope you don't mind.' He pulled his T-shirt over his head and threw it onto the table. 'It's baking out here.' Lying down along the bench, he revealed tanned skin and muscles that swelled and stretched with every movement. Lottie managed not to stare for about sixty seconds before giving in. If Cameron was relaxed enough to hold her hand and stroke her arm, surely she was free to stare at his body.

'So come on, as you're obviously showing it off, do you work out or is the body just from clean living and a physical job?' she asked.

'Do you like it?'

'I don't not like it,' she smiled.

'Then it doesn't matter whether I go to the gym or not,' he said.

'Do you ever give a straight answer to a question?' Lottie asked, lying back on her own bench and stretching out.

'Life's too short to be serious all the time,' he replied. 'I learned that the hard way.'

His voice had changed. Lottie was unused to hearing much except wisecracks from him. She sat up again and looked over the table top at his face.

'What happened?' she asked.

'I lost someone I loved. Cancer. She was too young, didn't deserve it – all the traditional clichés.' He turned his head and shielded his eyes to look at Lottie. 'Let's not ruin the afternoon. The sun's out and I want to enjoy it. What's your take on the case? I want to know why she did it.'

'The defendant?' Lottie asked, wanting to know who Cameron had lost and when, aware they were questions it was wrong to pursue when he had deliberately changed the subject.

'Maria,' he said. 'I'm making myself use her name. She's a person, not a thing. The prosecutor does that all the time, have you noticed?'

'We probably shouldn't discuss it,' Lottie said. 'I feel as if breaking the rules will result in some buzzer going off when I walk into the courtroom tomorrow.'

'That's just Tabitha getting to you,' Cameron said. 'I think they should hold the trial outside. We could sit on the grass and drink cold beer, get some perspective and take the drama out of it, although I'm not sure even that would be enough to mellow the haters.'

'The haters?' Lottie asked, as Cameron sat up and took a sip of his beer.

'Gregory, Agnes, Tabitha, even tattoo-man seems to have joined their clan and that's an alliance I wouldn't have bet on.'

'I think they're just shocked by what they're seeing and hearing,' Lottie said. 'Aren't you?'

He didn't answer, running his glass over his chest instead, sending rivulets of water trickling down towards his stomach. Lottie caught a group of girls at the next table staring open-mouthed.

'I think you have some admirers,' she said.

'I'd prefer it if there was no one here except you and me. I'm tired of sharing you.' He reached both his feet forward beneath the table to trap one of hers. Below the table her phone did a triple buzz in her bag, stopped, buzzed three more times. That was the alert from Zain's mobile, sending her a text. In less than a second she'd compiled a mental list of the possible subject matter of the text. Suggestions for dinner. A date for the calendar. A request to perform a specific domestic task.

That was about it. There would be no declarations of love, or expressions of gratitude. Not that he didn't love her, or wasn't grateful to her. Deep down she knew that Zain hadn't changed, but she had. She needed more than he was giving her. Lottie considered checking the text, knowing that whatever the content, the mood of the afternoon would be broken and she didn't want that. If all she had was a few seconds to feel alive and wanted, why would she destroy them?

Gently, slowly, but deliberately, Lottie pushed her other foot forward to grip Cameron's. They sat like that for several minutes, listening to the gulls screech overhead and watching day trippers on the sands below. Lottie wanted to stop time. She was content. She'd not yet done anything wrong, although she wanted to, more than she was comfortable admitting to herself. The desire to reach across the table and touch Cameron's hand was almost overwhelming. It was late though. Within the hour she'd have to be at Daniyal's childminder to pick him up.

'We should go back,' she said with a sad smile. 'I can't risk being late.'

'Ice-cream first, though,' Cameron said, handing her a twirling shell that gleamed pink inside. 'We'll stop off in Portishead on the way.'

'There's always time for ice-cream,' Lottie agreed, standing up.

Cameron held his hand out for her to pull him up off the bench, keeping hold of the very ends of her fingers as they made their way back to his van. Lottie considered pulling her hand out of his, but didn't. It was a gift, she thought, to feel so adored, and it was harmless. A sunny afternoon's toying, nothing more.

A few miles back up the coast Portishead was busy with tourists, bustling enough that neither of them worried about seeing anyone else from the jury. Bristolians knew better than to brave the seaside in the middle of the school summer holidays. Cameron detoured to a cash machine as they talked ice-cream flavours and chocolate flakes.

'Bollocks,' he said, banging the keypad, then ripping his card back out of the slot.

'Hey, I can pay for the ice-creams. It's not that big a deal,' Lottie joked.

'I don't need you offering me money,' Cameron snapped. 'Leave it, okay? This is none of your business.'

Lottie moved backwards, wrapping her arms around her waist, feeling the sting of his reaction as if he'd slapped her. For once, he wouldn't meet her eyes as she sought answers in his face. The heat had turned oppressive. Her skin was prickling uncomfortably and sweat was making a waterfall of her spine. 'All right,' she said slowly. 'I think I'd like to go home now.' She turned around, taking small, unsteady steps in the direction they'd come.

'Lottie,' Cameron said. 'Lottie, wait.' She carried on walking. 'Oh for God's sake, hear me out, would you? I didn't meant it. I never do.'

'We've been here before. You didn't mean it before, either. I don't need this. If I'm going to let a man to speak to me like that, it might as well be my husband, thanks.'

She kept going, increasing the length of her paces until Cameron had to jog beside her.

'Shit, I would never . . . I'm not him, Lottie. I'm not some bloke who sees you as a trophy to be taken out and polished occasionally. You're worth so much more. I shouldn't have spoken to you like that. It's not because I feel entitled to, okay?'

'I'm not listening to excuses. You're right. I am worth more and however great your body is, and however much you make me laugh, it's not enough to make me hang around while you

130

unleash your temper. You need to drive me home now. We're done.' She kept walking. Cameron jogged a few paces to block the pavement in front of her.

'Listen to me, would you? The person I lost – to cancer – was my fiancée,' he said. Lottie stopped. Cameron put his hands on his hips and glared at the ground. 'I missed a lot of work while she was sick. We got behind on the rent, and I was messed up for a while after I lost her. I was just getting back on my feet financially when I got called for jury duty, so now I'm not working again and, well, it's just a vicious circle to be honest.'

Lottie breathed in. It took her a while to figure out that she hadn't breathed out again. She was crying before she could reach out to hug him.

'I wish you'd told me before now,' she said. 'No one should have to cope with so much on their own. I'm so sorry.'

'A few months ago I realised I had to start again. Going out, making friends. It's scary getting close to new people when part of you is convinced you'll end up losing them, too. The last thing you want to do is freak people out talking about what you've been through.'

'You have to keep trying,' Lottie said.

'Forgive me?' he asked.

'Forgive you?' Lottie said. 'Are you kidding? I never even gave you a chance to explain. I guess it's not only Tabitha who judges too quickly.' She took his arm. 'Let me buy the ice-creams,' she said. 'Not because of the money, but because I need some sugar. Okay?'

'Sure, but next time's on me,' Cameron said. They walked arm in arm around the quayside to the ice-cream stand. 'Do something for me? Wear that blue summer dress tomorrow, the one with the buttons and the white straps. It's stunning on you. I haven't been able to get it out of my head.'

'I'm not sure it's even clean,' Lottie said, knowing it was in her washing basket. Knowing she would take it out as soon as she got home, wash it and tumble dry it. She would find time to iron it in the morning.

Cameron tucked a strand of hair behind her ear as they reached the van, other hand on her shoulder. He smiled sweetly, looking at his feet before he spoke.

'You're kinder than you should be,' he said. 'It's one of the reasons people underestimate you. That, and your face.'

He leaned closer, taking care not to touch her body with his, brushing her cheek with his own so slightly that all she could feel was the day's stubble taking hold. He kissed her where her cheekbone met her hair, releasing her shoulder immediately. It was a gesture of apology, Lottie thought, a suitable ending for an afternoon of contradictions. Or a beginning, the unstoppable voice in her head insisted. The end of flirtation and the start of something else. That moment when the slow dance ended and the boy asked you to go outside to catch some air. She had always known what it meant. Why was she trying to pretend it was any different this time?

She should be thinking about her husband, Lottie thought, as Cameron started the engine. She should be planning activities to do with her son at the weekend. Perhaps she should even be thinking about the court case. But the only thing on her mind was Cameron's words. Next time, he had said. There would be a next time to go out and enjoy each other's company, just the two of them. As Lottie considered all the reasons why it couldn't happen, she wondered how long she would have to wait until it did.

15

Day Six in Court

Lottie tried not to look at Cameron the next morning. She hadn't slept well and the lack of rest was revealed in shadowy half moons beneath her eyes. Every thought had been of him. As she had dropped her bra into the washing basket, he had been whispering to her. Whilst washing the dress Cameron had asked her to wear, she'd imagined his eyes on her body.

'Everything okay?' Zain had asked, catching her staring, lost, out of their bedroom window.

'Yeah, of course,' she'd said, forcing a smile to negate the rush of guilt at where her mind had been as she busied herself collecting stray items of discarded clothing from various corners.

'I don't suppose you've seen my blue shirt with the double cuffs?' Zain said, as he laid his trousers across the end of the bed rather than hanging them up.

'Have you looked in the laundry basket, or would you like me to do that for you?' Lottie asked.

'Is this about that dinner? Look, I'm sorry. I could have handled it better. There was just a lot riding on it and you were . . .' his words faded into a mumble.

'I was what?' Lottie asked. 'You might as well just say it.'

'Well, you were rude. Don't get cross again,' he said. 'I know you hate those evenings and it was a shame we were on that particular table, but I've never seen you quite like that.'

'Yeah, well, I've never been made to feel quite that inadequate and I didn't notice you rushing to defend me,' she said, picking up an abandoned pair of shoes and throwing them into the bottom of the wardrobe.

'They're my bosses, Charlotte. Could you not have just tried to brush it off? You know what, forget it, we're going round in circles. It looks as if my promotion's going ahead, so no harm done.'

'No harm done?' Lottie asked, dropping the gathered washing onto the carpet. 'Is that all you care about? No harm done to your promotion prospects, that's great. I'm so pleased.'

'Don't snap at me. One of us has to earn the money. It's not optional.'

'Did you ever stop to think that I'm capable of earning a wage too? Or that I might get bored here all day?' she asked, softening as she saw the confusion on his face. Zain had always taken care of her. Life wasn't exactly luxurious but she didn't want for much from day to day. She sank onto the edge of the bed, head in her hands. 'Listen, don't worry about it. I'm sorry too. I know you work hard for us. I'm tired and . . . I don't know . . . maybe I had a bit of PMT at the dinner or something.' She gave him a weak smile.

Zain laughed and patted her shoulder. 'That's so funny,' he said. 'I was thinking that was probably the cause. Bit more evening primrose oil next month maybe, or we'll have to make sure we don't have any plans to socialise.'

Lottie stood up, holding in the response she wanted to spit at him. Was that it? She expressed displeasure at being humiliated and talked down to, and her husband's only thought was PMT.

'I'll find your shirt,' she managed, setting one foot in front of another until she could bolt the bathroom door and let loose her silent rage into the mirror.

She'd left the argument there. Zain had been oblivious to her fury for the rest of the evening. Lottie had played at domesticity in the kitchen. Only reading a bedtime story to Daniyal had made her feel calm. Even then, she'd barely slept.

'Good morning,' Cameron said to Lottie as he walked into the jury room. 'How was your evening?'

As normal as that. Easy as pie. And yet, Lottie thought, nothing was easy for him at all. A year or so ago Cameron had lost the woman he'd planned to spend the rest of his life with. It hardly seemed fair that he'd had to perform jury duty. She was sure that if he'd explained to the judge . . . but how could he have done? It wasn't the place to bare one's soul and reveal financial hardships. Then she'd never have met him at all, of course, and however sympathetic Lottie felt for his plight, she couldn't regret that. Imagine sitting in that room with those people, with no Cameron there to make it all bearable.

'Fine,' she said. 'Yours?'

'Jack and I went out for a drink,' he said quietly.

Jack looked up from his cryptic crossword and smiled. 'We did,' he smiled. 'Not that it's easy being in public with him,' he told Lottie. 'I swear there were a couple of women actually drooling next to him. It was embarrassing.'

'Ah well, you've either got it or . . .' Cameron announced.

'Was he this insufferable last night, Jack, only I'm thinking that maybe those women were about to vomit rather than drooling over him?' Lottie interrupted.

'Have you noticed the Tabithas this morning? They've been in a huddle since I arrived,' Jack whispered.

'You're just changing the subject,' Lottie grinned.

'Maybe a little,' he smiled back, 'but they must be up to something. None of them even bothered glaring at Cameron when he walked in, and that's a first. I'm getting tea. Either of you want anything?'

Jack was livelier than Lottie had seen him since the trial had begun. They both declined the offer of a drink. She leaned over to whisper in Cameron's ear as Jack crossed the room. 'He seems chirpy. Did you put something in his drink last night?'

'He just needed someone to talk to. His parents are, you know, old fashioned, so his home life's not that much fun, and now he has to turn up to this mausoleum each day.'

'So you stepped into the breach and did the whole big brother, broad shoulders thing?' she smiled.

'Something like that,' Cameron replied, shifting his legs so that one of his thighs pressed against Lottie's.

She tensed to move away, stopped herself, and relaxed against him. His eyes met hers and for a few seconds neither of them spoke, both looking down as if the heat between them was a physical object that others might spot.

'It's okay, Lottie,' Cameron said quietly. 'Let me be what you need. I need you, too.'

The oxygen went out of the room. Caught in the chasm between ridiculous denial and the finality of acceptance, she stayed silent.

'This is enough for me. A friendship. The knowledge that perhaps, if you weren't married there might have been something more. I don't want to put you in a difficult position.'

She gulped air then did her best to speak, her voice husky with sudden dryness.

'I know,' she muttered, any hope of pretending confusion or ignorance evaporating into the heat. 'I never thought you'd try to take advantage.'

'Don't make me out to be too much of a hero,' Cameron winked. 'You can't expect me to behave myself forever. I'm only human.'

She was at a tipping point. For a second Lottie blamed Zain for what she was about to do. Insensitive Zain who had laughed and agreed when she'd mentioned PMT. Self-obsessed Zain who never thought to look for his own shirt when she could do it for him. Reliable, predictable, safe, she reminded herself; dull, her serpentine inner-voice hissed. Then there was Cameron. He was everything else.

'I don't recall having asked you to behave yourself,' Lottie said, standing to put away her magazine, ready to go into court. 'And I'm not sure it would make any difference even if I did.' Leaning down low in front of him, she picked up her bag from the floor, watching Cameron's eyes follow the bead of sweat running from her throat to her breasts. 'To be honest, I'm not even sure I want you to.' She walked out, knowing how that particular dress would swish around her legs if she worked her hips, knowing it was just short enough to tantalise, and in absolutely no doubt that Cameron was watching.

Her Honour Judge Downey glared at both Miss Pascal and Mr Newell.

'The prosecution calls Detective Inspector Anton,' Imogen Pascal said.

Anton was in the witness stand in a heartbeat. The jury had seen him in court every day, sitting behind Miss Pascal, whispering to her, handing over notes. Lottie thought she had seen an emotion flash in Miss Pascal's eyes just once, when DI Anton had left a hand on her shoulder fractionally too long, under the guise of getting her attention. It had looked like mild irritation with a hint of get-off-me-right-now.

No time wasting in court today, Lottie was pleased to note. If they finished early enough perhaps she and Cameron would have more time together. Just to talk, she told herself. Just to finish talking where they'd broken off yesterday.

'Could you describe the scene when you arrived at the Bloxhams' property?' Imogen Pascal asked the policeman.

'The defendant was standing on the front driveway with the chair leg at her feet. She'd been unwilling to put it down initially but had complied upon being asked. Mrs Bloxham seemed calm, almost surprised there was so much fuss. I asked her if she needed medical attention and she said she didn't. When I went into the kitchen . . .' he paused. 'I've been a police officer for fifteen years and I've never seen anything like it.'

Lottie caught Imogen Pascal's half eye-roll before the barrister brought her expression back under control and forced a polite smile. 'That's quite something,' Miss Pascal said. DI Anton had overplayed his hand, Lottie thought. It was too much. They had all seen Edward Bloxham for themselves. No need to big it up in the courtroom. Lottie turned to Cameron who gave a slight shake of his head, evidently feeling the same. 'Could you describe the scene on a factual basis for the jury, please, DI Anton.'

'Yes, right. The kitchen was almost immaculate, which made me wonder if the defendant had spent time cleaning up before realising that she couldn't get rid of the body and deciding to call the police instead.'

James Newell got to his feet, arms crossed. 'That's speculation, Your Honour. I wonder if Miss Pascal could explain in plain terms to DI Anton what the word factual means.'

Imogen Pascal narrowed her eyes at DI Anton and tried again. 'Just tell us what you saw with your own eyes, please, officer.'

'Sorry, yes, there was a body on the floor, face down. It's a large kitchen with a central dining table and five chairs around it. The man's head was facing towards the rear door that accesses the garden, and his feet were pointing diagonally towards the pantry. His hands were out to either side of his head. As I arrived in the kitchen the paramedics were starting to turn him over to secure a line for intravenous fluids.'

'Was anything in the kitchen disturbed?' Pascal asked.

'Nothing was broken. The only blood was in a pool on the floor, and covering Mr Bloxham's body and clothing. Mrs Bloxham obviously had blood on her hands and we sealed each of those in an evidence bag for forensic testing. The rest of the house was likewise undisturbed. There was no suggestion of a physical fight anywhere. There was an unbroken mug in the sink and a pile of post on the kitchen table. Apart from that it was all tidy.'

'Thank you, detective,' Miss Pascal sighed. 'And did you arrest the defendant?' she asked.

'I did. However, she fainted at the scene when I explained that the air ambulance was on its way to transport her husband to the hospital.'

'Fainted?' Miss Pascal enquired, sending a quick glance in the jury's direction. She's making sure we're paying attention, Lottie thought, pleased that she was starting to recognise the lawyers' tactics. 'Was the reason for that apparent?' the prosecutor continued.

'I'd say it was the shock of realising that her husband was still alive. It was clear from her phone call to the emergency services that Mrs Bloxham believed him to be dead.'

James Newell sighed loudly as he got to his feet. 'That's speculation,' he moaned to the judge.

Imogen Pascal nodded an apology, although the upturned corners of her mouth told Lottie that she was content the point had already been scored.

'What happened to the defendant next?' Imogen Pascal asked DI Anton.

'Having regaining consciousness, she was cautioned at the scene, then driven to the police station. At that stage Mrs

Bloxham was seen by a doctor to ensure that she was unharmed and fit for interview. After that we offered her a lawyer, as is standard practice. She said she didn't need legal advice.'

'Can you summarise the interview for us, DI Anton?'

'I can, I'll just consult my notebook.' He flicked through a few pages, then began reading. 'Mrs Maria Bloxham, aged thirty nine, was given her rights. I told her that she did not have to answer questions but that if she failed to do so the jury might take her silence into account as part of the case against her. I repeated that warning twice, and asked her to confirm that she understood what it meant. She did. I then proceeded to ask her questions about the injury to her husband.'

'What information did the defendant provide about the attack itself?' Miss Pascal asked.

'Absolutely nothing,' DI Anton said. 'She didn't answer one single question.'

'Do the Bloxhams have any children?'

'None,' Anton replied, pulling his shoulders back.

'And their financial situation, what can you tell us about that?' Pascal asked.

'There are substantial assets, both in bank accounts, savings, some stocks and shares. The house is in a good area, very sought after,' DI Anton reported.

'And who would benefit from Dr Bloxham's death?' Imogen Pascal hammered the point home.

'Mrs Bloxham. We tried to contact his family while he was in hospital, but he has no siblings and no living parents. The defendant is literally the only family Dr Bloxham has.' DI Anton shook his head slightly, adding emotion to his speech before glancing back momentarily at the dock. Lottie was glad it wasn't her sitting in there. If looks could kill.

'The defence is free to cross-examine,' Imogen Pascal said, sitting down.

James Newell took his time, finishing writing a note and consulting with the lawyer behind him before standing up. 'So by the time you interviewed Maria Bloxham, she had already called the police and explained that she had hit her husband over the head with a chair leg,' he said.

'Yes,' DI Anton said, pulling himself up straight.

'She'd handed over the chair leg as evidence,' Newell continued.

'I've said that,' Anton said.

'She had neither fled the scene nor made any excuses for what had happened,' Newell finished.

'Your point being?' DI Anton asked him.

'The point being, detective inspector, that Mrs Bloxham did not need to answer your interview questions because she had already fully confessed what had happened. You knew the how, the where and the when. So suggesting that the jury should hold her silence in interview against her is rather harsh, isn't it?'

DI Anton opened his mouth to answer, looked at Imogen Pascal who – Lottie noted – simply looked away, then shut his mouth again.

James Newell continued. 'Did you see a landline telephone in the property?'

'I don't believe so,' Anton replied.

'Did Mrs Bloxham have a vehicle at the property?' Newell asked.

'Not that I was aware of,' Anton said.

'And you say you investigated the couple's financial situation?' the barrister went on.

'Yes. The accounts and shares total around £380,000. The house has no mortgage, and is estimated to be worth between £750,000 and £800,000. In addition there are royalties from Dr Bloxham's books. That would all have gone to Mrs Bloxham, if her husband had died,' Anton finished.

'Is the implication that Mrs Bloxham might have hit Mr Bloxham over the head to have inherited all the money?' Newell asked slowly.

'It's a motive, yes,' Anton replied.

'But she immediately phoned the police and admitted what she'd done. Tell me, detective inspector, how she could possibly have thought she would get away with that?'

There was no reply, although DI Anton was looking increasingly fed up, and running his finger around the inside of his collar.

'About those bank accounts,' Newell went on. 'How many of them did Mrs Bloxham have access to, either as a signatory or by having the account in joint names?'

'I'm not sure, actually,' Anton said.

'Let me assist,' Newell replied, handing over a series of bank statements for the usher to give DI Anton who flicked through them. 'Can you answer the question now?'

'Uh, it actually looks like none of them,' Anton said.

'None, officer. All that money, a variety of accounts and Maria Bloxham did not have access to a single penny of it. Can you confirm that you found no accounts in her sole name?'

'We didn't,' Anton said.

'And was she insured to drive Mr Bloxham's car?' Newell asked.

'No,' Anton said.

'When you searched the house, what passports did you find?'

'Dr Bloxham's passport was located in his office. We didn't find one for Mrs Bloxham,' Anton said.

'So Maria Bloxham was not allowed access to money, nor was she allowed to drive, nor could she leave the country. There wasn't even a landline phone in the house,' Newell summarised.

'There was a mobile phone found in one of her shoes, hidden at the back of her wardrobe,' Anton responded.

'Did it have any credit on it?' Newell asked.

'No, but it might have had previously,' Anton said.

'And is there a record of any calls being made from it?'

'No, it was pre-paid. No billing. She was obviously hiding it from her husband,' Anton finished smugly.

'Thank you, DI Anton, it's very helpful to hear you draw that conclusion. Hiding it from her husband is exactly what she was doing. The pile of post you've said was on the kitchen table, who was that addressed to?'

'All the letters were to Dr Bloxham,' Anton confirmed.

'At what address?' Newell asked.

'I'm not sure. It didn't seem relevant at the time,' Anton said.

'Very well. No further questions,' James Newell said, sliding back into his seat.

'That is the close of the prosecution case,' Imogen Pascal said.

There was a flurry of activity as Tabitha waved a sheet of paper in the usher's direction, who moved to retrieve it and pass it to the judge.

'We have a request from the jury,' Her Honour Judge Downey told the barristers. 'They would like to visit the Bloxham's property. I don't suppose there can be any sensible objection to that. Miss Pascal, we will take a short break while you see if arrangements can be made. Members of the jury, please remain in your room until you have confirmation, after which you may leave the courtroom ready to reconvene tomorrow.'

'Bloody Tabitha,' Cameron whispered to Lottie as they left the courtroom. 'Jack was right that her little posse was up to something this morning.'

'Maybe it's a good thing,' Lottie said. 'It might help us set the scene more clearly, and I'm curious about it. I want to understand what their lives were like. It's true you never know what happens behind closed doors. This might be the closest we can get to seeing the truth for ourselves without either the prosecution or the defence putting their spin on it.'

'Yeah, sure, I agree. I was just hoping we could get another day off. Yesterday seems too long ago already. Here, you go ahead,' he said.

'Waiting for something?' Lottie asked him.

'No, I just want to be able to watch you walking.' Cameron got close enough to whisper in her ear that Lottie could feel his face brush against her hair. 'Just like you knew I did earlier.'

16

The jury deliberation room was sealed off from the outside world, relying instead on an ancient air conditioning system that was no match for the hottest day of the decade, as the newspapers were dramatically proclaiming. What little air was circulating was dry, visibly dusty and only slightly cooler than the outside temperature. The long rectangular table of deep cherry wood had become increasingly sticky, and the straight-backed chairs offered little in the way of comfort. Eleven of them sat around in their habitual places, sipping water and waiting for Cameron to reappear.

'I don't see why we can't leave the building,' Pan complained. 'They've got our mobile numbers. I could have walked to the shops, bought my wife's birthday present and been back by now.'

'Rules are rules,' Tabitha replied. 'The case is too important for us to be wandering off. The judge simply asked us to wait for confirmation of the visit to the Bloxham's house tomorrow. I'm sure it won't take long.'

The eye-roll equivalent of a Mexican wave circled the table, but no one bothered to respond to Tabitha's lecturing. That would only encourage her to add further commentary. The heat had them all at a loss. A crash the other side of their door preceded a stream of cursing. Tabitha pursed her lips but managed to say nothing for once. Lottie hid a smile. It was Pan who got to the door first and opened it.

Cameron grinned at them from the corridor, clutching two large saucepans full of ice. 'Ta da!' he sang as a spontaneous round of applause erupted.

Across the corridor another jury room opened and a head appeared in the space between door and frame. 'Do you mind?' an elderly man hissed. 'We're deliberating.'

Jack leaned to his right to whisper in Lottie's ear. 'See, it's not just us. Every jury has its Tabitha.' Lottie covered her mouth to hide a laugh, but her eyes were already on Cameron as he entered the room, tan lines showing from their illicit walk along the Portishead seafront the previous afternoon. Today his T-shirt was that bit tighter and she could see the point where the deep brown of his bicep reddened then blanched beneath his sleeve. The heat she felt inside was a match for the record temperatures outside. She focused on nibbling a snagged thumb nail, studiously not watching as he arranged the ice in central bowls for everyone to reach.

Around their side of the table, Cameron leaned between Lottie and Jack, stretching across to deliver dozens of ice cubes. Jack grinned at him, fanning himself.

'You are absolutely amazing,' Jack proclaimed, reaching for a cube and running it over the back of his neck.

Cameron took his time picking up the stray cubes that had attempted escape. Lottie tried not to look at where his T-shirt had risen above the line of his belt, exposing a slab of flat stomach, nor at the muscle definition lines that ran down from his abs into well-filled jeans. Every part of his body was so toned, it was hard not to stare. Harder still not to compare Cameron's body to her husband's spongy flesh, not fat exactly, just not . . . she searched for a word that was fair rather than gratuitously insulting. Just not in prime shape, she thought. Since hitting his mid-thirties, Zain's previously sleek body had first softened then expanded. Cameron took his seat to her right. Normal conversation resumed, pairs and trios forming to chat. Cam shifted his chair a fraction closer to hers, pouring himself a glass of water and settling in.

'I still have sand in my shoes,' he whispered. 'Do you think we'd get in a lot of trouble if the rest of them found out?'

The rest of them. At some point since that exhilarating, uncomfortable first day, the rest of the jury had become a separate entity to her and Cameron, save for Jack who was sweet but quiet. Day after day of moving from the courtroom to their allocated jury room, constantly waiting but rarely being informed of the reason for the delay. Hours of being forced together and finding allies, unable to explain it adequately – at all, in fact – to anyone else. It was like being on a government sponsored desert island.

'We didn't discuss the case details,' Lottie replied quietly. 'So I don't think we broke the judge's rules, although perhaps we strained a few of the extra ones Tabitha's made up. Where did you get that ice?'

'Used my natural charm on the catering staff. Don't let me forget to take the saucepans back later. Anything exciting happen while I was away?'

'I don't think anything exciting's happened to me for about a decade,' Lottie sighed. She looked away, embarrassed. That was too close to the truth. The jury room was no place for confessions.

'I'm pretty sure I can change that,' Cameron said.

He leaned forward, taking a handful of ice and dropping all but a single cube into his water.

'Have you got your book with you?' he asked.

'Yes. Why?'

'Open it,' he said. 'Get reading.'

'I don't . . .' He was already spreading his newspaper out on the table, finding the sports pages and settling down to pass the time.

Lottie shrugged, bemused. Yesterday they'd talked for hours. Now, it seemed, he just wanted to switch off. Perhaps he was regretting having told her about his fiancée. She opened her book and set her elbows on the table, trying to concentrate in spite of the sweat that was trickling down her back. Absolutely typical that she had to end up doing jury duty during a heatwave – the ice stung momentarily as it touched the inside of her right thigh. She whipped a hand down below the table to rub the spot, and connected with Cam's arm. Lottie stared at him. He didn't look up, apparently engrossed in his paper, giving only the tiniest shake of his head. She opened her mouth to speak, knew there was nothing she could say aloud, closed her lips again. Reopening her book, she glanced around the table. Jack was doing another crossword. Tabitha was holding court with her cronies. Pan was typing furiously into his laptop. Jen was filing her nails. No one seemed to have noticed.

When the ice touched her a second time she was ready for it. Cameron's little finger hooked the hem of her dress and lifted it ever so slightly as he rested his wrist an inch above her knee. The chill on her flesh was delicious. Tiny cascades of ice water ran down the inside of her thigh, making miniature puddles on the seat. Lottie didn't care. They would dry in a matter of minutes. She allowed herself a grin, keeping her eyes firmly on the page. Cameron's arm was completely still. Only his hand was moving, his fingers making a circular pattern over her skin.

It was fun. Nothing more. Cameron being Cameron, making even the dullest morning a playground for himself. She told herself not to take him too seriously. It was all a joke. The ice cube melted, the warmth of his fingertips quickly replacing the frozen water. Breathing out and feeling light-headed, Lottie contemplated the guilt she'd been ignoring.

Yesterday's trip to the pub had been nothing more than friendly. Holding hands as they'd walked to his van had been flirtatious. This, though, was a neon red line. It was the point at which she had to say no or start lying, both to herself and to Zain. Pan stood up and left the room as Tabitha started a conversation about local elections. Lottie bent her head further forward towards her book, hoping no one would try to speak to her, terrified that someone would notice what was happening.

Cameron reached forward again, his long fingers slipping deftly into the central bowl to grasp more ice cubes. Lottie watched him draw his hand slowly back, slipping one cube into his mouth, his eyes never wavering from the page. As his left hand disappeared beneath the table once more her stomach tightened, knowing what he was about to do. She closed her thighs as his hand reached them, concentrating on maintaining a neutral expression, finding the heat in the room suddenly overwhelming. The ice cube slid into the valley between her legs, moistening her skin, helping his fingers push her thighs apart. Lottie's eyes closed as a burning trail of want trickled through her from stomach to groin. His fingertips were firm but gentle as he ran his nails along her soft flesh, a millimetre at a time. She was all liquid. The air around her was short on oxygen. Flexing her toes, she commanded herself to stay still and not respond. When her legs parted she gasped, betrayed by her own body. Jack looked up from his puzzle book.

'You okay?' he asked.

'Yeah, great book.' She kept her focus on the page, knowing she couldn't look Jack in the eyes. 'Forgot where I was for a moment.' She leaned further over the novel, letting her hair fall across her face to cover her burning cheeks, ensuring Jack went back to his own entertainment. Her flushed skin might be due to the heat of the day. Perhaps she could even get away with blaming the heatwave for her faster than usual breathing. The thin cotton of her bra, though, was fighting a losing battle against her hardening nipples. She brought her upper arms inwards, covering the tell-tale profiles through her summer dress.

Cameron's fingers snaked up her thigh, his eyes flitting briefly across to meet her gaze. She imagined what he was seeing. Her pupils would be dilated, her lips full and red as blood rushed to the softer parts of her body, her skin glistening with perspiration that had nothing to do with the sun.

'Stop,' she mouthed silently to him. It would only make him more determined. She'd known that even as she said it. He was already turning away, his smile revealing carnivorous white teeth as he flipped his page carelessly.

Lottie took a deep breath and pushed herself backwards in her chair, away from his hand, wanting him to stop. Wanting him. Moving did nothing to deter him. His hand pushed on between her thighs, forcing her skirt to ride up until it barely covered her knickers. Twisting his wrist, he pressed his palm firmly between her legs. A fire raged inside her. His fingertips brushed her silk panties, and Lottie's heartbeat was a bass drum in her ears. It had been so long – too long – since she had reacted to anticipatory pleasure. The routine of marital sex had dried up any sense of longing, replacing it with Friday night expectations and Saturday morning sheet washing. This was an explosion of need and desire, coupled with an age-old sense of shame about being caught in such a wild state of arousal.

'Hot, isn't it?' Cameron commented to her, casually, as he circled his finger over the fabric of her knickers. Lottie raised a knuckle to her mouth and bit down hard.

The door opened abruptly and the court usher stood mopping his face with a handkerchief.

'Right, ladies and gentleman, the visit to the Bloxham house is set for tomorrow morning. Please meet here at 10 a.m. and you will be transported to the crime scene by minibus.'

Lottie tensed, suspended in slow-motion mortification, certain that everyone knew what was happening beneath the table. Then it was all movement. The closing of newspapers and shuffling of chairs. Cameron's hand slid back down her leg with a gentle pat on her knee. She forced one shaking hand to fold over the page of her book, not that there had been any reading progress since she'd opened it.

Jack stood up next to her, taking a last swig of water. 'I think I'm going to die of boredom if they don't hurry this trial up,' he said.

Lottie smiled, clearing her throat, nodding.

'I don't know about that,' Cameron said, standing up and pushing his chair beneath the table. 'I'm finding it all quite stimulating.' He smiled at Lottie as Jack walked away, before wandering off to retrieve his bag. Lottie waited the few extra seconds she needed until her legs had stopped shaking before doing the same. That was the end of it, she told herself. If it stopped now, there really was still nothing for Zain to find out. But beneath that was a growing sense of feeling more alive. Better still, of feeling wanted. Full-blown adultery remained a giant leap away, she told herself. She could take back control of the situation. It wasn't too late yet. Not quite.

17

Maria waited for James Newell on Broad Street opposite The Grand Hotel, wishing she was invisible as guests took afternoon tea and stared at her through the expanses of square glass. Relentless media coverage had her face plastered on every screen and newspaper, and some sensationalist internet group was calling her The Bristol Butcher. Sunglasses and hats did little to hide her identity. Behind Maria, the barristers' chambers was fronted by a line of arches proclaiming grandeur and gravitas. The whole street – solicitors, art galleries and the sorts of restaurants that still favoured ties – was an ode to a gentler life. Her defence counsel had proved kinder than Maria felt she had any right to, offering to drive her to Edward's house to collect some of her possessions. The visit was at her own request. She needed to move forward. No one understood what it was like, putting your life on hold while it took months for a trial to get started. The police had grudgingly agreed to let her into the house, but only once the prosecution had closed its case. When Newell's BMW hovered at the pavement's edge, it took a few seconds before she could move. This was normal life. People extended the hand of friendship, you accepted, returned the favour. The problem was that she had nothing to offer. They drove making small talk until they reached the house she'd last seen from the back of a police car. She had no desire to walk through the front door, although she was curious about the state of the kitchen. Did the police clean up, she wondered, or would there be a dried up pool of blood on the floor?

'Are you sure you want to go in there?' Newell asked, as they waited for DI Anton to arrive. 'I can request that the police officers to do this for you.'

'I'll be fine,' she said. 'I need some more clothes, and as I have no intention of ever living there again, I might as well clear out my belongings. If I get convicted, I'll never get the chance.' James Newell nodded but remained quiet, acknowledging both the truth of what she'd said and the possibility that the case might end badly. 'So how do you think the trial's going?' she asked, filling the silence.

'As well as can be expected. I'm sorry you've had to listen to people talking about you as if you weren't present in the courtroom with them. A trial can be a very impersonal process.'

'That's all right. You did warn me,' she said. 'I'm sorry you've had to be involved in the whole sorry affair.'

'This is my job,' Newell said. 'I get to walk away at the end of the day. I try never to forget that my clients can't.'

'What about the ones you think are guilty. Do you worry about them too?'

Newell relaxed against the headrest and closed his eyes. 'Guilt and innocence are such finite terms. Life rarely allows us to make such clean choices. I can't think of many clients over the years who fall squarely into either one category or the other.'

Maria thought about it as she stared in through the iron gates. Her own guilt was the cement between the bricks of their aesthetically perfect home. She had let Edward dominate her. In the early days, now that she looked back, she knew she could have left, only it was easier to have a roof over her head. It required no effort to have someone else pay for the food and the bills, to organise the car and decide what they should eat. Her life – however much she had hated it – had been built on her fear of going it alone. Perhaps she could have prevented the bloodshed, if she'd been stronger but by then Edward had deserved what he'd got. The moment the chair leg had connected with her husband's skull had been a victory.

'Are you going to be okay giving evidence, only you'll be cross-examined and you can't . . .' Newell fumbled the words.

'I can't lose my temper. I know,' Maria said. 'I'm sure I'd be just as quick to judge if I were on the jury.'

'Don't write those twelve people off too soon,' Newell said, undoing his top button and wiping sweat from his forehead. 'Juries are tricky beasts but I've found them remarkably perceptive over the years.'

'I'm not sure my case is one that many people could sympathise with. The older jurors won't even look at me, and when the younger ones do it's as if they're staring at a spider under a glass. They want to get a good look, but they wouldn't want me too close.'

'There's a long way still to go. Remember they haven't heard your side of it yet.'

'Thank you, James. I know you're doing your best,' Maria said softly as DI Anton pulled up. She wanted to reach out and pat her defence counsel on the arm, but checked herself. He was her barrister, not her friend. 'Let's get this over with.'

She got out of the car to meet DI Anton and the police officer accompanying him.

'Mrs Bloxham,' Anton said. 'There are rules. You will have to be accompanied in every room of the house and we will check every item you wish to remove. There will be no access to the kitchen or your husband's study. Is that agreed?'

'Absolutely,' Maria said. 'I was wondering, will Miss Pascal be joining us? I assumed you'd want her here, DI Anton.'

One side of Anton's upper lip lifted in a snarl before he could control himself. He narrowed his eyes at her. 'This is a police matter. I don't need a barrister here to make decisions. Let's get moving.'

He strode towards the house, the junior officer rushing to catch up, leaving James Newell staring at Maria.

'What was that all about?' Newell asked her.

'I don't think he likes me,' Maria whispered in reply.

'I don't think he does either,' he gave her a quick smile, then motioned with his head. 'Best not keep them waiting. After you.'

Maria made her way to the front door. She could hear DI Anton striding around upstairs, checking the bedrooms before allowing her access. It was foolish to wind him up but when you were at rock bottom you had to get your kicks wherever you could. Ribbing the supercilious detective inspector about his obvious hankering for Imogen Pascal was hardly the crime of the century – she'd already committed that – and at a deeper level, she was enjoying flexing her emotional muscles. It felt good to be unafraid, and to push back a little. It wasn't as if she had much left to lose.

Upstairs, she took a suitcase from one of the spare bedrooms, before walking into the room that she and Edward had shared for years. It was dusty and needed a good airing, but other than that it was exactly as she had left it. Lifeless and oppressive with bad memories. The most enjoyment she'd had in their double bed was imagining Edward dead. And here she finally was, even though he remained clinging to life. Maria decided to enjoy the moment. She had finally taken everything from him.

'What do you need?' DI Anton asked, arms folded across his chest.

'Clothes from my wardrobe.' She pointed at the door.

The police officer stepped forward and opened it. 'Anything you want, place on the bed for us to check. We'll pack it for you.' Anton said. It was an order rather than a suggestion.

Maria removed the clothes in sections, left to right as they were hung. Skirts first, then blouses and finally dresses. DI Anton and the assisting officer checked every pocket, ran their hands over each hem and seam, before folding them and putting them into the suitcase. For a second it was as if Edward were there, overseeing the activity, controlling her again. It's not him, she told herself. This is just standard procedure. My husband will never invade my privacy again. He'll never do anything again. That thought gave her enough satisfaction to quell her rising anger.

'Next?' Anton huffed.

Maria pointed to a chest of drawers. 'I need my underwear from in there.'

The officer opened the drawer and pulled everything out onto the bed.

'Is it really necessary to check every item?' James Newell asked. 'The prosecution has closed its case. You can't present any more evidence and you've already searched every inch of the house. This seems like overkill.'

'It's all right,' Maria shrugged. 'Let them check. I have nothing to hide. Why don't you wait downstairs, James. The fewer people that watch, the better I'll feel.'

Her barrister left the room as Anton and the other officer began checking. They went slowly enough to start with, eventually speeding up and throwing the pile of bras and pants into the case.

'Just some shoes now,' Maria said. She went back to the wardrobe and pulled a few pairs of clumpy old shoes out onto the carpet. No stilettos or heels or pretty pumps. Nothing stylish or shapely. Nothing that might have shown off her legs. Flat, wide and designed for maximum wear. Ed had sold his shoe choices to her on the basis of what was best for her feet. She had swallowed that lie in the same dumb way she had swallowed all the rest. The flat shoes he chose kept her shorter, never quite at his height, never able to look him directly in the eye. And they were cheap. That mattered too.

Anton and the officer bent to the floor checking the footwear, running their hands inside each one, making sure there was nothing they'd missed.

Maria backed towards Ed's bedside table and picked up the framed wedding photo she hated so much, shoving it between layers of clothes in her case while the police were distracted. Finally everything was agreed to and packed. The officer had the grace to lift her suitcase down the stairs and into Newell's car.

Maria stood in the garden for a minute, staring up at the house as DI Anton conducted a final check.

'I don't regret it,' she whispered to Newell as he waited patiently by her side. 'If I had to live that day all over again, the only thing I'd do differently is make absolutely sure he was dead.'

'Not a good idea, saying that sort of thing out loud. You're going to need the jury's sympathy when you tell your story,' Newell replied, putting his hands in his pockets. It wasn't a lecture. Maria appreciated the conversational tone. 'However you feel about your husband, you have to present yourself as the victim, not the aggressor.'

'I'm sick of being a victim,' Maria said. 'The jury will have to take me how they find me.'

'Is anything I say going to make a difference?' he asked.

She smiled into his warm eyes, wishing she'd married a man more like James Newell, wondering how different her life would have been.

'No, but I appreciate you trying. It's good to have someone looking out for me.'

He drove her back to the bail hostel and carried the suitcase to her room. Maria liked him. James Newell was a good man and a realist. He was so anxious not to reveal how hard it was going to be to win the case. It didn't matter. She already knew it would turn on the throw of a dice.

The cab driver picked her up half an hour later. They repeated the exercise of lugging the suitcase out of her room and into the boot of the taxi.

'Where to?' he asked as she settled herself in the back.

'Tallon Street,' she said. 'The underpass.'

He turned round, surprised. 'You sure you got the address right? There's no houses down there, and it's not altogether safe. Trouble with drugs and that's where a lot of homeless people go in the evenings.'

'I know,' Maria replied. 'It's the right address.'

They drove for fifteen minutes, caught in traffic lights and roadworks. Maria stared out of the window. Late afternoon and the bars were already full. Hoards of twenty-somethings sat on benches and enjoyed the slight breeze in the sweltering sun. Bristol was packed to its edges, it seemed.

Tallon Street bore no resemblance to the rest of the city. Whatever industry had once been there had deserted, leaving a row of empty units. It was too far from the centre to make it desirable but close enough that it could be reached by those wanting somewhere quiet and dark to do illicit deals. She had heard about it at the bail hostel, an unexpected source of useful information.

'Pull over here, this will do,' she told the driver. 'Could you get my case out for me please?'

He did as he'd been asked with nothing more than a shake of his head, but his opinion was written all over his face.

'Would you wait up the street for me? I won't be long,' Maria said.

'Five minutes, then I'll have to go for another fare,' he said, climbing back into the driver's seat. 'Be careful.'

Maria lugged the case into the mouth of the underpass. Whatever conversation had been passing between the bodies lying in various piles of sleeping bags and cardboard stopped immediately. She could smell urine and smoke. Pale orange lights covered in old cobwebs lit one side of the passageway ineffectively.

'Got any money?' someone asked her as she stepped around their feet.

'I'm sorry, I don't,' she said. 'I wanted to leave these clothes for anyone who needs them.' She left the suitcase at the side of the underpass, opening it to show there was nothing threatening contained within.

'Just clothes?' another person shouted from further in.

'And some shoes,' Maria said. She knelt down by a woman who was huddled lighting a cigarette. 'Could I borrow your lighter?' she asked.

The woman put it into Maria's hand without bothering to speak. From her pocket she took the framed photo of her and Edward on their wedding day. Bending back the clips that held it in its frame, she took the picture out, running her fingertips over the image of her face, shining with hope and love. Still innocent. Horribly unsuspecting.

She lit a corner of it, holding it in her hands as long as she could before letting the smouldering remnants drop to the floor.

'Thank you,' she said, as she handed the lighter back. By the time she walked out of the underpass, the contents of the suitcase were already being scattered.

It was what Edward would have hated most, she thought, as she walked back to the waiting cab. The clothes he had selected to keep her in her place. The clothes he had paid precious pounds for. The shoes he had known she hated. Gone to people Ed had nothing but contempt for. He lacked the basic human empathy required to see the homeless as more than just alcoholics and dropouts. As gestures went, she knew it was pathetic, but Maria felt better.

She could move on. It had been painfully slow, waiting for the prosecution to close its case so that she could be allowed in to the house to gather the clothing, but now it was done. The only photograph in which she and Edward had been captured together was ash.

18

Day Seven in Court

Her Honour Judge Downey, the barristers, police and court ushers met the jury outside the Bloxham's house. The bundle of photographs had revealed tiny slices of the property – a view of the kitchen, a section of the driveway where the chair leg had been dropped – but nothing had prepared Lottie for how grand it was. The gates were huge twirls of blackened iron that opened only when a police officer stepped forward and clicked a key-fob. They moved silently, as if by magic, skimming the top of the gravel by millimetres without disturbing a single stone. The garden was stunning if overgrown, but someone had committed endless hours to weeding and pruning in the past. The house itself was straight out of a lifestyle magazine, picture perfect, with large windows and curtains tied back to millimetre-accurate specifications.

'These people have too much money,' Agnes Huang said loudly, getting a sympathetic nod from Garth Finuchin and his tattoos in reply. 'How can only two people have lived here? It's built for half a dozen.'

'Just what I expected,' Gregory muttered. 'Exactly where I'd imagined Dr Bloxham living. And look at the garden. How lovely. What I wouldn't give to live here.'

'It's beautiful,' Lottie whispered to Cameron and Jack.

'My mother would approve,' Jack said. 'Although she would also point out that it's a relatively recent build, indicating new money, her words not mine. Very upper-middle class. I guess they don't get many attempted murders around here.'

'Probably not,' Cameron replied. 'This may be the most excitement the neighbourhood has ever seen. Come on, they're letting us in.' He pressed light fingertips into the small of Lottie's back as he let her go first into the garden. She went slowly, buzzing from the brief contact but wishing he would keep his hands off her when they were in the group. There was a limit to how much risk she was comfortable with.

Yesterday had been an aberration in her marriage, her behaviour wanton and disloyal. Her return home had been almost physically painful, as she had crossed the threshold into what should have been a haven of family life. Worse than the guilt, though, more disturbing and visceral, was the arousal that had pulsed through her all evening and all night. She had irritated herself, unable to sit still, finally cleaning the kitchen cupboards at 11 p.m., ensuring that Zain was in bed and asleep before taking her place next to him. Lottie had stared at his profile in the lacklustre moonlight that made it past the curtains. He didn't deserve what she'd done to him, there was no question about it. Zain had been sullen all evening, immersing himself in a set of sales accounts and hardly speaking. There was still the unresolved issue of trying for another baby, but Lottie wasn't backing down on that one, throwing Zain's carefully constructed life plan into disarray. She was almost jealous of how certain he was about the things he wanted. All she seemed to be doing was floating along on the tide.

Later today, she would tell Cameron things couldn't go any further. Yesterday had been too much. Her jury buddy was gambling less than her. Sleep had eluded her again, and in the morning she'd choked on a mouthful of toast when Zain had appeared unexpectedly in the kitchen asking where his wallet was. Casual flirtation was one thing, but where they were headed was too dangerous.

'Will Tabitha run a finger along the tops of the cabinets to check how good Maria Bloxham's dusting was, do you think?' Cameron whispered to her and Jack, at the back of the line.

Lottie giggled in spite of the tension she was feeling. 'I'm more concerned that Agnes is so jealous, she's going to drop prawns down the back of each radiator to make the place uninhabitable.'

'And Pan will be going through totting up the value of all the artwork,' Jack added. 'He'll probably leave his business card on the kitchen table.'

They sniggered together as they walked forward, lifting the grimness of the mood. In some ways it felt unreal, like walking onto a film set after watching a movie, Lottie thought.

'God, the Tabithas are going to absolutely love this,' she said quietly.

'When you're as close to death as that lot, you've got to get your kicks any way you can,' Cameron smirked.

One by one the jurors stepped inside the house, moving slowly through the hallway. The rules had been explained to them already. They could look but not touch. No photos were to be taken. Any questions had to be written down and directed through the judge at court the next day. The whole visit was to be on the record. At no time was any conversation to take place between any of the jurors and the court officials or police officers.

The hallway resembled an illustrated coffee menu, with shades of cream, beige and darker browns across walls and woodwork. Not one fingerprint, Lottie thought, no scratches either. No children had ever run through that hallway, dragging toys and lurching from wall to wall with sticky hands. Her jealousy at the simplicity of it all evaporated in the silence. Maria Bloxham had spent every day there alone. Her husband had his work. The jury had learned nothing about the defendant yet except that she had committed a single, brutal crime. Perhaps the boredom and quiet had finally driven her mad, Lottie thought. She could sympathise with that. Wasn't that exactly why she was playing such a dangerous game with Cameron now? She watched him whispering into Jack's ear as they approached the kitchen. Perhaps Lottie was making excuses. Maybe, as the prosecution had suggested, Maria Bloxham had been driven by selfishness or anger, like when she'd sworn at the psychiatrist and stormed out. It wasn't impossible that the unfortunate couple had simply argued once too often about the correct way to stack the dishwasher.

The jury convened in the kitchen, staring at the spot on the floor where Edward Bloxham had landed as if there was the possibility he could still be there. The brown stains in the tile grouting told a grisly story, and the heavy wooden kitchen table stood unused, with one chair missing from what was clearly intended to be a set of six. Lottie wondered what had happened to the other chair. Had it been broken in temper or by accident, and how long ago? Edward Bloxham couldn't tell them and perhaps it wasn't in the defendant's interests to be honest about it now.

'You may walk around the remainder of the house,' the judge told them, 'as it might later be relevant when the defendant gives evidence. You have thirty minutes, then I'll ask you to return to the minibus.'

The judge and barristers retired into the back garden, avoiding any possibility of being asked questions or overhearing the jurors' comments. For a few moments the twelve of them stood glancing around the kitchen, embarrassed to be the first to take advantage of the chance to poke around the empty house. Tabitha recovered quickest, opening the pantry door and having a good look inside.

'Look at that,' she breathed. 'So much cupboard space for just two people.'

'My kitchen would fit into this one four times over,' Samuel Lowry added with a nervous laugh. 'Whatever the Bloxhams argued about, it certainly can't have been money.'

'What I want to know is why she didn't use a knife instead of that great big chair leg,' Garth Finuchin joined in, opening up the cutlery drawer and whistling as he looked at the weaponry options available. 'She could have made damned sure she finished the job.'

'I'm going to check out the rest of the house,' Pan said. 'I'm not sure it really requires a full thirty minutes.' He returned to the hallway, from where he could be heard opening and closing doors as he went.

Lottie glanced around the kitchen. Sure enough, the pile of post DI Anton had mentioned in his evidence was still sitting on the kitchen table. She wondered just how far they were allowed to go in checking out the property, not that there was anyone in the kitchen she could ask. Making sure the other jurors were busy looking elsewhere, Lottie slipped the top letter off the stack and faced the wall as she slid it out of the envelope.

'Dear Dr Bloxham,' she read, 'I watched your latest video last night on encouraging slow worms back into our gardens. I hope you don't mind me writing to you, but I wanted to say how much I love your passion. I adore wildlife and never miss reading your blog. I live in the Bristol area, as I know you do, so perhaps you could let me know if you have any live events planned. Meeting you in person would make me so happy. I'm single, in my thirties, and I love to bake. I wonder if you could send me a photo? I've enclosed a return envelope if it's not too much trouble . . .'

Lottie folded the letter and pushed it back into the envelope, noting that it was addressed to an office suite in the city, presumably Dr Bloxham's place of work, before replacing it on the pile. It was a bit sickly, she thought, writing to ask for a photo. What the hell were they going to do with it? Pin it up in their greenhouse?

'Anything interesting?' Cameron asked her.

'Fan mail. Bit weird to be honest.'

'Let's do the tour,' he suggested.

'Good idea,' Lottie muttered. 'The sooner I'm out of here the better.'

Jack followed her out and Cameron brought up the rear, leaving the Tabithas to continue their hypothesising in the kitchen.

The first door past the kitchen was a separate dining room with a glass topped table and more comfortable looking chairs than the practical farmhouse style ones in the kitchen. After that was a spacious lounge featuring a fireplace at its centre, swept free of ash. Landscape paintings sat in frames on two walls, with a mirror on the third and patio doors onto the garden in the fourth.

'No photos,' Lottie said.

'Maybe it's a generation thing,' Jack replied. 'My parents only have photos of me and my brother, and his kids. None of themselves.'

'It's immaculate,' Cameron said. 'I mean really, strangely tidy.'

'You mean your house doesn't look like this? But I can just see you wearing an apron and holding a feather duster,' Jack laughed.

Cameron responded by good-naturedly punching Jack's shoulder. 'Hey, I have talents you can't even imagine. You should taste my toad-in-the-hole.'

'Not taking that bait,' Jack laughed as Lottie shook her head at the two of them.

They left the lounge and headed for the room opposite, which was smaller and evidently more lived in. Books lined the walls, and a mahogany desk took pride of place, covered in papers and notes. Silk curtains framed the window with a view into the front garden and a leather armchair faced the property's second fireplace, this one more showing signs of recent use, with partially burned logs waiting to be relit. A large television screen had been hung carefully on a bracket on one wall, and an impressive computer set up had been fixed to hide the cables and blend in with the sumptuous look of the room.

'Nice,' Jack said. 'That's quite a rig.'

'Must be expensive for them to have bothered putting a lock on an internal door,' Cameron said. 'You think they'd have been more worried about a burglar breaking the window to get in, given that it's on the ground floor.'

'There's only one chair,' Lottie said. Both men stared at her. 'I'm just saying, they couldn't have watched TV together here, not unless one of them sat at the desk while the other sat by the fire, and then they wouldn't have been facing the same direction.'

'There was a TV in the lounge though, right?' Jack asked.

'I don't think so,' Cameron said. 'No, actually I'm sure there wasn't.'

Lottie turned around, reading some of the books titles. 'These are all his books.' She picked up some of the notes from the desk. 'And notes about seabirds with some graphs. Do you think Mrs Bloxham came in here to watch television when her husband was working, so they could be together?'

'I guess that would've disturbed him,' Cameron said. 'I wonder where the key was left. No point keeping it on a hook in the hallway. If a burglar got in he could have opened up straight away.'

'It just seems odd. There's no sign of her existence here. Not a single book that might have been hers,' Lottie commented. It felt like a man's space, and more particularly that it was designed to suit Edward Bloxham's needs alone. She wondered if Maria Bloxham had found it a relief when her husband shut himself away, or if it was a barrier between them that exacerbated frustrations.

'Let's look upstairs,' Jack said. 'I bet there's another TV up there. Probably another lounge too, given that it was just the two of them.'

They took the stairs in single file, with Jack at the front and Cameron at the back. He brushed the back of Lottie's left calf as she climbed the steps before him, making her jerk her head back to make sure no one was around to have witnessed it. Cameron winked and grinned

'Don't!' she mouthed at him, wide eyed. It wasn't the time, and it certainly wasn't the place. If he kept on touching her like that, sooner or later someone would notice.

They met Pan coming down the stairs as they rounded a ninety degree bend.

'I'd say it's worth substantially more than the eight hundred thousand the police estimated, what do you think?' he asked them.

'Maybe, given the size of the garden,' Jack replied.

'Is the money really relevant?' Cameron asked.

'Just getting a feel for their lifestyle,' Pan responded, continuing down towards the ground floor.

'Told you so,' Jack grinned. 'Pan will have written a price on every item before we're finished.'

Just-Jen and Garth-the-tattoo were whispering in the first guest bedroom they came to, but stopped as they entered. That was it then, Lottie realised. There was now an us and them. She moved on. The unused bedrooms were all the same. Decorated in bland pastels, with floral bedding and little on the walls. No trinkets enlivened the furniture, no stray items of clothing lay discarded on top of beds or drawers. No hobbies or collections were evident. It reminded her more of a hotel than a home. Maria Bloxham had only just turned forty, yet the house could have belonged to someone a generation older. Perhaps Edward Bloxham had taken responsibility for the decorating – he was much older than her, after all – which raised the issue of why his wife hadn't contributed. Maybe it wasn't her thing. Maybe she just didn't care. But it felt odd for anyone to have lived so many years in a house that lifeless and old-fashioned, and to have done nothing about it.

One of the guest bedrooms had an en suite bathroom. Lottie wandered in there while Jack and Cameron went on a search for another television. Men and their priorities, she thought. Her attention was drawn to a slightly open drawer. Not something that would normally have seemed odd, but every other cupboard door and drawer had been fully shut, just as every curtain was perfectly restrained by its tie-back.

Feeling like an intruder, she opened the drawer a few inches and peered in. A pair of nail scissors, a packet of tissues and a hairbrush with a few strands of dark hair were all that it contained. The bin below had been emptied and a clean liner put in. The shower door was free of streaks and the taps were gleaming. Whoever had used the bathroom had been careful to clean up after themselves, and yet the room had been used recently enough that the obsessive cleaner had missed the slightly open drawer on their last visit.

After closing it, then thinking better of changing the state of the place and going back to reopen it a fraction, she followed Jack and Cameron's path into the main bedroom suite.

'Find what you were looking for?' she asked them.

'We've been avoiding the rest of the snoopers for the last few minutes,' Jack said. 'Thankfully they got bored up here, and have gone back down to stare at the bloodstains a while longer. Find anything exciting?'

'There was no note explaining why she did it written in blood on the mirror, if that's what you were after,' Lottie told him. 'Are you two done?'

'I am,' Jack said. 'I'm heading for the front garden for some sunshine. Coming?'

'In a minute,' Cameron said. 'I'm just going to wait for Lottie to have a look in this bathroom, then we'll be down.'

Jack disappeared down the stairs as Lottie wandered in to inspect the master en suite. 'It's a bathroom,' she said to Cameron as he followed her in, shutting the door.

'It is,' he said. 'Jack and I were surprised at how free of clutter it is. Usually you can't escape signs of life in a bathroom. Toothbrushes, perfume, razors – who puts absolutely everything away?'

'The whole house is like that, though,' Lottie said. 'Except for the study.'

'And what about that mirror?' Cameron asked.

'What about it?' she replied, turning to face the full-length mirror on the back of the door that Cameron was pointing to.

He walked behind her, reaching around to engage the door lock, and looking Lottie's reflection in the eyes. 'Do you see how beautiful you are?' He leaned his head down to run his lips from behind her ear to the place where her neck became her shoulder, tightening his arms around her waist.

She pushed him away, rubbing her hand across the skin he'd kissed. 'We can't do this,' she said. 'Not here. They're just downstairs and if we get caught . . .'

'I'm feeling ill, you came in to look after me and I asked you to lock the door,' he said, bringing one hand up to undo the tiny white buttons that fastened her dress down the front. She took hold of his wrist and held it away. 'We have a ten minute window. They're all busy discussing how palatial . . . I think that was Tabitha's word . . . this place is. Just relax.'

'I can't relax after what happened here,' she said, but her voice was already hoarse and her breath was coming faster.

'I think you can,' he said. 'I'm pretty sure I can help you.' Cameron ran his free hand down to the hem of her dress, pulling the fabric up over her thighs to reveal white lace knickers.

'Cam, this isn't right,' she said, releasing his wrist and pushing against his chest.

'If you're quiet, we'll hear anyone as soon as they set foot on the stairs. As for what happened in this house, there are only two people who know the truth. This room is just four walls with only you and me in it. I'm not going to waste a chance to show you how much I want you.' He turned Lottie around to face him. 'You're the only woman I've met – since my fiancée – who made me feel like this. Part of me thinks we were meant to meet, however bizarre the circumstances.'

Every last part of Lottie melted. Cameron pulled her against him, smiling as he brought his face to hers and parted her lips with his own, pushing his mouth down gradually harder until she let herself relax against him, kissing him back, her fingers gripping his shoulders. She pressed herself against him, feeling the iron of his body and the heat between them.

Cameron ran his lips along her shoulders, letting her feel the edge of his teeth before moving just far enough away to be able to see her fully. She wanted to be able to lie convincingly to herself, to believe that she hadn't imagined him looking at her just like that when she was dressing that morning. She saw herself through his eyes. The thin cotton and tiny lace tri-angles of her bra accentuated her hardened nipples rather than hiding them. She was panting by the time he brought up his right hand to mould it to her breast. Pressing his thumb firmly across the centre of her nipple, she groaned, winding her arms around his neck and stretching out her body for him to enjoy.

'Quietly,' she whispered, doing her best to listen for footsteps on the staircase, terrified by the loudness of her own breathing.

Pushing her back against the icy mirror, he slipped one dress strap off her shoulder, following with her bra, then moved his head down to take a nipple in his mouth, pinning her upper arms against the door. She held her breath, forsaking all thought of Zain, knowing she wouldn't stop Cameron, even more sure that she couldn't stop herself. Cameron moved his hand down from her left arm, hooking his thumb into the side of her panties, shifting them across as he sucked and licked her breast.

'We shouldn't . . .' she whispered.

'But we're going to,' he said, as he ran his fingers down her rib cage, past her stomach and over her groin.

He slid gentle fingers down to that burning part of her that had seemed to be sleeping for too long. If the day before had been an awakening then this was an earthquake. As he circled the edge of her clitoris with the lightest of touches, Lottie cried out, thrusting forward, desperate for more of him. She ran her hand up to his hair, pulling his mouth harder against her breast.

He slipped a finger inside her and she bit down on his neck to silence herself. Every muscle in her body was flexed. She opened her legs wider, desire controlling every part of her.

'I want you,' she panted.

'Not like this,' he said. 'I'm going to take my time. God, I can't think of anything but you.'

He slowly pulled away from her, moving her clothes back into place, kissing her neck and mouth as she closed her eyes, coming back to reality.

'Oh God, how long we've been?' she whispered frantically.

'Don't worry about it,' he said. 'I'll go down first and tell them you had an urgent phone call from your childminder. Okay?'

'Fine,' she said, straightening her dress.

'I wish it didn't have to be like this. I want to show you off, make it real,' he said.

'It's already real for me,' Lottie replied, stepping forward and kissing him, letting her tongue drift across his.

They pulled apart. 'You're amazing,' he said. 'Not just how you look or how I feel when I'm with you. You're funny and sensitive. I never thought I'd meet anyone like you again.'

She stared at him, shocked. She'd expected flirting, but not such an emotional declaration. The spark between them was undeniable, but beyond that Lottie had no idea how she felt. There was Daniyal to think about, and she couldn't even bring herself to consider how Cameron compared to Zain. Loud voices in the downstairs hallway made her jump. Now wasn't the time to start dissecting where their relationship was going, but she needed to give him something back.

'Maybe you just bring out the best out in me.' She kept her response neutral. 'You'd better go. Sounds like someone's on the way up. Keep them talking.'

He picked up her hand, turned it over, and kissed her palm. 'Give it a few minutes then come down,' he brushed his lips against her cheek.

She watched him go. What they'd done in the Bloxhams' house was wrong on every conceivable level, but she'd been too entranced with how Cameron made her feel to have resisted. Leaning against the doorway, adjusting her clothes, Lottie was already imagining how much better it would be next time.

19

Ruth sat in her car and stared at the shop where she knew Maria had topped up the pay-as-you-go mobile that had become a lifeline. The jury would be at the Bloxhams' house by now. She had huddled in the court's public gallery each day, in spite of Maria warning her off, arriving early to take the seat furthest from the glass dock, shielded by other onlookers and the press. Maria was within her rights not to want her there, not least because humiliation in front of strangers was preferable to your life being laid bare in front of people you knew.

Reading the jury's expressions as the evidence came out had become a miniature obsession. It was, after all, part of what she was trained to do and for the most part the news wasn't good. Ruth had spent a shameful night locating those jurors she could identify on social media after their names were read out when they were sworn. It had felt like going through someone else's underwear drawer. At least ten of the twelve had left footprints on the internet. Photos, comments, purchase reviews in their real names. It was shocking what she had been able to find out in just a few hours. The Greek businessman was high profile. There were some media pieces about sales he'd made in the art world. Tabitha Lock had won numerous Women's Institute prizes at different fêtes. Garth Finuchin had once run as a local councillor, independent to any mainstream political party. Gregory Smythe had written a letter to a local newspaper promoting gay rights. That one she hadn't seen coming – even she was subject to profiling on the stereotype of age and dress code, she realised. Other jurors had Facebook pages or Twitter feeds. Ruth wished she could say she had only checked them the once, but the small hours were now full of checking for updates, to see if any of the twelve had mentioned the case to the friends and family. None of her new found knowledge could halt the steady progress of the court case against her friend, however.

The prosecutor – Imogen Pascal – had made a masterpiece of what was an already overwhelming case. The hedgehog video had drastically reduced the jury's tolerance to hear anything but praise for Edward Bloxham. It would take a monumental effort for the defence to discredit him. Then there was Maria's unfortunate lashing out at the psychiatrist. Some of the jurors had reacted strongly to that. The foreperson – Tabitha Lock – had been the most overt in her facial expressions. Others had followed suit, albeit more guardedly. There had been pursed lips, frowns and marked shock. Only four of the twelve had been able to take Maria's abusive language to the psychiatrist in their stride. It didn't bode well for the verdict, but Maria's reaction had been understandable and the questioning had plainly not been as innocent as the psychiatrist had pretended. Asking a woman if she was premenstrual or menstruating was an intimidation tactic designed to humiliate. He had intended to throw her off her game, getting either an emotional reaction or a confused denial from her. Either way, he would have followed up with a more probing question had Maria not suddenly decided to put the psychiatrist in his place. As much as Ruth wished Maria could have handled his questions more levelly, she was right not to have played his game.

Ruth checked her watch. Lunchtime. Just enough time left to get to the cashpoint and withdraw more cash before picking her mother up from the Active About Dementia group she attended each week. After that her two year old twins would need picking up and the rest of the day would be lost. Ruth hadn't intended to drive past Maria's house. Quite the opposite. Somehow though, her car headed off in that direction. She slowed before passing the driveway. A minibus sat outside, one wheel left carelessly on the pavement. The jury was still inside then, inspecting the scene of the crime. The kitchen wasn't the only room in the house where human misery had been wrought, though. Far from it.

Maria had been phoning her once a month for nearly a year by the time Ruth managed to broach the subject of her sexual relations. It had lurked there, unspoken in so much of what had been discussed before, but Maria always edged away when Ruth asked about it. Then there had been one particular day when Maria had called sounding so unlike her usual self that Ruth had not immediately recognised her voice.

'He wanted me last night,' Maria had growled, her voice guttural, as if her vocal chords were twisted with rage. Ruth's stomach had dropped.

'Are you hurt?' Ruth had asked first. Physical safety was always the primary concern. Psychological damage was the poor second cousin. There were worse things than death, though. She had counselled enough rape and abuse victims to be sure of that.

Maria had laughed. The sound had been nothing short of a horror movie special effect. For a few moments, Ruth had been genuinely scared, as if some demon had taken over her client's body and could deliver itself through the phone line.

'Maria, can you tell me about it?' Ruth had asked. 'You don't have to, but it might help.'

'It was normal between us at the start. That's the thing about Edward. He's a terrible person but a brilliant actor, it turns out. These days he likes me to play dead. I'm not even sure I should complain about it. It's the only part of our lives together that isn't a lie.'

'That must make you feel . . .' Ruth struggled to find sufficiently bland words, 'less than human.'

'It makes me feel the way he wants me to feel. I lie on my face. He likes me to have my arms down at my side. I'm not allowed to move or make any noise. At first it was a game. I'm not sure how I was ever stupid enough to play along. He would have me lie there in bed, pretending to be asleep, then move on top of me. He said it turned him on, the thought of screwing me in my sleep. Then I asked for something different, to be allowed to lie on my back. He made some excuse about the angle of our bodies being more comfortable if he was behind me. I just . . . I just accepted it. Do you know what's more awful than getting fucked whilst having to pretend you're dead? It's knowing you're getting fucked that way because you were too stupid and too weak to have stopped it.'

'You're being too harsh with yourself. This is how coercive control works. It's slow, incremental. It plays to the parts of its victims that lack confidence and it steals their voice. How often does he do this?' she asked.

'Three times a month. Four if he's got a new contract, a big pay cheque or a good book review. He seems to like it more when he knows my body doesn't want him. I think he enjoys having to force himself inside. Hurting me. Sometimes his weight gets too much for me and I can't draw breath. He counts the seconds when I'm not breathing. I think the only reason I'm still alive is because the thought of me dying excites him so much that he . . . you know . . . finishes.' She broke off, the sob scratching her throat like sandpaper. 'I cut myself every time after he makes me play dead, last night included. I know I shouldn't have done it. I don't know why I did. I think I just wanted to prove to myself that I was still alive. For a while when he was on top of me, pushing and shoving, heaving, pressing my body into the mattress while I kept my mouth shut, I wondered if I maybe I really had died and was stuck in a living hell with him.'

'Maria, I'm worried for you,' Ruth had quietly. 'I'm concerned about what you might do. Forgive how patronising that sounds, but . . .'

'You could never be patronising,' Maria whispered, the first spark of warmth resonating in her voice. 'Don't worry about the cutting. I did it as a teenager. It's a skill you never lose, apparently, knowing just how deep to go without losing too much blood and understanding what pain you can tolerate. I would cut myself a thousand times rather than have him touch me again.'

'I can come and get you,' Ruth had said, sufficiently emboldened by desperation to offer to break all her own self-imposed rules. 'Give me your address. This has gone on too long. You have to leave him.'

Ruth knew she was lecturing, offering real world help that often wasn't wanted and wasn't the answer. Getting personally involved. But something in Maria's tone and words haunted her. Sometimes listening to the bare hopelessness of her voice was like talking to an entity from beyond the grave.

Ruth's drive to the cashpoint didn't take long but it was far enough to get her worrying about her money situation again. Not her overall bank balance. Her father had made sure she wouldn't want for anything. There was enough money in savings accounts and investments to last her for decades. The problem was that those accounts weren't easily accessible and she was depleting her current account almost to nil. Those sorts of withdrawals might be noticed. Certainly they were out of kilter with her normal spending. Making a mental note to transfer some of her savings into her current account, she withdrew another five hundred pounds and stuffed it in her purse.

By the time she arrived at the Active About Dementia centre, there was a woman standing outside glancing at her watch, a bright green tabard marking her role as official. She began walking towards Ruth's car before the engine was even off.

'Mrs Adcock?' she asked as Ruth opened her car door.

'Miss Adcock,' Ruth corrected. 'Is my mother all right?'

'We've been trying to phone you,' the woman continued. 'You didn't pick up.'

'Is my mother all right?' Ruth repeated, calmly but firmly.

'Yes, well, she's being given a sedative by our nurse. There was a bit of a to-do,' the woman murmured. 'Would you like to come inside and have a chat about it over a cup of tea?'

'I think as you were waiting for me out here, we'd best get on with it,' Ruth replied. 'What happened?'

'There was a slight disagreement with Mr Baskins who wanted to help your mother finish a jigsaw puzzle. She took offence when he picked up some of the pieces.' The woman stopped talking. Ruth summoned an additional measure of patience.

'And then?' Ruth asked.

'Then your mother punched him in the face. Rather harder than any of us thought possible, actually. His bottom lip was badly split. There was quite a lot of bleeding . . .' The woman let the last word drag. Ruth realised there was more to come. She waited. 'Also, your mother broke one of his teeth in two. Mr Baskins has been taken to the hospital for emergency dental treatment.'

'Right,' Ruth breathed out heavily. 'What sort of shape is my mother in?'

'Not injured at all,' the woman declared.

'I meant emotionally,' Ruth said. 'How did she react to the incident?'

'She said Mr Baskins should go and stand in the corner. After that we took her into a separate room and the nurse took over. I'm afraid this means we can't continue to accommodate her at our sessions. I am very sorry.'

'You saying you're sorry doesn't help. My mother needs contact beyond the immediate family, and stimulation from other places and people. You know dementia sufferers can be prone to violent outbursts,' Ruth said, hands on hips, aware that she was looking and sounding confrontational, but finding it impossible to ease up. 'They rarely understand or remember what they've done. They're certainly not responsible for them.'

'Quite so, but I have to consider the well-being of all our patients. I don't mean to speak out of turn, but if your mother's condition is worsening now might be the time to consider permanent hospitalisation. It's only going to get harder for you to look after her at home.'

'I'll manage fine, thank you,' Ruth said, pretending calm. 'It's not hard for me. I love her.' She walked past the woman and began pushing open the centre door.

'I only meant . . .'

Ruth let the door fall shut behind her before the woman could finish her sentence. Institutionalising her mother was unthinkable. However tough it was going to be, Ruth was determined to care for her until the end. She walked down the corridor to the nurse's room, stopping outside to listen to her mother humming a nursery rhyme.

'Hello, Mum,' she smiled opening the door. Crossing the room to hug her, she noticed the blooming bruise on the back of her mother's knuckles. 'How are you feeling?'

'I didn't get my pudding today,' her mother said. 'It was rhubarb crumble. My favourite.'

'How about I make it for you tomorrow? There's some rhubarb in the garden. You can have custard or cream with it, whichever you prefer,' Ruth said, slipping her mother's cardigan over her shoulders.

'Can I have ice-cream?' her mother asked.

'Of course you can,' Ruth replied as she guided the older woman out towards the car.

'Ruth, I think perhaps I did something bad today. I can't remember what it was, but people looked at me as if I had. Did I?' Tears brightened the corners of her mother's eyes, and Ruth's watered in return.

'No, darling. You didn't do anything bad. You couldn't possibly have done. Now let's get you home.' Ruth settled her mother gently in the car, wishing – as she did every day – that her sister Gail was still alive. Perhaps without that tragedy, their mother would never have succumbed to dementia, and Ruth would have been able to share the pain of seeing a proud, intelligent woman reduced to childlike helplessness and confusion. Fastening her seatbelt and kissing her mother on the temple, Ruth wondered how much time they had left together. Not long enough was the simple answer, and the last thing Ruth could afford was to have that time together shortened. The thought of losing another person she loved was unbearable.

20

Day Eight in Court

The first cool day in weeks left a sticky wetness in the air. Lottie had chosen jeans and a powder blue hoodie to start the new week, partly because of the sudden drop in temperature, but more importantly as a nod to the cascade of guilt she'd endured through the weekend. No more dresses that showed off her legs to attract Cameron's attention, and no more starchy skirts and blouses to try to fit in with the Tabithas. It was time to be herself.

She'd kept her mobile switched off all day Saturday, dreading the thought of contact with Cameron, knowing it would throw out her mood even further. By Sunday morning she'd been unable to stand not knowing what texts or voicemails might be waiting, and succumbed to temptation. Worse than anything she'd imagined, Cameron hadn't attempted to contact her at all. Of course, she had told him not to, citing the need for separation between him and the place where she had to be a good mother and maintain the pretence of normality with her husband. But still, she'd thought, perhaps a simple text saying . . . Saying what? she asked herself. Thanks for the grope in the bathroom. Must do that again soon. What could Cameron possibly have to say to her? By Sunday evening her own neediness was irritating her, as was her inability to look her husband in the eyes. She was skittish and snappy. Grabbing her phone she took matters into her own hands.

'This has to stop. Too risky. Just friends, okay?' she texted him, locked in the bathroom to make sure there was no chance of Zain catching her, and turning her phone off again the second she'd finished.

'Charlotte!' Zain called her from the lounge as soon as she exited.

She shoved her mobile in her pocket and went to see what he wanted. 'Yup?'

'My mother emailed. She's coming to England for Christmas,' he said, making notes on a pad as he spoke, ever immersed in his work.

'When you say Christmas,' Lottie replied through gritted teeth, 'how long do you actually mean?'

'Just three or four weeks. Pakistan's a long way to come. She's got to make the journey worthwhile and she hasn't seen her grandson for eighteen months. It'll be nice for Daniyal.'

'And how long were you planning on taking off work during that time?' Lottie folded her arms and leaned against the door frame.

'I should be able to get a whole week this year. You need to confirm what date suits you for her to arrive. Mid December would be best. Closer to Christmas the flights get too expensive.'

'So I'll be driving her around and entertaining her for the other three weeks, will I?' Lottie asked. Zain finally looked up.

'I'll do my bit when I'm not at work. Did you have plans for December already?'

'Don't take the piss,' Lottie said. 'It's fine for you. You're the golden boy. All she does is criticise the way I cook, how I clean, everything I do with Daniyal . . .'

'Come on, Lottie, you're being oversensitive. It's not that bad.'

'And you're being ignorant. Of course your mother can come here – it's your house – but you're looking after her. Maybe I do have plans for December. It might have been nice if you'd at least asked me first.' She span round grabbing her car keys from the hall table. 'I'm going to the supermarket. Daniyal's having his nap. Check on him if you can be bothered to tear yourself away from your paperwork.'

'Charlotte, we should talk about this!' he called after her as she slammed the front door.

An hour later she'd returned home and apologised half-heartedly. Zain was entitled to have his mother to stay, even if the thought of listening to her mother-in-law's griping left her cold. It was just another bed for her to make, more meals to cook, no big drama. And nothing to look forward to. That was the problem. Once jury service was over, Lottie was going back to the same old, same old and she was dreading it.

Pulling the ends of her sleeves down to cover her hands and her hood up around her neck, she made herself as physically unavailable as she could, and prepared for a new week battling both her own desire and Cameron's advances. As she walked into the jury room, Jennifer grabbed her arm and began whispering in her ear.

'Tabitha's asked for an official meeting,' Jennifer rushed. 'She's in a bit of a flap.'

'Oh God, what is it now?' Lottie groaned, rolling up the sleeves of her hoodie again. Even the rain hadn't reduced the temperature in the court building enough for it to be comfortable.

'Well, apparently,' Jennifer said, drawing it out as Lottie stared lovingly at the urn of tea that was destined to stay hot only for another ten minutes or so, 'she has reason to believe that two of us on the jury have been dallying – her word – out of court together.'

Lottie's tongue was suddenly glued to the roof of her mouth. Jennifer had constructed a mask of melodrama and was wearing it instead of her normal face. The world was moving in slow motion and the room was too loud. Had someone heard or seen them at the Bloxhams' house? Perhaps it was from the café in the Cabot Centre. Jack was the only person who'd spent much time with her and Cameron. Surely, she thought, he wouldn't have been gossiping with the Tabithas. Lottie's hands were damp and her throat was dry.

'Who?' Lottie finally whispered, in her mind grabbing Jennifer's face and squeezing an answer from her mouth. Tabitha would make sure everyone found out. They would be reported to the judge, and publicly humiliated. She and Cameron would be ordered off the jury. Zain would find out somehow, it was inevitable, and there was no way she'd have the strength to lie to him if he questioned her directly. The tacky brown carpet at her feet was suddenly a bed of mud from which she couldn't seem to move.

'Don't know who's involved,' Jennifer said. 'Tabitha wouldn't say, but we'll find out as soon as everyone's here. That's Pan arriving now, which makes twelve. This should be interesting.' Jennifer took her seat at the table, tapping her fingers on the wood, barely able to keep the glee from her face. Nothing like a bit of scandal to start a new week, Lottie thought. Only this was an ending, not a beginning.

Cameron's face appeared from behind Garth-the-tattoo, waving with a newspaper and greeting her with a wink. Lottie shook her head, motioning towards Tabitha who was deeply engaged with Samuel and Agnes. In response, Cameron took his time looking her up and down, raising his eyebrows appreciatively.

'Good, we're all here. There is a matter we need to consider prior to going into court so I suggest we all sit down and get started,' Tabitha officiated.

Lottie tasted stomach acid in the back of her throat. Cameron had no idea what was coming and there was no way she could warn him now without being obvious about it. They had to deny it, or figure out who knew and what their agenda was. At the very least she had to make sure Cameron didn't react aggressively towards Tabitha. If he handled it badly, Tabitha could and would make both their lives very unpleasant indeed, humiliating them by reporting it to the judge being the least of Lottie's worries.

Cameron was last to sit down, spending as much time as he could choosing biscuits, no doubt with the aim of frustrating Tabitha. Lottie coughed to get his attention but only succeeded in getting Agnes to offer her a mint to suck.

'Good,' Tabitha said as Cameron finally took his seat. 'It has come to my attention, for the second time, that two among us are becoming more friendly than the rules permit.'

At last Lottie had Cameron's attention. He frowned at her, then turned his full attention to Tabitha. Lottie's hands were shaking beneath the desk, one leg tapping an involuntary beat on the floor.

'I hesitate to bring this up publicly but we all know we're only supposed to be communicating within this room . . .'

'Why don't you just get on with it?' Cameron interjected. Lottie took a sharp breath in. This was exactly what she'd worried might happen. He was completely reactive, all the time, ice or fire with very little in between.

'Fine,' Tabitha replied curtly. 'As it concerns you, Mr Ellis, I'll be happy to get on with it, as you suggest.'

'Is there no way this could be handled more discreetly?' Lottie cut in. Every head turned to stare at her. 'I mean, do we really need the whole round table showdown? It seems a bit harsh.'

'No. I want to hear,' Agnes Huang snapped, to a general round of nods.

'I think we all have the right to know what's going on. The rules apply to everyone equally,' Gregory Smythe chipped in. One of Lottie's nailed snapped against the underside of the table. She bit down hard on her bottom lip, aware that she could no longer trust herself to speak.

'The Cabot Centre is, it seems, a very popular venue,' Tabitha announced.

Lottie's stomach heaved. It was inevitable that they were going to be noticed sooner or later. How stupid of them to meet in the city, knowing other jurors were in the area. Would the judge be told in public, in front of the press, she wondered. What if the whole trial had to be cancelled and the local papers printed her name? The room began to spin.

'I hope Mr Finuchin won't mind me saying it was he who saw you, Mr Ellis, over the weekend out with Mr Pilkington, in quite a severe state of drunkenness apparently.'

Lottie stared at Tabitha. 'Cameron . . . and Jack?' she blurted, her stomach dropping with relief, leaving her dizzy and nauseous.

'My concern is actually the drunkenness,' Tabitha pulled herself as upright as she could in her chair. 'Loose lips sink ships.'

'This isn't the Second World War, and Jack and I going drinking together has no relevance to this trial,' Cameron said.

Lottie directed her attention towards Jack, who was looking completely unperturbed at Cameron's side.

'We didn't talk about the case,' Jack said. 'Not when we were sober, not even when we were drunk.'

'You both looked completely bloody pissed to me,' Garth Finuchin muttered. 'I bet you can't remember anything you said to each other.'

'Problem solved then,' Cameron grinned. 'If we can't remember what we said to one another, then no harm can have been done.'

'It's hardly feasible that you spent the evening together without discussing the case,' Tabitha responded, her face increasingly stern as Cameron failed to respond with any sincerity. 'The rules are that we only talk when we're all together in this room. We've discussed it before.'

'So when I see you and Greg . . .' Cameron said, folding his arms and leaning back in his chair.

'It's Gregory, thank you,' Smythe interrupted.

'Whatever you like,' Cameron continued. 'When I see the two of you in the corridor chatting on your way in and out of the building, that's breaking the rules. Right?'

'I don't think it applies within this building . . .' Tabitha replied, gritted teeth muffling the consonants.

'Okay, so when I see Agnes and Samuel saying an extended goodbye outside the court building at the end of the day, that's not allowed either?' Cameron smiled at the two offending jurors. Lottie wanted to shake him. She might have been off the hook, but the near-miss adrenalin was still rendering her nauseous, and Cameron winding Tabitha to breaking point wasn't helping.

'You're being deliberately obtuse,' Tabitha raised her voice. 'What if you'd been seen by someone from the court or the defence team? They would object and then we might all get sent home.'

'So this isn't about the rights and wrongs of my having an evening out with Jack, it's about you wanting to keep your place at the head of this jury and passing judgment on Maria Bloxham. You know what I hate most about this conversation? It's being accused of breaking the rules by someone who isn't even vaguely trying to hide the fact that she's already convicted and sentenced the defendant in her own mind.' Cameron stood up and walked to the tea urn, turning his back on Tabitha who stood to respond.

'Take that back!' she shouted.

'Take it back? What are you, eight years old? You really think none of us hears you tutting in court or sees you rolling your eyes?' Cameron laughed.

'I'm entitled to my opinion the same as you are,' Tabitha said, her voice wavering for the first time. Lottie sat forward, holding her breath. Cameron needed to get himself in check. He finished pouring himself a drink and was stirring it slowly as he walked back to stare Tabitha in the face.

'Actually, you're not. Not at this point. Perhaps you weren't listening quite as well as you thought you were, but we're supposed to hold all judgment until we've heard both sides. You're not supposed to develop sympathies with one team or another until the end point. We're here to assess information and remain as impartial as possible. Only you were swayed by that pathetic little hedgehog video and by the dear old dribbling doctor. You fell into every trap the prosecution set for you. It was to be expected. Imogen Pascal knows who the easy targets on the jury will be. I'm sure she had you pegged as a pushover from the second she saw the flowery skirt and pearls.'

There was a moment of silence before Pan stood up and coughed. 'I, er, need make a call to Milan and the line's bad enough already. I wonder if we could all quieten down a bit for a few minutes. It really is very important.' He left the table and wandered into a corner, laptop in one hand and mobile in the other. Lottie could have kissed him.

'Maybe we should leave it there,' Samuel Lowry murmured. Everyone stared at him. It was the most commanding thing he'd done since they'd been selected for jury duty.

'Good idea,' Cameron said, taking his tea and the newspaper back to one of the more comfortable chairs and motioning for Lottie to join him. She gave a brief, small shake of her head. There had been more than enough drama and speculation for one morning. Lottie wasn't prepared to add any more fuel to the fire.

Instead, Jack joined Cameron and the two of them sat chatting happily, perfectly able to ignore the polar temperatures emitted from the Tabitha brigade who were still sat at the far end of the jury table. Lottie's phone buzzed in her pocket. When she saw the sender was Cameron, she looked across the room. His eyes were focused on his own mobile.

'You okay?' he texted.

'Sure. Was worried though. Best keep a low profile,' Lottie replied, taking care to delete both her own and Cameron's texts as she went.

'Doesn't affect us. Jack and I can go for a drink. Don't let Tabitha intimidate you,' Cameron typed, giving her one brief glance. Jack leaned across to whisper in Cameron's ear and got a burst of laughter in response.

Lottie wished she could be sitting there with them, instead of the micro-no-mans-land she found herself in. 'I'm not intimidated. Just sensible. No point making enemies,' she typed.

Cameron looked up after he'd read it, staring at her for several seconds, his eyes alight with the glow from his screen. 'Are we okay? Got your text Sunday. Wanted to respond in person,' he sent.

'Tough weekend. Worried we'll hurt people.'

'What about what we want?' he texted.

'I don't want to get caught. Certainly not by the Tabithas. They'll make trouble.'

'These idiots don't matter. Do you know how incredible you are?' Lottie read the text with her heart thumping. Cameron made her feel strong and independent. What the hell did Tabitha think she was doing, upbraiding him and Jack for going out for a drink together? Lottie wished she'd spoken up on their behalves, regretting her fear-induced paralysis. She opted for the next best thing: stoicism after the event.

'You're amazing for standing your ground. What did you & Jack get up to?' she typed.

'Cinema, beer, curry. Mostly beer.' Cameron cast a sideways look at Jack who was flicking through a weighty textbook. 'He needed a friend & a laugh.'

Lottie shot a curious look towards Jack. 'Something wrong?'

'Tell you in person,' Cameron replied. The door opened and the usher announced that the trial was about to start again.

One by one, they put away their phones, laptops and reading material, filing out into the corridor. Lottie caught Cameron as they brought up the rear of the line. 'Jack's okay, right?' she asked.

Cameron rubbed his forehead, looking around to make sure no one else was within hearing distance, before moving closer to whisper into her ear. 'He told me confidentially, but I know you can be trusted and Jack needs all the support he can get. Jack's gay and he just told his parents. They've reacted badly, and tried to ban him from announcing it publicly under threat of not financing his studies.'

'That's awful,' Lottie muttered as they walked slowly down the corridor towards the jury entrance to the courtroom.

'They're old fashioned and feel embarrassed socially, apparently. Anyway, Jack needs their financial backing and doesn't want to drop out of uni, so he's stuck. Don't say anything, will you?'

'Of course not,' Lottie said, touching Cameron lightly on the arm. 'Thanks for telling me though. I'd like to help if I can.'

'You can help me by agreeing to see me this week. Spending the entire weekend without you was hell, especially after Friday,' he grinned.

'Quiet!' Lottie mouthed as they walked forward to take their place in the jury rows.

'Say yes then,' he whispered to her as they sat down. Lottie tried not to grin and had to cover her mouth as she failed. It was easy to text and say she didn't want to see him from a distance. Rejecting him when he was next to her was impossible. 'I'm taking that as agreement,' Cameron said as they picked up their pens and notepaper, ready to start the new day.

James Newell stood up and looked across briefly to see that they were all settled, before addressing the judge. 'Your Honour,' he announced confidently. 'The defence calls Maria Bloxham to give evidence.'

21

Time stopped. Everyone was waiting for her to stand up. Maria glanced around the courtroom at the sea of faces, anticipating what she might say. Each of them had expectations, preconceived ideas of the sort of person she was. The press had their pens at the ready. The judge was flicking through her notes. The jurors – twelve little birds perched on parallel wires – were waiting for something like justification. How could she have done it? Would she do it again, given the chance? And Ruth was there, too, trying to hide at the back of the public seating. Of course she hadn't been able to stay away. She'd never been able to leave Maria to her fate and today was the culmination of it all. It had been years in the making. Only Imogen Pascal didn't turn to see her stand up, legs a little wobbly in spite of the sense that she had nothing left to lose. Maria straightened her white shirt and brushed her straight black skirt down before leaving the dock. One of the dock officers accompanied her to the witness stand, presumably to make sure she didn't make a sudden attempt at escape. They didn't realise she already had. James Newell smiled reassuringly, and Maria understood that he was assessing her readiness for what she needed to do. It was all down to her now. The case would be won or lost on the strength of the story she told. Maria kept her eyes down and her voice level as she was sworn in.

'Ms Bloxham, could you explain what happened the day you were arrested?' he asked. Maria opened the set of photographs in front of her, running her fingertips over the images of the injury to Edward's skull, a dull sense of pleasure stirring in her stomach.

'Do you need some water?' Newell prompted, his voice a little louder.

Maria looked up. Everyone was staring. 'I picked up the chair leg and hit him with it,' she said. 'I wanted him to die.'

The jury froze mid note-taking while the journalists scribbled harder and faster. Someone in the public gallery let go a small sob. One of Edward's multitude of fans, Maria guessed. The judge issued a delicate cough, staring at James Newell. His face was as unresponsive as the most professional of poker players. Imogen Pascal looked her directly in the eyes for the first time since the trial had commenced. A current passed between them. The real battle had begun. The prosecution would twist every word, wring the evil out of every adjective she used, lay traps weaved of clever questioning to trip her up. Which was why Maria had decided it was best to simply deliver everything Imogen Pascal wanted to hear up front.

'All right,' Newell said slowly, one finger massaging a small circle on his temple. There had been a plan. Something close to rehearsals so that Maria knew the order his questions would come in. She'd gone through her answers with him. Now she was off script already. She felt sorry for him. It wasn't a simple case and she wasn't an easy client, but Maria was done playing intellectual chess. 'Perhaps you could start at the beginning instead? How did the day you were arrested begin?'

'It didn't begin that day,' Maria said.

'I see,' Newell replied softly, the sideways tilt of his head an acknowledgment that Maria was going to do things her own way and that all he could do was let her. 'Start from the point you feel is relevant to what happened between you and Dr Bloxham.'

Maria rubbed the pale band of skin where her wedding and engagement rings used to sit. She could sunbathe for a decade, she thought, and the sickly whiteness would never tan. It was just one scar among many. The first sign that her life was destined to be lived in misery had been when Edward had chosen that ring. It was as good a place to start as any. She told the tale slowly in plain terms. The memories though, came hard and fast, knocking down the internal walls she'd spent years constructing. The retelling might be a gateway to madness, but even madness was preferable to numbness after so long.

'I was overwhelmed when he asked me to marry him,' she said, choosing a spot on the wall to address. 'At twenty-one I had no close family and Edward filled that gap. I thought I was the luckiest girl in the world.' That was the whole truth, perhaps even an understatement. 'Edward was good at romance before we were married. He proposed to me in the Cotswolds. It was during a midnight picnic in a meadow, under the pretext of badger watching. Such a beautiful night. There was a lake on one side and a woodland copse on the other. I was head over heels. It was even a full moon. I'm not sure if he planned that or it was a coincidence. Either way, it was magical.

'I remember it so clearly. He poured me wine, just half a glass. Edward didn't like women drinking too much. His own was full when he toasted us. He kissed me, told me I was perfect for him, everything he'd spent his life looking for. At that stage I was still stupid enough to believe he meant that in a good way.'

'How do you think he meant it, in hindsight?' Newell asked.

'I know exactly how he meant it. He wanted someone naive. I was without family and easily impressed. Almost alone, save for a couple for friends. He became the guiding influence in my life effortlessly. Edward wanted someone he could dominate, so he was right. I was perfect for him.'

Imogen Pascal leapt up. 'This is speculation and hypothesis. The defendant cannot be allowed to say whatever she likes about the motives of a man who is unable to respond.'

James Newell moved a few steps along counsel's bench to respond to her, stage whisper style. 'Sit down.'

Imogen Pascal glared at him, but she was reaching for her seat.

'Mr Newell,' the judge intervened. 'I was inclined to agree with you, only in a more polite fashion. This case is emotive enough without you two losing your tempers. Don't make me tell either of you again. And Miss Pascal, the defendant is answering a serious charge. You will allow her to do so without further interruption. Continue. If a line is crossed, I'll deal with it.'

Newell took a sip of water and pulled his gown back up over his shoulders. He managed to give Maria a reassuring nod before returning to his questions.

'You were telling the court about the night Dr Bloxham proposed. Please carry on.'

'Yes,' Maria said. 'Edward.' She allowed herself to slip back to that night. The irony was that she'd thought it was the best of her life when actually it was the start of the end. 'He laid me back on the rug, propping himself up on one elbow to look down at me. "Darling Maria," he said. "I want you to know I'll dedicate myself to providing for your every need. I'll be your friend, your partner, lover, advisor, everything you need." I realised what was coming then and I was amazed. Not that he was proposing, but that he'd chosen me. He had a PhD and I'd only passed A-levels. He was published, and had even been on television a couple of times. To me he was a sort of celebrity. Edward had everything planned to the last detail. He'd taken the ring from the jeweller's box I guess it came in, and fitted it into a geode. When I pulled the halves of the rock apart, the purple crystals glittered in the camping light. It sounds pathetic now, but I thought it was the most beautiful thing I'd ever seen. It was like discovering an ancient treasure. Edward took my left hand and pushed the ring – it was a small diamond solitaire because he said my fingers were so slight that a large stone would have looked clunky – onto my finger.' Maria winced remembering the pain it had caused.

'The band ground against my knuckle, grazing off a sliver of skin. My face must have showed the pain because he looked irritated with me and asked if I didn't like it. I told him I adored it, and I meant it. I wanted to get married and I . . . I loved him. Truly. I explained that the ring was a bit small but that resizing it wouldn't be a big deal. He told me he'd asked the jeweller to make it tight, based on the size of another of my rings. His exact words were, "I never want it to slip off. I don't want you to lose it, just like I never want to lose you. Hopefully you feel the same."

'I told him I did, one hundred per cent. Rather than go against his wishes, I said I'd get used to the ring. I lost weight for years during our marriage. That ring was so small it never budged. During the summer months my finger would swell until I thought it would burst.'

'Did you ever ask again if you could have it resized?' Newell asked.

'Often, in the early years of our marriage. I learned by his moods that the suggestion was offensive to him. In the end it was easier to put up with the pain from the ring than the emotional backlash of complaining about it.'

Imogen Pascal stood up. 'Your Honour, we've been here some time hearing the details of what sounds like an idyllic and romantic proposal nearly twenty years ago. I wonder if we could move onto events which have some actual bearing on the attempted murder?'

James Newell prepared to answer the objection, but Maria cut in before he could get there, her voice shrill enough to shatter glass.

'These events are relevant because, like everything else in my married life, that ring was designed to cause discomfort. The size of it was planned as a daily reminder that I was tied to him. I couldn't get rid of it any more than I could get rid of my husband, and he wanted me to feel it every hour of every day.'

'Mrs Bloxham . . .' the judge cautioned.

'It's Ms Bloxham,' Maria interrupted her loudly. 'I don't want the title any more than I still want that engagement ring. I had to get it cut off my finger. Even that was painful, like every aspect of getting rid of him has been.'

Her Honour Judge Downey glared at her, taking a moment before responding. This time Newell managed to get a word in first.

'I apologise, Your Honour. Giving evidence is obviously traumatic for my client.'

'Your client needs to be aware that she must speak through you, both to me and to Miss Pascal,' the judge replied. 'On this occasion I'll deem the matter of relevance to be satisfied, but I won't be so lenient with the next outburst. Carry on, Mr Newell.'

Maria picked up a biro that had been left on the witness stand in front of her. As James Newell organised his notes, she unscrewed the end and removed the ink cartridge, snapping the clear plastic casing in two. She needed to be able to concentrate, to stop getting lost in the intensity of the memories and control herself.

'Could you describe the early part of your marriage?' Newell asked.

Maria slid the shard of plastic as hard as she could into the palm of her hand, forcing herself not to release her grip on it as she focused her eyes back on the wall opposite her. The pain was clean and clear. It wiped out everything else. She blinked a few times, breathed deeply and took herself back to the years of confusion and denial.

'It was series of disappointments,' Maria said. 'Everyone and everything seemed to be letting me down, except Edward. He was good at that, picking me up after I got knocked down. It took me years to realise that he'd orchestrated the damage to make sure he was the only person I had left.'

'Is there a specific example that comes to mind?' Newell asked.

'My best friend,' Maria smiled as she pushed the plastic a millimetre deeper. She hadn't allowed herself to remember that particular loss for years. It had signalled the end of every contact she had beyond Edward, and a period of extraordinary grief. 'Andrea. We used to have a night out together once a month. Edward tolerated it before we were married, but not for long afterwards. To start with, Edward told me he wanted his new bride to himself in the evenings, given how hard he was working during the day. I was flattered, rather pleased actually. It's nice to feel so wanted. I explained it to Andrea, making excuses sometimes for not being available, but the truth is I turned down her invitations with something like pride. It seems pathetic now, how much I loved our routine. I would get home from work, cook dinner, light a fire and put his favourite newspaper on the coffee table ready for him. He used to tease me about it.' She swallowed hard, feeling all eyes on her, the humiliation of her loyalty sticking like thorns in her throat. Picking up the glass of water with a shaking hand she tried to get past it.

Newell saved her. 'You were saying he used to tease you? Can you remember how, specifically?'

She nodded. 'Sometimes when I brought his slippers, he'd say, "Good dog," or he'd pat me on the head. I thought it was affectionate, you know? A private joke between us. I told Andrea about it. She was supposed to laugh, agree with me about how sweet it was. When she didn't I was offended. Cross. I think seeing her face when I told her confirmed a sneaking suspicion I'd had that Edward was laughing at me, not with me. I blamed Andrea for not having a sense of humour. In fact, I told her she was desperate to find fault with my husband. After that I barely saw her. There was too much tension between us.'

'So did you and Andrea lose contact at that point?' Newell asked.

Maria took a breath, looking across to the jury. A few of them had crossed arms. She didn't seem to be making any headway with them. The younger ones were interested, leaning forward ready to take notes. The jury foreperson was whispering to the older man next to her. She wondered what they expected from her. Was she supposed to cry and pour her heart out to them?

'Ms Bloxham? You were telling us about your relationship with Andrea,' Newell prompted her.

'Yes, sorry,' she said, 'We did lose touch, but only after I'd seen her one last time. I'd been married about a year. She waited for me outside work one evening. I was intending to walk to the bus stop when she called out my name. She hadn't warned me that she'd be there, but by then she'd stopped phoning me.'

Maria could still see her, bright red coat and smiling face, beaming as if nothing was wrong at all.

'She asked where my car was parked and I told her I'd got rid of it as Edward said it would never pass the MOT. Andrea didn't comment on that which was completely unlike her. Usually she'd have said something about Edward bossing me around. At the time it was a relief that she didn't make a big deal about it. With hindsight I should have known straight away that something was wrong. I told her I had time for a coffee as long as I didn't miss my bus. I gave my best friend the grand total of twenty minutes after a decade of friendship.' Maria smiled at her own stupidity and shook her head. 'I didn't deserve her anyway. She was only trying to warn me.'

'Warn you about what?' Newell asked.

Maria raised her eyebrows. 'Him, of course. She saw through him from the very start. I guess she was less naive than me, but desperation is blinding. Andrea told me she missed me. I think I told her I missed her too, but maybe that's just wishful thinking. I hope I did. I remember being worried that if I missed my bus, Edward's dinner wouldn't be ready on time. He didn't like that.'

Maria could still fell the warmth of Andrea's arm, the last time she had ever slid it through Maria's so they could walk together to a nearby café. The sense of her being so near, so loving, brought tears to her eyes. Losing Andrea had been her own fault, not Edward's. What a price she'd paid for that stubbornness.

'We ordered hot chocolate. It was always our treat. We met working a Saturday job together as teenagers, at a chemist's. After that, Andrea got a degree online and I had a string of administrative jobs. We made small talk for a minute. She asked how I'd been. I . . . I lied. I told her life was wonderful. It was too hard to admit how unhappy I was, and I was still at the stage when I thought that perhaps it was my fault for not being a good enough wife. Anyway, Andrea didn't say anything but it was obvious from her expression that she didn't believe me. I snapped at her.' Maria rubbed her forehead. 'Why do we do that to the people we love?' she asked, addressing the question to James Newell. He met her eyes patiently, waiting for her to continue. 'Then Andrea asked after Edward, and I was embarrassed. I knew by then, you see – what he was. Not all he was capable of. Not how devious he was. That would be giving myself too much credit. My naivety was still a work in progress. But I knew he had a mean streak. He could be cruel. And I'd begun to feel the loss of control Andrea had warned me about. The money, the car, my friends. He didn't like it when I made suggestions about what we ate or did. Around then, the dates are a bit fuzzy, he'd decided I shouldn't drink alcohol at all. Not that it was a big deal, but it reinforced that he was behaving more like a parent than a partner. I knew I'd given away control of my life.

'Of course, I pretended everything was wonderful, told her Edward took care of everything, which at least was true. She just stared at me. Andrea had these huge blue eyes. Beautiful. I'd been waiting for her to say something about Edward and eventually I couldn't bear it any more. "Go on, then," I said. "Say what you're thinking. You never could hide anything."

'Andrea looked hurt, but not surprised and she said that was because she'd never needed to hide anything from me before. She told me she loved me. That was worse than her pity. I knew she loved me, and yet I'd chosen Edward over her and actually I was starting to suspect that he didn't love me at all. Not in a normal way. Not how I wanted to be loved. Even then, when she was reaching out to help me, I was still too proud to let her.

'I pretended I had no idea what she was talking about, playing for time and trying to figure out what to say to her. Andrea put her hand over mine, and I wanted to grip it. I wanted to throw myself into her arms and tell her I was lonelier than I'd ever been in my life. I didn't, obviously, or I wouldn't be standing here today. So I played dumb and made out she was making a fuss about nothing.'

Only that wasn't true. Maria had done something worse. Making a show of trying to recall the moment to the jury, she could hear her actual words at scream pitch in her mind.

'I'm fine. Better than fine. Unlike you, I have a husband and a beautiful home. Is that why you're being such a bitch?'

Andrea had gasped. The victory had lasted just seconds. Everyone thought they knew better than her. Maria the weakling. Maria who needed guidance. The young woman who could never make up her own mind. She got enough of that condescending bullshit from her husband. She didn't want an additional helping from the one person who was supposed to have her back.

'We argued,' Maria told the jury calmly. 'It was silly really. She was only trying to help.'

The truth was something she was less proud of.

'Come on, Ria,' Andrea had said. 'I'm on your side. Everyone makes mistakes, I just don't want to see you regret yours for the rest of your life.' There had been tears in her eyes. Maria knew her friend was fighting not to break down completely.

'We probably shouldn't talk about Edward any more,' Maria had replied. 'You obviously aren't rational when it comes to him.'

'This isn't about me,' Andrea's voice was low and husky. 'I know this is bad, Maria. I can feel it. Just leave. Come and stay at my place while you get on your feet again. You don't even have to go back there. We can buy you new clothes, shoes. Whatever you need.' She'd reached out a hand across the table, resting it on Maria's shoulder.

'Would you just fucking quit it? I don't need your help. I'm not sure what you think you know, but you're wrong. I'm happy. Maybe you just can't cope with being replaced.'

Andrea's hand flew off her shoulder as if she'd been stung. Her eyes closed and her head fell. Maria felt the shame of her nastiness like a burn that would scar her forever.

'I'm sorry,' she muttered. 'I didn't mean that. I'm overtired. Shit, I'm going to miss my bus.' She grabbed her bag and reached for her purse, faltering as she realised that Edward hadn't budgeted for her to buy extras like the hot chocolate.

Maria looked back at James Newell, trying to get past the awful memory of ripping into her best friend.

'Andrea paid for the hot chocolate. She had to. Edward was setting me an allowance by then. I wasn't allowed extras to buy myself anything. I took sandwiches for lunch and had a weekly bus pass so I didn't need cash. As we were leaving Andrea told me she'd been accepted into the army. She was due to leave for Sandhurst within the month. In spite of our argument, she promised to post me her new contact details once she got there. The army had always been her dream. I hadn't even known she'd got around to applying. I told her I was pleased although I was shocked that she was actually leaving, and a bit jealous. She was escaping, properly. From Bristol, from meaningless little jobs. From me.'

'How did the two of you leave things?' Newell asked.

'She told me I was still her best mate, and she tried to hug me.' Maria frowned. 'I don't think I hugged her back. By then I was frantic about not missing my bus, and hurt that she was leaving. I just didn't know how to tell her that. Also, I knew Edward would hate me hugging her. That sounds stupid, I know, but he was very specific that no one else should touch me. Anyone at all. I ran for the bus, wishing I could go back and start the evening again. It didn't occur to me that it would be the last time I'd see her.'

'Do you need a moment, Ms Bloxham?' the judge asked.

Maria shrugged, looking confused. The court usher stood up and offered a box of tissues to dry her face. She hadn't even realised she'd been crying.

'Thank you,' Maria said, cleaning herself up.

'That's quite all right,' the judge smiled kindly. 'Continue when you feel ready.'

Maria took a deep breath. 'On the bus, I toyed with the idea of not telling Edward I'd seen Andrea. It seemed ridiculous, feeling uncomfortable about spending time with an old friend, but Edward had never taken to Andrea. The atmosphere between them had been stilted, almost competitive on Edward's behalf. I'd persuaded myself it was charming, Edward wanting me to himself. Any sensible woman would feel lucky, I thought. When I got home, I prepared dinner as normal, put some washing on and lit the fire, making sure there was a glass of red wine breathing so he could enjoy it as soon as he came in. He was very particular about how his wine should be served. By the time he came through the door, I was bursting to tell him about Andrea, to stop myself from blurting it out later on, which would only have caused a worse argument.

'I kissed him on the cheek, then took his briefcase and overcoat. "You'll never guess what happened to me today," I said. "I ran into Andrea as I was leaving work. Isn't that odd?"

'"You just ran into her?' he asked. 'That hardly seems credible. How long has my wine been breathing?" I remember thinking, maybe that was the end of the conversation. Perhaps he would leave it there. I was so relieved. I told him his wine had been breathing for half an hour, only it was maybe just fifteen minutes. I was wondering if he'd notice the difference.

'"So where exactly did you run into Andrea?" he asked. I knew by his tone of voice that he already suspected something was wrong. I decided it was easier to just be honest about it, so I told him she was waiting for me at work, but I made a point of being clear that I hadn't known she would be there. If he thought I'd made plans without telling him in advance he really would have been cross. He asked what she wanted, made some comment about us gossiping and wasting our time, then kicked off his shoes and took his wine into the lounge. I realised I was expected to follow him.

'I explained that she was off to join the army and fiddled with the firewood so I could keep my back to him. It was easier not to tell him everything if I didn't have to look him in the eye. It didn't work. He asked what I wasn't telling him and I tried to brush it off. That was my mistake. I said he was being silly. Edward didn't like being called silly. He found it offensive. I apologised at once, but then he accused me of deceiving him about my conversation with Andrea. Looking back, I must have been a wreck. I bet he knew there was something wrong from the moment he stepped through the door. He was just waiting for me to spill it. I was always so nervous around him.'

Imogen Pascal folded her arms and tilted her head back, staring at the ceiling, pretending to be bored, knowing the subliminal message she was sending to the jury was that they should be feeling bored too. This was a distraction, her body language told them, just so much fluff to dull the final blow. Maria told herself not to let it get to her. This was her moment. If she let Miss Pascal win now, all her careful hours of deciding what to say – and what to omit – would have been for nothing.

'Edward looked me up and down, this smug little grin on his face. "You forgot to put your apron on," he said. "Just look at you: what a mess. Your face is flushed, not in an attractive way. I know you, Maria. You can't lie to me. What did Andrea say? Something about me, I suppose. She could never stand the fact that you'd found a husband and she hadn't. Nothing uglier in a woman than jealousy. Come and sit next to me." He patted the couch next to him. I didn't want to sit down. Edward was always at his nicest right before he taught me a lesson.'

'Taught you a lesson?' Newell queried.

'His words, not mine, as if I was a naughty schoolgirl. He liked to make it clear how ignorant I was. I think that was his favourite word for me. I told him I needed to change my skirt as I didn't want to get soot on the leather. He said I should do as my husband told me. He quite often referred to himself in the third person. He added that there would be plenty of time for me to clean the sofa later. He was smiling as he said it, but his face was pinched and hard, as if the muscles were seizing up. I sat down. "There's something I should have told you and I regret not having done so at the time, but I'd made my mind up to protect you from it," he said. "At our wedding, Andrea, I believe having had too much to drink, took me aside. She was ranting about how you should have chosen a dress size up, how your hair didn't flatter your face, I didn't really pay much attention."

'I tried to interject, but my mouth wouldn't make any sound. It didn't sound like Andrea. I couldn't see how she would do that to me. Not behind my back. After a while I asked if he was sure. He said – and I recall this word for word – he said, "I'm afraid so. Put enough drinks inside a woman and her tongue lashes like a snared snake." Then he told me she'd offered herself to him. His phrasing. To start with I decided I must have misunderstood his meaning. I thought about it for a while, tried to imagine it, but I still couldn't believe it. I tried to clarify if something had actually happened between the two of them. He swore to me he'd never touched her.

'Eventually it all sank in – the reality, not Edward's version. I told him Andrea would never do that to me. I didn't accuse him of lying, I never once had the courage to do that in our whole marriage. I did tell him he must have been mistaken though.'

She looked up. The courtroom was completely silent. Even Imogen Pascal was listening now. Maria had her back to the row of journalists but for once their pens were still. Everyone wanted to know how her husband had retaliated.

'Edward wasn't the sort of man you corrected,' she said. 'That didn't only apply to me. I saw the replies he wrote to people who left bad reviews of his books and articles. He was unforgiving.

So he asked me if I was forcing him to reveal the sordid details, knowing I wouldn't be able to stand it. There's no doubt in my mind that he'd have been extremely imaginative if I'd called his bluff. I simply told him that I believed Andrea loved me, and that it made no sense for her to have betrayed me.

'He leaned close into my face, really close, and said, "What is it I have to do to prove my dedication to you, Maria? I provide for you and take care of you. You have this house, money when you need it . . . what do you want? Why am I suddenly someone who can't be trusted?" That was when I made the most serious mistake I had until that point in our marriage. I told him that his version seemed unlikely . . . given that Andrea had never even liked him. I regretted it before I'd even closed my mouth. The look on his face was pure venom.

'"Yet you continued to be friends with her? You faithless bitch," he shouted, standing up. I could smell the wine on his breath, and his shoulders were up. He looked like an angry bull. I apologised. I remember being scared, properly scared for my safety, for the first time. He seemed so out of control. He lowered his voice, almost to a whisper, and leaned over to talk right into my ear. "You remained friends with a whore who pretended to hate me because she couldn't have me, and you did nothing to end your relationship with her? We need to make some changes, Maria. I need to straighten up your priorities. I'll eat dinner and decide on a strategy. You'd better go upstairs and consider how you've behaved and what you can do to improve yourself."

'I went. Even now I'm not sure why, but I was so used to doing as I was told that refusing seemed impossible. There was a moment when I considered arguing with him, but everything he'd said was right. I had stayed friends with Andrea knowing how she felt about Edward. In my heart I knew she hadn't made a pass at Edward. Even if she'd liked him, she wouldn't have done that to me. At the same time, I didn't want to believe that my husband would lie to me about something so hurtful. I'd agreed to spend my life with him. The last thing I wanted to believe was that he would be that cruel and manipulative.'

She paused, picking up the glass and realising it was empty. No one moved. Every person in the court was on the edge of their seat. This was what power felt like, she realised. Knowing that an audience hung on your every word. It occurred to her that she could say whatever she wanted next. The point, though, was to stick to the truth, or as close to it as she could get. The fewer lies she told, the harder it would be for Imogen Pascal to prove she was lying.

'What happened next?' Newell asked.

Maria sighed. 'As I reached our bedroom, I realised I was going to be sick. Fortunately I hadn't eaten dinner, so it wasn't that bad, but by the time I got off my knees in the bathroom Edward was watching me from the bed. He pretended to be concerned at first, told me to sit down on the bathroom floor in case I was ill again. I did as he suggested. My stomach was still cramping. Then he told me he'd left me a gift in the bathroom cupboard, below the sink, on the lowest shelf.

'I opened the cupboard door, not knowing what to expect. Edward wasn't given to buying gifts. There was a tiny blue plastic case on the shelf, two inches long and an inch wide. I flipped it open with my thumb nail.'

'What was inside?' Newell asked quietly.

'Blades,' Maria replied blandly. 'Disposable razor blades.'

'Why did your husband buy you razor blades?' Newell's voice was louder now, focusing everyone on the answer she was about to give.

'To cut myself,' she said, pulling the plastic pen shard from her hand and closing her fist over the wound to stop the bleeding before anyone noticed it. 'He knew I'd cut myself as a teenager. We met when he was volunteering at a charity that offered support to self-harmers. Edward stopped as soon as we started seeing each other. Said it was a conflict of interests for him to be involved with me and in a position of trust. I fell for that, at the time.'

'What do you mean, you fell for that?' Newell asked.

Maria smiled and shrugged. 'I was exactly what he wanted. Lost and pathetic. If I had to sum myself up back then, I'd say I was controllable. Everything Edward ever dreamed of.'

Imogen Pascal was on her feet in a heartbeat. 'Your Honour, this is being presented to blacken the jury's opinion of the victim.'

'It's part of the Bloxhams' history,' Newell countered. 'And it will be backed up by the remainder of Ms Bloxham's evidence.'

'There's no way for the prosecution or Dr Bloxham to answer these accusations. This is an entirely unique case. As such I ask that the jury be told to disregard this evidence,' Miss Pascal persisted.

This time Maria was more careful to ask the judge's permission before answering, raising her hand before she spoke.

'Yes, Ms Bloxham,' the judge said, adjusting her wig slightly, getting some cooler air below the horsehair.

'The reason there's no one who can back this up is because Edward planned it that way. I was never supposed to talk to anyone about my life. There weren't meant to be witnesses. Had there been, I'd have found a way to leave him years earlier.'

The judge leaned back in her chair, fiddling with her pen lid and taking her time considering the arguments. Maria waited.

'All right,' she decided. 'Miss Pascal, the test is relevance. As far as I can see, the evidence Ms Bloxham is giving goes to her perception of the state of the relationship so I'll allow it. Be careful Mr Newell. I'm not going to allow an outright character assassination of Dr Bloxham. Keep to the point.'

Newell nodded. 'Ms Bloxham, without assuming what was in your husband's mind, would you explain exactly what happened?'

'As I stared at the blades, Edward said, "I know this makes you feel better." He'd asked me extensively about my history of self-harming. During our first few dates we didn't really talk about much else. He seemed so understanding. I remember feeling grateful that I'd found someone who would accept me for who I was, without seeing me as damaged or a liability. I'd explained that cutting helped me feel in control of my life, as well as providing a release for a lot of negativity. I found it very hard to stop. I guess you could say I was addicted for a few years. That night, Edward was fully prepared, though. He'd even bought wound dressings and antiseptic spray. He told me he was willing to let me do it because he knew I needed it. He actually gave me permission, as if I should have been grateful.

'I wanted to fight it. Andrea helped me stop the first time, but she was going off to the Army and I'd been so horrible to her that I couldn't imagine she'd want to be my friend any more. It was just me and Edward. That's all I remember thinking. Just him and me forever. I took a blade from the case and got a good grip on it. It was hard, my fingers were sweaty, so I took a bottle of talcum powder from the cupboard and coated my hands. It was like riding a bike. I sat with my back to the wall. You have to take precautions in case you pass out. Once I'd found a clear patch of skin on my thighs, I got ready to cut. He told me I was a good girl. His voice sounded distant. The only part of myself I could feel was my fingers. I used my forefinger and thumb to stretch the patch of skin so the cut wouldn't snag, then I secured the blade with my thumb against my folded fingers. That gets you a good side angle, which keeps the cut shallow and limits the bleeding. I knew if the cut didn't heal well it might require medical treatment and I didn't want that. All those prying eyes and advice. I'd had enough of that the first time around. By then, I needed it. I was so upset and confused. Cutting myself had always given me a sort of relief. I knew it would make me feel better. It was that fast. After all that time having stopped, I touched one blade and I was hooked again. I didn't even try to argue with him.

'Edward asked if I was ready. I recall wanting to slam the door, to have the moment to myself, but letting him watch was a price I was prepared to pay, so I did my best to ignore the fact that he was there, leaning down low over my leg and just concentrating on that. I blew on it to get rid of any stray particles. It was an old habit. Then I sliced. The cut was the length of my thumb.'

In her mind, Maria could see it as if she was right there, all those years ago. Scarlet beads blossomed and spread, tiny rivulets of relief. No one had ever understood it was nothing short of an orgasm. The build-up, the moments waiting for the sensation to drive home, shuddering, eyes closed as the peak of the agony passed and soothing, healing blood brought her to rest. Nothing else mattered for a few, too brief, seconds. No one else existed. She was safe from the world. Everything was back under her control. The jury wouldn't understand the terrible ecstasy of it, and she wasn't stupid enough to try to explain it. At best they would think her mentally ill. At worst, she would come across as some sort of psychopath-in-waiting, which was exactly what Imogen Pascal and DI Anton wanted.

'Edward interrupted once he'd seen enough. He said I should feel better after that, then reminded me to clean up the blood and talcum powder. I nodded at him like some pathetic mutt, so grateful. Isn't that awful? Just so incredibly grateful.'

She looked up at James Newell, that part of her tale complete. 'He never hit me,' she added, looking at Imogen Pascal. Part of the deal Maria had made with herself was this. She wouldn't lie about anything Edward had done. No exaggeration, no creativity. She didn't need to. All she needed to do was omit. 'He didn't need to get violent when he could get me to cut myself. Sometimes it felt like a punishment, other times it was more of a reward. Most of the time it was when I'd argued with him and he needed to feel in charge again.'

'How often did you cut yourself during the marriage?' her barrister asked.

'Sometimes once a month. During the worst times it was once a week. They got . . . deeper.' Maria ran her hands down over her thighs, feeling the dappled landscape even through the material.

'How else did Mr Bloxham control you?'

'It was incremental,' Maria said pinching the bridge of her nose as a migraine tried to blacken the edges of her vision. 'The first night I cut myself, he told me in bed that I wasn't coping properly and he didn't want me to go back to work. No notice period, no explanation. He phoned my employer the next morning. I didn't fight him. I was so confused at having self-harmed again that I thought he might be right. I wasn't sure I could deal with any stress given what he'd told me about Andrea as well.'

'What about your marital finances? Who handled those?' Newell asked.

'He did, of course,' Maria gave a tiny laugh. 'I didn't earn any money after that so he said it was best to close my bank account. Edward did the shopping on the way home, then later in our marriage he had it delivered when he'd be at home.'

'By the end of your marriage, what contact did you have with the outside world?'

'None,' Maria replied smoothly. 'He made sure I had no one to run to.'

'And the intimate aspects of your marriage?' James Newell asked quietly. The courtroom was so silent, Maria decided she could have heard a feather drop, never mind a pin. Was it really so fascinating, hearing the grotesque details of a person's private life? Bloodshed was captivating, but apparently sex was what really made people sit up and listen.

'For the first year, like everything else, it seemed relatively normal. Could I get more water please?' The usher hurried over with a fresh jug and refilled her glass. 'When things started to change, his requests seemed playful. At first it was just putting a blindfold on me and asking me to stay quiet. I was okay with that. I figured lots of people had those sorts of fantasies. Sometimes he wanted me to act scared.'

'Could you be more specific?' Newell prompted.

Maria rubbed her eyes with her good hand. It was draining. The remembering, the retelling, reliving it all. 'He wanted me to ask him to stop, to be kind, not to hurt me. But he didn't get . . . you know . . . really seem to enjoy that. He never seemed satisfied. That was when he tried something new.'

'Which was?' Newell asked.

'Having me lie with my face into the pillow.' Maria could feel the blood draining from her face. Her vision was fuzzy and the air felt thin. 'He had strict rules. No talking. No movement. The first time, he was more excited than I'd ever seen him.'

'I'm sorry to have to ask for details, but what exactly did he do to you?'

Maria closed her eyes and told it as quickly as she could. There was no point dragging it out.

'I would be naked, roll onto my stomach. He would take his time opening my legs, taunting me. Sometimes he spoke, sometimes he didn't. Then he would lie on top of me. He was heavy, only I wasn't allowed to complain. That was against the rules. He used to get very angry about that. When he was ready, he would have sex with me. It could be hard to breathe so I learned to take long deep breaths whenever I could. If I broke the rules, he wanted to start all over again and it just took longer. Even after he'd finished, I had to lie there completely still and quiet until he said I could move.' She raised a hand to her throat, parched in spite of the water. There were tears on her face that hadn't been there a minute ago. Maria didn't allow herself to look at anyone else in the courtroom. She didn't want pity.

'Ms Bloxham,' Newell was practically whispering. 'Did you consent to having sex like that?'

'I objected occasionally, then I learned not to. It wasn't worth it. His moods were so unpleasant afterwards. Soon I just put up with it, like everything else. I didn't like it. I didn't want it – didn't want him. But I didn't fight him off. If I was good, he let me cut myself afterwards.'

'I see. And did you—'

'There was one other thing,' Maria interrupted him.

'Go on,' Newell encouraged her.

'Afterwards, when he got off me, he liked to lie by my side and stare at my face. He gave me one extra instruction then. He liked me to have my eyes open, not to blink, no facial expression allowed. Everything had to be slack.'

'As if you were dead?' James Newell asked. The air in the courtroom was electric.

'I object. Mr Newell is leading the witness,' Imogen Pascal leaped into action.

Maria was in no mood to let the prosecutor take the moment.

'Just like I was dead,' Maria confirmed. 'Almost as if he had killed me.'

Imogen Pascal sat back down. She had intervened too late, and she knew it. It was all Maria could do not to smile.

Newell waited a few seconds then cleared his throat before beginning again. 'Now, Ms Bloxham, could you explain exactly what happened the day you were arrested?'

There was an audible out-letting of breath from people around the courtroom. They were relieved not to have to hear any more details of her sordid sex life. Maria didn't blame them. If she could have her own memory wiped, she would. Tipping her head back to stare at the ceiling, she registered the damp hair at the nape of her neck and the tension in her shoulders. The jury shifted in their seats before the next set of revelations began. DI Anton leaned over the desk to whisper in Imogen Pascal's ear.

'All right,' Maria said, happy to be on the home stretch. 'I'll tell you about that day.' It had begun, like all life-defining days, she supposed, exactly the same as any other. 'Edward went to work in a foul mood. One of my tasks was to respond to what he called his fan mail. He said I hadn't written long enough letters, and there was a spelling error in one. I had to handwrite them and sometimes I ran out of things to say. Anyway, he wanted them all redone.'

The reality of Edward's fury was both more chilling and more subtle. The days when he was happy had been few and far between in the past two years. Maria knew why. As much as Edward had been the agent of his own misery, she still got the blame for it. There were no more tenterhooks. She had submitted to him completely. The sense that her life couldn't get any more meaningless had liberated her from the nervous wreck she was through her mid-thirties. She had no further to fall, and that knowledge was like valium. Maria spoke only when spoken to. She never fought, never argued. Every rule was complied with. Sometimes in the evening she would find that she'd sat and stared at a blank wall for an hour or two without any sense that time had passed.

'Before he left,' she told the jury, 'he told me I needed to recognise how lucky I was. He said he'd be generous if I got all his letters perfect, and let me have access to the blades that night, as he was sick of me moping around. For the last five years of our marriage he'd hidden them. He said he was concerned that I'd attempt suicide if I wasn't supervised. Two cuts, he said that morning. For some reason he'd decided I was allowed a double treat. Only he knew my legs weren't up to that. By telling me before he left, he was ensuring I'd spend all day thinking about it. I did, too.

'I spent the morning cleaning, doing washing, the usual chores. I spent a bit of time in the garden but not much as I knew the letters would take me two or three hours. As I sat down at the kitchen table to start writing, I felt blood trickling down the outside of my thigh. A recent cut had pulled apart. The scar tissue was too damaged to knit together any more. That was when it dawned on me. I wasn't going to heal. I went to the bathroom and poured surgical spirit on the open wound. I barely even felt it sting. I remember wanting to just rip the skin off my legs and let it bleed.'

Maria looked at James Newell who met her eyes calmly. She was doing all right. Imogen Pascal had her head buried in a file. DI Anton was sitting chest puffed and arms folded. It didn't matter what she said, he would never believe her.

'Did you dress the wound?' Newell asked.

'Three times,' Maria confirmed. 'Each time it just bled through the dressings. By the time I finally got it to stop, I knew I couldn't risk cutting myself any more and even if I did, it was pointless. It had stopped making me feel better months earlier. It was just a spectator sport for Edward. I'd only carried on cutting because it was easier than explaining to him that I no longer wanted to. I'd finally hit rock bottom.'

The courtroom was too hot. The air conditioning was whining with effort and Maria couldn't find any fresh air to breathe. She allowed her eyes to close for a few seconds. DI Anton tutted. Even with her eyes shut, Maria knew from the direction of the sound and by the tone that it was him.

'I didn't want to die,' she said. 'In spite of how unhappy I was and how hopeless I felt, I wasn't ready to let go of life right then. But I knew, not just imagined or suspected, I knew he wouldn't stop until I was dead. There was nothing left of me to break or control. I did everything I was told . . .' as far as Edward knew, Maria added in her head. 'All that remained was for him to watch me die, a blade in my hand, on the bathroom floor. I wasn't sure how much longer he was prepared to wait, but he was encouraging me to cut myself more and more often. That morning, when he told me I could cut myself twice, I knew he was hoping for something extraordinary. He was driving me towards death. Edward knew I couldn't cut myself safely any more. The truth is, I was scared that I might just give him what he wanted. It would have been declared a suicide, but that was never how it felt to me. My choices were to run away from him knowing he'd have me committed, or to stay and have him drive me to self-harm until I finally bled out.'

Maria forced herself to look towards the jurors to finish her story. This was their moment, what they'd turned up for day after day in the stifling heat. James Newell had told her to address them in the most personal way as she could.

'I tried to do a good job answering his letters but I was jittery. I drank endless cups of tea trying to calm myself down, telling myself I'd imagined the edge in his voice, checking every now and again to see if the wound on my leg was scabbing over, but it just got more painful as the afternoon went on. I was thinking up ways to placate him. The house was immaculate. I was even wearing clothes I knew he liked, and I'd made sure my hair was neat and tidy. There was steak in the fridge and I'd peeled the vegetables. I know it sounds as if I was carrying on as normal, but I didn't know what else to do. I was trying to persuade myself that everything was fine, but it wasn't. There was a clock counting down inside my head. I could already feel the blade in my hands. Edward would be sitting on the bed, giving instructions and offering advice. As he got more excited, he would stand in the bathroom doorway for a better view.'

Maria looked at the judge who was leaning forward, her chin in her two hands, elbows on the desk.

'He hated me,' Maria said. 'That's what it took me years to figure out. I don't know why. I never got to the bottom of it, and I would never have dared ask what made him the way he was. But he had nothing but contempt for me. Perhaps that was my fault. Maybe what he really needed was a woman who would stand up to him. If that's right, then he picked the wrong partner. That day, though, I could feel his hatred like a cold wind through the house.

'Edward came home early. He did that once every few months but usually when he had particularly good news and wanted to tell me all about it, a television appearance or a mention in a national newspaper, something like that. Those days he was chatty when he came through the door. He liked me to sit in the lounge and hear the details, blow by blow. That day he must have sat in his car a while before coming in. I heard the gates open and the tyres on the gravel, but the front door didn't open for a good few minutes.'

Lie.

'When he did finally come in, there was an edge to him. He was tightly wound and gleeful, but not in a positive way. I was hoping I'd misread it, waiting for the announcement that he'd got a new book deal or stopped a greenfield building project from happening. I remember standing in the hallway, wishing he'd say something. When he smiled it was as if there was nothing left alive inside him.'

Truth.

'He didn't explain why he was early so I covered his silence with what I had planned for dinner. I was in the middle of washing up the tea cups in the sink, so I went back into the kitchen to stop him staring at me. When he took his jacket off, I could see sweat rings on his shirt at his armpits. That was unusual for Edward. He was obsessive about hygiene, so whatever he'd been doing that day must either have been either very strenuous or he was more excited than I'd ever seen him. I think that was the final straw. I knew I wasn't imagining why he was home so early. If I had to describe it, I'd say it felt like a grand finale. I know that sounds dramatic . . .' Maria gave the judge a look, 'but it was as if he was waiting for something big to happen.' Her Honour Judge Downey gave her an encouraging nod.

'I did what I could to calm the atmosphere. I began showing him the letters I'd rewritten. I asked if he'd like me to read them out to him after dinner for his approval, but he wasn't interested. After that I offered him coffee, or an early glass of wine. I'd had his favourite red breathing since lunch time so he wouldn't have anything to complain about. He declined that too. I remember him going to the kitchen sink and scrubbing his hands with hot water as if he was preparing for something. I kept the conversation going but it was one way. He was practically ignoring me.'

Another lie. Perhaps the biggest so far.

'I said I might do another hour's gardening to get out from under his feet. It occurred to me that I might be safe if I could just get outside. He stared as if he hadn't heard me. His face was flushed and he was breathing fast. Not like he was ill, more like an athlete firing up the adrenalin before a high jump, if that makes sense. Eventually he said, "No gardening this afternoon." That was it. His decision. I wasn't to go through the back door. So I asked if he'd like his dinner early, said I could start cooking immediately.

'He told me to stop fussing and that I needed calming down. That was when I looked at the kitchen clock, and I wondered what time my death would be recorded. I wasn't sure how long Edward would leave it before calling an ambulance.'

Not a lie, only borrowing from a different timeline. Maria had looked at the kitchen clock so many times wondering what the circumstances of her death would be. Every time she cast the net of her imagination, it ended in blood. That time, for the first time, the blood she was imagining wasn't hers.

'It was no surprise when Edward told me he would see me up in the bedroom. In fact, it was almost a relief, you know, that I hadn't been going crazy and imagining it all day? If he hadn't told me to go upstairs, I'd have been waiting all night to see what he had planned. It was the confirmation I needed of his intent and I felt those blades calling. Edward knew it, too. He must have seen the look on my face, because he smiled genuinely for the first time since coming through the front door. I was close enough to him to see his pupils dilate.'

True. Absolutely true.

DI Anton, arms folded behind his head, let out a huff of laughter. The judge glared at him. The jury, as one, didn't move an inch. Every eye was fixed on her. Imogen Pascal turned her head just enough give the police officer the evil eye. Not out of courtesy to me, Maria thought. Just to avoid the disapproval of the judge, and perhaps the press. Miss Pascal was all about the image. It didn't matter any more. Maria was nearly through her part in the charade, for better or worse, and if she screwed up now, DI Anton's attitude would be the least of her troubles.

'I knew I couldn't do it again. I couldn't sit on that bathroom floor and let Edward feed off my pain and misery. If I didn't cut in the wrong place, I would end up cutting too deeply or just . . .' she took a deep breath, her eyelids fluttering as the memory of what might have been tried to swallow her, '. . . just slice the blade across my neck and be done with it.'

'Are you suggesting you were at the point of committing suicide, or that you knew continuing to cut yourself at that point was putting your life at risk?' Newell asked.

'Either. Both.' Maria shook her head. 'Edward believed I'd lost the will to live. I had no self-worth left, no joy, no purpose. He'd achieved his goal. I think he expected me to kill myself. He certainly knew that the damage to my legs was bad enough that continuing to cut was a real danger.

'I was conflicted at that point. There was this voice inside me saying Edward deserved to be left explaining to the police how his wife had bled to death on the bathroom floor. Only he was too clever for that and he knew it. He'd have said he was on the phone, or on his computer, or in the garden. There would be a reason why I was dead before the paramedics could get there. And it dawned on me then how well it would feed into his love of publicity. Poor Dr Edward Bloxham, whose mentally ill wife committed suicide, leaving him to find her body on the floor of their bathroom. Poor Dr Bloxham who had been so stoic for so many years, coping with his deranged wife. Poor Dr Bloxham who would need consoling. He would also need another wife. There was no way he was going to cook and clean for himself. That was the thing. If I killed myself he'd simply have filled my shoes and while that wasn't my problem, the thought of me escaping only to leave another woman walking straight into his trap, to endure what I had . . . I couldn't do that. He wanted me dead.' She paused. 'Actually that's not entirely accurate . . .' She had practiced this line in her head a thousand times waiting for the trial. She knew exactly how it needed to be delivered.

'He wanted to watch me die. My death, I think, was just going to be a side effect of him getting the thing he desired the most. It didn't matter to him if I cut myself too hard deliberately or if it was a side effect of the cutting. He'd spent our whole marriage building to that point. That was when I knew, if I didn't kill him, I would walk up those stairs to my death. So I went to get a clean dishcloth from the pantry to wipe up the last tea cup that was still in the sink, and that's when he spoke again. He said, "You could always try a different part of your legs, maybe the softer skin. Fresh skin. Towards the inside of your thighs. Virgin territory. Would you like that, Ria?"'

She'd always hated it when Edward called her that. Only Andrea was supposed to call her Ria. It had been their pet name for each other – Ria from Maria, and Rea from Andrea. The jury didn't need to know that, though. Not how angry she'd been that afternoon. Furious enough, in fact, to have killed.

'When he suggested I try the softer skin, all pretence was gone. He wanted me to slice closer to the large artery. More blood, harder to apply pressure, less chance of it being able to clot before I passed out. He was smiling when he said it, and flushed. Excited. Inside the pantry, I had no idea what I'd grabbed. It could have been a tin of beans or an old saucepan, I just pulled whatever was nearest. I didn't realise exactly what it was until it was all over. The leg had been there from where a chair had broken a few weeks earlier. The rest of it was in the garage. Edward had been meaning to fix it.

'When I stepped out of the pantry he was staring out into the garden, waiting for me to do what I'd been told and go up the stairs. I always went first. It was a master of the house thing with him. He ordered, I obeyed, readied myself. Then he could just walk into the moment and enjoy it. I'm not sure he knew I was still in the kitchen, to be honest. When I think about that moment now, I see it in black and white. I don't know why.'

Maria did know why. She knew perfectly well. Want to show people you were dissociated from your feelings or acting

223

outside your body? You saw it in black and white. Some people had described an out-of-body experience, seeing themselves doing something in the third person. That, she thought, was probably a step too far. The library was an amazing source of information if you were looking to read up on psychology.

'I walked up behind him, raised the chair leg and swung it down on his head. I don't remember hearing anything. There was this buzzing inside my head, and all I could feel was fear. I was scared of what would happen if I didn't do it. Really terrified, like I'd never been before in my life. Edward didn't say anything or turn around. It was a good connection. He sort of . . . crumpled. I stood there a while, I don't know how long. Everything was silent then – as if I'd gone deaf. I must have been in shock because I remember staring out into the garden a while.'

True. The garden had been looking glorious.

'When I came to my senses, I walked into the hallway, took Edward's mobile from his jacket pocket and phoned the police. I told them what I'd done straight away, but by the time they arrived it felt unreal. I was relieved and horrified all at once, but I was glad to be alive, for the first time in years. And I knew I didn't have to cut myself again. I knew I wasn't going to die that night, and that was all that mattered. After nearly twenty years of keeping everything a secret, I just couldn't find a way to explain it in the interview.'

22

There was no mistaking the look on Imogen Pascal's face as she stood up to cross-examine. She was out for blood. James Newell had repeatedly reassured Maria that court cases were never personal for the barristers involved, but winning was clearly personal for Miss Pascal. This was a high profile case, and one the prosecutor did not want to lose.

'Mrs Bloxham,' Pascal started, pausing briefly, but Maria was ready for that one. The prosecutor wanted her to lose her temper. She was determined not to. 'You've painted an extraordinarily unpleasant picture of your husband's character. Do you accept that he was very highly regarded in his professional life?'

'I do,' Maria nodded.

'And that he had no previous criminal convictions indicating any propensity towards violence or dishonesty?'

'I'm sure that's right.' Maria kept her eyes on the desk in front of her.

'So you're the only person who has ever made an accusation of this nature against Dr Bloxham,' Pascal continued.

'As far as I know,' Maria said, keeping her voice neutral. Imogen Pascal was going to follow whatever script she'd written. Trying to score points off her would be futile. All Maria had to remember was not to engage.

'Except for your friend Andrea, of course? Is she going to be appearing as a witness in your defence?'

Maria froze. Andrea, the grief at her loss, was her Achilles heel. It must have been apparent to Imogen Pascal as soon as Maria had started talking about her.

'Most of what Andrea knew about Edward, she'd only heard from me. I didn't feel like I'd left the relationship on good terms. It's been nearly twenty years since we spoke . . .'

'I see, so even your friend Andrea couldn't have given the court any independent evidence. It would all have been what you'd fed her. That explains why she's not here.'

Maria took a shaky breath, giving Miss Pascal the opportunity to continue.

'Well, let's see what see we can agree on. So you met Dr Bloxham when he was volunteering at a charity that offered support to self-harmers. How did you find out about that group?'

'Andrea made enquiries. She thought I needed help to ensure I didn't lapse.'

'Dr Bloxham was volunteering there before you started attending?' Miss Pascal clarified.

Maria nodded.

'You'd accept that this is further evidence of his decency and public mindedness then?'

Maria laughed.

'Is something funny, Mrs Bloxham?'

'You really can't see it?' Maria grinned. 'He was there looking for someone. He found me. It wasn't some happy coincidence. Nothing in Edward's perfectly planned life ever was. He wanted a woman he could control, so he went out to find someone broken. And I think – I *know*, having lived with him for so many years – that he was entranced by watching me cut myself. He wasn't volunteering to help other people. He was only helping himself.'

'You're saying his very presence there was part of some greater plan to get into a relationship with a woman who self-harmed?'

'Yes,' Maria replied firmly.

'May I ask if you've ever been diagnosed with paranoia?' Miss Pascal asked.

'I have not,' Maria said. 'I'd never seen a psychiatrist until this court case.'

'So you would accept then, that it's possible you are suffering from a mental state such as paranoia but you've just never been diagnosed.'

Maria made tight fists with her hands, and the blood began dripping from the wound again. 'I'd think I'd know if I was suffering from a mental illness,' she said.

'Really? You've spent most of your adult life cutting yourself. Perhaps that deserved a diagnosis?'

James Newell stood up. 'The defendant can't answer questions like that. Could we move on?' he asked the judge.

'I'm not crazy!' Maria blurted. 'That's what Edward told me everyone would think. It's not true and it's not fair!'

'Please calm down, Ms Bloxham, no one's saying you're crazy,' the judge reassured her.

DI Anton murmured something unintelligible into the ear of the officer next to him and they both laughed. Maria wanted to slap him.

'I can move on,' Imogen Pascal agreed. She'd got what she wanted. 'For the duration of your marriage you were housed in desirable accommodation in a nice area, and you were not required to earn money to contribute to the household financially?'

'It was the house my husband chose for us. I wasn't allowed to go out to work after the incident where Andrea turned up,' Maria replied.

'And we're back to your absent friend Andrea again. The way you told that part of your story was as if you believed her rather than your husband, who had done nothing before then to make you suspicious of his motives. Would you agree that sounds somewhat paranoid?'

'By then he'd persuaded me to give up my car, was dictating what we would eat and had already refined my clothing choices to what he deemed acceptable. It might be the benefit of hindsight, but I don't believe Andrea made a pass at Edward at our wedding. I believe she was trying to warn me against him only I was either too stubborn or too desperate to see clearly at the time.'

'You said Andrea promised to get in touch when she joined the army. Did she?' Pascal asked.

Maria shook her head. 'No. I wasn't expecting to hear from her for a month or so, and I was distracted. When Edward encouraged me to start self-harming again, for a few weeks I was pretty much consumed by it. It took me a while to realise that we'd stopped getting post altogether after that.'

'I don't see the relevance,' Imogen Pascal tapped her pen on her hand and cocked her head.

'Edward had decided to have all our post redirected to his office. He didn't discuss it with me. When I asked him about it, he said it was to reduce my stress and because it was easier for him to deal with the post at his desk,' Maria said.

'So once again, he was acting in your best interests and handling all the household correspondence, meaning one less responsibility for you,' Pascal replied. Maria didn't have to look up to know she was smiling. It was right there in her voice.

'Actually it meant I had even less contact with the outside world. Not even junk mail. Edward told me there had never been any personal post for me. At the time I told myself that perhaps it was because he'd been telling the truth about Andrea. Later on I realised it was just another way of controlling me. I'm sure Andrea sent me her details. I believe Edward shredded the letter so I couldn't get in touch with her.'

'You keep using the word "realised" Mrs Bloxham, but it wasn't realisation, it was your own assumptions and beliefs. There's no proof of anything you've claimed in this courtroom, is there?'

Maria gritted her teeth. She'd asked for one simple courtesy, and Imogen Pascal couldn't even manage that. Innocent or guilty, every man or woman had a right to be treated with dignity. She took a deep breath and did her best not to shout. 'I'd prefer to be called Ms rather than Mrs. It was mentioned earlier.'

The judge nodded her agreement and peered at Imogen Pascal over her glasses.

'You are still married though, aren't you? So legally you're still Mrs Edward Bloxham.' Miss Pascal smiled politely at her.

Maria gripped the sides of the witness stand, her injured hand a bright white ball of pain.

'I'll be issuing divorce proceedings. It's just a bit more complicated when . . .' Maria broke off. Imogen Pascal had dug a hole for her and she fallen straight in it.

'When the defendant has been so brutally attacked that he can't answer legal proceedings for himself? Is that what you were about to complain about?'

'Bitch,' Maria muttered under her breath.

'Ms Bloxham,' the judge cautioned her. Apparently Maria hadn't been quiet enough. 'This may be stressful, but I won't tolerate the use of bad language or abuse in my courtroom. If you can't exercise some restraint, I will have no choice but to . . .'

'Your Honour, it's not a problem. Please don't intervene on my behalf,' Imogen Pascal cooed, looking more reasonable then ever.

Maria watched as the jury foreperson gave the prosecutor an approving smile. Manipulative bitch, Maria amended to herself. She'd underestimated Imogen Pascal.

'So be it, if you're happy to continue. You've been warned, Ms Bloxham,' the judge said.

Imogen Pascal shook out her gown, head held high, and kept her voice sugary. 'At what point did you suddenly start to distrust Dr Bloxham?' she asked.

'There wasn't a single point, that's not how it worked,' Maria replied, failing to keep the irritation from her voice. James Newell gave her a sharp look. 'Edward was brighter than that. If I had to put a day on it, I'd say it was when he had the landline removed from the house. That was two years after we got married, and by then I had very little contact with the outside world. I wasn't going out at all unless it was with him at the weekend. He didn't want the expense of the home phone as well as his mobile. That was his explanation.'

'So did lots of people phone you regularly before that? Was the landline an important part of your day?' Pascal asked, her voice almost jaunty. Maria glared at her.

'No. No one ever phoned me, but it was there in case of an emergency,' Maria said, forcing calm into her voice in spite of the sense that she was being mocked.

'In case, say, you needed to phone the police. You managed that perfectly well with your husband's mobile after you'd assaulted him so it's not true to claim you were completely cut off from the world, is it?'

'That was the only time I ever touched his mobile phone,' Maria said. 'It was his personal property, not for me to touch.'

'So he had a password or screen security, did he, to stop you using it? If that's the case how did you call the police?'

'No password. He didn't need one. He knew I wouldn't break his rules. I wouldn't have touched it under any other circumstances,' Maria replied.

'All right,' Pascal said. 'So let's take a look at your claim that you were completely cut off from the outside world. There was a television in the house, right?'

'Yes, but . . .'

'Let me finish, please, Mrs Bloxham.' Maria bit her tongue and tried to concentrate. Her feet were feeling numb and the blood that had run down her hand was crusting in the heat. 'There was also a computer in the house. Presumably you know how to send emails and use the internet. It's pretty much impossible to be out of social media circulation in this day and age. In fact, some people would say you were lucky, if indeed your claims were true.'

A titter of laughter from the police officers in court followed the jibe. Maria knew it was designed to throw her off-balance. Imogen Pascal wanted her to lose her temper in the same way she had with the psychiatrist.

'Both the television and the computer were kept in Edward's office. They weren't for me. I wasn't allowed in there. He locked the door whenever he went out,' Maria said.

'You weren't allowed in his office? Ever? You never once set foot in there? But Ms Bloxham, you were thirty-nine years old when this incident occurred. You'd been married for nearly two decades? Are we really supposed to believe you never once entered your husband's study?' Miss Pascal's voice went up a pitch with incredulity. Maria wanted to tell her what she could do with her questions. She wanted to throw the glass of water at the prosecution barrister's superior face and storm out. Instead she picked out the reassuringly bland spot on the wall and imagined she was talking to Ruth, who had never failed to believe her or questioned her. Imogen Pascal might be speaking, but it was Ruth's voice she needed to hear.

'I was allowed in just once a day . . .'

'I'm sorry, we've gone from you never setting foot in the study to you being allowed in once a day. That's a big leap, Mrs Bloxham. Do you even know what the truth is any more or have years of boredom and paranoia completely distorted reality for you?'

'No!' Maria shouted, catching her temper halfway through the word so that it died in her throat. 'You interrupted me. I was saying Edward let me in there once each day while he was there, to clean out the fireplace, empty his waste paper bin, and vacuum as necessary. I meant I never went in there alone. The only time I touched his computer was to dust it.'

'Come now, are you really claiming you weren't allowed to watch the television at any time in the last twenty-odd years?' Imogen Pascal huffed.

'I was allowed to in the first couple of years of our marriage, but Edward didn't like it. He said it was bad for my brain and created unreal social expectations. He watched it, though. I could hear it through his study door in the evenings.' She remembered sitting on the hallway floor once listening to the canned laughter of some comedy, wishing she could be allowed to watch it too. She'd asked his permission the next day to be allowed some television time, perhaps one evening a week. Edward had laughed and asked what it was she thought she needed comic relief from, given the fact that she had no strains or worries in her life. The conversation had been closed.

'I'd like to ask you about a mobile telephone that police found hidden in one of your shoes in the bottom of your wardrobe.' Miss Pascal reached behind herself and an officer slid a clear plastic bag containing the mobile into her hand. It was given an exhibit number and passed by the usher to Maria. 'Is this yours?'

'It is,' Maria said, risking a glance in the direction of the jury. A couple were whispering to one another. Some were shaking their heads. Imogen Pascal had scored some points.

'So, far from being cut off from the outside world, you actually had your own personal mobile device. Who paid for it and who paid for the credit for you to make calls?'

'I paid for it. I never made any calls though,' Maria muttered.

'But you didn't have access to money. How could you possibly have bought yourself a phone?'

'I saved up coins I found around the house. Back of the sofa, in Edward's pockets when I was doing the washing, that sort of thing,' Maria replied.

'So you were stealing from your husband? He didn't know you were taking those coins and spending his money on phones?' The prosecutor managed to mix the perfect level of concern and disbelief as she rammed her point home.

'Not phones, just one phone,' Maria said. 'I never had the courage to make any calls. There was no credit on the phone when it was found.'

'But your story seems to change whenever a question is asked. Why is that?'

'Nothing's the way you're making it sound,' Maria said, forcing herself to look Imogen Pascal in the eyes.

'Or perhaps you're lying,' Imogen Pascal countered.

James Newell stood up. 'Miss Pascal needs to limit herself to questions. My client is not here to be engaged in an argument.'

'Quite so,' the judge agreed. 'Move your questioning along, Miss Pascal.'

'Let's move to the crux of the matter then, shall we? Are you claiming that you struck your husband a blow intended to kill him, in self-defence?' Miss Pascal asked, sliding off her glasses dramatically as she completed her question, then tossing them onto the desk and leaning back against her seat, arms folded.

'I am,' Maria replied simply.

'You actually believed that you were sufficiently under his power that he could have persuaded you to cut yourself so seriously that you would have died?'

'I did. I still do,' Maria said, knowing it sounded far-fetched, steeling herself against the barrage of questions that would follow.

'But you weren't locked in the house. You spent each day in your garden, so you could get in and out of the back door. When the police arrived at the scene, you'd opened the front door. How is it possible that attempting to kill a man was a safer option than simply walking out? You said yourself, he never hit you. He never laid a finger on you. Why not just leave?'

Maria sighed. It was a reasonable question. It was, in fact, the same question she'd asked herself month after month and year after year of a marriage that had chipped away at her soul until there was practically nothing left.

'I had no one else. Nowhere to go. No money. No job. To start with, that was a good enough reason for staying, back when things weren't so bad . . .' Maria began.

'So you were just using your husband for what you could get out of him at that stage?' Pascal interjected.

'I'm sure that's the way you want to present it to the jury,' Maria snapped. James Newell raised his palm a few inches off the desk, nothing dramatic, but it was the signal they'd agreed that she had to calm herself down. Maria took a breath. 'I was a lost young woman, quite naive, and I was scared. Later on, when things became unbearable, I did try to leave.'

'Try to leave? Is he supposed to take responsibility for all your failings? You're an educated woman. You speak well, and you clearly understand these proceedings. You've told the court you were in employment during your early marriage, so you could have got a job and supported yourself. You weren't entirely dependent on your husband, although perhaps you chose to be.'

'I didn't choose any of it! Not one single day. Choice is about knowledge and free will,' Maria shouted.

'But Mrs Bloxham, there's no evidence of any of this. No proof of a single word of it. Not one witness is here to tell the court about Dr Bloxham's alleged bad treatment of you. How and why is the jury supposed to believe you?'

The jurors were staring at her. And the judge. Maria turned slightly to see if Ruth was nearby, instead meeting the sea of journalists' eyes. They were waiting for an answer, only there wasn't one. There just wasn't.

'I don't know,' Maria muttered. 'I just . . .' Her voice trailed off.

Imogen Pascal let the silence hang for thirty seconds before continuing. 'All right. Well, you've already stated that Dr Bloxham never laid a finger on you, so you acknowledge he never physically prevented you from leaving, in which case I can move on.'

'He threatened to have me committed to a mental hospital,' Maria blurted, desperate not to lose the argument entirely. 'And there was the sex.'

'Which you accepted you consented to. How much did you stand to inherit in terms of marital assets if Dr Bloxham died?' Imogen Pascal continued.

'Actually Miss Pascal, I think the jury should hear what the defendant has to say about the alleged threat to have her committed,' the judge intervened.

Miss Pascal nodded at Maria. 'You were saying?'

'We'd been married about five years when I first told Edward how unhappy I was and that I was leaving. He said everything I knew he would, so I was ready for it – how I wouldn't cope on my own, how he wouldn't support me financially – I told him I didn't care and that I'd made my mind up. He got cross, more angry than I'd ever seen him before. I went upstairs to pack a bag and he came after me. He said that if I ever left him, he would have me committed. He said he'd accuse me of attacking him and say I was a serious suicide risk. He even . . . he pulled up my skirt and pointed at the scars on my thighs. I had a history of cutting that was detailed on my early medical records, so he knew he could prove long-term self-harm to a psychiatrist if he had to, and the scars by that time were fresh and so much worse. As bad as living in a house with Edward was, at least I had relative freedom. I wasn't being drugged or locked in one small room every day. It's what I've always been most scared of, people thinking I was a danger to myself because of the cutting. He knew that, and I knew he wasn't making hollow threats. He'd sooner have seen me institutionalised for life than let me leave him. He repeated the same threat regularly during the remainder of our marriage, whenever he sensed that I was rebelling against his control. That's why I stayed.'

James Newell smiled at her kindly, gently, from his position nearer the jury. Maria looked along their row, knowing she needed to be brave enough to make eye contact to have any hope of them believing her. Not all, but a few of them met her eyes: the two younger males, and two of the females. It was a tiny victory, but a victory nonetheless.

'I was asking you before how much you stood to gain if Dr Bloxham died,' Pascal continued as if she had never been interrupted. 'Are you able to put a figure on it?'

'I never even considered it,' Maria said. 'I have no idea what my husband has in terms of assets apart from the house, and I don't know if there is a mortgage on that or not. I hadn't dealt with finances for two decades. I hardly ever left the house.'

'But you stood to inherit substantially in excess of one million pounds,' Imogen Pascal said. 'It's ridiculous to say you had no idea how wealthy Dr Bloxham was.'

'I never dealt with the money. I didn't see one bank statement. How was I supposed to know how much money he had?'

'You've already told us how. You knew he was constantly in work. He was at pains to tell you about his book deals and television appearances, articles in magazines. You knew all about the planning applications he consulted on and his university lecturing. Your evidence on that has been most compelling. Are you about to say you thought he did all that for free?'

'I didn't say that,' Maria replied, her cheeks flushing.

'So he was being paid well and you didn't live a lavish lifestyle. Were there expensive holidays?'

'There were no holidays at all,' Maria growled.

'And only one car to run. No children. No other obvious expenses. Frankly it's preposterous to suggest you didn't realise there were savings,' Miss Pascal continued.

'I didn't say there weren't any, I just didn't know exactly how much . . .'

'You've told us Dr Bloxham was careful with money though. Liked to save rather than spend, that's the impression we've got. Right?'

'Um, yes,' Maria said. She felt faint. This wasn't how she'd imagined it going.

'So you were living in a beautiful house, with low expenses, and your husband had a good income and liked saving. You knew the two of you were well off, didn't you? That sort of money is a pretty good motive for attempting to kill someone, wouldn't you agree?'

'It wasn't my motive,' Maria replied plainly.

'Really? You see, you've had the benefit of years to plan this. You've clearly built up a certain amount of resentment towards Dr Bloxham, perhaps disappointment at how little you've done with your life . . .'

'He took my life away from me. I didn't resent him, I hated him. He belittled me and threatened to have me locked up,' Maria countered.

'Yes, you hated him, and you're a woman with a temper, aren't you? You don't like to answer questions, you don't like to be challenged. Your behaviour with the psychiatrist is clear evidence of just how reactive you are.'

'That was his fault. He was goading me. He wanted me to talk about the most intimate parts of my life, to draw up a report for your benefit. I agreed to talk to him and he was vile!' Maria knew she was raising her voice, but there seemed to be nothing she could do about it.

'So you swore at him and walked out. Forgive me, Mrs Bloxham, but the woman who was able to stand up to a highly qualified professional with no difficulty at all seems to be a far cry from the poor, pathetic, emotionally abused victim you're choosing to pretend to be in court today!'

Newell was on his feet before Maria could respond. 'Miss Pascal is going to have to apologise for that,' he said.

'I'm not apologising for cross-examining effectively,' Imogen Pascal bit back.

'Cross-examination comprises asking relevant questions, not being abusive and insulting. Let's try and comply with at least a few rules, shall we?' Newell said.

'It's all right,' Maria said.

'Just wait a moment please, Ms Bloxham,' the judge said, raising a silencing finger in her direction.

Maria looked from judge to prosecutor to defence as they continued to argue, bemusement on the jurors' faces, whispers from the public gallery. Stepping down from the witness box while the prison guard was distracted by the contretemps, moving to the side where the jury could see her, and keeping her back to the public and press benches, she raised her skirt until it was just a couple of inches below the line of her underwear.

James Newell noticed first, the argument dying on his lips.

'Maria,' he said, dispensing with formalities and using her first name.

'Ms Bloxham,' the judge peered over the edge of her bench. 'You must retake your place immed . . .' The prison guard finally caught up and reached out to take hold of Maria's arm, pulling her back towards the witness box. 'Let her go,' Judge Downey instructed. 'Can all members of the jury see this clearly?'

One by one, the twelve of them nodded.

Maria held her skirt up long enough to make sure no one would forget the mess that was her thighs. The skin was discoloured from white through pinks and angry reds to browns where the scar tissue was harshest. The texture was thick impasto oil-painting brushstrokes that raised right off her legs. In some places the scars had failed to knit together fully, leaving jagged red seams like lava flow. The judge let the jury take their time before coughing politely and speaking again. 'For the court record, Ms Bloxham is showing the court the substantial scarring between her knees and the fronts of her thighs on both legs. I hope both counsel will agree it can be described as extensive.' Newell and Pascal both nodded. 'Thank you. You may go back into the witness box now.' Maria did as she was told. 'Miss Pascal, continue cross-examination.'

'Ms Bloxham,' Imogen Pascal used her preferred title, presumably not daring to anger the judge again so soon. 'Why did you not give this explanation to the police as soon as you were arrested? They have no record of you pointing out the damage to your thighs.'

'I couldn't cope at that stage. I was in shock over what I'd done, and I was still concerned that I might be declared a danger to myself and locked up. Edward had spent so many years convincing me that was what would happen, it took a long time for me to have any faith in myself.'

'Isn't the truth that he was deeply concerned about you, and trying to protect you from being committed to a mental hospital?'

'No!' Maria shouted.

'Didn't he oversee your self-harming as a gesture of kindness, to make sure you never took it too far?'

'What? How can you say that?' Maria slammed the desk.

'And all the time you were planning and plotting to kill him. You just waited for that one perfect moment when he turned his back, then you struck,' Pascal continued.

'That's not true,' she hissed.

'And the real victim here is Dr Bloxham, not just for the crater you put in his skull, but for having years of generosity and care repaid with a bloodbath and endless lies.'

'I told you what it was like, what I went through! How would you have felt, trapped inside that house, abused, treated like a slave . . .'

'And you had a much earlier opportunity to explain your version of events when you saw the psychiatrist. He could then have evaluated what you had to say. You still chose silence over explanation.'

'Professor Worth didn't want to be persuaded. I knew as soon as I met him that whatever I said, he was going to conclude that either I was mentally ill or just plain dangerous. I assumed I'd just be giving him more reasons to say I should be locked up,' Maria said, her own anger deflated by the looks on the jurors' faces, which even now were slack with shock at what she'd shown them.

'But Dr Bloxham never held the blade, never made a cut. He never forced you to cut yourself or threatened you if you did not. That's right isn't it?'

'It was more complex than that. He used psychology as a weapon,' Maria replied, feeling naked and vulnerable once more.

'So you could have thrown the razor blades out of the window, or even, and think about this a moment, or even just said, "No, I'm not going to cut myself any more." That's right, isn't it?'

'I was desperate, and I guess addicted by then, and so unhappy that it was my only escape. He knew I'd never say no to him,' Maria muttered.

'Ah, so that's the truth of it. It was easier to bludgeon your husband to death, or so you intended, than to deal with your own addiction. You intended to kill him, you did your utmost to kill him, all because you enjoyed self-harming too much to exercise the mental strength to stop. Isn't that the reality of it?'

'The reality?' Maria blurted. 'My reality was cleaning and cooking and sitting alone while he relaxed in the only room in the house where there was noise and colour and light. No friends, no colleagues, no neighbours. Gates that bastard had built to lock the world out and to keep me in. My reality was living every day with a man who expected adulation on tap. I answered his fan mail, for God's sake! I spent half my life on my knees cleaning fireplaces because he preferred open fires. Do you think he ever said thank you? Do you think he ever made me a cup of tea? Every single day was the same. Prioritise Edward, don't annoy him, think of ways to please him. Don't be offended when he called me his lapdog. Don't answer back when he told me my cooking was shit. Persuade myself that him checking my dusting was actually him being interested in my life. Why the hell should anyone, anyone in the fucking world, have to live like that? It's like I've just woken up from the coma I've been in half my life!' she shouted. 'You want me to tell you I'm sorry? That hitting Edward was a mistake. Well, I'm not and it wasn't!' Maria slammed her fist into the witness stand, sending the booklet of photos flying, and upending the glass. 'The truth, in case you're actually interested, is that I hated him. The only reason I'm here is because I finally gave as good as I got.'

Imogen Pascal put down her pen, closed her notebook and smiled warmly at the judge. 'No further cross-examination,' she said. 'But I am applying to recall the prosecution psychiatrist, Professor Worth. Given the details now revealed by the defendant which she chose not to share with our expert, it seems only right that the jury hears a professional assessment on how they relate to the case. We won't be able to get him here tomorrow, so I have to ask for an adjournment for a day, but he's available the day after that.'

'It's a reasonable request. Adjournment granted. Have Professor Worth here at 10 a.m. the next day. Counsels' speeches to follow thereafter,' Judge Downey decided. 'The jury may leave the courtroom now.'

They filed out with much shaking of heads and muttering as Maria watched, rueing her final words, knowing she had played straight into the prosecution's hands. Perhaps it was natural justice. She had to pay some price for what she'd done. Until now she'd maintained a little hope that the penalty wouldn't be quite so great.

23

Lottie awoke still seeing the scarring on Maria Bloxham's thighs, terrified in that befuddling fusion of dreams that her own body was equally scarred. She scrabbled beneath the sheets, running her hands across her still smooth skin before coming to her senses and sitting up. Zain was zipping up his case.

'You all right?' he asked, slipping his wallet into his jacket.

'Bad dream,' Lottie panted, rubbing her eyes. 'You should have woken me. I'd have made you breakfast.'

'That's all right, I'll stop and get some on the road. It's a good job they've given you a day off. Jury service is obviously exhausting you,' he smiled.

'More than you know,' Lottie said. 'When are you back?'

'Tomorrow evening. Call the mobile if you need me,' he said. 'I should go.' He left without kissing her goodbye and Lottie was glad. She could hardly bear to let him touch her these days, torn between guilt and longing for Cameron, and the desire to escape the trappings of domesticity. A night without Zain was exactly what she needed to clear her head and decide what she really wanted.

'Mummy, can I have chocolate for breakfast as daddy's gone?' Daniyal grinned from the doorway.

She opened her arms to him and he ran for the hug. 'Well, now,' she said, mussing his hair, 'I think maybe a little bit of chocolate if you promise to eat a bowl of fresh fruit. How does that sound?' He grinned and raced off to the kitchen. 'Quickly though, we've got to be at your childminder's in an hour,' she shouted as he disappeared. It was bad of her, she thought, sending Danny to childcare when she wasn't in court, but they'd been given too little notice for her to cancel. At this stage she'd have to pay for him anyway, and the truth was that she was looking forward to having a day to herself. It was such a rare treat. She had nothing planned other than a hot bath, maybe a movie in bed, and no housework at all.

By the time Cameron texted her, she had already dropped a moaning Daniyal at the childminder's. He claimed to have stomach ache, but Lottie suspected it was more a case of knowing she was at home and doing his best to have the day with his mum. Not today, she told herself. She wasn't giving in. It was time she started treating herself to some alone time.

There was a moment when Lottie considered simply deleting Cameron's text or turning off her mobile, but neither were long-term solutions. He wasn't going to be put off that easily, and she was flattered. It was good to feel eighteen and free again, even if reality was much more complicated. The near miss with the Tabithas had left her shaken. Having Cameron by her side in the courtroom was as reassuring as it was physically distracting. The conflict inside her raged on. She just needed to be firm with him, that was all. Zain was away, Danny was being looked after, and she wanted some peace and quiet. She rang him.

'Hey you,' Cameron said brightly. 'I wasn't expecting to hear your voice. What are you up to?'

'Not much. You?'

'Trying to get yesterday out of my head and failing,' he replied. 'I just needed to talk about it. I don't suppose you can escape into town for a while and meet up? We have to be able to find somewhere the Tabithas won't spot us.'

Lottie checked her watch. 'Probably not a good idea,' she said. 'Zain's away overnight. I've got to pick Daniyal up at five. Also, there's no way we should risk being seen together in town. The Tabithas have eyes everywhere.'

'Fair point,' he said, 'but I really would like to talk.'

'We're talking now,' she laughed.

'I know, but it's not the same. Yesterday was . . . I don't even know how to describe it.'

'I know,' Lottie said quietly. 'I feel the same. It was hard to listen to. And her thighs . . .'

'Don't,' Cameron sighed. 'I couldn't get them out of my head all evening. Please Lottie. I need you. If Zain's away, why don't we meet nearer to your house?'

'Because then we're likely to bump into someone I know from round here. Seriously Cam, I think it's unwise.' The thought of what might happen if they were alone together remained unspoken. Like a drug, having tasted it twice, she wasn't sure she could deny herself it again. She did want to talk though. The trial was burning a hole in her mind, and no amount of hot baths or TV was going to distract her.

'How about I bring food to you, then? At least that way we definitely won't be seen in public. I'll even park in the next road so no one sees my van. Give me an hour?' Cameron asked. In the background Lottie could hear him pick up his keys.

'I don't know,' she murmured. 'It might be a bit weird.'

'I'd suggest mine, only I'd need a week's notice. I'm not the best at tidying since . . . you know.'

Lottie jolted at the thought of him living alone in the space he'd once occupied with his fiancée, arriving home to the emptiness. 'Sure,' she said, making her mind up. 'Come on over. My neighbours are all at work anyway but it might be better if you left the van out of the drive. See you in an hour then.'

It was amazing that an hour could pass both so fast and so slowly. She checked her watch every five minutes, changing her clothes three times, redoing her hair, and putting on too much make-up then taking it off again, all the time telling herself nothing could happen between them. Or at least that nothing should happen between them. Assuring herself that she wasn't so disloyal as to let Cameron touch her in the house she shared with Zain. He just wanted to talk about the case. She did, too. Damn Tabitha and the stupid rules. After court yesterday the jurors had said their goodbyes quietly, each one of them lost in their own thoughts. Even Cameron had been distracted and quiet. Lottie thought Jack had been close to tears. She had focused on getting back to Daniyal and looking after him, doing her best to block out the day. Now it was hard to think about anything else. It was just as well the judge had adjourned until tomorrow. Lottie wasn't sure she was ready to set foot in the courtroom again just yet. The doorbell rang while she was still throwing make-up back in the bathroom drawer. She ran down to open up with butterflies in her stomach and a hesitant smile on her face.

Cameron entered quickly, a plastic bag in each hand. 'Hope you're hungry. Which way's the kitchen?'

'How many people did you think you were feeding?' she laughed, pointing along the hallway to the end. Cameron went ahead of her.

'You know what it's like. You pick up strawberries, then you see the raspberries, and before you know it a simple baguette and cheese lunch has turned into a royal banquet. So here you go, Your Majesty. All we need is plates and cutlery. No cooking required.'

He was so thoughtful. The food was amazing, ideal for a summer lunch, and Daniyal would love finishing all the fresh fruit they couldn't eat. How typical of Cameron to know instinctively what she would like.

'So how are you feeling after yesterday?' he asked, dipping a chunk of bread in hummus.

'Actually I had a nightmare about it. The whole thing was so intense. Now I don't know what I feel. When Maria Bloxham was talking I felt really sorry for her, but then when Miss Pascal was asking her questions, the defendant's version of events started to sound ridiculous. How is it possible that she didn't ever walk out? Whatever he'd threatened her with, did she really need to kill him? It's kind of hard to understand how their whole life together ended in that one awful moment.'

'But the skin on her legs . . . I wouldn't wish that on my worst enemy,' Cameron said, pouring Lottie a glass of Prosecco.

'Just a small glass,' she said. 'I have to drive later, remember?'

'I can't believe she'd have done that much damage to her skin if she hadn't been massively unhappy for years. And remember the lock on his study door? I thought it was weird when we visited. No TV anywhere else in the house. No landline. What she said about her life made sense to me.'

Lottie took a handful of grapes and some brie, sipping her drink as she thought about it. 'The problem is that we haven't heard any version except hers. The story that no one else ever went into their house gives her an excuse for smashing his skull in, and it means no one can contradict her. I did wonder what Dr Bloxham would have said about it, if he was still able to speak.'

'I thought she seemed honest,' Cameron said, selecting the largest of the strawberries and offering it across the table to Lottie. She bit into it, laughing as red juice dribbled down her chin.

'Her scars though,' she said, sobering up again as the memory hit her. 'Surely you've got to be pretty disturbed to do that. Unbalanced. Maybe she is paranoid, like Miss Pascal suggested. What if Dr Bloxham kept a lock on his study door to have somewhere he could get away from her? What if she really couldn't cope with the pressure of work and he was left with some reclusive wife who just never left the house? How the hell are we supposed to reach conclusions when the two options are polar opposites?'

'I think if she was that crazy, her legal team would be running a defence that involved pleading she was insane or something. Their house might be worth a small fortune but it gave me the creeps. It was so empty. I reckon I'm a pretty good judge of character, and I thought he was a smug git on that hedgehog video. Can you imagine letting him touch you?'

'Oh that's gross, don't say things like that!'

'Why not? I think you need to be human about it. I'm not interested in what the lawyers say. I know how I feel, that's what matters, right?' Cameron ripped off a chunk of baguette and grabbed the butter.

'Well, I've reached no conclusion about any of it yet. I seem to change my mind every hour. I guess I'm just hoping that somehow, by the end, it'll be obvious who's telling the truth.'

Cameron smiled at her, wiping his hands on his jeans and walking around to her side of the table to kneel in front of her. 'Let's not think about it any more today. It's our day off and I say we've both earned it.' He picked up her right hand and brushed his lips over her knuckles. 'And although I promised myself that I was only coming here as a friend, seeing you sitting in the sunshine with strawberry juice on your lips, I know I'll never forgive myself if I don't kiss you.'

'Cam . . .' Lottie whispered as he slid his free hand into her hair and gently pulled her head towards his. 'We shouldn't,' she added just before her lips found his. She pulled away after a few seconds. 'This is my family home. I'm not comfortable.' But his lips were warm and his body was hard. He was so full of life and exciting, completely at odds to the horrors of the case that was consuming them, and so very different to her conventional marriage.

'It's just bricks and mortar,' Cameron said. 'Family is people, not a place. Does Zain really feel like family to you right now?'

No, Lottie thought, not prepared to go so far as to say it aloud.

'Did you have this planned all along?' she asked him.

'Can we agree that it might have been in my subconscious?' he grinned. 'And maybe, if I'm honest, it's lonely going back to an empty flat each night. Being with you makes me feel part of something again.'

Lottie melted inside. She felt exactly the same. The gulf between her and Zain had been getting wider and wider.

Cameron slid his arm around her back to bring their bodies closer together. Lottie tried to keep her body apart from his, but he was already between her legs, crushing her against him. His tongue was brushing against the tip of hers, exploring but not pushing, inviting but not intruding. She knew she should stop him. It was Zain's house and Daniyal's home. But Cameron's hands were soft and warm, the tips of his nails running down her spine, making her arch her back and press her mouth more firmly against his.

He pulled back, framing her face with his hands and staring into her eyes. 'I can't stop thinking about you,' he said. 'I've tried Lottie. I know you have a family, but I don't know how to stay away from you.'

'Me too,' she said, tears filling her eyes. 'It would have been easier if we'd never met.'

'Don't say that,' he murmured, gently wiping the droplets from her cheeks. 'I'll never regret finding you.' He leaned forward and put his mouth against her neck just below her ear, brushing the delicate skin with his teeth, tasting her, as Lottie tipped her head back and let him consume her. She didn't regret it either. How could she regret feeling this alive again? It was as if they were meant to be together. Fate was to blame.

Cameron stood up, taking her gently by the hands so that she joined him.

'Spare bedroom?' he suggested.

Lottie hesitated. Going with him into the spare bedroom meant passing Daniyal's bedroom door. It would be half open, the way he always left it. Good Dog, his beloved cuddly toy, would be sitting on the end of his bed. His pyjamas would be folded on his pillow where she'd left them. The photo of her, Zain and Daniyal at a safari park would be smiling down from the wall.

'I'd rather stay downstairs,' she said, running one hand down Cameron's arm, distracting herself from thoughts of her family with the knowledge of what lay beneath his shirt.

Running his hands up from her hips, he gripped the edges of her top and inch by inch raised it, staring at the skin revealed beneath. Lottie swayed against him.

'No, stay back there,' he said. 'I have to look at you. I want to burn every part of you into my brain.'

Lottie let him look as if she were on a pedestal, loving the pure desire on his face.

Her mobile rang.

'Leave it,' he said.

'I can't. I have responsibilities, remember? Just one minute.' She dived into her handbag and grabbed the phone. The childminder was calling. 'Yeah, hi. Everything okay?'

'Not really. Daniyal says he feels sick. I was wondering, if you weren't too busy, perhaps the best thing would be for you to collect him,' the childminder said.

'Has he actually been sick?' Lottie asked.

'Well no, but he is pale and . . .'

Lottie rolled her eyes. Danny knew she was at home. She should have realised he'd try this. 'Give it an hour and see if he perks up then,' she suggested. 'He's probably just been jumping up and down too much.'

'I don't think that's it,' the childminder said. 'He really is quite insistent.'

Lottie looked at Cameron. If he weren't there she'd have gone to fetch Danny in a heartbeat, but today . . .

'Call me back if he gets any worse,' Lottie said, adding, 'and thanks for letting me know.' She hung up.

'Problem?' Cameron asked.

'Danny's a bit off colour. I'm sure it'll pass,' she said, drowning her guilt in another mouthful of Prosecco.

'Come here then,' he said, pulling her back towards him and putting warm lips on her neck. Arms up,' he ordered, tugging the pink cotton over her head and throwing it onto a chair. 'If I could have created a woman from scratch, she'd have been you.'

Lottie put her fingers on his top button.

'One minute,' he said, scrabbling in his pockets to remove his keys and mobile. 'Let me just silence this thing.' He pressed a couple of buttons and abandoned everything next to the sink. 'Now, if I'm not mistaken, you were about to take my shirt off. Is that right?'

'Maybe,' Lottie laughed. 'Did you have any objections?'

'Only that you don't do it too slowly. I'm not sure I can't wait much longer to feel my body against yours,' he grinned.

She made quick work of his buttons, slipping the shirt from his shoulders, taking her time to enjoy the sight of him as much as he'd enjoyed her. Cameron grabbed her wrist, spinning her round so she was standing against the kitchen table, pushing her hair to one side and running his tongue up the nape of her neck, as he undid her bra strap and flicked the lace off her shoulders. Wrapping his left arm firmly around her waist, he stared down at her breasts from over her shoulders, sliding his right hand down her neck, along her collar bone, and over the upper swell to her nipple, circling the pink flesh until Lottie couldn't stand it any more.

'Let me turn round,' she panted. 'I want to touch you, too.'

'Not yet,' he said, moving his hand down to the button of her jeans, popping it open and following with the zip. Lottie looked down, watching his hands shifting the denim down over her hips, letting it fall from her thighs to the floor where she picked up each foot in turn and kicked her ankles free.

'You still seem to be overdressed,' Cameron laughed, dipping his fingertips gently beneath the silk of her panties. 'You must be far too hot in those.'

'You're wearing a lot more clothes than me,' Lottie replied, gasping as he ran his hand over the top of the material to explore between her legs. 'How about we even things up a bit?'

'I guess that's only fair,' he said, letting her twist in his arms to face him and strip off his jeans.

'Seriously . . . no underwear? Were you that sure this was going to happen?' Lottie shook her head.

'Nothing like that, just too warm for layers, that's all. Speaking of which, let me help you with those.' He ripped the panties down then picked her up, sitting her on the edge of the table, gently parting her legs to stand between her thighs, bringing his mouth back down onto hers, pushing his tongue harder against hers.

Lottie wrapped her legs around him and let him lower her down onto the table, amidst the crumbs and stray blueberries.

'Make love to me,' Lottie murmured, tightening her legs around him.

'You sure about this, Lottie?' Cameron asked, lifting his head from between her breasts to look her in the eyes.

'Yes. I want you, and I don't want to wait any more,' she said, raising her pelvis to meet him, pulling herself onto him, crying out as she met the rhythm of his movements. Her mobile began buzzing with a text message alert as she gripped Cameron's body with her legs.

He held her hip with one hand and wrapped his free fingers in her hair, as he moved faster inside her. Lottie groaned, her breath as hot and dry as the sunshine blinding her through the garden windows. She came first, shuddering against him. Cameron answered her cries with a guttural groan, arching his back and thrusting harshly, falteringly, before collapsing onto her.

They stayed like that, recovering, catching their breath with foreheads touching, smiling, before Cameron pushed himself off the table to stare down at her.

'You're like some Roman goddess, surrounded by fruit,' he laughed. 'And I think most of the strawberries may be crushed under your shoulders.'

'Didn't even feel them,' she grinned. 'Sounds as if I've got some cleaning up to do.'

'No, you don't,' he said. 'You get to go and take a long, hot shower while I clean up. What sort of man would I be if I let you do all the work?'

Her phone buzzed again. Lottie sat herself up and stared at the food carnage around her. 'Damn, where did I put my mobile?' she asked as she stood up to search for it, avoiding squashing berries underfoot. 'That's quite some mess we made. Oh shit. The childminder's trying to reach me again. I missed a call when we were . . .' Being too noisy to hear the ringtone, she thought.

'It'll be fine,' Cameron said, wrapping his arms around her from behind as she reread the frantic sounding text message.

'Kids are sick all the time. Five minutes from now, he'll be running around again. He probably just ate too fast.'

'I guess,' Lottie said.

'Hey, she's a childminder. They're trained to deal with this. If you'd been in court, she'd have had to deal with it anyway. What's the difference?'

'That's true,' Lottie said quietly.

'So don't rush off. She'll phone back if it's serious,' he kissed her ear gently. 'Let me clean this up then I'll join you. Go get the water hot,' he said, winking as he began picking berries off the floor.

Lottie watched as Cameron swept the debris from the table and into one of the bags. He was amazing, she thought, and better than that, she felt amazing too. Also, he was right. If the case hadn't been adjourned for a day, the childminder would just have coped. She was only phoning because she knew Lottie was at home. What harm could it do to take a shower and enjoy the moment? She was in no fit state to leave the house, or to see Daniyal, not yet anyway. She drifted to the stairs, telling herself not to look at the family photos on the walls. Zain would never find out, and what he didn't know could never hurt him. Just as along as she was careful.

Five minutes later she was showered and getting dressed again. Cameron wandered in to join her, looking around the bedroom appreciatively.

'This is nice,' he said. 'Really comfortable. Did you design it yourself?'

The sight of him naked in the doorway Zain had entered thousands of times, was a bucket of ice to her conscience. Cameron standing in the space her son ran through to kiss her good morning. Her lover in the bedroom her husband had paid for, and had decorated himself in Lottie's favourite colours.

'Yeah, listen, Cam. I can't leave Danny any longer. I know I said we'd shower together but I should get going.'

'Hey, don't panic,' he said, sitting on the bed and reaching a hand out for her.

'I'm sorry. I'm just not okay with you being upstairs. Let's go back down . . .'

'Lottie,' he said. 'You're freaking out. What we just did isn't something you need to feel guilty about. I care about you.'

'Yeah, I know. I care about you too,' she said, pulling on trainers. 'But it wasn't right to leave Danny when I could have gone to get him. I'm just going to do my hair, and please don't take this the wrong way. I really appreciate lunch, and you clearing up, but I need to speed up. Could you let yourself out? Please don't be mad.'

'Hey,' he said, standing up and kissing her lightly on the cheek. 'I'm not the kind of guy who gets mad. Not ever. You can count on me.' She waited until she heard him click the front door shut before tidying the covers where he'd sat on her bed, then dragging a brush through her hair before running for the door herself. Bad mother, she thought. That's what I've become. A bloody terrible mother, in fact. It was never going to happen again.

24

Maria sat in Queen Square park and threw crumbs at the pigeons. The tree-lined green with a horseman at its centre and a star of pathways was always busy but people rarely sat still there for long. It was more a passing-through kind of park. She saw Ruth coming from a distance, with her unmistakable bold steps and broad shoulders. Taking a seat on the same bench as Maria, Ruth stretched out her long legs and closed her eyes in the sunshine.

'Is this casual enough for you?' Ruth asked.

'Almost too casual,' Maria laughed. 'You can look at me, you know.'

Ruth rolled her head to smile at her friend. 'I won't ask how you are. I was in court yesterday. I can't imagine how it must have been dissecting your private life in public. Did you sleep?'

'A little. I really don't want to rehash yesterday. How are the twins?'

'Maria, you need to talk about it. The prosecution is recalling the psychiatrist. You're going to have to listen to more of his rubbish. I'd like to prepare you for what he's likely to say,' Ruth said, extending her arm halfway along the space between them, not quite daring to reach out all the way.

'I need a friend now, not a counsellor. Let me hear about you instead. Professor Worth will say whatever he's going to say. You can't stop it.'

'But you can't react . . .'

'Like I did yesterday? I know I shouldn't have lost my temper. I seem to be doing it more often these days. I think I'm catching up on years of repressed emotions. How's your mother?'

'Still screaming at people out of the car window. Last weekend she deliberately dropped a box of a dozen eggs at the supermarket to see what sound it would make. Most of the time she still thinks my father's alive. The worst of it is telling her each time that he's dead. Seeing the look of grief on her face over and over again is tough.'

'Thank goodness she's got you,' Maria smiled. 'What about Lea and Max?'

'They still haven't figured out that being twins isn't a competition. I've got to be honest, dropping them off at the nursery is something of a relief at the moment. They're climbing every chair, sofa and chest of drawers they can find, and food has become a weapon. Two years is not the easiest age.'

'Do you remember the call when you told me you were pregnant? I think I was more excited than you. That news kept me going for months.'

'I remember hearing the change in your voice. You were so supportive when I said I'd chosen IVF. Everyone else thought I was crazy having children with no partner.'

'Now look at you, still running the helpline while you organise a whole family on your own. I'm surprised you get a moment to yourself,' Maria said.

'Listen to you giving me a lecture,' Ruth chided gently. 'I like the new hairstyle. Does it feel strange after so long to be in control of your own life?'

'It feels as if I just got out of prison,' Maria said.

Ruth's face registered the awful irony of the sentence. 'We can still tell the court you were in contact with me,' she said. 'I'm the one person who can back up what you've said about how he treated you. The prosecution's building its case on the basis that you're making up how bad things were. Contemporaneous complaints would counteract that.'

'No, they wouldn't. If you tell the jury I was able to save up for phone credit, sneak out of the house to the shop, and make contact with you, it'll just support the case that I was strong enough to have left him. You were the someone I could turn to. All my claims that I was completely alone in the world would be undone.' Maria smiled. 'It wouldn't work and you know it. The conversations you've recorded are proof of what I said to you, but they're not proof of what was actually happening. The prosecution will tell the jury that it was just the ramblings of a disturbed mind, or that I was attention seeking. They'll twist it – I can hear Imogen Pascal's voice right now. "So Mrs Bloxham, you leave the house to buy phone credit, but you couldn't get yourself to a domestic violence shelter, or to a doctor? That hardly seems credible."' Maria was pleased with her impression of the prosecutor, but Ruth wasn't smiling.

'Coercive control is complex. It's different in every single case. You were in no position to make reasoned, rational decisions. Very few victims have an understanding of how much jeopardy they're in until it's too late.'

'It still boils down to my word against his, and given that he can't speak the jury are naturally going to feel suspicious of me. James Newell still has to make a speech to the jury. I have faith in him.'

'The prosecution gets to make a closing speech as well, and Imogen Pascal isn't going to be kind. There has to be something more I can do,' Ruth raged, her hands curled into fists in her lap, as large as a man's.

Maria felt sad for her. Nothing about Ruth was delicate or feminine, neither her body nor her face. Finding a partner who didn't judge her looks had proved impossible, and the family she'd always wanted had been elusive until she'd taken the decision to try IVF. Not that a husband was the answer to everything, God knew Maria was living proof of that, but the desire for companionship, for warmth at night, that 24-hour best friend, was a crucial part of most adults' life plans. Ruth was no different.

'There's nothing you can do except watch. Let me do this on my own. I'm prepared for the consequences.'

'What if I'm not? You reached out to me. I said I'd always be there to help.' Ruth slapped angrily at a stray tear as Maria abandoned their agreement not to get too close to one another, sliding along the bench to take her friend's hand.

'Go home. Kiss the twins from me. I'll get to meet them one day, whether it's twenty years from now or next week.' She gave her friend a swift hug then stood up to leave. If she only had a few days freedom left, she wanted to spend them walking and seeing the world. There would be plenty of tears to come if things went wrong.

'I can't let you be convicted, Maria,' Ruth said, staring at the ground, sounding not dissimilar to a stubborn child herself.

'Respect my wishes, Ruth. I've left Edward behind. Go home and enjoy your family this evening, for me. Love every minute of it.'

Maria took the opposite exit to the path Ruth chose, forcing herself to keep her head up and look at the trees and sky rather than the ground. The end of the trial was imminent. Once Professor Worth had done whatever additional damage he could, it would be down to the lawyers' speeches, the judge's summary of the case, then the verdict. She had waited so many months for the trial to start, it seemed impossible that it was nearing a conclusion already. After that, it was prison or freedom. Turning her face into the sun, she determined to enjoy what might be her final day outside. A gentle breeze was blowing in from the south. It was still hot but not too humid, and the birds were soaring above her. Somewhere inside her though, a clock was ticking away the hours until her fate was decided. She'd been trying not to think about incarceration, but it was looming too large now to be ignored.

In all likelihood she'd end up at Eastwood Park Prison, north of Bristol, in Falfield. A couple of months ago, she'd looked it up on a computer in the library, amused to see she could learn anything from cookery to salon services, and manicures to industrial cleaning. At least the inmates could look beautiful as they poisoned a meal for their lovers, knowing exactly how to clean up the carnage afterwards. It seemed less funny now. Walking was good. That was how she would fill her afternoon, she decided. See as much as possible, take it all in. If she was destined for a cell, she should walk while she still could.

25

Day Nine in Court.

Lottie was running late. Daniyal was completely recovered, except that he hadn't wanted to get out of bed. His previous sickness, as far as Lottie could tell, had likely been caused by drinking orange juice followed immediately by milk. The childminder had been offish at her late arrival to collect him, but had softened when Lottie offered women's problems as a vague excuse.

That morning, Daniyal had dressed himself in heavy jeans and a woolly jumper. Lottie had forcibly removed the winter outfit and replaced it with shorts and a T-shirt. Breakfast had been reduced to tantrums from them both. By the time Lottie had calmed him down, she should have been dropping him at the childminder's. Having finally wrestled him into his car seat, the tears began again.

'Danny,' she'd said, 'this isn't like you. What's the matter, sweetheart? Can you tell Mummy?'

'Everything's wrong,' he'd said. 'I want Daddy to come home.'

That had stung. Daniyal had always been more clingy with her than his father, not that parenting was a popularity contest, but it was the first time he'd needed anyone except Lottie to make him happy.

'Daddy will be home tonight. We can have dinner together then do something fun,' she'd said, starting the engine and trying to keep a smile on her face. She wasn't feeling it though. The whole house had felt soiled by the time she'd returned with Daniyal the day before.

'You won't. It won't be fun. You and Daddy don't laugh. Nothing's fun.' He'd folded his little arms and glared out of the car window.

Lottie's throat had constricted. Was her misery so obvious that even her three-year-old had felt it? Not just felt it, but she'd unwittingly passed it along to him, infecting him with her sadness. She'd tried to speak but found that she couldn't. For a while in bed last night, she'd relived the scene with Cameron in the kitchen, before reverting back to what was really on her mind. She had left a sick child with the childminder rather than interrupting a sex session with a man who probably thought of himself as her lover. Was that why Daniyal was longing for his father now? Zain had been gone twenty-four hours and already her son felt the void in the house, that apparently she was too self-absorbed to notice or fill at the moment. Lottie had turned the engine off and climbed out of the driver's seat, opening Daniyal's door to lean in and hug him.

'Honey, I'm so sorry. Mummy's just been so busy. It's no excuse. I think I got too tired. You know what it's like when you get really, really tired and then everything goes wrong?' Daniyal had given a grudging nod, allowing her to dab his tears with her sleeve. 'Well, I've nearly finished being busy now, so we can concentrate on laughing and being a family again. How does that sound?' She fought to keep her own tears from falling.

'You and Daddy together? Promise?' Daniyal persisted.

'I promise,' she said, hugging him extra tight.

They'd driven to the childminder's making small talk about squirrels and daisies, but Lottie was shaken. Leaving a quiet but compliant Daniyal for the day, she'd had to pull into a lay-by to dry her guilty tears and compose herself.

What was she doing? She'd taken a risk which could have been the end of everything. Cameron had come into her home, and they'd sex on the kitchen table, the heart of their home, the centre of everything she loved. It was madness. She wanted to go straight back home, drag the table out into the garden and burn it. The problem was that she couldn't change a single thing. Zain could never, ever find out what she'd done. She had to behave like she always did if he wasn't going to suspect. Any lapse could mean the loss of everything she cared about. Daniyal, her home, her life. As much as she'd thought she was sick of it, right now she would do anything to turn the clock back a month. Glancing in the mirror she realised what a wreck she was. Mascara had clumped in her eyelashes and smudged. Her lipstick had bled around the edges. The hair she'd spent thirty minutes straightening was oily with sweat. And still she had to go to court. Taking a deep breath she pulled out into the traffic and followed the line of cars into the city centre. Her affair with Cameron had to end. No more excuses or giving in to lust. Daniyal was all that mattered now. She couldn't change what she'd already done, but she could make sure it never happened again.

Outside the court building, Lottie fought her way through the crowd of protestors that seemed to be growing every day, arriving in the jury corridor with a few minutes left before she was needed. She decided to hide in the ladies toilets, using her time to delete several flirtatious texts from Cameron without answering them. He'd sent a few the previous night too. Those she'd read but not responded to. Now it was cleaner not to know what was on his mind. She didn't want any more memories of him than she already had. Waiting until she heard the other jurors entering the courtroom, she followed at a distance, giving Cameron a vague smile as she took her seat next to him.

Professor Worth was getting settled into the witness stand for the second time, adjusting his tie before taking the oath again.

'Thank you for coming back,' Imogen Pascal cooed. 'Evidence came to light during the trial that the prosecution would like you to comment on. Have you read the transcript of the defendant's evidence?'

'Indeed I have,' the psychiatrist replied, slipping off his glasses and polishing them. Lottie looked to the dock where Maria Bloxham was rubbing what looked like a large scab on her left palm and paying the witness no attention at all. 'My first comment would be that she had the opportunity to discuss self-defence with me. Had that been what was foremost in her mind, I'd have expected her to feel compelled to have shared it. In addition to that, the psychology of self-harm is complex. Often it's a cry for attention which is why it's so prevalent in teenage girls.'

Of all the people a teenage girl would want to confide in, Lottie thought, it wouldn't be him. She knew she would never have opened up to Professor Worth. He was too smug. Maria's position was different though. Charged with attempted murder, surely she'd have told her tale to whoever would listen, if only for the record. What did she have to lose?

'Self-harm, the process itself, is often secretive and private while it's happening. I note also that Mrs Bloxham claims her husband watched her self-injuring. That means he would had to have been able to tolerate seeing her inflict and endure pain, and do nothing about it. More than that, she suggested it was at his instigation, yet I've found nothing in his history that indicates such a high level of abusiveness in his personality. No previous convictions, no prior complaints from former partners, nothing but glowing references from people he worked with. Quite the opposite, in fact. I believe he used to volunteer with a charity who offered counselling and advice for self-harmers, suggesting an advanced level of empathy and concern for the condition. That seems like quite compelling evidence to me that the defendant's version of events is skewed, to put it neutrally.'

'Is it possible Dr Bloxham was a markedly different person in public and in private?' Pascal asked.

'Possible but unlikely. Most people can sustain an act for a limited period of time, but not long-term. The defendant accepts Dr Bloxham was never directly physically violent to her. It would take a monumental amount of self-control to be manipulative and cruel, as the defendant suggested, but never to cross the line into physical abuse. If the victim in this case managed that, it would be the first time I've encountered such highly developed psychopathy in my career, and I have to tell you, there's not much I haven't seen.'

'Is it possible for one person to persuade another person to hurt themselves badly enough to risk death, even when they are unwilling, do you think?' Pascal continued.

The judge was staring at the psychiatrist. For once, Lottie noted, she had even put down her pen, and had her hands folded on top of her notepad. This was the crucial question, she realised. The case turned on this. Lottie glanced at Cameron who was uncharacteristically pale, leaning forward in his chair, glaring across the courtroom.

'Technically, and there are all sorts of caveats to this, but technically yes. That, of course, is a very different question to whether or not I believe that is what happened in this particular case.'

'So let's deal with the first part of that answer and then move on to the second, Professor,' the judge interjected.

'Quite so,' he smarmed. Lottie concluded that she hated him, even though there was no particular logic for it. 'There are instances where one person has become so influential in another's life that they've persuaded them towards suicide, although the victim is usually tending towards it in the first place and the persuader simply provides affirmation. Other examples include the sort of extremist brain-washing that's evident in the case of suicide-bombers, or online suicide challenges aimed at teenagers. If a person really does not want to harm themselves critically though, it would in my opinion be difficult to force them to do so without some form of physical intervention.'

'And in this particular case?' Miss Pascal asked.

'Having had the benefit of meeting Mrs Bloxham, albeit briefly, I fail to see that someone with her strength of personality could have been forced to do anything she did not wish to do. She certainly found it easy enough to decide not to answer my questions when it didn't suit her. I gather that she formulated a plan to conceal small amounts of her husband's money over a period of time and then to purchase a mobile phone which she also hid. That's manipulative and organised, and it's at odds with her claim that her life was under threat. As she accepts there was never any threat of physical violence from her husband, I fail to see what she thought would happen if she simply refused to self-harm. When we assess the effect of pressure on a person, we also consider the consequences. That allows us to form a view of how rational a person's actions are. If the threat of consequences is real – for example, if a gun is being held to your head – then violent acts in self-defence are understandable. In this case, I see no such evidence. I simply do not understand how Mrs Bloxham can claim she was in immediate danger, at least not from anyone except herself.'

'Do the claims she's making tell you anything about Mrs Bloxham's current mental state, professor?' Imogen Pascal asked, raising herself to her full height and crossing her arms.

'One of two things. Either the defendant is deeply calculating and prepared to lie shamefully to get away with this crime, or she honestly believes what she's told the court in which case it's feasible to conclude that she is suffering serious paranoia which might make her a continuing danger to society.'

'Thank you, Professor Worth,' Imogen Pascal gave a small bow of her head then sat down.

Taking his time getting up, James Newell adjusted his wig and flicked through a folder before he was ready to ask his first question.

'Deliberate self-harm is addictive behaviour, isn't it?' Newell asked simply. There was a general sitting up in court, a shifting of focus. This was more interesting, Lottie thought. The defence barrister pitting himself against the prosecution witness.

'Quite often, yes,' Worth agreed.

'Because it offers temporary relief from stress or depression in the same way that drugs and alcohol might,' Newell suggested.

'Absolutely,' Worth said.

'So Dr Bloxham providing his wife with the razor blades was not very different from him buying a heroin addict a stash of drugs. That addict might be able to use the drugs safely and restrict their intake, or they might have a bad day and suddenly take it all at once, risking death. What's the difference?'

'The difference is that a skilled and experienced self-harmer like Mrs Bloxham knows how to avoid self-harming too dramatically, and can avoid serious injury,' the professor replied.

'But addiction is unpredictable. It's a downward spiral in almost every case. The severity of the damage to Ms Bloxham's thighs makes it pretty plain that her addiction is out of control, don't you agree?'

'I didn't see the scars but I'm willing to accept that assessment, although I don't see the relevance of what you're asking.'

'Really?' Newell asked, a frown creasing his forehead as he drew his head back, staring at the psychiatrist. 'You don't see that her husband buying her razor blades,' the volume of the barrister's voice began to rise, 'and repeatedly encouraging, even instructing her to cut herself, is a form of physical violence? Dr Bloxham may not have wielded the blades, but he abused his knowledge of his wife's addiction so despicably that he might as well have done. That's the reality, isn't it?'

Professor Worth fiddled with the bundle of photos on the desk in front of him. 'I'm not sure I can . . . I mean, it's a matter of fact and degree. It would depend on the facts. I'm not even convinced her husband knew Mrs Bloxham was self-harming.'

'You think it's possible he didn't look at or touch her thighs for the entire duration of their marriage?' Newell snapped back. The psychiatrist didn't answer. 'For the sake of argument, let's consider Dr Bloxham as a loving husband who cared about his wife and who wasn't controlling and tormenting her. If someone you genuinely loved was self-harming to a dramatic extent, what would you expect to be a reasonable course of action, Professor?'

'A referral to a general practitioner who could assess the medical situation and put appropriate expert assistance in place,' Worth said.

'But you've seen Mrs Bloxham's medical records, haven't you?'

'I have,' Worth agreed.

'Did she ever see the GP about the self-harm?'

'She did not,' he answered quietly.

'Was there any note in the records that Dr Bloxham had ever contacted his wife's GP to report deliberate self-harm?'

'No,' Worth agreed again.

'And do you recall the date of Mrs Bloxham's last contact with her GP? I mean for anything at all – coughs, colds – anything.'

'I'd have to check my notes to be accurate, but I do recall noting that Mrs Bloxham hadn't seen her GP for more than a decade. It might be, of course, that she either had no complaint in that time, or that she didn't want the doctor to question the damage to her thighs.'

'Or it might be that her husband didn't want her to have access to an outside professional in case she started telling someone what her life was like. That's a possibility too, isn't it?' Newell finished.

'Almost anything is possible if you don't care about actual proof,' Worth said. 'I can only tell you what I saw. Mrs Bloxham was not sheepish and downtrodden, quite the opposite. She was angry, confrontational and aggressive. I saw fury rather than fear. That was my professional opinion at the time, and nothing I've learned since then makes me change my assessment. If anything, I'm even more concerned that she may be suffering a serious psychiatric illness which makes her dangerous and could have led to her attack on Dr Bloxham. Sadly, I can only help people who want to be helped.'

'No further cross-examination,' Newell said, retaking his seat.

As the judge began thanking the psychiatrist for having taken time from his schedule to return to the courtroom, Lottie was distracted by Cameron pulling a slip of paper from his pocket. He motioned to the court usher, who did a quizzical double-take then stalked over. Cameron whispered in his ear, then the usher made his way towards the court clerk, who stood up and passed the paper to the judge.

'One moment please,' the judge directed in Professor Worth's direction. She handed the paper back to the clerk who took it first to Imogen Pascal who read it, stretching her jaw to one side and gritting her teeth, before getting her game face back on and smiling politely. After that James Newell was allowed a look. Lottie watched his eyebrows raise slightly, before he glanced along the double line of jurors. He wanted to know who'd written the note, Lottie thought. She was desperate to ask Cameron what was on it, but that would mean leaning closer to him. The judge took the note back from the usher and looked around the court. 'It appears that there is a note from the jury. I see no objection to putting it to this witness as it arises from Ms Bloxham's evidence.'

'Who wrote that? No one asked me,' Lottie heard Tabitha mutter below her.

'Shhh,' Pan responded, already poised with his pen and notebook.

'Professor Worth, the question reads, "What is the psychology behind a male instructing a female partner to pretend to be completely unresponsive during sex?"'

The psychiatrist looked uncomfortable, directing his gaze in Imogen Pascal's direction for guidance. The prosecutor gave a slight shrug of her shoulders and looked back down at her file. He hadn't been prepared for that question, Lottie thought. Cameron had though. She wondered when he'd decided to ask the question. Before they entered the courtroom, that much was clear. No one else might have noticed, but Cameron hadn't picked up his notebook all day which meant he'd drafted the question in advance.

'Again, this is based only on what Mrs Bloxham said. There's no independent evidence that this ever happened,' Worth began.

'I'll deal with that, if you wouldn't mind just explaining the psychological aspects please,' the judge said, tersely.

'Of course. In broad terms, asking a partner to play dead indicates primarily a desire to dominate them. They can't respond, move or object. They also can't express any physical desire or pleasure themselves so there might be an underlying issue of wanting the sex to feel non-consensual,' he paused. No one in the courtroom moved. 'At a very obvious level, it might be role-play for someone interested in necrophilia, having sexual relations with the dead. Taking the psychology to an extreme it is also possible that the dominant partner has fantasies about killing. Not necessarily their actual partner, but killing in general.'

Lottie was distracted by DI Anton leaning forward and whispering manically in Imogen Pascal's ear. She waved him away and he sat down, red faced, obviously cross. James Newell looked back towards the jury once more, catching Lottie's eyes. She gave him the briefest smile as he turned away again.

After that they were dismissed, citing the need for legal argument in the afternoon. Lottie hadn't waited for Cameron in the hallway between the court and the jury room, pacing ahead instead, only surprised by the fact that he hadn't caught up with her. They were due a conversation, but it wasn't one she wanted to have until she was a sensible distance from their fellow jurors.

'Need to talk,' she texted him, knowing what a huge understatement it was. She needed to do the talking and for him to listen. If she tried dealing with the problem on the phone it would never feel properly resolved. Cameron had to understand how serious she was, and for that she needed to be looking him in the eyes. Feeling sick with nerves, she waited for his response as she packed her bag in the jury room.

'Sounds perfect,' he replied. 'Lucy's on Harbourside? Thirty mins?'

'Great,' she responded, waving a nonchalant goodbye to her fellow jurors and exiting the court building, heading for the old dockside. Even in poor weather the collection of bars, restaurants and artsy cinemas made Harbourside a haven for twenty-somethings, but in the sunshine every spare inch of the high walls above the water became a bench for students, tourists and those with time on their hands, complete with picnics, fast food, wine and beer. They lined both sides of the waterway, chattering loudly and basking in the golden afternoon light.

Lucy's café was between an Italian restaurant and a late night bar, with just a few tables outside and featuring gaudy plastic covers, but it made the best coffee in Bristol. Lottie chose seats inside away from prying eyes, keeping her back to the window. Cameron arrived ten minutes later looking tired but happy.

'Hey gorgeous,' he said. 'I don't suppose I'm allowed to kiss you in public. I'll just have to settle for imagining it instead. I didn't even get a chance to say hello to you at court this morning. What a day!'

'It really was,' Lottie played along, wishing he would keep his sunglasses on as she tried to figure out how to say what was needed. 'What was that you did in court today? Tabitha nearly had a fit, one of us deciding to do something without her express permission.'

'Tell me about it. I had to escape before she could insist on another disciplinary committee meeting. I'm guessing I'll be for it tomorrow morning,' Cameron smiled.

'You got the note out of your pocket, though. It was already written. When did you decide you were going to ask a question?' Lottie smiled at the waitress who delivered the drinks she'd already ordered.

'In the morning, before we went in. Professor Worth was obviously going to side with the prosecution so I thought I'd even up the odds a bit. Did the trick, didn't it?'

'Yes, but you keep saying the Tabithas have already made their minds up to find her guilty. It's starting to sound as if you've made your decision already too. Surely we should all be keeping an open mind?' Lottie took a sip of coffee, and tried to ignore the unwanted images that were flooding her mind from the previous afternoon.

'I think I'd rather talk about us,' Cameron said, brushing her knee with his hand beneath the table.

Lottie jerked away. 'Cam, don't,' she said.

'Okay, too public, I apologise,' he said. 'It's hard not to touch you.'

'We can't,' Lottie said quietly. 'It was a mistake. My mistake. I've got too much to lose. This morning Daniyal was . . . it doesn't matter. The fact is that the trial's almost over and this has to stop. I'm sorry. There's no excuse for the way I behaved yesterday . . . and before that . . . but I don't want to risk my whole marriage. I love my son too much to play games like this.' Cameron ran his hands through his hair and stared down into his coffee. 'Please say something.' She pushed her sunglasses onto the top of her head, revealing tear-filled eyes. 'I need to know you're okay with this . . . with me.'

'So what, you were just fucking with me?' he hissed. 'What am I supposed to say? Yeah, sure Lottie, it didn't mean anything so fine, just dump me. I never had you figured as the sort of woman to treat other people like trash.'

'That's not fair. My son needs his father and a stable home environment which I'm not providing at the moment because all I've been thinking about is you. I can't let everyone I love be destroyed,' Lottie fired back.

'Everyone you love? Meaning Zain as well as Daniyal? When did that happen? After everything you've said about being unhappy and unappreciated. Has it occurred to you that perhaps you misled me?' Cameron whispered. 'I lost the last person I loved forever, Lottie. You knew that before you got involved with me. Am I really supposed to accept that you think it's okay to just drop me now that you've realised there might be consequences?'

'Oh God, Cameron, I'm sorry,' Lottie sighed, sitting on her hands to try to stop them shaking. 'I didn't mean it to end like this. Actually, I never intended for it to start . . .'

'I love you,' he said. 'As stupid as that sounds after such a short time, I know I love you. We can't give up on each other so easily. I won't let that happen.'

She stared at him, tried to pick up her cup to fill the silence with action, but failed.

'Cam . . .' she breathed.

'Don't say anything,' he said. 'Not right now. Give me a couple more days before you decide it's all over, that's all I ask. I promise not to hassle you if you'll do that for me. Just think about it.'

'It's not that simple,' Lottie blurted. 'Zain's not a bad man but if he finds out that we've . . . I don't know what he'd do. Daniyal was born in Pakistan. If Zain decides to punish me he could put him on a plane and disappear. You're right. I didn't think about the consequences until we'd already taken it too far, but I'd be lying if I said we had a future, and I don't want to lie to you.'

'I'll look after you and Daniyal, Lottie. I won't let Zain hurt either of you. Just agree to think about it a bit longer. Please? I know there's a lot at stake. There is for me too.'

He looked desperate, Lottie thought. What had she done? Not only risking the ruin of her own life, but Cameron's too. She only had to get through to the end of the trial. After that she and Cameron wouldn't see each other anyway. He'd be back at work and she'd be looking after Daniyal again. That would be the break from each other they needed to make their separation painless. Away from the stress and intensity of the courtroom, Cameron would get their fling into perspective. She'd never imagined he would develop feelings for her so quickly – the brusque, jokey carpenter who'd begun jury duty filled with anger and irritation. Lottie had been completely wrong about him. He was more sensitive and needy than she could ever have imagined. A cooling off period wouldn't be such a bad thing for her, either. The whirlwind needed to settle.

'All right,' she said. 'I'll think about it. Just a couple more days. Then you'll agree with whatever I decide. No more argument, okay?'

'Fair enough,' he said. 'As long as I know I'm still in with a chance.'

26

Day Ten in Court

Maria stared through the crack in the ladies' toilet cubicle door. Imogen Pascal was washing her hands and staring at herself in the mirror. In spite of the humidity, she was dressed to kill. Her midnight blue suit, skirt just above the knee, tight-waisted jacket, might as well have had the designer label still swinging on the outside. It said money, class, confidence, and it was hard not to be impressed. Maria was, quite genuinely. She had wondered at length about Miss Pascal's private life. Would she ever have children or was her career going to be the love of her life? Had she realised yet that DI Anton stared at her constantly, or was she completely unaware?

Maria was under no illusions that the prosecutor hadn't wondered about her in such human terms. No doubt the only question in Miss Pascal's mind was how many years' imprisonment marked the appropriate sentence for the attempted murder of a spouse. Her closing speech, like every meticulously plotted part of the trial, would no doubt be killer – pun intended, Maria joked to herself. Nothing anyone could do now. What would be, would be.

She couldn't hide any longer. James Newell was waiting for her. Imogen Pascal was applying unnecessary fresh lipstick as she exited the cubicle. Maria took the sink closest to the exit door.

'Good morning Miss Pascal,' she said. It was, after all, ridiculous to pretend they didn't know each other.

'Mrs Bloxham,' the prosecutor nodded stiffly.

'Ready to give your speech?' Maria asked.

'We can't talk, I'm afraid. It's not proper. Nothing personal.' She recapped her lipstick and pulled a comb from her handbag.

'It's not personal? Is that really what you think?' Maria asked, knowing she should keep her mouth shut. Mr Newell would be furious with her. But it was personal. She was a human being. How could anyone say anything so insensitive?

Imogen Pascal thought better of doing her hair and went to pass Maria and exit. Maria stepped in front of the door, checking no one else was with them in the toilets, but the other cubicles stood empty.

'You need to let me pass,' Pascal said.

'Why? So you can have me sent to prison without a scene? So you don't have to face the fact that I'm a human being with feelings? Did it ever occur to you that I might be innocent or do you just not care?'

Imogen Pascal took a few steps back. 'I'll call security if I have to. I'd rather not. You're obviously under a lot of stress right now.'

'A lot of stress?' Maria shouted. 'You mean you actually noticed? How kind of you.'

'Mrs Bloxham, this could stop the whole trial. Is that what you want?'

'I want you to look at me and see a real person, not just a set of papers or a chance to score a few points. I want you to stop playing games at my expense. How does that sound?' She slammed a hand into the wall. Two dryers roared into life, blasting unwanted additional heat into the room, and a bundle of paper towels fell to the floor.

'I'm going to explain something, then I'm walking out of here. If you attempt to stop me I will have you arrested. This is my job. I could just as easily have ended up defending you as prosecuting. I don't choose my cases, they're given to me. I understand this is personal to you, but to me it's a process. I simply play my part in it. You will get convicted on the facts, not because of any trickery on my part. This has been a fair trial. The judge has been impartial and you have an extremely competent barrister. If you don't like being here, maybe you should take a good long look in that mirror and ask yourself why you are. The answer to that is nothing to do with me.'

Imogen Pascal strode out, showing no sign that she'd been disturbed by what had happened. Maria felt a grudging respect for her accompanied by the erratic pounding of her heart, wondering if even now the prosecutor was hurrying to find DI Anton and have her arrested again. She suspected not. At this stage, the trial would have to be abandoned and restarted, and Imogen Pascal wanted to finish it. Maria was certain of that. Glancing in the mirror, she saw a stranger looking back. Where did the hopeful young woman go who would never have been so aggressive to another female in the ladies' toilet, of all places? It was Edward she was angry with, not Imogen Pascal. With the thought came a sudden rush of shame. She wanted to apologise, explain that the heat and tension was getting to her. Too late, though. Her case was being called through the public address system. James Newell would be getting worried about her. Splashing cold water over her face, she tidied her hair, ripping off her tights and throwing them in the bin. It was too hot for nylon. She would just have to look dishevelled. Maybe that was the right approach anyway. She was never going to be one of life's Imogen Pascals. And if the case went against her, she was never going to be anybody at all.

'Ladies and gentlemen of the jury,' Miss Pascal began her closing speech, 'let's look at what is not in dispute in this case.

The horrific and very nearly life-ending injury suffered by Dr Bloxham. The weapon, a chair leg with a bolt sticking out. Who dealt the awful blow? The victim's wife. It's not even in dispute that she intended to kill him. So why are you here?'

Maria kept her head straight, just as James Newell had instructed her, glancing only from the corners of her eyes in the jury's direction. They were listening intently, every one of them edged forward on their seat, most scribbling notes and providing exactly the audience the prosecutor craved. The younger man on the end, next to the pretty young woman he'd spent so much time looking at, was different to the rest. His arms were folded. His notebook remained closed on the desk in front of him. It was he who'd sent the note to Professor Worth that had both delighted and embarrassed James Newell, causing him to apologise repeatedly for not having thought to ask the question himself.

'You are the arbiters of truth,' Imogen Pascal announced dramatically. 'And what's unusual in this trial is that you don't even need to decide which side is telling the truth. The reason you don't have to decide that is because one party has been deprived of his voice, deprived of his right to put his case, almost deprived of his life entirely. Mrs Bloxham was at liberty to say whatever she wanted about her life with Dr Bloxham. She didn't know that when she was interviewed by the police, of course, so she stayed silent. Her husband might have recovered and been able to give his own version of the facts. But by the time we got to court, by then she knew Dr Bloxham was never going to be able to gainsay a single word she said, which is why she suddenly painted him as a black-hearted manipulator. The question is, do you believe her? Do you believe that the woman who told the psychiatrist – Professor Worth – to go "Fuck himself" was so downtrodden that she never once felt able to simply leave her husband? The woman who thumped the witness stand as she gave evidence. The woman who – and I do not seek to make this about me – but the woman who was unafraid to call me a bitch, right in front of both you and the judge.'

Imogen Pascal turned her head to stare at Maria in the dock.

'The woman who stood up in the dock and shouted that her husband hated hedgehogs. Do you think Maria Bloxham only developed that temper since attempting to kill her husband, or do you agree with the prosecution's assessment, that the defendant's overwhelming aggression played a key part in her attack on her husband? And what about her icy calm when the police arrived to find her still clutching the chair leg? There was no sign of the self-professed terror that she might have been just minutes from death. No trembling hands. No tears. Did she really only use what force was needed to knock him out so she could disappear into a domestic violence shelter, for example? Or did she aim to kill, and use as much force as she possibly could? Did she feel remorse once the danger was passed and the police were there to help her, or did she only faint when she realised her husband was still alive? You already know the answer to those questions.

'As for the money – the very substantial amount of money Mrs Bloxham stood to inherit – even she couldn't maintain her initial lie that she had no idea Dr Bloxham was well-off. Of course she had an idea what the house was worth. She admitted knowing her husband had savings. Do you really believe she hadn't given that a single thought? This woman, who had been kept, wanting for nothing throughout her marriage, who was never once harmed by her husband, has weaved a tale so fantastic, it's hard to see where the fantasy elements start and stop, but fantasy it is, ladies and gentleman. The defence cannot produce one witness – not one – to back up her version of events.

'The prosecution says her defence is not only a pack of lies, it is an unbelievable excuse for attempting to rid herself of a husband with whom she was bored, and from whose death she stood to gain substantially. Do not be swayed by the sight of her thighs. We all have scars, some internal, some external. We do not all turn to violence, or attempt to commit a murder. Do not be swayed by the cleverly told tales of a sad life. Remember that she lived in relative luxury, you yourselves having visited the house and locality. Keep at the forefront of your mind what you know about Dr Bloxham. His good character, his work on behalf of endangered species and the environment, his fight against large-scale development. Recall the sound of his voice as he held that baby hedgehog. And finally, ask yourselves this. Which version of events is the easiest to believe? Because as a rule of thumb, you can often trust that simplicity is the closest thing to reality. Can you believe the word of a woman who lost her temper and contradicted herself? Who didn't explain her defence at either the first, or second, opportunity, but who waited until she had it all figured out months later? Trust your senses. The injuries. The self-confessed hatred the defendant harboured towards the victim. That, you might conclude, was the most truthful part of everything she said. Thank you.'

The two most elderly jurors glanced at one another, shared a nudged elbow. In her mind, Maria could hear them saying what a good job Imogen Pascal had done. Wasn't she clever? Didn't she managed to say exactly what they'd been thinking all long? All they were missing was a nice cup of tea and some shortbread biscuits. The pretty young woman was pale and drawn, more so than she had been throughout the trial. Had jury duty affected her so badly? Not nice to have to decide another person's fate. And the very young man, stick thin and always dressed in ill-fitting clothes, was biting his nails again. Maria used to do that as a child, before she'd found a more precise channel for her nervousness. Not that she would recommend it to anyone else.

James Newell was getting to his feet now. Maria liked him. She'd thought it impossible that she might ever warm to another man again, but he was caring, sweet and entirely genuine. She sat back and waited for her barrister to do what he could on her behalf.

James Newell smiled at the jury, made a point of looking each one of them in the eye, and relaxed into his speech. 'Good morning,' he began. 'It's been a difficult trial, no mistaking it. You'll probably be glad when it's all over. It's hard to look at photos like these,' he picked up then released the bundle of photographs, 'and equally upsetting to have seen the state of Maria Bloxham's thighs. I'll concede that seeing Dr Bloxham in this courtroom was distressing, even for those of us who deal with such cases all too regularly. In spite of all that, I'm going to ask you do something which runs contrary to all that emotion. I need you to take a step back and consider the hard evidence. I'm going to recap some crucial parts very briefly. Maria's name was not on the mortgage . . .'

Imogen Pascal was standing before Newell could get another word out. 'Your Honour, my learned friend is aware it's not good form to refer to his client by her first name.'

'And as Miss Pascal found it so difficult to remember to refer to my client as Ms Bloxham rather than Mrs on numerous occasions, I shall refer to my client as I see fit in my closing speech,' Newell said warmly to her, although there was no mistaking the steel beneath his tone.

'Let Mr Newell continue uninterrupted, Miss Pascal,' the judge directed.

'As I was saying . . . Maria's name was not on the mortgage. She has no bank account. She has no car. No access to money unless it's small change down the back of the sofa. No access to a landline and no mobile with any credit in it. The prosecution hasn't disputed any of these facts. How many of you have none of those things? How many of you know anyone who has none of those things? So I ask you, what sort of home life do you think Maria lived? Who among you has not visited your GP in a decade? Under what circumstances can you imagine that happening? Much has been made of Maria swearing at the psychiatrist, but consider this. If she did suffered the sort of manipulation and torment that she's described to you, her reaction to Professor Worth makes complete sense, particularly given her husband's threats to have her committed. That was no baseless threat either, given the extent of her self-mutilation. You can easily see how her worst fear might have been realised. She would have escaped from the house with no bank account and no access to money, with no community ties and no place to go. Dr Bloxham would have said she was a danger to herself. Frankly, he could have said anything he liked. Years of coercive control stripped Maria Bloxham of the tools of independence the rest of us take for granted. Social media, jobs, contact with the outside world. Savings. A phone. Of course she believed she would end up institutionalised if she tried to leave her husband.

'And as for her behaviour in court, who wouldn't find this process distressing and stressful? Her reactions have been normal and human. They show that she is emotional, not cold and calculating as the prosecution would have you believe. As for the scars on her upper legs, they are all the evidence you need to be sure that she was self-harming for years. There's no doubt that she was telling the truth about that. Did Dr Bloxham know? How could he not have known? Did he do anything about it? It appears that he did precisely nothing. Wouldn't you have tried to help the person you loved when they were inflicting so much damage on their own body? Unless, that is, you were responsible for it. Unless you were the sort of person who liked their partner to play dead during sex. Unless you were the sort of person who, over a period of years, cut their partner off from the rest of the world and controlled their every move. I urge you to accept Maria Bloxham's version of events. It's the only version that makes sense. She knew that it was her or Dr Bloxham, kill or die. She did what she believed to be necessary at the time to escape him before it was too late, because a cage – no matter how beautiful, no matter what the postcode, no matter how great its value – is still a cage. She'd been locked in hers far too long.'

Newell finished his speech softly, the courtroom entranced, and the mood didn't break until he'd sat down. Maria risked a glance towards the press and the public gallery. Ruth had come to watch the death throes of the trial and was dabbing her eyes with a handkerchief. Journalists were scribbling madly in their notebooks, perfecting their copy ready to exit and send emails back to their editors. Then the court doors burst open and a crowd began noisily to fill the court.

'Justice for Dr Bloxham!' one of them shouted.

'Send her down,' someone else began to chant. Others joined in. The noise was deafening. The heat of the protestors' bodies raised the temperature even further. They stank of body odour from standing outside in the sun, and two of them were shirtless and shoeless.

'Silence,' Her Honour Judge Downey ordered. 'I will have quiet in this courtroom immediately!' The protestors showed no sign of complying, and police officers intervened, trying to ring-fence the intruders into one area.

'Lock up the Bristol Butcher!' one woman shouted, quoting one of the trashier headlines of the day.

'Get additional security up here right now. Usher, escort the jurors back to their room. Mr Newell,' the barrister stood up, doing his best to ignore the shouting. 'I'm afraid I must remand your client in custody over the luncheon adjournment for her own protection.'

Maria was hurried to her feet and taken through the rear door of the dock, down the stairs, with a prison guard at either side of her. Behind her the shouting continued until they reached the cells where layers of metal and concrete made it impossible to hear anything except the complaints of her fellow prisoners.

Her cell, 8' by 12' was basic in the extreme, containing only a metal bench on which she could lie if she felt sufficiently sure about the hygiene of the previous occupant – she didn't – and a chair bolted to the wall. Not designed for comfort, only as somewhere for you to await your fate, it was still a glance into what her future might hold.

The corridor beyond stank of that crossover point between urine and disinfectant. Something that resembled the reek of school dinners added a top-note, unidentifiable stewed meat and green vegetables that had sat too long in boiling water. The walls had been marked by people who had found stray pens, nothing intelligible. Just a desire to feel alive by leaving a minuscule piece of themselves there, before being moved on. Most of them would have been transported to a prison from the court cells. She'd heard all about it from her fellows at the bail hostel. Women's prisons, she'd been told with gleeful darkness, were so much worse than men's. Psychotropic drugs were widely used to calm down the population. Bullying was extreme. There would be a settling in period that would see her pushed to her limits. One woman at the bail hostel had reported being pinned to a wall while she had boiling water thrown over her torso. She had the scars to prove it. Speaking of which, Maria's own scars would be on full display in the showers. That was going to get her a certain amount of unwelcome attention. Prison would be quite some leap after nearly two decades alone except for Edward. Sharing a single room with one or two other women, no peace, no quiet, was a curious thought. Getting to know other women intimately – she shuddered to think how intimately and under what circumstances – was unsettling. The idea that her every movement would be dictated to her by the guards and the governor, perhaps some new version of Edward, was horrific.

James Newell appeared in the doorway. 'You okay?' he asked as the guard unlocked to allow him access.

'I'm fine,' she smiled. 'Think I'll pass on today's lunch offerings though. What happened upstairs?'

'Looks like an animal rights group who were staunch followers of Dr Bloxham. Stop the badger culling, protect the countryside, prevent new housing on green plots. That sort of thing. It's really not about you. They just saw an opportunity to promote their agenda in front of a lot of journalists and took it. As the judge is summing up this afternoon, there are a number of television cameras gathered outside. We'll have to make special arrangements to get you in and out of the court building from now on.'

'It's a shame, straight after your speech. I though you did brilliantly. The jury was really listening.' Maria braved the bench and sat down, wrapping her arms around her waist and wishing she was alone. It was easier to be brave when you didn't have someone looking at you with so much pity. 'There was a conversation I told you I didn't want to have before the trial. I think it's time now. How long will I get if I'm convicted, now that the judge has heard all the evidence?'

'You're sure you want to do this now? You were adamant before that we should just focus on the verdict. Why the change of heart?' Newell asked, taking off his wig and letting it flop in his lap.

'Probably the act of being escorted down into the cells and sitting behind a locked metal door while I waited for you,' Maria said. 'Don't worry, I'm not about to go into meltdown, but I do think now might be the time to prepare myself for the worst.'

He nodded, rubbing his hands together as if he was cold. To be fair, the cells were the coolest place Maria had been since the heatwave had started. Somehow the relief from the burning temperature wasn't as pleasant as it should have been.

'It depends on the view the judge takes of your evidence. If she accepted that you'd been abused over a sustained period but that you still didn't have sufficient reason for using such extreme violence, she might be inclined to give you a reduced sentence, say between five and ten years given that you have no previous convictions.'

'And if Judge Downey thinks I'm a lying, cold-blooded would-be murderess who wanted her husband's money?' As Maria asked the question, the reality hit her hard. She was a liar, and those lies had been told stone cold sober to suit her purpose. She hadn't hesitated once.

'Given the severity of Dr Bloxham's injuries, you'd be looking at a sentence in the region of twenty years,' he said, looking her straight in the eyes as he delivered the news. Credit to him, Maria thought, he didn't flinch, but then this was just part of his job. 'You'd serve approximately two thirds of that.'

'That's what I was expecting,' Maria replied. 'I just needed to hear you say it. I'll be fifty-four years old when they release me. That's a tough age to be starting a new life. Listen, I could do with some time alone. Do you mind?'

'Sure,' he said. 'We'll be going back into court in half an hour. The judge will sum the case up this afternoon. I'll tell the guards to bring you some coffee, okay? You should at least try to drink something.'

She waited until he'd left to let out the sob that had been hovering in the back of her throat. Fourteen years in prison, staring at walls like these, praying for anything to alleviate the boredom. Fourteen years without a garden to tend.

If there was any justice in the world, Edward would be painfully aware that he was trapped inside his own prison cell, hearing life beyond his reaches that he could never rejoin.

'No regrets,' she said aloud. 'I chose this.' And if her future held prison, it would also hold another blade, bought or made. Either from the prison kitchens or the medical store, perhaps fashioned herself from a piece of plastic. Maria wasn't afraid of pain. She'd made an art form of it. Watching the blood flow from her body was preferable to spending fourteen years in a cell. Of course, it had also been preferable to spending the next fourteen years with Edward, which was how she'd ended up here in the first place. The next time she cut herself she would have to be less afraid. Prison or freedom weren't the only two options. Death was everybody's inescapable future. It was up to her if she chose that path earlier than nature had planned. Edward disabled, and her bleeding to death anyway. There was a certain circularity to it. What went around came around, she thought.

27

The courtroom had returned to its usual atmosphere of calm by the time the jury retook their seats. Lottie had avoided Cameron over lunch, positioning herself at a table between Agnes and Jennifer. Jack and Cameron were laughing in a corner, and Lottie was relieved to be away from them. There had been a tangible tension amongst the twelve of them, knowing the moment for which they'd been gathered was imminent, and as a result all conversation relating to the trial had ceased. Even Tabitha had been reduced to small talk rather than bossiness.

Her Honour Judge Downey waited until they were all comfortable before starting to speak. She turned her body to address them directly, crinkling her eyes at the corners as if to set them at ease, keeping her voice level and low. 'Ladies and gentlemen of the jury, at this point it is my job to sum up the evidence you've heard, and to tell you about the law,' she began. What followed was a detailed review of what each witness had said and of the exhibits they'd been shown, from the video of Dr Bloxham, to the medical and forensic evidence, and finishing with the defendant's version of events. Lottie made the odd note, but she'd written most of it down as the trial had progressed. Instead she watched Maria Bloxham through the slightly misted glass at the back, wondering how she felt now. Lottie was no lawyer, but it was pretty obvious that a guilty verdict meant the defendant was going to prison and probably for a long time. She tried to imagine it. How often would you get visits? If she ended up in a cell, would Zain be allowed to bring Daniyal to see her? How many partners actually stood by their spouses during a prison sentence? Not that she could conceive of doing anything bad enough to justify getting locked up, but until a couple of weeks ago she'd thought she would never be capable of having an affair either. It was amazing how life took you by surprise.

The court door opened quietly, and three men entered. The judge paused, obviously wary after the protest before lunch, but the males simply sought seats in the public gallery and sat down, doing their best to look unobtrusive. That wasn't easy given the size of them. All three were easily over six feet tall, and two of them had the sorts of physiques more commonly seen in wrestling arenas. Imogen Pascal and James Newell exchanged a querying look, shrugging at each other. Newell turned back towards the dock and caught Maria Bloxham's eye, but she too shook her head blankly. Lottie glanced sideways at Cameron waiting for him to meet her eyes and make some sort of sarcastic comment, but his attention was fixed rigidly on the judge as if he hadn't noticed the incomers at all.

'That brings me to the law,' the judge continued. 'It is the prosecution's task to make you sure beyond a reasonable doubt that the defendant attempted to kill Dr Bloxham, and that the force she used was not used in reasonable self-defence. You should decide what her state of mind was when she dealt the blow. Did she honestly believe that her life was in danger? Do you believe she felt she had no alternative? Could Maria Bloxham have taken a less serious course of action? In considering that, we do not expect people who act in self-defence to carefully weigh the minutiae of the force they use, but the amount of force cannot be out of all proportion to the risk that they perceive. The defendant does not have to prove anything. If there is any doubt in your mind as to whether or not the defendant is guilty, that doubt must be exercised in Mrs Bloxham's favour, and it will be your duty to find her not guilty. The prosecution must prove to you that the defendant did not act in self-defence. I would like you to reach a unanimous verdict, which means you should all agree. You may send notes with questions to me via the usher, or notify the usher when you have reached a verdict.'

Imogen Pascal stood up and slid quietly along the barristers' bench to whisper in James Newell's ear. He nodded quickly and turned round to whisper to the people seated behind him.

'Your Honour, Mr Newell and I have agreed, in consultation with the police, that the jury ought to be sequestered in a hotel until a verdict is reached. Given the seriousness of the incident with the protestors in the courtroom today and the continuing public interest in this trial, it seems possible that there might be intimidation attempts or improper advances.'

The judge directed her attention back to the three larger-than-life men who were still watching the proceedings.

'What does sequestered mean?' Lottie leaned to her right and whispered to Jennifer, hand covering her mouth.

'It means we all get locked up in a hotel together until this is over. No going home, no going out.'

'Oh my God! Can they really do that to us? I mean, can't we object?'

'You can try,' Jennifer replied. 'I'm not sure I'd be brave enough.'

'All right. Members of the jury. Given the high profile nature of this trial and the earlier protest, I am ordering you to be kept in a safe place that will not be publicly named. All arrangements will be made for you. Once you are told the name of the hotel, you may notify your partner or a friend who will be able to bring you an overnight bag. The remainder of this afternoon will be spent organising this so you should remain in the jury room until then. The usual rules apply however. You may only deliberate to reach a verdict when all twelve of you are together in the court building, and I should warn you that there are penalties for breaking these rules. Usher, you may take the jury back to their room.'

They stood up and began to move towards the door, the business of the court resuming before the door had even closed.

'Miss Pascal,' Lottie heard the judge say. 'Given the nature of this case, can you confirm whether or not the prosecution will seek a second trial if a verdict cannot be reached?'

The door swung shut. They never stopped, Lottie realised. All the hours that she and the other jurors had spent tucked away in their room waiting, the barristers had been arguing points of law. It made you wonder just how much the jury hadn't been told, and why information was kept from them.

'So you're going to get Zain to come to the hotel and bring you a toothbrush then?' Cameron whispered in her ear. He'd waited for her in the corridor and walked behind her as they made their way back to the jury room.

'I don't have any choice, do I? What about you? Is there anyone who can bring you a bag?'

'My neighbour has a key. I'm sure he'll help. Seems like a good opportunity for us to really talk things through, don't you think? I'm just hoping Tabitha and Gregory are on a different floor or I swear they'll be holding a glass to the wall.' He smiled, but it was half-hearted.

'You're not yourself,' Lottie said.

'You're avoiding me,' he whispered, putting a hand on her arm to stall her in the corridor before she could enter the jury room. 'Tell me you feel the same way about me as I feel about you and I'll be fine.'

'This isn't the time or place. We should get into the jury room with the others before they start gossiping.'

'Promise we'll find a way to be alone tonight,' Cameron said. 'We still need to talk.'

Lottie sighed. It wasn't the way she'd wanted to do it, but if she had to put her foot down, at least there would be privacy. 'I'll text you my room number. Best leave it until midnight to make sure everyone else is asleep though.'

The court usher entered the jury room behind them, waiting until everyone was silent before announcing their next destination.

'Rooms have been organised for you at the Marriott Royal Hotel. You may drive there if you have cars in the city already, alternatively taxis are waiting to transport you. Please use the next ten minutes to contact whoever needs to know where you'll be staying.'

Lottie made the call to Zain she'd been dreading.

Hi,' she said. 'Tell me you're nearly home.'

'I am,' he said. 'Is something wrong?'

'You could say that. The judge has decided the whole jury has to stay in a hotel until we've reached a verdict. I can't come home so I need you to collect Daniyal from the childminder then pack a bag for me and bring it to the hotel. I'll text you the details.' He sighed. Lottie could imagine him in his car, some current affairs programme on the radio as he drove, tapping his fingers on the wheel in frustration as she broke the news. 'Sorry,' she added.

'Don't apologise, it's not your fault. Daniyal will be upset you're not going to say goodnight to him.'

'I'll phone him instead. They can't stop us from talking to our children. I'm hoping this will all be over tomorrow. There's plenty of food in the fridge.'

'We'll cope. It's a shame though,' he paused. 'I'll miss you.'

Lottie felt the lies she'd been telling rise in her throat, threatening to choke her. She couldn't speak. Facing the wall, she dashed away tears, wondering how she could have risked so much for so little in return.

'Anyway, do what you have to. I'll sort everything else out.'

'Zain,' she blurted before he could hang up. 'Me too. I know I've been a bit distracted with the trial. I'll make it up to you when this is over.'

'Just come home soon,' he said. 'That'll be enough for me and Danny.'

Lottie rang off, her hands shaking. Her marriage could be saved if she didn't mess up again. As long as Zain didn't find out what had happened with Cameron and she got her priorities straight, her world didn't have to collapse. Perhaps this was the wake-up call she'd needed to help her see how lucky she was. Not only that, but Daniyal had coped fine without her. Maybe she should look for a job, or even do a college course. It was time. There was no reason she couldn't salvage something positive from the near wreckage she'd created.

The hotel, a grand old Victorian building near the Cathedral and a couple of minutes walk from Harbourside, provided a private room for the jurors to eat in away from other guests. Lottie's bedroom was extremely comfortable, and the bathroom was the largest she'd ever seen. There were worse places to get stuck for the night, she thought, even if it didn't exactly feel like a holiday with police officers stationed at various points around the place.

Pan was on his laptop throughout the meal, with Gregory making pointed comments about how rude it was to use technology whilst dining. Agnes spent an hour moaning about what everyone else considered excellent service and wonderful food. Lottie tried not to stare at her watch throughout, desperate to be able to retreat to her room and get away from the others.

Garth Finuchin had decided to park himself next to her at the table, and had spent most of the time regaling her with tales of how Bristol used to be and how much he disliked it now.

'Too many students,' he said. 'You can't drive through the city on a Friday night without some drunk pillock falling onto the bonnet of your car.'

'We have a similar problem in the countryside,' dog-obsessed Samuel joined in. 'Our local pub is on a regular cycling pub-crawl route. The number of people we've had throwing up cider onto our front garden. I've notified the police on several occasions.'

'Could I just say something?' Tabitha waited for quiet. 'While we can't discuss the evidence, I thought we should agree a timeline for tomorrow. My suggestion is that we compare notes on each witness, including the judge's review of the evidence. After that, we can decide on the relevant issues. Also, there are some exhibits I'd like to see again, so we could send a list of those to the judge. We can probably get through all that by lunch time.'

'This is getting ridiculous,' Pan cut in. 'We've heard the evidence multiple times and I don't need reminding about any of it. I'm expected in Edinburgh the day after tomorrow, so as far as I'm concerned, we should take a vote on the verdict first thing tomorrow. Let's see what the majority of the group thinks and then debate. If we're sensible, we can be out of court for good by 1 p.m.'

'I'm in no rush. It's a nice hotel. We've been stuck in that court for ages. I say we review all the evidence. I want to make sure I get my decision right,' Agnes said, tucking into a third helping of the dessert she'd recently complained about.

'You'll have to forgive me if I don't feel the need to review the evidence simply to get an additional night in a hotel. Some of us have jobs to get back to,' Pan snapped, finally closing his laptop and glaring at Agnes.

'So you're worth more than those of us without posh jobs, is that it?' Garth asked.

Lottie dropped her head into her hands. 'Let's not have another row. What we're doing here is too important for that. There's a lot at stake. For what it's worth, I think we can just review the evidence when aspects of it come up that we don't all agree on.' She looked at Cameron, waiting for him to let Tabitha have it, but he sat with his arm crossed and his mouth shut.

'Surely we only need to focus on the prosecution's case,' Jack said. Everyone at the table turned to stare at him. He spoke so infrequently that Lottie suspected most of them had forgotten he was even there. 'The judge said Maria Bloxham didn't need to prove anything. The way I understood it, the prosecution has to prove its case, including the fact that it definitely wasn't self-defence.'

'Now hold on a moment. The judge didn't use the word definitely. Beyond a reasonable doubt is not the same thing as being definite. One can apply common sense to fill in the gaps,' Gregory said, raising his voice above the various mutterings.

'We're not supposed to be doing this now,' Pan said, standing up. 'I have more work to do, so we'll start fresh in the morning.'

'Shouldn't we listen to Tabitha?' Jennifer asked. 'That's why we elected her, right?'

'I don't have to listen to anyone at 9 p.m.,' Pan said.

'Neither do I,' Jack grinned, getting to his feet and grabbing his jacket. 'See you at breakfast.'

'Hold on,' Lottie said, raising a hand to keep everyone there a moment longer. She was sick of the backbiting. More than that, she wanted to get back to her family and ongoing chaos wasn't going to help. 'We're deciding someone's future, and it's got to be done right. Even if Dr Bloxham won't understand the outcome, he deserves a fair trial too. I'm as fed up with being at court as the rest of you, but Tabitha's right that we need some sort of plan. It'll save time tomorrow, Pan. This isn't going to be a quick, easy decision. I haven't even started to make my mind up about how I feel about the case. Every time one witness makes sense, the next one comes along and changes my mind. We're need to be logical, avoid repetition, not be drawn into arguments, and I agree that I'd like to see the exhibits again.' She glanced around at the faces. No one was arguing with her yet. She had no idea where the sudden decision to take control had come from, but it felt good.

Cameron coughed. 'Such as?'

'All of them, really. I'd certainly like to see the video of Dr Bloxham again now that I've heard what the defendant said about it, just to see if any of it rings true,' Lottie said, speaking slowly and clearly. She was fed up with listening to everyone else's views. Hers were no less valid.

'You know what? I think we're all over-tired. It's been a long day and I've had enough,' Cameron stood up and put on his jacket. 'Let's agree to keep our powder dry until tomorrow, shall we?'

'Can I suggest . . .' Samuel started to say.

'Suggest all you like, mate,' Cameron said. 'But we're leaving.' He walked out with Jack trailing behind him. Pan used the opportunity to exit too, and Garth Finuchin took a packet of cigarettes from his pocket and made towards the nearest exit. Lottie wasn't sure what had happened. She felt scolded. Cameron was clearly fed up, and not just with the usual Tabitha bunch. He hadn't been himself all day, and now he'd practically stormed out. She'd texted him her room number earlier as agreed. What she didn't know was whether Cameron was going to turn up at her door at midnight or not, and if he did, what sort of mood he would be in.

28

The knock on her door came earlier and louder than Lottie had been expecting. She opened it ready to drag Cameron inside, reminding him that there were other jurors on the same floor as her. Instead she found Jack standing outside her door, grinning and holding a bottle of red wine.

'Got glasses?' he asked.

'Um, come in,' Lottie replied, moving aside to let him enter, turning her head to avoid the alcohol fumes. 'It's kind of late. Have you been drinking non-stop since dinner?'

'Yeah, Cameron and I stayed in the bar after everyone else went to bed. Fancy a glass? It's Merlot.' Jack was opening cupboards to find glasses before she could reply. Lottie looked at her watch. She still had half an hour before Cameron was due to turn up and there was obviously something on Jack's mind. 'Sorry to crash your room but I'm just over the corridor and I saw you coming out of here earlier. I'm too wired to sleep.'

He unscrewed the bottle cap and dropped it on the floor, then began sloshing wine between two glasses, with a fair amount landing on the table. Lottie grabbed a handful of tissues and mopped the spillage before it could drip on the carpet.

'So where's Cameron?' Lottie asked as Jack handed her the wine. Perhaps a drink was what she needed, she reasoned. Nothing wrong with a bit of Dutch courage before she made sure Cam knew exactly where she stood.

'He got a call on his mobile and had to go down to the parking area underneath the hotel.' Jack burped then laughed. 'Sorry about that. Should never mix beer and wine. I guess Cam's friend was late delivering his overnight bag.' He threw himself down onto Lottie's bed, spilling yet more wine onto his shirt. 'I can't believe this is nearly over. You remember the first day? I was so nervous, and to be honest I was in a really bad place, then I met Cameron – and you . . .' he raised his glass in a toast to her, 'and now I don't want it to end. Cam will go back to work, I'll be back at uni and we won't see each other as much.'

'I'm ready to get back to real life,' Lottie said, picking up the bottle cap before taking a chair. 'The jury duty thing has been interesting but I need to get away from the misery. I'm not looking forward to tomorrow at all. I reckon it's going to be a series of arguments. I'm surprised Cameron managed to keep quiet this afternoon.'

'He's amazing, isn't he?' Jack said. 'Can you keep a secret?' He sat bolt upright, beaming.

'Sure,' Lottie smiled back, watching the glass in Jack's hand sway back and forth, hoping her duvet would survive his visit. She really didn't fancy sleeping in a bed that reeked of spilled red wine, but at the same time she didn't want to stop him talking. He'd had such a hard time with his awful family. If Jack was about to come out to her, she had to make sure she reacted the way he needed her to, with warmth and reassurance.

'I think I've fallen a little bit in love with him.' He clapped a hand over his mouth and looked mock horrified. 'Shit, I can't believe I actually said that out loud.'

Lottie shut her eyes, wondering if she'd heard right. 'Do you mean in love with Cameron?' she checked.

'Yes. God, yes,' he bounced to his feet again. 'We've been spending a lot of time together after court, and it was so awful when Tabitha made that big fuss about us going out that evening but actually I was kind of pleased someone had seen us. Until then I felt as if I was imagining it, but he's such good company and really funny. He seemed so closed off to start with then when I really got to know him, I realised he's just as scared and confused as the rest of us. Can I put some music on?'

'Best not. Don't want to wake whoever's in the next room,' Lottie said. 'Jack, are you sure about this? Falling in love takes time. You have to be sure you really know someone . . .'

Lottie downed the remainder of the wine from her glass and considered the kindest way to burst Jack's bubble. Cameron's attempts to help him out during a bad patch had obviously backfired. Lottie hated to be the one to bring Jack off his high but she couldn't leave him to get his heart broken without trying to minimise the damage. She poured the remnants of the bottle into her own glass figuring it was best to finish it before Jack did. He found the remote control and began channel surfing to find the hotel's selection of radio stations. Lottie took it from him and switched it off again.

'Jack, you know Cameron's straight, right? I mean, I know for sure he really likes you. He told me you've been having a bad time lately, but I'm worried you might be getting your signals mixed. It's hard when you like someone, especially a man as attractive as Cam, not to blur friendship with something more, but I'm scared you'll end up disappointed.' She put her hand on his forearm and squeezed.

'No,' Jack said, sliding his arms around her and hugging her hard. She did her best to keep control of her drink. 'Me and my big mouth. Cam told me not to say anything to you but there's no one else I can tell. I know he hasn't been in a relationship with a man before and nothing's happened yet . . . but I can feel a spark between us. It's the intensity in his eyes, and how close he holds me when he hugs me goodnight after we've been out.'

Oh fuck, Lottie thought, pulling away from Jack. 'Have you told him how you feel yet?' she asked.

'I'm pretty sure he knows,' Jack said, picking up the empty wine bottle and tipping it to find any last dribbles. 'He's talked a lot about feeling trapped inside his own sexuality, how women judge him by his looks and treat him like a piece of meat, how he can't go to a bar without girls throwing themselves at him. He's sick of it. I know he's looking for something different.'

Lottie's stomach shrivelled. If Cameron really was looking for permanence, maybe he wasn't going to let her go as quickly and easily as she needed him to. She checked her watch again. Ten to twelve. She had to get Jack out of her room. He'd have way too many questions if Cameron turned up. It was clear she wasn't going to be able to persuade Jack that he'd got the wrong end of the stick. Cam would have to do that himself. Just one more awkward conversation to have. Maybe she shouldn't have drunk the wine after all, she thought.

'I should get to bed,' she said, looking pointedly at her watch. 'But Jack, think about it. Cameron may have been friendly and caring, but he's in a difficult place. I probably shouldn't talk about this, but he lost his fiancée to cancer a while ago. I think a lot of what he's said to you might be coming from a pretty dark place.'

'Yeah, that was awful, right? It wasn't his fiancée, though, it was his sister who died,' Jack said. 'And don't worry, he told me all about it. He says that's what made him realise he had to live life freely, you never know how long you've got left. Did he tell you he and his parents nursed his sister the whole time. It made them closer than they'd ever been as a family. He wants to introduce me to them.'

Lottie stared at him. There were so many questions she wanted to ask. Jack had to be mistaken, but right now she didn't want anyone else to witness Cameron turning up at her door. Her world was teetering on the edge of disaster and the fewer people who were involved, the better.

'I see,' she said, walking to her door and opening it a few inches. 'Well, I'm glad you and Cameron have grown so close. I really am tired now, though. Sorry. Would you mind?'

'Sure, sure. Thanks for listening, Lottie. Cam said you were a proper mother figure. He was right.' Jack gave her another unstable hug, kissed her wetly on the cheek then headed out, leaving Lottie standing uselessly in the middle of her room, the empty glass dangling from her fingertips.

'Mother figure?' she asked her reflection in the mirror on the back of the door. Was that a reference to the fact that she had a child, or because she was a few years older than Jack? Either way, it didn't feel much like a compliment.

She took her glass into the bathroom and rinsed it out, trying to get her head round the fact that she and Jack had such different accounts of Cameron's recent loss. He had clearly told her it was his fiancée who'd died, no doubt about it, yet Jack had seemed so sure. Perhaps Jack had only heard what he'd wanted to hear. She'd been guilty enough of that in the last three weeks. Wishing she could just turn off the lights and fall asleep, Lottie listened as footsteps from along the corridor approached her room.

29

A single knock, low and gentle, announced Cameron's arrival. Lottie steeled herself. Their fling had to end now. No more excuses. No getting sidetracked by lust, or caught up in Cameron's declarations of love. She opened the door. He walked straight past her and kicked the door shut.

'I should have realised you'd be drunk too,' Lottie said.

'Was I supposed to stay sober for you? You stopped answering my texts yesterday and you've been avoiding me all day, so I figured I was going to need a few drinks for this conversation.' His voice was ice.

Lottie had forgotten about that. Of course he'd known what was coming. That was what his bad mood over dinner had been about. Cam opened her minibar and took out a bottle of beer. She considered stopping him. The last thing she needed was a bar bill, but if it would calm him down then maybe it was a small price to pay. She walked to the chair and sat down purposefully. 'Jack was here a few minutes ago. He's got the wrong idea about you and him. I'm worried he's going to get hurt,' she said as he popped the lid.

Cameron drank half the bottle in one go then grinned at her. 'Who's been gossiping then?'

'It wasn't deliberate. He thinks . . . God help him, Cam . . . he thinks he's in love with you.'

'Shit happens,' Cameron said. 'He'll survive, maybe even wise up a bit.'

'That's harsh. He just mistook you paying him some attention for a different kind of feeling. You told me he's confused at the moment.'

Cameron walked to the window, ripping the curtains open and staring down to the street below. 'Wow, I really am good. He's a nice kid but you're more my type.'

'Could you shut the curtains please?' Lottie asked.

'What, you think Tabitha's standing out there with binoculars checking on us?' he laughed. Lottie took a deep breath. Cameron was being a jerk but she had to take responsibility for the situation she found herself in. If he was drunk, that was partly her fault. She walked over and gently closed the drapes. He smiled down at her, wrapping one arm around her waist. 'Hey, I'm sorry, gorgeous. Can't we just be like we were? You were so much fun then.' He went to kiss her. Lottie pulled away.

'Did you know how Jack felt about you? Only you don't seem that surprised about it, or concerned.'

'He's a kid. I can't help it if he got the wrong idea. You, on the other hand, didn't misread me at all. You knew straight away I wanted you. Fuck me, it's hot.' He stripped off his T-shirt and tossed it on the floor. 'Want to join me?'

Lottie sighed. Nothing was going the way she'd imagined it. Cameron threw himself onto her bed, stacking the pillows behind his head and settling in.

'We can't do this any more, Cam. I thought about it like you asked me to, and I reached the same decision. I have too much to lose. Daniyal has to be my priority. I can't destroy his happiness for my own sake. I know you'll understand.'

'How?' he asked, finishing his beer and tossing the bottle across the room towards the bin. He missed. Lottie fought the desire to get cross.

'How what?' she asked.

'How can you be so sure I'll understand? I might not. Maybe I'm not prepared to accept that decision.' His lips were curled into a sneer. Lottie felt a shiver of discomfort. It was the alcohol talking, she told herself. This wasn't the Cameron she'd come to know. He wasn't callous or cruel. She just had to appeal to his softer side.

'Hey, this is hard for me too,' she said, perching next to him on the bed. 'If things were different, if I wasn't married, you and I could have had a real future. But you knew about Daniyal from the start. You know how much I love him. I can't risk losing that.'

'Don't lecture me about loss,' Cameron shouted. 'You knew my fiancée died but you played with my feelings and led me on without a second thought.'

Lottie stared at him. His face was the picture of grief, contorted with pain, but his eyes were shining. Her discomfort bloated.

'You fiancée or your sister? I'm confused. You gave Jack different information. Pretty detailed though, something about you and your parents nursing her until she died?' she said quietly.

Cameron narrowed his eyes at her, grinding his teeth together before bursting into a fit of laughter. He doubled up on the bed, clutching his stomach.

'Shit, you two really did have a good long chat, didn't you? Congratulations, Charlotte.' She glared at him. He'd never used her full name before. 'It didn't occur to me you and Jack would compare notes about that. Actually, the tragic tale of terrible loss was based on truth, but not my own. It was a friend's girlfriend. Amazing how using the c-word makes people do whatever you want. You were practically grovelling at my feet.'

She rose on unsteady legs, staggering away from the bed. None of it made sense. Why lie to both her and Jack? Was he so drunk he was just spouting nonsense, or was he winding her up, punishing her for hurting him? Had she grovelled to him? That's not how she remembered it. And he'd lied about the cancer. Bile rushed, bitter and nauseating, into her throat. She had no idea who the man on her bed was, but the Cameron she thought she knew, who'd promised he would never hurt her, was nowhere to be seen.

'I don't think this is the right time to try and sort this out,' she said, keeping her voice soft and non-confrontational. 'You should get some sleep. I'm not sure what's going on, but you're not yourself and . . .'

'I'm not myself?' he snorted. 'Really? What the fuck was that about earlier, wanting to watch the frigging hedgehog video again? Are you trying to make things a thousand times worse?' He lurched to his feet and ripped the minibar door open again, grabbed two small bottles of whisky from the rack.

'That's enough,' Lottie said. 'You're going to have to pay for those. I want you to leave. You're too angry to be rational. Maybe this is easiest anyway. There's no point talking any more.'

'Oh we've got a lot more talking to do, Lottie. You need to understand what has to happen tomorrow.' He ripped the caps off the miniature bottles, downed the first and sat on the floor with his back against the wall, staring at the contents of the second bottle.

'What the hell are you talking about?' she asked, raising her own voice. He was showing no sign of leaving, and there was no way she could get rid of him if he wouldn't go voluntarily.

'We agreed that we were going to vote not guilty. Now suddenly you want to start reviewing the evidence to help make up your mind?' he slurred.

'I didn't agree anything and I don't see what business it is of yours whether I say Maria Bloxham's guilty or not. You know what, Cam, I was actually worried about talking to you tonight because I was really starting to care about you and I didn't want to hurt your feelings, but you just made this an awful lot easier. We're finished for good. You've got problems and I'm fed up with being on the receiving end of this crap.' Lottie started walking towards the door, reaching out for the handle.

'I wouldn't do that if I were you,' he said, shaking his head.

'Do what exactly? Kick you out of my room? Actually I can, and if you don't want to go willingly there are several police officers also staying here overnight who'll be more than happy to help,' she bluffed, stopping just short of the door and wishing she felt as positive as she'd sounded. Cameron kicked off his shoes, clearly going nowhere.

'Come on Lottie.' He stretched his arms above his head with a yawn, showing off his muscles. 'I came here to offer you a carrot. Don't make me get the stick out instead. That would be a lot less fun.' He took his phone out of his pocket and rested it on his lap.

'I want you to leave without a fight. We've got to be around each other all day tomorrow, so I'd prefer it if there wasn't any bad feeling,' Lottie said, wondering why she felt the sudden desire to get the hell out of her own room.

'That's more conciliatory. You're nicer like that. Given that you've already decided to dump me, though, I might as well be straightforward with you. Tomorrow, you'll vote the same way I vote. You don't need to anything else except keep your mouth shut, not cause trouble, and make sure at the crucial moment you find Maria Bloxham not guilty.'

Lottie stared at him. He sat with his hands behind his head, staring her straight in the eyes, suddenly more sober than he'd been all evening. She realised she didn't know him at all.

'Why?' she asked quietly.

'Before this evening, I was hoping you'd just do it because I asked you to,' he smiled.

'So that was the carrot. What's the deal with the stick?' She felt nauseous. The red wine was curdling in her stomach and sending a fountain of acid towards her throat.

'Come here,' he said, standing up and holding out his hand.

'No. No more bullshit,' she replied, fighting tears. 'Just tell me what's really going on.'

'You need me to spell it out for you? I thought you had more brains than that,' Cameron smirked.

'I don't think you did, actually. You thought you could seduce me and that I'd be so obsessed with you that I'd do whatever you told me to. I ruined it by breaking up before we'd reached a verdict, apparently.'

'You see, I knew you were bright.' He walked to stand directly in front of her, looking down into her eyes. 'Listen to me. If you don't do what I've asked you, your husband's going to get a visit he'll never forget. If I time it right, he'll be at the airport with your little boy before you've finished the weekly shop. I forget, is it a Pakistani passport your son has? I was pretty bored during those conversations.'

Time stopped. Her world turned upside down. Everything she'd believed to be secure and known was melting. Cameron's face was twisted and hateful. She wanted to run to her son's bedroom and wrap him in her arms, but she was stuck in some Hotel California style of hell and there was no way she could leave. The adrenaline rush hit her like a train. The options were fight or flight, and the latter wasn't feasible. She sucked in the biggest lungful of air she could get and focused on the red-hot rage that was bubbling inside her.

'Get the fuck out of my room,' Lottie said, storming over to the table and grabbing the empty wine bottle. She turned it upside down and smashed the end of it against the window sill, thrusting it in Cameron's direction. 'You fucking low-life. How dare you threaten me with that. My husband won't believe you. I'll say you're bitter because you tried it on with me and I said no. He'll be more than ready for you.'

'Oh, Lottie. You're growing balls now? Bit late, to be honest.' He pointed at his mobile, left on the floor. 'Pick it up. There's a file open. Just click the arrow.'

'No,' she said. 'I'm not doing anything you tell me. We're done. You're a piece of shit. I guess it serves me right, but I'm done.'

'Yeah, you are,' he said, ignoring the smashed bottle end and leaning down to pick up the mobile.

He held the screen in front of her face and pressed play.

'Make love to me,' Lottie heard herself say.

'You sure about this, Lottie?' Cameron replied, his voice slightly muffled. As Lottie recalled, that was because he'd been kissing her breast at the time.

'Yes. I want you, and I don't want to play games any more,' she demanded. What followed was largely groaning and the sound of dishes hitting the floor.

'Turn it off,' she hissed.

'Really? It's just getting to the good bit. You should hear yourself when you're properly turned on. It's quite impressive. Zain's a lucky man.'

'Don't say his name,' Lottie muttered.

Cameron laughed loudly, switching off his phone and putting it back on the bedside table. 'You hypocrite. You were texting me from his work dinner, making plans to see me, wearing the clothes I asked you to wear. Do you remember letting me touch you under the table in the jury room or did I just imagine that?'

'It was a mistake,' Lottie said. 'I was confused.'

'I don't think your husband's going to accept that as an explanation when he hears you asking me to fuck you in his kitchen, on the kitchen table where you serve his meals.'

Lottie froze. The edge of her vision was a grey fog and there was a noise like angry bees in her head. 'You wouldn't,' she said. 'I have a child.'

'You think I'd lie about a dead fiancée and flirt with some gay kid to get him to do what I want, but somehow I'm above playing this tape to your old man? That's the desperation talking. Put the bottle down.'

'No,' she said, raising it level with his face.

'You want to play?' Cameron grinned. 'Shit, I wish you'd been more like this during sex. Would have been a hell of a lot more interesting.' He walked towards the door and opened it a crack.

For one blissful second Lottie thought he might just leave. Instead he put his mouth to the opening and began shouting. 'Yes, you're amazing, do it! God your tits are beautiful!'

'Shut up!' she shouted.

'Oh yeah, that's right. Get on top. Ride me. Go on Lottie, fucking ride me . . .' he yelled at the top of his voice.

She threw the bottle to the floor, sprinting for the door and slamming it shut.

'All right,' she said. 'Just stop. I'll do whatever you want.' She put her back to the door, tears flowing unchecked down her cheeks.

'Good girl,' he said. 'Although that was fun. Do you think Jack heard? Maybe he'd be interested in a threesome.'

'You're going to crush him. But not until you've got what you wanted from him, right? Can I ask why?' she whispered.

'You cannot. Need to know basis only,' he said, slipping his phone back into his pocket. 'I should leave you to clean up. Careful with that glass. Sleep well, Lottie. I need you well behaved tomorrow.' He picked up his T-shirt and slipped his shoes back on, whistling as he moved around her room. Lottie watched him in the mirror. She was shaking.

He was a monster, capable of anything. The audio file on his mobile would spell the end of her marriage. Zain wouldn't wait around for any sort of explanation. She would lose every-thing. Her son would grow up not knowing his mother. How long before he forgot her face, the sound of her voice? There was no way she would win the legal battle if Zain took him to Pakistan. The audio file was all the evidence it would take to damn her completely.

'G'night sweetheart,' Cam said, planting a kiss on her mouth before leaving.

Lottie threw herself against the door, double locking it then sinking to the floor. She got her fingers into her mouth before she could scream out loud. There had been more than enough noise coming out of her room for one night.

It was obvious that Cameron had been planning this from almost day one. None of it had meant anything to him, yet she'd risked absolutely everything. She'd been taken for a fool. A willing fool, though. That was worse. So little resistance. He must have laughed himself to sleep after fucking her on the kitchen table.

What stung most was that she'd believed his declarations of love, and even indulged in her own admittedly teenage fantasies of what life with him might have been like. Cam playing football in the park with Daniyal. Her and Cam on holiday, soaking up the sun on some distant beach. She had betrayed Zain in her daydreams, in her sleep, and in the flesh. But Cameron's motiv-ation was the real mystery. Why risk so much for a woman he didn't know? He hadn't even wanted to be on the jury at the start. Not that it mattered now. Cam's choices were his problem. She just had to comply and keep her family intact. Her head was a mess. All she wanted was to call a taxi and run home to hide, but that could only happen once she'd been a good girl and obeyed orders. Lottie crawled to her bed, dragging the covers over and hiding from the world. The hard truth, she thought, was that she deserved everything she'd got, and then a bit more.

30

Day Eleven in Court.

'Right,' Tabitha said, ticking items off a neatly written list. 'We've seen the exhibits again and reviewed the evidence. Touching briefly on the judge's summing up, the prosecution must prove to us beyond a reasonable doubt that Mrs Bloxham is guilty. She does not have to prove her defence to be true. There was also the visit to the house to bear in mind.'

'Do you think it'll go on the market now?' Agnes Huang butted in. 'Only who would buy it after what happened there?'

'He didn't die,' Garth said, sighing loudly. 'It's not as if it'll be haunted.'

'I reckon he could die any time,' Agnes replied. 'There's a thought. If he dies, will we be brought back to do this all again, only with a charge of murder.'

Pan coughed loudly. 'Let's not get distracted,' he said. 'The house was clearly worth enough to make money a potential factor, even without the savings accounts. Plenty of people have killed for less. The defendant wasn't very good at answering questions on that. She changed her story a few times.'

'She didn't change her story,' Jack said loudly. 'The prosecutor kept tripping her up.'

'You can't get tripped up if you're telling the truth,' Gregory added loftily. 'I agree with Pan. The finances might be a motive.'

'I was wondering why she didn't tell the prosecution psychiatrist what she told us in court. I'd have leapt at the opportunity to put my side of it as soon as possible,' Jennifer said.

'That works both ways,' Bill Caldwell noted. He was mopping his head continuously and his handkerchief was a dripping ball on the table. 'If she was guilty and it was all a plan to get the money, she'd have told the psychiatrist as much as possible to get him on side. Why swear at him? Makes no sense.'

'It does if what she told us is the truth,' Cameron added. 'Did anyone actually consider that?'

'Yes, you're all looking for holes in the defendant's story. We're supposed to be looking for the flaws in the prosecution's case,' Jack said, crossing his arms and looking ready to take on the world.

Lottie couldn't bear to watch. He was a different person to the shy boy she'd first met. Cameron had made him bold, given him a purpose. As soon as the trial was over he'd be tossed aside like trash. She hadn't even been able to make eye contact with Cameron, avoiding breakfast completely. There was a hard knot of hatred in her stomach, and her pulse was noisy in her ears. The first thing she'd done on waking up was phone Daniyal to tell him how much she loved him. Zain had seemed distant, although perhaps she had imagined that. He'd packed her bag thoughtfully, with cool clothes, her favourite perfume, and the make-up she preferred. Until then, she hadn't realised quite how well he knew her.

'The point about the psychiatrist for me was that she wasn't at all afraid of swearing at him. How are we meant to believe she never once stood up to her husband?' Tabitha asked.

'I swear at my husband all the time. The man's an idiot!' Agnes laughed.

Gregory glared at her. 'I'm not sure that's relevant,' he muttered.

'I for one never use language like that,' Tabitha went on. 'It's certainly not ladylike, and to a professional man, as well.'

'Her gender's not on trial,' Jennifer noted. 'It wouldn't matter if it were man or a woman swearing. The point is that it seems there are two sides to Maria Bloxham. Is it possible that the act of trying to kill her husband was so liberating that she suddenly found some new strength?'

Lottie stared at her. The woman she'd so casually and ignorantly thought of as Just-Jen was much more. The full hypocrisy of her judgment hit her. Jen was insightful, bright and open-hearted. She wasn't just an anything. The truth was, Lottie realised, that she'd been judging herself, then unfairly labelling every comparable woman in the same terms. There was nothing quite like low self-esteem for making you drag everyone else down to your level.

'Sorry, but we're not here to psychoanalyse the defendant,' Pan said, tapping impatient fingers on the desk. 'Let's get back to hard evidence. If she didn't strike him in self-defence it was either for the money, because she's a dangerous crazy person, or because she just plain hates him. I'm erring towards the money.'

'Of course you are,' Jack said. 'There is more to life, you know.'

'Let's not get personal,' Tabitha interjected.

'I'd say staring at a man's caved-in skull is fairly personal,' Garth Finuchin said.

'Can I just say, the term crazy person is not politically correct. Could we decided on a better term if we're going to discuss that aspect?' Samuel piped up.

'Oh, for Christ's sake. We don't need to discuss that at all. The prosecution hasn't proved Maria Bloxham is suffering from any mental illness, so you can't convict her on that basis,' Cameron growled.

'Fine,' Tabitha said coolly. 'We're going round in circles. I suggest we all make a list of the key three issues. I'll compile them and we'll focus our debate on those.'

By lunchtime Lottie was exhausted. Dark shadows beneath her eyes betrayed the sort of night she'd had. Jack tried a few times to engage her help on his side of the argument but her heart wasn't in it. Her freedom of thought had been curtailed. What point was there in her pretending to have an opinion? She had no idea if Maria Bloxham was innocent or guilty. The trial process had been a seesaw. All that mattered was that she kept on Cameron's good side and got out as quickly as possible.

At 1 p.m. she was sitting with a plate of sandwiches on her lap that she had no intention of touching. She'd managed three cups of black coffee during the morning, her stomach not strong enough for the addition of milk.

'Hey, how you doing?' Cameron smiled warmly as he sat down next to her. She stared at him, open-mouthed. No words would come. 'Did you get any sleep? Kind of looks like you had a rough one.' He looked around, checking who could hear him, Lottie realised. She braced herself. Something new was coming. 'So here's the thing.' He kept his voice low enough for just her. 'The court has to think we've been working hard to make our minds up all day. They need at least ten votes, one way or the other, for a majority verdict. When Jack, you and I maintain a not guilty verdict, they won't be able to convict her. It's a numbers game. The prosecution said in court yesterday they wouldn't seek a retrial if we couldn't reach a verdict, so we just have to hold firm and it'll all be over. Make it convincing, though. Maybe try to eat something. You're going to need to speak a few times this afternoon. When I said keep quiet I didn't mean act like you got struck dumb overnight. Pretend you haven't made your mind up yet. Don't make anyone suspicious, okay?'

Lottie nodded.

'You need to smile at me and pick up a sandwich now,' he said, putting a hand on her forearm. She forced the corners of her mouth to comply and raised a sandwich in one shaking hand. 'Take a bite Lottie. I want to see you've got control of yourself.' He squeezed her arm, gently at first, then tighter and harder until she forced the bread into her mouth and began to chew. 'Relax. It'll all be over soon.' He winked at her, showing perfect white teeth as he grinned. 'I like that skirt, by the way.' He leaned across to whisper in her ear. 'Reminds me of what I did to you with the ice cube.' The sandwich turned to rock in her mouth. 'I wonder how your husband will react when I describe that to him. Maybe it'll excite him. I'm getting hard again just thinking about it. Don't fuck up this afternoon.' Lottie dropped the sandwich back on her plate as he walked away to rejoin Jack.

By 3 p.m. they'd rehashed every aspect of the evidence, Jack and Garth had narrowly avoided coming to blows, Samuel had been reduced to tears and Agnes had been asked to stop shouting at least ten times. Lottie commented every fifteen minutes. She was checking on the clock.

'It's nearly the end of the day,' Tabitha said. 'This might be a good time to take stock of where we are with the verdict. Shall we have a show of hands?' There was a general round of tired nodding. 'Right. Hands up please if you believe the defendant is guilty.' It was slow but the hands went up. All except the three of them and Pan. 'We're split then,' Tabitha said, noting the decision in her book. 'The judge urged us towards total agreement. May I ask which parts of the evidence you're undecided upon?'

'All of it,' Cameron said loudly. 'And there's no way anyone in this room is going to persuade me otherwise. Doesn't matter how much time we spend here.'

'Me too,' Jack backed him up.

Lottie felt everyone's eyes on her. She took a deep breath, knowing she had to speak and that seconds were passing.

'I agree with Jack and Cameron,' she managed eventually.

'Really?' Tabitha asked. 'Only you've been talking about the evidence as if you weren't quite certain. Are there any questions you want to raise that we could answer for you, any parts of the trial you found hard to follow?'

'None of it was hard to follow. I'm not some stupid kid you need to patronise,' Lottie barked. There was a general intake of breath. 'Listen, I kept an open mind. I considered the arguments. Maria Bloxham said she acted in self-defence. The prosecution hasn't proved to me that she didn't. The psychiatrist was arrogant and I don't blame her for swearing at him. Is that enough for you?'

'More than enough, thank you,' Tabitha said, sniffing.

'Self-defence? Hitting a bloke with his back turned? You lot are just bleeding heart liberals. Where the hell did common sense go?'

'It's called rule of law,' Jack replied.

'Learn that phrase at university, did you? Good luck with real life.' Finuchin pushed his chair backed noisily from the table.

'Most of us have been able to see sense,' Gregory said. 'I'm struggling to understand why you can't see it from our point of view.'

'Perhaps because we actually understand the phrase innocent until proven guilty,' Cameron snapped. 'Would you like me to explain it to you for the hundredth time?'

'No need for that,' Tabitha said.

'What makes you better than us?' Agnes demanded.

'How I would love to answer that,' Cameron sneered at her.

'Pan? What it is you're not clear on?' Tabitha attempted to bring the table back to order.

'I'm on the fence, so not guilty seems the only fair decision. That said, if it was going to swing matters one way or the other and conclude proceedings . . .'

'You cannot make a decision just so you can get out of here quickly,' Gregory admonished.

'That's not what I was saying,' Pan replied, rubbing his eyes. 'It just seems we're stuck.'

'I suggest we write the judge a note,' Tabitha said. 'She'll advise us. It's too hot to stay in here any longer.'

They were called into the courtroom twenty minutes later, all reconvened in their usual places. Lottie kept her head down, much closer to Cameron than she wanted to be. He was making her skin crawl. She knew the only reason he hadn't really exploded at the Tabithas was because he had the numbers he needed with her and Jack. Crossing her fingers, she waited for the hell to be over. Surely the judge had to dismiss them if they were adamant that they couldn't reach a verdict. They'd been at it a whole day.

'I've received a note from the jury,' the judge announced to the lawyers when everyone was settled. 'It seems they are divided in proportions that would not be resolved by my issuing a majority direction of either 11 to 1, or even 10 to 2. Any suggestions from counsel as to how we proceed?'

'I'd invite Your Honour to give the majority verdict now, to attempt to move things along,' James Newell said.

'I agree,' Imogen Pascal joined in. 'And I should add that we reviewed our position overnight and have decided we will list the case for a retrial if this jury cannot reach a verdict, although we'd obviously like to avoid that scenario given the costs.'

'You're fucking kidding,' Lottie heard Cameron mutter. He sat upright and frowned across the courtroom towards the public seating. She followed the line of his eyes, noting that the three huge men who'd appeared yesterday were back again. Other than that, the seating was populated only by the same crowd who'd been in court on and off throughout the trial.

Someone was controlling him, she thought, sharing information and telling him what to do, unless he was working for the defendant directly. His fingernails were digging into the padding on the seat arms. As Lottie watched, it began to rip. He was stronger than Lottie had ever imagined. All those hours working with his hands, the hands Lottie had spent nights fantasising about, had made him lethal. She imagined those fingers around her throat and knew there was no way she would cross him. Cameron Ellis wasn't just dangerous. He was totally out of control.

'Very well,' the judge said, checking her watch. 'Members of the jury, it's been a long day and you've obviously worked hard. You may return to your hotel for the night. Tomorrow you will begin deliberating again, but I will accept a majority verdict from you. You may go.'

The usher stood up to see them out. Lottie looked back at Cameron who was still staring across the court. She scanned the crowds again to see who he was so interested in, but by then he was on his feet and following the rest of the jurors.

'Your room, tonight, 9 p.m.,' he hissed as he stalked past her in the corridor. 'And don't be a bitch and not answer the door, or I'll speak to your husband instead.'

James Newell's head was uncharacteristically low when he walked into the conference room. Maria kept her hands folded in her lap, trying to come to terms with the latest blow.

'They're just going to keep on bringing me back until they get a conviction, aren't they?' she asked.

'They'll try once more, if this jury can't reach a verdict,' Newell corrected her. 'I know this isn't what we'd hoped for. The jury is obviously deadlocked at the moment. The judge will give them the whole day tomorrow to try to make up their minds, and if not the case will be listed for trial and we'll start over.'

'I'm not sure I can do this again,' Maria said, chewing her nails. 'Sitting in the dock like a lab rat with everyone staring at me.'

'You can't plead guilty just to avoid a second trial. That's what the prosecution wants. I suspect that's why Imogen Pascal announced their change in position in front of you. They don't really want the expense of retrying a case they might still not win. She's trying to force your hand.'

'But Professor Worth will be so much better prepared next time. He'll have all the answers in place to condemn me before I've even given my version of events. You know that,' Maria said, standing up and pacing.

'You'll be better prepared too. Don't lose heart now. Let's get through tomorrow and see what happens. There's no point worrying yet. I meant to ask you – the three men who went into the public gallery. Are you quite sure you don't know them? The timing was . . .'

'Strange, I know, but I'm afraid I have no idea who they are. Certainly not the type Edward would have been friendly with, and I didn't organise rent-a-crowd support.'

'No,' Newell laughed. 'Probably just interested members of the public then. Nonetheless, be careful on your way back to the bail hostel. They looked organised, if you know what I mean.'

Maria waited in the conference room until the last of the journalists had given up on getting a photo of her, and disappeared. She had prepared mentally for the case to end either that day or the next. The thought of starting from scratch was intolerable. Metal flashed in her mind. She needed some relief. The tension was like a boil that needed lancing. One more day, she thought. Twenty-four hours and it should be over. Twenty-four hours and she might have been sentenced. Back wearing clothes other people chose for her. Eating food other people decided upon. Sleeping in a bunk not knowing what might happen in the hours of darkness. Her fortitude was shrinking with every passing minute.

She was tired of proving herself, and exhausted at the preconceptions the press had been allowed to spout. What was it about being female that meant you were assumed to be hysterical, given to flights of fancy, or just a plain old liar? She was fighting to be believed on every single fact, yet from the second Edward's qualifications had been read out in court, he'd been put on a pedestal. The difference between men and women suddenly seemed less like a chasm and more like a continental divide. It wasn't just about the unequal pay, preferential promotions, and everyday sexism that she'd read so much about in the papers. It was the sense that women needed less gravity, breathed a lighter version of air, that somehow they were less substantial in every way. A man could hit a woman and be an alpha-male. A woman who hit a man was a shrew or a she-devil. Women being deceptive seemed to be the presumed normal state. She'd thought life with Edward had prepared her for any eventuality. Not for this trial though, and not for prison either. Spending the second half of her adult life behind bars was suddenly unthinkable.

She had to go past the pharmacy en route to her hostel. Her discipline and resolved evaporated. Not one cut since she'd been arrested and here she was, needing it again, longing for the simple, clean pain to end the nightmare. Just a single slice and it could all be over, she thought, as she left the building and headed for the shops. It wouldn't even hurt. She could wrap herself up warm, maybe sit in the bath tub. If she took a handful of paracetamol first, she could just fall asleep as the water turned red.

31

Ruth went to check on her twins for the fifth time that evening. As usual, she'd put them to sleep in their separate beds, and now they were snuggled up together in one, arms wrapped around one another. Max was sucking his thumb and Lea was playing some invisible piano with her fingers on top of the covers. Both were smiling in their sleep. They'd spent the evening decorating their grandmother with stickers. Ruth's mum had sat through the arts and crafts session, happily accepting that every visible inch of skin was going to end up plastered in a cartoon character, sparkly star or rainbow. For once there had been no spilled drinks, no tantrums, no yelling of obscenities. Odd really, given Ruth's own mood, that their house was so serene. She wanted to scream. The prospect of there being a second trial if the jury couldn't agree on a verdict was barbaric. Maria had suffered enough.

Certain that the house was settled for the night, she locked herself in her office, taking out one of her journals from the filing cabinet. It documented her final call from Maria. At the time Ruth had made her notes, she'd had no way of knowing that Edward Bloxham was just two hours from being air-lifted to a hospital. She opened the relevant pages, noting how bad her handwriting was, but then she'd been upset when she was writing her notes. Her recall of that particular conversation was almost word perfect, but she reread her notes anyway, poking at the soreness of it all.

Maria had called at lunchtime. By that stage, Ruth had put Maria's mobile number into caller recognition on her phone. She'd answered quickly, hoping Maria was having a rare good day.

'Hi Maria,' she'd said. 'How are you doing?'

'Not really doing . . . at all,' Maria had replied. 'Saying goodbye now, Ruth. No more calls.'

'Why?' Ruth asked, putting down her coffee and picking up her pen, scribbling down Maria's words.

'He says I can cut myself again tonight.' Maria had long since stopped saying her husband's name. Ruth always knew who "he" was. There was no one else in Maria's life. 'I'm going to. I'm just not sure I'll be able to stop. The pain helps. I can forget everything. I think I want to forget now.'

'Maria, you're worrying me,' Ruth had said. 'You mustn't let him make you do this. The self-harm is so dangerous, especially when you're feeling like this.'

'You've been a good friend. I know I never got to see you in person, or thank you properly, but I always knew you were there when I needed you.'

'I can send help. You need to get out. Right now. I can call the police . . .'

'He'll have me locked away. He's got it all planned. I've never gone to the doctor, just cut more and more. I can't get away from him. He'll still control my life. I'll be told I'm depressed and paranoid, a danger to myself. The funny thing is, I know I am.'

'This isn't right, Maria. Please, I can't do nothing.'

'I don't want anything,' Maria had said. 'Just to hear your voice.'

'I have your address. Do you remember you gave it to me before when you were really scared? You promised you'd let me help if it got bad enough. This is it, Maria. It's now. You have to give me permission to get help. I can call the police, or an ambulance. Whatever you need.'

'No one will believe me. Sometimes even I think I've made it all up in my own head. I don't want to argue with you, Ruth. Maybe he'll have changed his mind by the time he comes home.'

'You could pretend to be ill. Just go to bed, tell him you were sick today. You said he hates to be around illness. He'll leave you alone.'

'Not this time. I don't want to play games any more. It's all right, really. I'm all right. You've been so . . .'

The mobile phone beeped. What little credit Maria had left was gone. Ruth stared into the receiver of her landline, furious and terrified. She knew better than to intervene when she'd been specifically told not to. And what had Maria really said? That she was going to cut herself again. They'd been there before. If she called the police, they would attend at a house to find a woman who would say nothing was wrong. There was no injury to justify calling an ambulance. Any intervention meant that Edward would realise Maria had been in contact with someone and then he'd search the house from top to bottom until he found her phone.

So Ruth had done what she did at the end of every call. She'd faithfully written up her notes, careful to recall the wording used as precisely as possible, noting inflection and what she'd been able to assess or diagnose about her caller's psychological state. Ruth had always been good at that, at hearing the precise emotions in people's voices, in assessing their strengths and weaknesses by the things they said or didn't say. Reading people was her gift. By the time she'd finished her notes, she knew one thing with absolute certainty. Maria no longer cared about living. The call was no cry for help. It was the last contact she would ever have with anyone except Edward.

32

Cameron was sober. Lottie wasn't sure if that was better or worse. Either way, he was in a foul mood. The steak knife she'd concealed in her sleeve on leaving the hotel restaurant was hidden beneath her pillows. It was true she couldn't say no to him coming to her room, but she could at least arm herself. She sent the last ten minutes reading and rereading a text from Zain.

'House empty without you,' it read. 'Danny and I told your photo about our day. He can't wait to have you home. I know things have been hard. So much work pressure I forgot to pay you any attention. Let's book a holiday soon. Good luck tomorrow.'

Lottie had phoned to say goodnight to Danny, and Zain had been on speakerphone, but somehow texts allowed you to say things more clearly. The guilt was consuming her. Fear of the possible consequences of her stupidity was making her ill. Just one more day, she told herself. If she could keep it together for just one more day . . .

That was when Cameron had slunk in, his eyes narrowed to slits, looking as if the whole world was his enemy. He threw himself into the chair and put his head in his hands. Lottie stayed next to her door, leaning against the wall and waiting for him to speak.

'We can't let this go to a retrial. You're going to have to persuade them to side with us,' he snarled.

'You're insane,' Lottie replied. 'How the hell am I supposed to change their minds? We've only got Pan on our side and he'll flip as soon as it means he can get back to work. But Tabitha, Gregory and Garth? That's not happening.'

'You have to,' Cameron said slowly. 'Fuck!' he shouted, bursting from the chair and kicking the side-table hard enough to send it flying. Smashed glass skittered across the floor. Lottie put a shaking hand on the door handle. 'Don't you dare open that bloody door,' he commanded.

'I don't know what you expect me to do,' she cried. 'You said just stay quiet and vote not guilty. I did everything you wanted. This is nothing to do with me.'

Cameron breathed out hard and shoved his hands in his pockets. 'We need a plan. They won't listen to me. I've had too many run-ins with that snooty dog Tabitha. If we keep Pan on our side, that's four of us. Six more need to say not guilty and we're safe.'

'Safe how? What is she to you?' Lottie asked.

'She?' Cameron looked confused.

'Maria Bloxham. You're so determined she should be found not guilty. I don't get it. At the start of the trial you wanted to be released from jury service. How did you end up this involved?'

He rubbed his temples. 'Yeah, well, it turned out that jury service offered a way to solve all my problems, at least until Imogen fucking Pascal changed her mind about the retrial. Anyway, that's not your problem. You need to figure out how to get enough jurors to vote not guilty or your husband gets a life-changing surprise. I hope you like Asia, because that's where you'll be headed for contact visits, if you get any.'

Lottie bit back the desire to either scream at Cameron or beg for mercy. Neither was going to work. He'd played his strongest hand with the audio file. Tonight he was a mess.

Not just desperate, but scared. Really scared, she realised. It was like looking at herself in a mirror.

'You're in trouble,' she said. 'So you can give me as many orders as you like. You're right, Zain probably would divorce me. He might try to take Daniyal, but maybe not. He's proud, but not vindictive. What I think is that you've got just as much to lose as me. That question you pulled out of your pocket for the psychiatrist. You didn't write that. Where did it come from?'

'An interested party. Does it matter? It didn't make any fucking difference.'

'The same someone who asked you to help Maria Bloxham? They obviously thought it was the right question to ask, so it might help us too. I just want to know what's in it for you. If you're expecting me to sort this shit out, I think I have a right to know,' she said.

He sat on the edge of the bed, picking his nails. His face was ashen. 'There are some debts. No big deal. If I'd been Maria Bloxham, I'd have smashed in that bloke's head for the money too.'

'You really don't believe it was self-defence,' Lottie whispered, 'but you're still prepared to force Jack and me to say she's not guilty.'

'I couldn't give a flying fuck what happens to her. This is about my life, my problems.' He stood up and ran at the wall. 'Shit!' he shrieked, kicking the plaster. 'Shit, shit, shit!'

Lottie stood up straighter. 'Your life's in danger. That's what those three men were doing in court, the ones you wouldn't look at. Is that who you met in the parking area last night? No wonder you were so pissed off when you came up here.' She paused, thinking it through. 'You always were short of money. Now it makes sense. How much do you owe?'

'Enough that the interest alone is going to cost me my right hand – maybe both hands – if I don't pay it,' he yelled, striding across the room and grabbing her by the throat. In half a second she was against the wall on her toes, struggling to breathe. 'And if you're so fucking smart all of a sudden, you might want to concentrate on sorting out how we do this.' His face was millimetres from hers. His spittle was flying into her eyes. The edges of her vision began to blur as she flapped her hands uselessly against him. Then she was on the floor gasping for air, scrabbling away from him into the corner.

She waited until her vision returned to normal, watching him as he stood, forehead leaning against the wall, banging his head softly every couple of seconds and muttering to himself.

'So you're being paid to fix the jury?' she rasped. 'No result, no cash. You take a one-way trip with the nice men who want to redecorate some unused warehouse with your brains?' she smiled.

'If you don't shut the fuck up, I'll finish what I just started,' he bared his teeth.

'No, you won't,' she whispered. 'you need me. There'll be questions if I have bruises on my throat in court tomorrow.'

'Cunt!' he shouted, aiming his aggression at the wall instead and knocking a picture to the floor.

Lottie walked across the room, picked it up and hung it back on the wall.

'You should go,' she said. 'If anyone's reported a disturbance you can't be found in here. The whole jury would end up being sent home.'

'Not yet,' he muttered. 'You think you're in control again, don't you? That little glint in your eye. Knowledge is power, or some such crap. I think you need to remember who's in charge and I plan to help you with that.'

'I know what's at stake,' she said. 'You haven't exactly been subtle about it.'

'Get on the bed,' he ordered.

She met his eyes. 'No.'

'Okay,' he said. 'If that's how you want it.' He took his phone from his pocket. 'You really should be more careful with your mobile. I got your husband's number from your contacts list when you were in the shower. You remember that time I did all the cleaning up after we screwed? Did you really think I was scraping berries off the floor out of the goodness of my heart?' He waved his mobile in the air. Lottie saw Zain's number flash up, Cam's thumb over the dial button. 'Last chance,' he said as she started to cry. 'Now get on the goddamned bed.'

'All right,' Lottie said. 'Just switch the phone off, okay? I'll do what you say. I get it. You're in charge. What are you going to do?' Her voice was shaking, and she was freezing cold in spite of the heat.

'To you?' he laughed. 'Nothing. With you? That's a different matter. We've done plenty already.' He pulled his shirt off and threw it on the floor. 'Why so shy now?' She perched on the edge of the bed as he threw himself down and stretched out. 'Don't be silly. Come up here. Let's get comfortable.'

Lottie shifted backwards, her muscles a bundle of knots, goosebumps on her arms. She sat next to him, staring at the opposite wall.

'What is it you want?' she asked.

'I want to give you a reason to believe Maria Bloxham,' Cameron whispered in her ear, licking the inside of it delicately. Tongue like a snake's, she thought. 'One you won't forget. What I can promise you is this: Once she's out of the dock, I'll destroy that recording. It all ends then. It's a little incentive for you not to get any ideas like rebellion or independence. Now take your clothes off.'

'You don't really want to make me do that,' Lottie pleaded.

'You did it voluntarily a couple of days ago.'

'Fuck you,' Lottie said flatly.

'You already did. Do you need me to help?'

Lottie sat upright, ripping off her T-shirt, and stripping her jeans down. 'Underwear too?' she asked.

'Oh yeah,' Cameron licked his lips.

It wasn't clear what he was capable of. Lottie had no point of reference for understanding him. This wasn't the Cameron who'd reassured her. It wasn't even the same man who'd humiliated her so cruelly in the jury room before they'd become friends. This was a deviant creature without conscience and entirely unpredictable. He needs me alive, she told herself. More than that, he needs me unharmed. She could taste regret in her mouth. All the ways it could have gone differently. If she'd let Zain write a letter to get her out of jury duty. If she hadn't been so desperate to make friends. If she hadn't been so easily impressed by Cameron's easy charm and good looks. What was that phrase . . . you only regretted the things you didn't do? Well, that was bullshit. She was alone and helpless, with a man who had gone from adoring to terrifying in just two or three quick steps. All she had left were scraps of pride and she was damned if she'd let them go to. He could punish her, abuse her, but she sure as hell wouldn't give him the satisfaction of seeing her break.

She summoned what little resilience and toughness she had left, papering over the cracks of her terror. 'If you're going to rape me, you'd best get on with it quickly. I'm not sure how much longer I can stay awake.' She folded her arms across her chest, determined to look Cameron in the eyes. If she had to submit, she wasn't going to cry. There would be no begging. She'd brought herself to this low, after all. What a way to learn that particular lesson.

'Lie down, Lottie,' he said quietly. 'You really are beautiful. I never lied about that.'

'I don't understand why you're doing this.'

'You will. Roll onto your stomach,' he ordered. She managed to hold back the tears until she put her face into the pillow. 'Just stay there, completely still for me, whatever I do. Say nothing, do nothing. It seems you need some extra motivation to do what I need, so here you go. I want you to play dead for me, Charlotte. That means I can move your arms, your legs, your body and you can't resist. You're powerless.'

Lottie held on a few seconds longer before the first sob escaped her. The thought of being used like that, no more than a slab of meat, was repulsive. It was the opposite of everything human and decent. Her body began to shake as he ran his hand from her shoulder, slowly, really feeling her skin, letting his fingertips drift over the rise and fall of her buttocks.

'Please don't,' she cried.

'Shhh,' he whispered close in her ear. 'You're dead. Crying's against the rules.'

'I'm going to do whatever I want to you. I like it when you're like this – pliable, easy, no effort on my part. It's what you were intended for. Can you feel that now?' He picked up one of her legs and moved it towards him, leaving her open and exposed. More than anything else, she felt vulnerable, more than she had in her entire life. Anything could happen at any second. Lottie was petrified, horrified by her own impotence.

'Wait there,' he said. 'I just need a moment.'

His weight shifted off the bed. Lottie listened for some clue as to what he was doing. There were footsteps, the rustle of clothing, he picked something up off the bedside table. Lottie braced herself, regretting every second, every thought she'd had since first walking into Bristol Crown Court. If she could turn back time, she would give anything. Anything at all.

Her bedroom door slammed. Lottie cried out. She held her breath. Nothing.

'Cameron?' she sobbed.

Nothing. She counted to sixty, keeping it slow in her head, then shifted to look to the side of the bed where he had been. Pushing herself up onto her elbows she turned slowly, expecting him to be in the chair, staring at her, waiting for her to move, to screw up, so he could punish her. It was empty. She snapped her legs together so hard it hurt, grabbing the duvet and covering her nakedness. Stepping off the bed she stumbled, smashing her knee on the bedside table, crawling two steps before making it upright. More tiny footsteps to the bathroom door, not wanting to look, unable to resist. Was he trying to trick her? She pushed the door fully open. It was empty. Running to the wardrobe she checked there too, then behind the curtains.

He was gone. His phone and keys had disappeared. He'd picked his shirt and shoes up off the floor. She was alone. Throwing herself at her door, she locked it and drew the safety chain across. He'd undone it so silently she hadn't heard a thing.

The shock sent her to her knees. She rested her head against the wood, reeling, sickened. Minutes passed before she managed to stand again. By the time she reached the bathroom, she was retching. Back on her knees, holding her hair away from her face, staring into the toilet bowl. Fifteen minutes later she was running a bath. Her hands wouldn't stop shaking. She realised she was talking to herself, saying soothing words usually reserved for Daniyal, reassuring herself. It was safe. He was gone. Only she had to see him tomorrow, maybe the day after that. Then who knew. He still had the recording.

Lottie filled the bath as deep and hot as she could get it, moving away only to raid the minibar, knowing she'd make herself sick again if she wasn't careful, but she had to drown his voice out of her mind. The heat of the water was good. She sat at one end of the bath, her knees drawn up to her chest, legs clamped together, drinking neat gin, no less violated for the fact that technically she hadn't been. In her head, she could hear Maria Bloxham's voice describing how it had been for her, being subjected to what undoubtedly amounted to rape month after month, year after year. Lottie recalled the defendant's face as she'd talked about it, the sheer loathing for her husband etched into every line and wrinkle. The same way it must now be imprinted on hers too, she thought. True hatred didn't fade. She already knew she would wish Cameron dead every day for the rest of her life.

He had proved his point. She would do whatever he told her to do. There was no question about it. Picking up the soap again, she began to scrub her skin. It would take all night to scrape the feeling of dirt away, and he hadn't actually done anything. It no longer mattered what had motivated Maria Bloxham to attack her husband. If she wanted his money, she was owed it, Lottie thought. If she'd struck the blow from anger rather than fear, good for her.

Tomorrow was a no-brainer, just as Cameron had intended. She would protect her son and protect her marriage, and do as she'd been told. At least now she could do that with a clear conscience. Maria Bloxham didn't deserve a prison cell. She deserved a fucking medal. If Lottie were as brave, she'd have picked up a lamp and smashed Cameron's skull with it too. She allowed herself a few moments to imagine the scene. Then she could have wiped the audio recording and the police would have been none the wiser. Self-defence, she imagined herself saying. He was trying to rape me. I had no choice. The words echoed in her ears, her own voice blending bizarrely with Maria's. We had no choice. No choice at all.

33

Day Twelve in Court

The twelve of them sat around the table. The heat had taken a turn for the worse, or possibly it was their tempers raising the temperature. Either way, Lottie was losing hope. The cuts to Maria's thighs had been her main argument. It was obvious the woman was living in misery, she'd argued. And why had her husband not got her help?

'Perhaps she's just mentally ill. That was one of the options the psychiatrist gave,' Garth Finuchin had countered. 'You don't know that her husband hasn't spent the whole of his marriage putting up with her deranged imagination, then one day she just lost it and bashed him over the head. Sounds more likely than that nonsense she told us.'

'What about the lock on his study door?' Jack offered.

'It was where he kept his notes and computer,' Gregory said. 'Perhaps he didn't want them disturbed if she was that paranoid. She might have just chucked everything on the fire one day. I'm giving Dr Bloxham the benefit of the doubt, especially as the poor bastard can't speak.'

'Because she hit him!' Agnes Huang added, gleefully and needlessly. There were murmurs of consent from around the table.

Lottie wanted to bang her head on the desk. Pan had stopped paying attention completely and looked ready to side with whoever could get him his freedom fastest. Samuel wasn't unsympathetic, but simply nodded in agreement with whoever was speaking at the time. Agnes was digging in for a fight and was content to stay there another week. Garth Finuchin was a lost cause. It seemed there was no card that trumped the sight of a grown man cuddling a baby hedgehog, turned drooling wreck. It had affected them at a deeper psychological lever than Lottie knew how to reach.

She stared at Cameron. What she did know was that being on the same side as him wasn't helping. Grabbing her mobile, she texted beneath the table.

'Change your verdict. Disagree with me.' She tapped send.

Cameron ignored the buzzing. She kicked him beneath the table until he pulled his phone from his pocket and glanced down to read the message. He raised his eyebrows and gave a brief shake of his head.

'Just be yourself,' she typed again. 'The real you. Don't hold back.'

He shot a nasty look at her, then shrugged. Lottie considered what she was about to do. It was desperate, much too close for comfort, and underhanded. And there was nothing else left to try.

'The thing is, I know Maria Bloxham is telling the truth,' Lottie began.

'So now you've got some sort of psychic connection with her, do you? That's convenient,' Garth mocked.

Lottie glared at him. 'I know, because when you've also experienced what she's been through, it's impossible not to see the signs in other people.' Her voice was wobbly, but it shut Garth Finuchin up, Lottie thought, waiting for Cameron to engage his brain and join in. The Tabithas had grown to dislike Cameron enough that Lottie needed him against rather than with her, if she was to garner any sympathy at all.

'Oh come on,' Cameron chipped in. 'I'm all for deciding the case on its merits, but I don't buy the whole sisterhood bullshit. Why don't we just stick with the law?'

'Mr Ellis, that's very rude. We agreed at the start not to let this get personal. I have to ask you to let Lottie speak,' Tabitha admonished. Lottie could see the hate on his face.

'Fine,' Cameron folded his arms. 'Just keep it relevant, would you?' he aimed at Lottie. She narrowed her eyes at him, no acting required.

'What Maria said about being controlled, it's not as unusual as you might think,' she began, wondering how she would get through it without breaking down or throwing up. 'It's what bad relationships are made of. One partner gets jealous or makes unreasonable demands. Some men choose women who their instincts tell them won't fight back. They like vulnerability. The strength those men give you at the start is hard to let go of, so you compromise. When you're told your boyfriend doesn't like a certain friend, you find a reason to avoid them. When he says you look great in red, you go out of your way to wear that colour.' She recalled the dress she'd worn because Cameron had liked her in it. She intended to cut it up the second she got home. 'When he says he hates it when women are lazy about shaving their legs, you make damned sure you never let it go that extra day.'

'Oh Lottie,' Jack said. 'Are you sure you want to tell us this? I had no idea.'

'Thank you, Jack,' she replied, not quite able to meet his eyes. He had plenty of hurt yet to come. He just didn't know it yet. 'I need to do this.' She cleared her throat and made her voice fractionally louder. 'It's tiny things to start with. Stuff you don't recognise as controlling but it's there, wrapped up as compliments and polite suggestions. Before you know it, you've made changes you never anticipated, and all the time you tell yourself it's because you love him. The truth is, you don't want to lose him, because by then, you've stopped seeing your friends as much. You've ignored the advice from your family and you don't want to look stupid.'

'It's a bit of a stretch from there to attempted murder. What the defendant described was something totally different. I'm sure you think you have some sort of feminist expertise here but really . . .' Cameron sounded bored.

'Shut up, I want to hear,' Agnes interrupted him. 'Did this really happen to you, Lottie? Was it your husband?' She sounded all too delighted to be getting some gossip.

Lottie felt grubby already, and it was only going to get worse. 'I can't say,' she replied. 'I have too much to lose.' That, at least, was the unadulterated truth.

'This is a safe space, dear,' Tabitha said gently. 'It sounds as if you've been through difficult times.'

'You'd be amazed at how bad it gets before you realise you're in an abusive relationship. You make excuses. He's under pressure. Money's tight,' she threw a glance in Cameron's direction. 'Your family's not supportive enough. He doesn't like Christmas or Easter or the summer, or whatever season it happens to be. Then he hits you for the first time. He hits you and it's terrifying and awful but then he cries in your arms and says he's never done that before. So you think, maybe it was my fault. Suddenly he's the boyfriend he was right at the start. Flowers appear for no reason. There are trips to the cinema. He's warm and kind. Then it happens again, and here's the reality. You know, from the second time he hits you, that it's really not you. You know it's him. But by then you feel so worthless that you can't see your way out. You're probably telling yourself it's because you love him. But you stay because it's easier and less scary than leaving. He's got you, and it's like drowning in mud.'

'Lottie,' Jennifer said, reaching out a hand and touching hers. 'How awful. You should have said something before now.

Sitting through this trial must have been heartbreaking for you.'

'Could I point out that even the defendant in this case makes it perfectly clear that Dr Bloxham never laid a finger on her. Not once. I've no time for men who hit women, but I've got to agree with Cameron here. I'm not sure how relevant this is,' Garth Finuchin said.

'Thank you, finally,' Cameron muttered.

'I think we should keep listening to Lottie,' Jack said sweetly. 'If she's prepared to give us her insight, we should respect that.'

Lottie smiled at him. 'Thank you. The relevance is that Dr Bloxham didn't need to hit his wife. He had something much more powerful to use against her. He knew she'd been cutting herself from an early age. When other men might have used their fists, he handed over a razor blade. He never needed to hit. He was much more devious. It also meant she could never go to the police and claim that he was violent, but try to see it through my eyes. Every cut on her legs was the equivalent of a black eye or a broken rib, just even more psychologically damaging. There's no other difference.'

There was silence. 'That's horrible,' Jennifer said eventually. 'I'm so sorry.'

'That question to the psychiatrist,' Lottie said. 'You need to know about that, too.'

'Ah, but you didn't write that. I saw Mr Ellis pull it out of his pocket,' Gregory huffed.

Lottie was ready for it. 'You're right. I was too embarrassed to hand it over myself, so I wrote it before we went into court and asked Cameron to hand it over for me. I suppose . . . I just couldn't face you all questioning me about why I wanted to raise that particular issue. It was too personal.'

'Go on,' Tabitha said softly.

Lottie clenched her hands together and focused her eyes on the table. 'When Maria Bloxham talked about her husband asking her to play dead while he . . . you know. I realised then that she couldn't have made it all up. By the time you get to the stage in your relationship when you'll pretend to be dead on command, you've lost control over absolutely everything. He'll tell you you're not allowed to move. That only he can move your arms, your legs, whatever he likes. He'll tell you that dead people don't cry, so you can't either. Normal people don't do that. If someone loves you, they want you to respond to them.' She took a deep breath and let the tears in her eyes fall unchecked. 'There's no consent when you pretend to be dead. It only happened to me once, and I'll never forget it. I'll never get over it. But I can tell you this. Maria Bloxham was raped every time her husband asked her to play dead. She was abused and violated. I completely understand how close she was to cutting herself too deeply to survive any longer.' Lottie looked up, and met every other juror's eyes, one at a time slowly, not sparing herself from Cameron's gaze. He looked away. 'When a man does that to a woman, he takes everything from her. Power, free will, choice, and life. He takes away the idea that you are actually alive. Maria Bloxham tolerated that for years. I don't blame her for hitting that man on the skull with the first thing that was handy. I don't blame her, because that's exactly what I want to do to the man who did the same thing to me.'

Jennifer put an arm around Lottie's shoulders and hugged her. Tabitha took a handkerchief from her sleeve and dabbed her eyes. Samuel made a dash for the men's room. Garth Finuchin sat, head down, silent for once. Agnes Huang was biting her nails. Lottie allowed herself to be comforted, Jennifer whispering meaningless but kindly meant nothings. Ten minutes later they were all sat back around the table.

'How can you be sure she didn't just research all this? She seemed clever enough to me. If you've been through it then other people have, too. There must be plenty of books in the library on it,' Andy Leith piped up.

'Hey, I hadn't thought of that. What if he's right?' Agnes joined in.

'Did you not hear a single word Lottie just said?' Jack asked, incredulous.

'We're not questioning Lottie's word,' Garth said. 'That doesn't make it self-defence. It still isn't enough to make me sure Maria Bloxham couldn't just have left her husband instead of trying to kill him.'

'That's a fair point,' Samuel echoed, changing sides yet again.

'I want to say one last thing,' Lottie sniffed. 'I tried to decide this trial, to the very end, on the basis of all the evidence. I kept an open mind. You'll remember it was me who suggested watching the video of Dr Bloxham again. No one can say I prejudged. What I have to tell you all is that you can't know the sort of man he was from how he seemed in public. That's not how this works. Abusers can be charming. Mine was clever and he seemed completely normal at first. If they weren't, they'd never be able to get a woman into a relationship in the first place. So forget everything you think you know about Edward Bloxham. We have to give Maria the benefit of the doubt, because for the life of me, I cannot see how she could have lied so convincingly about what she suffered. The prosecution certainly hasn't proved to me that she didn't act in self-defence. Not one bit.'

'Thank you Lottie,' Tabitha said gently. 'Does anyone else want to add anything?'

'Only that I think now would be a good time to have another vote,' Pan said.

Credit to him, Lottie thought. The man knew how to use timing to his advantage, and it had saved her from having to propose it.

'Show of hands then. Those who find the defendant guilty?' Tabitha said, just seconds before the door opened and the usher entered, asking for them to reconvene in the courtroom.

34

Maria stood up in the dock as she'd been directed. She looked around for something to steady herself on, but there was nothing. The jury foreperson stood too. Taking her time, Maria studied the tension on the faces of the journalists, assuming they wanted a guilty verdict. That would make for a better story, of course. James Newell and Imogen Pascal had their backs to her, but DI Anton had turned around to gloat, keen to witness her defeat. He smiled at her. She gazed blankly back. Finally she looked at the jury. Only the young woman was staring at her. Maria could have sworn there were tears in her eyes. Sorrow perhaps, about either what they'd decided she had done to her husband, or perhaps for the sentence she was about to serve.

'Have you reached a verdict on which you are all agreed?' the court clerk asked the foreperson.

'No,' the lady replied.

Maria's stomach lurched.

'Have you reached a verdict on which at least ten of you are agreed?' the clerk went on.

'Yes,' was the reply. Maria looked at Ruth in the public seating, already in floods, the back of one hand pressed firmly against her mouth.

'Do you find the defendant, Maria Bloxham, guilty or not guilty on the charge of attempted murder?'

There was silence. The jury foreperson looked along the lines of other jurors before addressing the judge.

'Not guilty,' she said, 'by a majority of ten to two.'

At that point the judge took over, although Maria couldn't hear a word of it. Ruth was openly sobbing in the public gallery. James Newell turned back towards the dock and beamed at her. The jurors were being thanked for their service. Maria smiled her thanks to those who looked her way, tears streaming down her cheeks.

'Ms Bloxham,' the judge said. 'You have been found not guilty of the charge. I'm pleased to say, you are now free to go. Officer, please release her.'

'Thank you, Your Honour,' Maria muttered. 'Thank you.'

Suddenly the door to the dock was being opened, and a gentle hand on her arm guided her out of her glass prison. Maria remained at the back of the court as the proceedings concluded, blood pulsing violently, the top of her scalp tingling as she struggled to breathe normally.

Imogen Pascal was whispering furiously to the police officers behind her, all hands on hips and squared shoulders. Detective Inspector Anton was shaking his head, and banging the end of a pointed finger on the desk. Maria looked away. She'd had enough confrontation to last her a lifetime. Journalists were already leaving the court, ready to run to cameras and make calls. The world was about to be told that she had been acquitted. Then James Newell was at her side, leading her out of the courtroom and into the public area beyond, finding a consultation room where they could talk in peace.

'How are you feeling?' he asked her as he shut the door.

'I'm not sure yet,' she smiled. 'It hasn't sunk in. But thank you, really. You've been so kind.'

'That's what we're here for. You're free to go, and also to leave the bail hostel. No more curfew, no more rules. I should stay away from your husband, though. Visiting him in hospital would be inadvisable.'

Maria laughed, only it turned into tears. Newell offered her a crumpled but clean handkerchief.

'You should also see a solicitor as soon as possible about a divorce and the matrimonial finances. I guess you won't want to go back to live in the house,' he continued

'Never,' she said. 'Can I ask . . . did you believe me? You said you did, only I wondered why.'

'I don't get paid to believe people,' he laughed gently. 'Let me put it like this. I hated that video of your husband with the hedgehog. I couldn't really explain why. Just my gut reaction. Do I think you told me the whole truth? Did I believe you never once used that mobile phone they found in your shoe? Those are more complicated issues, best left.'

'I'm sorry,' Maria said, and she meant it. Lying to James Newell had been so much worse than repeating those lies to the jury. He had trusted her. It didn't matter in the grand scheme of things, but she regretted it nonetheless.

'We're not going back through it now,' he reassured her. 'The point is this. If you were to ask me, do I believe justice was done today, I could put my hand on my heart and say yes. I think that's all that matters. Is that what you wanted?'

'It is,' she said. 'Being believed is important. It might sound silly, but that legal test thing . . . the prosecution has to prove its case, the defendant doesn't have to prove their innocence . . . that's all well and good. But what I understand now, is that you actually want someone to look you in the eye and say, yes, we believe you. Not that it wasn't proved, but that we think you're innocent. Otherwise, it's as if maybe you just got away with it. Maybe it was just that niggling doubt that made them return a not guilty verdict.'

'Maria,' Newell said. 'You know in your heart whether you're guilty or not. It doesn't matter what anyone else thinks or says. Please take care of yourself. It was a pleasure meeting you.'

He gave her a brief, hard hug before tilting his head in fare-well and leaving. That was it for him, Maria realised. Another case over. On to the next. No big drama. She wandered back out into the public area, looking for Ruth, expecting her friend to be ready to leap into her arms. Fifteen minutes later, when she was nowhere to be found, Maria decided it was time to clear her things out from the bail hostel. Perhaps Ruth had to rush off to collect her mother or the twins, she thought, perplexed and a little hurt. She picked up her bag and left Bristol Crown Court to fight through the protestors and the press for the very last time.

Lottie followed Cameron, hoping he wasn't headed anywhere dangerous. She really didn't want to run into the men he owed money to, but she had to make sure Cam understood it was over. He had to stay away from her for good. It wasn't hard to stay concealed amidst the tourists and worker lunch trade, but she still had to resist the impulse to walk crouched down. Cameron sauntered through the city back towards the hotel, presumably to pick up his bag, but at the last moment entered the Cathedral instead. Lottie couldn't remember going inside as an adult. It was as intimidating as it was beautiful, and the very last place in the city she'd expected her blackmailer to go. For a moment she was tempted to give up and run away. The thought of talking to him, of being near him for another second, was sickening. Her family was what mattered, though. Their peace and well-being. Lottie would endure any amount of discomfort to make that happen. She entered as quietly as she could.

Cameron was taking a seat in a side chapel as Lottie watched, mobile in hand, from behind a pillar. He'd done his bit, now he wanted payment. She'd known he wouldn't be prepared to wait. No doubt less pleasant people would be arranging to meet him later. The woman who turned up and took the seat next to his was tall and well built. Lottie recognised her as having been in the public seating in court, kicking herself mentally. Without a doubt, she was also the woman from the Cabot Centre café. At the time, Cameron had persuaded her that she was being paranoid, but there were few women so tall. Sunglasses had prevented her from taking in the details of her face then, but now it was clear. Cameron had set the whole thing up to prove he was getting results. And he had, Lottie thought. Probably more than he'd ever thought possible.

The woman put a supermarket bag on the floor, nodded at Cameron, then stood up to leave. Lottie walked forward, as if to go past her, putting one hand on her arm.

'Stay right there,' she whispered. 'I just took a photo of the two of you together, so don't suddenly decide to bolt or I'll have the police on you in minutes, and your friend Maria Bloxham will be straight back in that courtroom.'

The woman was shaken but she stood her ground. Cameron was still flicking through the contents of the bag, counting quietly when Lottie refilled the space next to him.

'What the fuck are you doing here?' he asked.

'Making sure you can never play that recording to anyone. Also, ensuring I can give the police every single detail I need to if you come anywhere near my family, should you happen to get into debt in the future and decide I'm your next cash machine.'

Cameron swung around, grabbing her face in one hand and squeezing hard. She grinned at him in response. He let go abruptly, pushing her away.

'I said I wouldn't use that recording once it was over,' he muttered.

'And I'm supposed to believe a blackmailing bastard who used me the way you did?'

'It helped you do what I needed,' he said.

'You made me implicate my husband in the worst kind of abuse. It doesn't matter that what I said stays in the jury room. The lies I told were despicable.'

'It's over. We all walked away,' Cameron growled.

'Is that what you think, you piece of shit? That I can just walk away from what you did? You want to know what I learned doing jury duty? I learned that you don't have to get someone's dick shoved inside you to be raped. I hope you get in trouble again, and I hope someone else makes you feel as helpless as I did. I hope they hurt you until you wish you were dead. Now listen to me. I will tell the police everything that happened if I ever see you again. You'll go to prison for a very long time. Say you understand.'

'Fine,' he said. 'Once my debts are paid, I'm leaving the area.'

'Good. Don't come back,' Lottie told him, standing up. 'And let Jack down easy. He's got my mobile number so I know he'll call me. Tell him you're not ready, tell him you're not good enough for him, I really don't care. Just don't hurt him any more than you have to, you fucking loser.'

She walked as slowly as she could manage back to the waiting woman as Cameron slunk past them, head down.

'So it was you who paid him to get the not guilty verdict. I was wondering how he had so much information,' Lottie said. 'There were twelve of us. How did you know who to pick?'

'Cameron tried to avoid jury service from the start. Online profiles make it easy. It only took me ten minutes to find out he'd recently been declared bankrupt. There were photos of him with a variety of women. A couple of the girls were wearing matching tops. The logo was from a casino. Once I knew he needed money it was simple. I guess I'm not bad at reading people,' the woman replied quietly, head down. Lottie saw the tears on her cheeks and wondered if she was scared of discovery, or something else. It didn't really matter. Lottie was all out of sympathy.

'No, you're very good at it. You picked a man who had no scruples about flirting with a student who was already having problems admitting his sexuality publicly, and who blackmailed me to get me to do your dirty work.'

'I'm so very, very sorry. I didn't tell him to do that. If I'd known . . .' the woman whispered. 'But you did the right thing. Maria Bloxham was innocent. She didn't deserve to go to prison.'

'I didn't deserve to be abused for it either,' Lottie said, letting every emotion show on her face. 'You think you're good at reading people? Read me. I've been through hell. I deserved some of it but not as much as I got. Did he tell you what he made me do?' The woman shook her head, eyes on the ground. 'He made me lie on my bed naked, legs apart, and play dead. Is that why you don't think Maria Bloxham deserved to go to prison? For what it's worth, I agree, but now you get to live your life knowing you inflicted the same horror on someone else. So next time you decide to play the good Samaritan, think about the collateral damage. You have no idea how much pain you've caused. Not a fucking clue.'

The woman sank onto a chair, head in her hands, crying. Lottie watched her for a minute, satisfied to have had her say, then made her way towards the exit. Her hands were trembling and her stomach was a knot of pain, but she'd done it. Cameron was sorted. The woman who'd paid him had been taught a small lesson in consequences. And Lottie had taken control. She'd finally stood up for herself. She'd been brought as low as she could imagine, to utter desperation, but somewhere in the mud and muck of the previous twenty-four hours she'd found a strength she hadn't known she possessed. Pushing her hair back from her face, she walked back out into the sunshine and fresh air. It was time to go home.

35

Maria stood in the back garden kindling a bonfire to burn the few clothes she still had left from the duration of her marriage. As sentimental as it was, she'd also come to wish farewell to her plants. There was nothing she wanted from inside the house, but cuttings from her favourite flowers would be a good start to her new garden, wherever that might be.

Staring through the windows into the kitchen, she marvelled that her new life had been so violently born. She could still see Ruth standing in her kitchen, having turned up uninvited. That was Maria's fault. It should have been obvious that Ruth would be unable to hear the desperation in her voice without taking action. Part of Maria had willed her friend and counsellor to come, not that she could have foreseen how it would end. She wondered if she would do anything differently, if she could have that day all over again.

Careful, sensible Ruth had parked a road away so no neighbour would notice her vehicle and make a passing comment to Edward. She had buzzed from the gate. Maria remembered thinking one of the neighbours must have failed to stay in to take delivery of a package. It happened once or twice a year. On opening the front door to look down the driveway, she'd recognised Ruth immediately even though they'd never met. Six foot tall, with the broadest shoulders she'd seen on a woman, a wide nose, straight set eyebrows, and the kindest eyes, smiling at her. Maria had opened the iron gates and let her in, knowing it was foolish. Having Ruth in her house, feeling a sense of companionship, was the worst thing she could possibly do. How could she hide it from Edward when he got home? Those few minutes of human contact, of having someone walk into her life who cared about her, would be both defining and soul destroying, the second they were over.

Maria made tea. They stood in her kitchen and talked. Ruth had pleaded with her to leave. Maria had made excuses why she couldn't, like she had for so many years. When you were broken it took too much effort to pick up all the pieces of you and carry that weight somewhere else. Then the sound of the gates rolling over the gravel of the driveway had come again. Edward was home early. It was a trick he played, randomly, every few months. Today though she knew she should have foreseen it. He was too excited about the prospect of his evening with her, at watching her part her own flesh for his gratification, to stay away any longer.

'You can't be here,' she whispered to Ruth. 'He'll punish me. It'll make things worse.'

'Maybe it'll make things better if he knows you've spoken to someone,' Ruth said.

'No! You don't get it. Please, please, Ruth. Oh God, it's too late. Just get in the pantry and stay quiet. He'll go up for a shower in a few minutes and I'll let you out of the back door.'

'Maria, I won't let him hurt you any more . . .'

'You have to do as I say. You can't just walk in here and make decisions for me,' Maria hissed.

'You're right. I'm sorry.' There were already tears in Ruth's eyes. 'Whatever you want. I won't make a sound, I promise.'

*

Ruth stood in the pantry, her back against the wall, trying to quieten her breathing, convinced she sounded like a freight train. A minute later there were footsteps, and the sound of briefcase catches being opened.

'Edward, you're early, that's nice,' she heard Maria say. Ruth had never heard her voice so delicate. 'I rewrote the letters for you. I hope you'll like them.'

'Stop blathering,' Edward told Maria. His voice was exactly as Ruth had imagined it. Superior, demanding, patronising. It was almost as if she could see through the pantry door to the scene unfolding in the kitchen. 'You remember what I promised you?'

Maria nodded.

'Say it,' he said.

'I can cut myself tonight,' she whispered.

'That's right,' he said. 'Only not tonight. This afternoon. I came home early for your sake. Aren't you lucky?'

'Yes, Edward,' Maria muttered. 'Thank you. I hope it didn't put you out.'

'Well, I suppose I'll have to work late tomorrow, but I'm prepared to make the sacrifice.'

Ruth could hear the enjoyment in his voice. Make Maria cut herself, then make her say thank you for the privilege, then make her apologise because her husband had to work late. Her hands were fists in her pockets and she was biting her bottom lip to keep from crying at the horror and injustice of it all.

'Two blades tonight, good and deep,' Edward's voice rumbled, theatrically. He was loving it. 'You must put plenty of towels down to soak up the blood. I thought as an extra I might film the event, make it a special evening. We've never done that before. Would you like to see it how I see it, Maria? Would you like to be able to watch yourself after it's all over? To really wallow in it? I think you'd like that a lot.'

349

Ruth gagged, bundling her jumper into her mouth to stop the noise. Dr Edward Bloxham was everything Maria had said he was and more. She knew he was excited just from the way he was enunciating his words. She'd have put money on him being physically aroused. But it wasn't some cheap thrill. It was a carefully conceived plan, executed over years. It was nothing less than incremental murder.

'If you think that's a good idea,' she heard Maria reply faintly.

'I do.' He walked to the sink. 'Two cups?' he asked. 'What the hell's this? You're getting so slovenly these days that you're not even bothering to wash up one cup before getting yourself a second drink? What is it exactly that I work hard all day for? Presumably you've been sitting around dreaming the hours away, achieving nothing. This is what happens when I get home early. I find out your nasty, dirty little habits.'

'Sorry,' Maria whispered. 'I just forgot. I don't know what I was thinking. It was a mistake.'

Ruth was reaching for her mobile phone, wondering how to adjust the settings so that it made no sound as she dialled.

'It certainly was. Perhaps we need something extra tonight to remind you who's in charge here, Ria.' He made a show of contemplating his decision, walking to stare through the glass in the back door out into the garden, arms folded, chin high, the master of his own tiny world. He kept his back to her as he delivered his judgment. 'Perhaps playing dead again will help you appreciate being alive. I think you've forgotten how lucky you are to live in this house with me. Go upstairs.'

'Yes, Edward,' Maria said.

'You'll cut yourself until I say stop. And afterwards you'll tell me how grateful you are and how lucky you are. Until I decide you really mean it.'

Ruth heard the words cut, grateful and lucky, but in her mind she saw her sister, Gail, wired up and comatose in a hospital bed. The sister she hadn't been able to save. The sister who hadn't even been able to talk about her awful life. And Gail's husband, who knew where he was now, abusing someone else unchecked because no one had done anything about it. But Maria had reached out. She had asked for help. And Ruth was right here, right now. This time there was something she could do. She reached her hand around for whatever was nearby – a frying pan or a rolling pin – whatever. What she found was solid and wooden. Just light enough to lift easily but heavy enough to send a message. And Edward needed to get the message. He needed to learn there were consequences. Maria deserved to be protected from him.

She pushed open the pantry door and saw Maria's face slacken. Raising the broken chair leg above her head, she noticed the metal screw protruding from its end and winking in the sunlight. Then she brought it down hard and heavy, and there was the slightest movement of air. It caught Maria's hair, wafting across her forehead. The sound was extraordinary, like halving a cabbage with a butcher's knife. No sound came from Edward's mouth at all. His upper body spun slightly, then his legs registered the blow and he crumpled, collapsing face forward onto the floor. Ruth just stood there, blood dripping down the chair leg towards her shaking hands.

'What . . . what . . . did I . . .?'

Maria stepped forward, staring into the gully in her husband's head. A pale worm of grey matter was oozing from a crack in his skull.

'You should go now,' Maria said, taking the chair leg from her, fascinated by the tufts of hair that had caught in the screw.

'Gail?' Ruth asked vaguely, staring at Maria, but not seeing her. Not properly.

'Ruth, pull yourself together,' Maria said. She sounded calm. So calm that Ruth hardly recognised her voice at all.

'We have to call someone,' Ruth said. 'The police, an ambulance. We have to explain.'

'No,' Maria said, putting a gentle arm around Ruth's shoulders. 'You can't say you did this. They'll lock you up, Ruth. Who'll look after the twins and your mother? They'll be sent to institutions, foster care. You know awful how it'll be.'

'But I can't run. They'll find me. It'll only make things worse,' Ruth said, her voice wavering with dawning realisation as she stared at the man on the ground.

'Not if they're not looking for anyone. You did this for me. I can tell them how my life was. Now that he's dead, I can do that.'

'I killed him,' Ruth sobbed, doubling over and clutching her stomach.

'No, you didn't. You saved me,' Maria said. 'I wish I'd had the guts to do what you just did, years ago. Give me that. Not for your sake, for my own.'

'No. I won't let you . . .'

'I'll say it was self-defence. I won't be lying, not really. I have a chance to persuade them. You don't. I want you out of my house, right now. You'll have to go over the back fence to the passageway behind the garden, but you're tall enough to make it.'

'Maria . . .'

'Think about Lea and Max, and your mum. That's all. You think about them, and you go.'

She looked at Maria, shock rendering her woozy and nauseous, but her friend was right. Even in the midst of the carnage, she knew it. 'I'll find a way to make sure you get out of this. I'll do whatever I have to do, Maria. I promise you won't go to prison.'

'Just go,' Maria said. 'I need to sort the kitchen out before I call the police.'

Ruth went, leaving Maria washing up the second cup from the sink. She jumped the fence and walked as normally as she could to her car.

In the house, Maria made sure there were no footmarks on the floor other than hers and Edward's. Then she picked up the chair leg from where she'd rested it on Edward's head as she'd cleaned, and ran her hands up and down in the blood and gore to make absolutely sure all trace of Ruth was destroyed. Finally she stared outside a while, appreciating her garden as she counted enough minutes for Ruth to be long gone. The last thing she did was to push the pantry door shut with her elbow as she left the kitchen, on her way to finally say the words she'd dreamed of so often. Dr Edward Bloxham, her husband, was dead.

36

Lottie's mobile rang as she was walking back to her car. It was Jennifer. She'd forgotten that they'd even exchanged numbers, it seemed such a long time ago.

'Hey Lottie, whereabouts are you? I was hoping to say goodbye in person,' Jen said brightly.

'Not far from the court, on my way to the car park. You don't need to worry,' Lottie replied

'Actually I'd like to, if you don't mind. I didn't get a chance at the court, too many people dashing off. Meet me at the court entrance? Five minutes.'

'Sure,' Lottie said. 'Why not?' It was on her route back to the car, and a distraction from what she was going to say to her husband. She was about to embark on a lifetime of lying. Frankly, delaying that, even for just a few minutes, seemed like a blessing.

Jen was already waiting when she arrived, wearing a red and green knitted cardigan in spite of the heat, with an equally bright smile. She hugged Lottie hard, in a motherly way. Like a proper mother, Lottie thought. Not one who had sex while her child was throwing up at the childminder's. Not the sort of thing Jen would ever do.

'I wanted to tell you, that was one of the bravest things I've ever seen anyone do. To open up to a load of virtual strangers, and to be so honest after what you've been through. I know we've been on that jury together, but we still don't know each other very well. Anyway, I respect you. And I'm here if you ever need me. I hope whatever you've gone through is in your past.'

A lump in Lottie's throat was threatening to stop her from responding.

'Thank you,' she croaked.

'Don't you cry, you'll start me off again,' Jen said. 'Look at us, silly things. Come on, I'll walk you back to your car.'

'That would be nice,' Lottie said, wiping her face with her sleeve as Jen linked arms with her and they got moving.

'Driving back over the suspension bridge are you? Traffic will be dreadful at this time. Just building up to rush hour now.'

'That bloody bridge,' Lottie laughed, glad to be thinking about something other than Cameron Ellis for a moment. 'I must have done four different projects on it at school, for history, geography, maths and physics. I know more about Isambard Kingdom Brunel than my own mother.'

'Ah, but he didn't really design it,' Jen said happily.

'What are you talking about?' Lottie asked. 'Of course he did.'

'Not the bits that mattered. A woman called Sarah Guppy patented the designs for the pilings in 1811. Imagine that! She didn't even have the right to vote, but she was an engineer and an architect. Brunel only joined the project years later. Without her, that bridge wouldn't be standing today.'

'How could I not have known that?' Lottie asked, shaking her head.

'I'm a bit of a nerd about it. Apologies if I'm boring you. I'm writing a paper on Sarah Guppy for my history degree at the moment. Only a distance learning course, but still. Keeps me busy.'

Lottie stopped walking. 'All you said was that you were a housewife. Why didn't you tell any of us?'

'No need to make a great big fuss about every little thing, is there? Anyway, I'm still a housewife first. That's what I take the most pride in. It doesn't mean I'm not anything else. This your car, is it?' she asked, as Lottie stood with the keys dangling uselessly from her hands.

'Um, yes, it is,' Lottie said. 'Thank you, Jen. I'm so glad you rang me. Do you think you'd mind if I kept in touch. I mean, you're obviously busy, so I won't hassle you . . .'

'Hassle away, anytime. I'd love that,' Jen said. 'Speak soon, yes?' She kissed Lottie's cheek and walked away.

Lottie climbed into her car, keys sitting in her lap. Jen wasn't what she'd seemed. Lottie's own prejudices had reduced her to something less. She felt ashamed of all the times she'd thought of her as Just-Jen. How could she have diminished another person to such a low status, and based on what . . . a few sentences of introduction? In fact, nothing inside the jury room had been what it first appeared. Cameron wasn't what he'd seemed. Jack had been duped and lied to. Lottie had been determined to hate the woman at the Cathedral who'd given Cameron the motive and opportunity to use her and Jack, only her heart wasn't in it. The woman's tears had been real, her sorrow genuine. If nothing else, the trial had taught Lottie something about reading people. She was certain – well beyond a reasonable doubt, or whatever the legal phrasing was – that Maria Bloxham had spent her life forced to live someone else's lie. Her rage in the witness box hadn't been a symptom of anything except the deeply felt frustration of injustice. She was no more insane than Lottie. If that was a good enough reason to lock someone up, then there would be many more candidates than there were cells available.

Now Lottie was about to go home, and pile up yet more of that deceit in her own life, through fear, and a lack of self-respect. She was taking away her husband's right to choose his future. The thought made her sick. Worse than that. It would make her less than she really was.

She started the car and followed the trail of vehicles to the suspension bridge. Jen was right. It was blocked all the way across. It took her another forty-five minutes to get home. Zain was already there, and just about to go and fetch Daniyal from the childminder's.

'Hello you,' he said, kissing her forehead.

Lottie hugged him once, briefly. She knew what she had to do. She'd had enough lying for a lifetime.

'Zain,' she said. 'I need to tell you this, and we'll work out what to do. I'm not asking for forgiveness because I don't deserve that, but you do deserve the truth. I love you. And I love our son more than life itself. I was unhappy and feeling trapped. I think I lost all my self-worth somewhere along the line. That's no excuse for what I did, but it's part of the facts. I had an affair with another juror. It's over now and I regret it more than I will ever be able to tell you. But I won't lie to you. I just can't. So when you're ready, however long that takes, I'd like to know if you'll give me a chance to fix it. And if we can't fix it, then maybe we could try starting again. I want to be your wife, but it has to be on both our terms. Equally. You take all the time you need to hate me. I just wanted you to know that it cannot possibly be more than I already hate myself. And I'm sorry.' She lifted her chin and looked her husband straight in the eyes. 'I'm so very, very sorry.'

37

Maria sat in her car outside the solicitor's office and looked at her watch. Ruth dashed across the street and hopped in, avoiding the sleet. Winter was bringing as much cold as the summer had heat, and the roads were treacherous.

'Sorry I'm late. You ready?' Ruth asked.

'To sign my divorce papers? Do you really need to ask?' Maria smiled.

'It's freedom from him finally, legally, not to mention financial independence. You must be feeling a bit emotional,' Ruth said.

'I suppose I am a bit, but it's not that big a deal. He's still there, rotting away in some hospital. Do you think he understood the outcome of the trial? Do you think anyone even bothered to communicate it to him?'

'Probably not. What would have been the point?' Ruth looked at her watch. 'We should go.'

'One more minute,' Maria stared at the grey sky. 'Listen, I've been thinking I might go away for a while, take a trip. See something of the world. Good idea or bad idea?'

'Well, you'll certainly be able to afford it. Once you've signed those papers, you'll have six hundred thousand pounds in your bank account. Even after you've bought a house, that's more than enough to fund a long trip,' she said.

'But?' Maria asked. 'Come on, I can hear it in your voice. What are you worried about?'

'The nightmares,' Ruth said. 'I haven't been listening deliberately, but I can hear you in the guest room. It's perfectly normal. You know my view. You're suffering post-traumatic stress disorder which probably requires treatment. I'm concerned that you might not cope very well in unfamiliar places.'

'You mean you're worried I might not cope without you,' Maria said.

'I mean . . . yes, without me. I want to take care of you, Maria. After all you did for me. What you risked.'

Maria reached across to take her friend's hand. 'Ruth, I know you think I did that for you, but you can rest easy. I've had a lot of time to think about the trial and the possibility of being found guilty, and my reality isn't so selfless. Yes, I wanted to protect the twins and your mother from what would have happened if they lost you. And yes, I felt responsible for what happened even though I hadn't hit Edward myself. You were in my kitchen for me, because of me. You didn't choose the path you took that day. There was absolutely no way you could have come to court as a witness on my behalf. You'd have been cross-examined into a corner, and admitted everything. You're too decent a person, and lying isn't in your nature. But you need to understand that in large measure I took responsibility for Edward's injury from sheer bloody-minded hatred. I didn't want him to have the win. The idea of him taking you from me would just have been another victory, whether he'd have comprehended it or not. The loathing I feel for him isn't temporary, it's not post-traumatic anything and it's never going to leave me. It's part of my DNA now. So don't go polishing my halo too often, all right? I've been driven by emotions my whole life – by nerves, and fear, and a lack of confidence – but hatred turned out to be the one thing that gave me strength. Perhaps a little too much, looking back on how I behaved in court.'

Ruth wiped away quiet tears as Maria withdrew her hand.

'So we're quits,' Maria continued. 'Your gorgeous children are all the therapy I need. Even your mother makes me laugh more than I have in years. You've opened your home to me, and you saved me from him. You always seem to forget that. If it weren't for you I'd either still be in my living hell or I'd be six feet under. Let's both move on. We can't change any of it. I need to embrace life. I know better than most people how precious it is.'

'Yes, you do,' Ruth leaned across to kiss Maria's cheek. 'And you deserve to be happy. Go on your trip. We'll be here when you get back. It is time to move on. I needed to look after you to assuage my own guilt. If you can let go of your past, I guess it's time for me to let go too. Do you have any idea where you want to go?'

'Yes,' Maria smiled gently. 'I thought I'd start in Germany.'

'Really? That's a bit random. I imagined you saying Australia or America. Is there something specific there you want to see?'

'Not something. Someone. I've been making enquiries with the army. Andrea was stationed there for a while when she first joined up. It seems she met a German man and they married, so once she left the forces, she stayed there. She's living in a town called Königswinter on the Rhein river. It has a castle.'

'That sounds lovely,' Ruth said softly. 'Although it's been a long time. Not to be negative about it, but people change. Have you . . .'

'Spoken to her?'

Ruth nodded.

'No. She has no idea that I've been looking for her. I need to do this in person. There's so much to say that I wouldn't know where to start in a letter. If she doesn't want to know me any more, I'll understand, and I'll move on. I just need a chance to tell her how sorry I am.'

'That's very brave of you,' Ruth said. 'And you're right. It does sound like a good place to start. I can understand you wanting to take back some of what was taken from you.'

'The rain's stopped,' Maria said. 'Now, I'm going in to sign my divorce papers, then you and I are going out to lunch. We deserve it. The only rule is, we're not to say his name. No talk of trials or lawyers or courts. We're going to pretend we're old friends who met at a yoga class or something utterly normal like that, and we can people-watch until it's time to pick up the twins. Agreed?'

'Agreed,' Ruth said, opening the car door, then pausing. 'You know I'd do it all again for you, don't know? If I was back in that cupboard now, I'd grab that chair leg and hit him, probably just a little bit harder.'

'You wouldn't have to,' Maria smiled. 'The only regret I have is not doing it myself. If I could turn back time, believe me, I would.'

Acknowledgements

I need to start by having a quick chat with the lawyers. I took a few liberties with procedure in this book and I'm asking you to forgive me. The truth, as we know, is that most trials contain few surprises and I'm afraid that doesn't make for very suspenseful fiction. So forgive me, and try to read like a reader rather than as if you were reading a brief. Know also, at a time when the criminal bar is under worse financial and time pressure than ever, that you are appreciated. The work you do ensures that our streets are safer places, without compromising on justice. It's not glamorous, you work the night shift 4 or 5 nights a week, and half of all you do effectively goes unpaid. If it were not for my outstanding agent, Caroline Hardman, I would still be there with you, travelling endless miles each day, never putting my children to bed at night, and sacrificing my weekends to reading unused material. Caroline, for giving me a chance at second career, and for making it possible to write this book, you have my everlasting gratitude (and free drinks whenever we're together).

This story, though, is Sam Eades' baby. Trapeze gave me a green light and let me write about extremely difficult subject matter, supporting me when the book took on increasingly relevant topics in the age of the #MeToo movement. Sam is one of those editors whose boundless enthusiasm lifts a book from the page until it burns in the imaginations of all those she tells about it. I consider myself privileged to have worked with you on this, Sam. Your insight, instincts and intellect are formidable.

It takes a team to publish a book though, and here are the publishing world's A-listers who got Degrees of Guilt onto the page, into the shops and into the hands of readers. Jen Breslin on marketing, Claire Keep in production, Sophie Wilson – my line and copy editor – who has the patience of a saint, Debbie Holmes on design, Susan Howe and the fabulous rights team, Paul Stark with the audio team. Thank you all for making the process look so easy.

I would also like to thank the lovely Matthew Scott (known better on Twitter as @Barristerblog) who offered me advice at the very start of writing this (all mistakes are my own, though) and who has given continual support to my writing from the get-go. To the folks who make Bristol Crown Court a friendly, welcoming place to work, and a great place to set this trial, you make a difficult job look easy every day. And to David, who put up with me while I was a barrister and who thought life would get easier when I stopped, until I decided to write books for a living – don't give up hope. I'm sure one day we'll have a normal life together.